JUST LIKE THEM

TRACY BROEMMER

Just Like Them

By

Tracy Broemmer

Women's Fiction

Published by Tracy Broemmer

Edited by Susan Schmitz (First Edition), Lexie Broemmer (Second Edition)

Cover Photo: Deposit Photos

Cover Design: Redbird Designs

Copyright © First Edition, 2011 Second Edition, 2019

ISBN#: 978-1-951637-04-0

―――――――――――――――――――――――――

Prologue

―――――――――――――――――――――――――

OCTOBER 2010

Teel

THE BLOOD HAD SPLASHED over her arms and her shirt and even splattered her face, and she thought of the miscarriage. The second one, the way the blood had soaked through her shorts and then streaked her legs.

The girls didn't even know about the miscarriages, and so she found it funny that she would lie in bed and chase sleep and think about those babies. Keegan was not the middle child, no matter how you looked at it, and so it wasn't about birth order.

There had been three of them, one before Rachel and two between Rachel and Keegan. The first had been hard. So hard to be young…Well, they'd gotten married a little later and gotten pregnant a little later but still…In terms of pregnancies and motherhood, aren't you always young the first time?

She and Bobby had wanted that baby so badly, and she'd ignored her mother's advice and purchased baby clothes and blankets and newborn diapers and then one day, just after the end of the school day, she'd sat at her desk grading English worksheets and felt a twinge in her belly.

The twinge hadn't bothered her. But by the time she left the school to go home to Bobby, she'd been in the grips of full-blown abdominal cramps, and she'd known that baby wasn't meant to be. Her second pregnancy had ended with beautiful Rachel, and she and Bobby had given her the moon anytime she'd reached a fat little hand for something and made a noise that resembled anything like *Daddy* or *Mommy*.

The miscarriage with the blood—the bad one—came when Rachel was just a year old. And though she'd told Bobby it was silly to blame himself, she often wondered if by making love too soon after Rachel and getting pregnant so quickly, if they'd done something to hurt her body or her chances of carrying a baby to term. Intellectually she knew that was ridiculous. Though doctors didn't advocate for women to get pregnant immediately after giving birth, it did happen, and most women and babies were fine.

She'd been further along than the first miscarriage, and she'd suffered through what seemed like hours of labor pain and Bobby had taken her to the hospital. Dr. Cash had said there was nothing he could do. The blood was so sticky and thick, and she remembered how it had seemed unfathomable that this blood had once been part of her baby.

The blood today had been warm like that, and a little sticky, but not thick. If she breathed too deeply, she could still smell the cloying scent, and she gagged, and then Bobby stirred in his sleep. She didn't want to wake Bobby. He had to be on site at six a.m. so he needed his sleep, and besides, what good would it do for Bobby to be awake? He'd held her earlier, until she'd finally drifted off to sleep, but dreams woke her, and she couldn't decide what was worse: the dreams or being awake and feeling the blood splash over her.

Funny that she would be thinking of those babies now. God knows there was so much she should be thinking about. And yet, no amount of thinking was going to change anything. Part of her thought she should get up and figure out how to help Keegan, but then part of her wondered just what the hell could be done to help Keegan. Exhausted, with her body aching from lying awake so long, she rolled to her back and turned her head on her pillow to look at Bobby.

He wore his age so well. Even now, after the blood—there had been buckets—and dealing with Keegan, and the looks her colleagues were sneaking in the hallways, she could look at him and see how attractive he was. She didn't quite feel the stirrings of desire she normally would, but that was okay. Not tonight.

Maybe it was just the blood. The sudden onslaught of warm, sticky blood would disturb anyone, and so maybe it was just the tactile memory of the miscarriage and maybe that's why she couldn't sleep for thinking of her babies.

The second one was a boy. She'd failed to give Bobby a son, though he'd never complained. He loved the girls just as much, if not more than she did. They'd have named him Robert Michael, after Bobby, if she could have carried him to term and given birth.

Maybe it was the pregnancy test stick she'd used just this morning, before the blood.

Maybe it was Keegan. Fear of losing her. Or maybe it was the fear that they already had lost her.

Chapter 1

Teel

TEEL ALEXANDER STIRRED in her sleep and wondered what the siren meant. In her dream world the siren made no sense; she was sitting on the deck with her sister, Eve, drinking coffee and there was no siren. It didn't go away when she reasoned, in that half–awake state, that it should not be there. Instead, it got louder. Louder still, until finally it sounded like it could shatter the windows in the house and maybe rend their bedroom down the middle, and Teel was instantly awake. She hadn't heard the rain when she was sleeping, but now she did. The bedroom flashed blue and red and then bright white and then blue and red again.

Still in the throes of sleep, she rubbed her eyes and listened to the rain ping against the windows. Thunder rolled, but it was so distant, she knew it wasn't a storm that awoke her. When the siren finally burrowed deep inside Teel and truly woke her, she threw back the comforter, climbed out of bed, and ran to the window on Bobby's side of the bed. Not just any siren. It was an ambulance, and it was in her neighborhood. It had to be close for it to be so loud.

"What's going on?" Bobby mumbled, head still mostly buried in his pillow. Lying on his stomach, he lifted his head and then as he heard the siren, he propped his body up on his elbows and looked toward the window. Teel knew he couldn't see her, not yet. It was too dark in the room, and he was still fuzzy with sleep.

She knew the instant the siren pierced his sleep stupor. Fully awake now, she could see him clearly in the bed. His whole body tensed, and he rolled out of bed and reached for her.

"Teel? What happened? Are you all right?"

"I don't know where it is," she answered, and he leaned close to her to look out the window over her shoulder. She was tall, but he had her by at least a foot. Still, the alternating blue and red lights painted emergency on their neighborhood, but the ambulance itself was not in sight.

In boxers and a short-sleeved undershirt, Bobby took her hand and pulled her from the bedroom. The central air was still on; it was September but still ungodly hot outside. The air was not running right now, and yet, Teel shivered as Bobby led her to the front of the house to the window of the dining room, where they stood side by side and stared in horror at the ambulance parked in the middle of the street just a few houses south of theirs.

The bare windows afforded them a painfully good view of the ambulance and the lights coming on in houses up and down the street. At the back of the ambulance, the doors stood open, but there was no one in sight. In her mind, Teel walked the neighborhood and wondered who the ambulance would take away. The Strattons were older, but not elderly, and Teel couldn't really imagine either of them suddenly dropping dead of a heart attack. Mr. Edgar, he was certainly of the age when he might die in his sleep, but as far as Teel knew, he hadn't been living in the house for the past two or three months.

"What's going on?"

Teel, still shaking, as much from that quirky adrenaline that had spiked to life inside her the second she'd realized it was an ambulance siren as from being cold, turned to see her oldest daughter approach. Rachel looked awake, even at this hour, and suddenly Teel wondered exactly what time it was. Nineteen years old, Rachel attended the city university but lived at home, and Teel and Bobby had abolished some of the house rules in her case, such as curfew. Not that it mattered. Rachel was a homebody; most nights she chose to stay around the house and study or read.

In pajamas, and yet looking very much awake and self-possessed, Rachel stepped up to the window beside Teel. Bobby must have noticed that Teel was shaking, because he stepped closer to her and put his arm around her shoulders.

"I wonder if it's Marlena Howell," he said quietly, and Teel thought he could be right, even though she'd forgotten about Marlena. Fifty-something Marlena had been diagnosed with a brain tumor earlier in the summer. Teel hated to think that, and yet, as far as this neighborhood went, an ambulance in the wee hours of the morning was off-the-charts weird.

Bobby reached past Teel and laid his hand on Rachel's shoulder.

"Is Keegan sleeping through this?"

"Keegan could sleep through a heavy metal concert." Rachel's flat voice revealed no emotion.

"What time is it?" Teel wondered aloud, but no one answered her. She looked back over her shoulder but from her position by the dining room window, she couldn't see the green numbers of the clock on the microwave in the kitchen.

"Oh my God." This time Rachel's voice carried something heavier than disbelief and still not as loud as shock. Teel looked back to the window and saw two EMTs manipulating a gurney down the cobblestone driveway at the English house. Of course from this distance and in the darkness, she couldn't see who was on the gurney.

"It's Marin," Rachel said softly, just as Teel saw Jeannie English hurrying down the driveway to catch up with the EMTs. Not wanting to believe it was Marin, but already sagging against Bobby with knees far too weak to stand on, Teel tore her eyes from Jeannie and searched the drive and the yard and the front porch, hoping she wouldn't see Rick. If she didn't see him, then maybe he was on the gurney and not Marin. Teel didn't want to believe it was Marin.

"Oh, God." The words just kind of escaped in a painfully sharp sigh, because there he was. Rick was running from the porch to catch up with Jeannie and that left only fifteen-year-old Marin to be the person on the gurney that was now being loaded into the back of the ambulance.

Chapter 2

TEEL

THEY'D GONE BACK to bed after watching the paramedics load Marin into the ambulance and Rick help Jeannie climb up into the back to be with Marin and then hurry back to the garage, no doubt to get the car and follow them to the hospital. It was just after two; Teel couldn't tear her gaze away from the alarm clock on the nightstand on Bobby's side of the bed. She lay awake and listened to Bobby in the bathroom. She knew when he came back to bed and kissed her she would taste the chalky fruity Tums he'd just chewed and swallowed.

Rachel had stood at the window even after the ambulance was gone and Bobby had gone to the bathroom and Teel had gone to the kitchen for a glass of water. But just minutes later, when Teel crossed back over the hardwood floor to tell Rachel she should go on back to bed, the girl was gone. No fanfare, no drama—she was just gone. Rachel had always been a very quiet adult personality packaged in her gangly, skinny child's body. When she'd turned 15, she'd begun to grow into her body, and by 17, she was beautiful, with razor sharp cheekbones, stormy gray eyes, and a lithe body.

Teel wondered now, as Bobby turned the light off in the master bath and came back to bed, how Keegan would have acted if she'd been the one to see Marin being put in an ambulance and taken away. They weren't really friends, hadn't been since grade school. But still, there was another layer of shock that wound its way through you when you knew someone involved in a tragedy.

Tragedy. Teel sighed and shook her head. It didn't have to be a tragedy. Maybe it was an attack of appendicitis or something.

"What?" Bobby asked as he slipped into bed and moved closer to her. Lying on her side, she leaned back against him.

"It doesn't have to be something awful," she mumbled.

"I'm sure she's fine." He slid his hand over her hip, his fingertips just under the elastic of her panties. "Maybe it was an appendicitis attack or something."

She turned in his arms then, and his fingers slipped further inside her panties as her lips found and kissed his. Their lovemaking was tender and quiet, and Teel couldn't help but think, as Bobby moved over her and brought her to the brink, life-affirming.

———

THE ALARM WENT off at five, but when Teel rolled over to her back, Bobby was already up. She lifted her head from the pillow to see the sliver of yellow light from under the closed bathroom door. She could join him in the shower. She didn't want to, though. Not this morning. She turned over on her stomach and thought of the way his hands had touched her just hours ago. The way he always touched her with so much love and need that it almost burned her skin.

The air was running now, and she pulled the comforter up over her shoulders. Snuggled in and closed her eyes. And saw the surreal scene from last night. The ambulance lighting up the neighborhood. The paramedics pushing the gurney over the cobblestone driveway. Jeannie and Rick racing after their daughter who was being taken away in an ambulance.

She sighed and stretched her legs, inviting a Charlie horse into her calf. Quickly, she jumped out of bed and paced around the bed until it eased. It had nothing to do with age, and yet, as she shrugged into her robe and padded out to the kitchen to start the coffee, she couldn't help but think how it sucked to get old.

The house was dark and quiet, beyond the can lights she dimmed above the kitchen counter. She made a full pot of coffee because lately even Keegan had started drinking a cup before she went to school. Teel wasn't sure it was necessary, but when picking her battles, this seemed like a lesser one.

She wondered if Rachel had gone to sleep right away after the ambulance had left and they'd all gone back to bed. If Rachel might be more upset than she'd let on. Story of their lives—Rachel folding each life experience into a tiny inch by inch square and tucking it away inside, the way a young girl might hide a small token of love in her blouse, just inside her bra, and close to her heart.

Bobby was done in the shower, but Teel turned and went down the other hall to the girls' rooms. Keegan's door was shut, but Teel eased it open silently to check on her. Keegan lay curled into a ball on her right side, and her long eyelashes lay against her cheek. Angel. Teel had always thought both girls looked like angels when they slept. Not really under-standing why but feeling it necessary, she leaned over her daughter and listened to her breathe. Touched her lips to Keegan's temple and then backed away when Keegan stirred and flopped over to lie on her back.

She tiptoed out of the room, even though Keegan would have to get up soon, and went to check on Rachel. Probably she shouldn't. Probably, since Rachel was 19 and a college student, Teel shouldn't be allowed these sorts of privileges of motherhood. It was probably not cool for moms to look in on their sleeping, college-student children. And yet, of her daughters, Rachel was the one who would not object to her mom in her room watching her sleep.

Rachel slept on her stomach, arms up under her pillow. Her room, typical of Rachel, was immaculate. The only thing that might be considered out of place was the book on her nightstand, and yet, Rachel was seldom seen without a book, so Teel didn't really consider the book out of place. Teel walked further into the room to see the title. She enjoyed reading, but she never seemed to have as much time for it as Rachel. It was a huge book, probably at least seven or eight hundred pages. A family saga. Historical fiction. Rachel would read anything. And what thrilled Teel, who had been a teacher for twenty-two years, was the way Rachel wanted to discuss what she read. To dissect everything, though not in a bad way. To understand a character's motivation. To commiserate with a character when he or she was in an untenable situation. To question a writer's facts and yet forgive an inaccuracy if the story was compelling.

Content now, after seeing that both girls were okay, Teel went back down the hall. She understood that checking on the girls was a reaction to what she had seen last night. There was no reason either of her girls wouldn't be okay. The smell of coffee greeted her as she entered the open kitchen and living area. If Rachel had beaten her to it, she'd have made cinnamon coffee. Teel liked it, but Bobby preferred plain black coffee, the stronger, the better.

Bobby stood at his sink in white boxer briefs. He was still lean and wiry. Teel loved that under his clothes he was hard and muscular, and that it was her little secret. She approached him and pressed her body against his back. He was still hot from the shower.

"Mm." He closed his eyes and let his head drop back when she slid her arms around him and leaned into nip at his shoulder blade. "Not today, babe. I have a meeting on site in less than an hour."

"I know." She drew her hands up over his bare chest and couldn't resist fanning his nipples with her thumbs. She laughed and stepped away when he groaned.

"You're wicked," he said to her and pointed at her in the mirror. She took a towel from the linen closet and hung it on the bar of the shower door.

"Me?" she asked as she slipped her robe off and tossed it on the whirlpool tub. He watched her in the mirror as she took her nightshirt off and let it fall to the floor. Never able to walk away from her when she stood bare-breasted before him, he groaned, turned his shaver off and set it down. He cupped her breasts in his calloused hands and then bent to kiss her.

He was ready, and they might have time for something quick, as they did many mornings before he left for a construction site and she left for school. Teel leaned into him, pressed her breasts against his chest and gave herself to the kiss. Bobby Alexander hadn't been her first lover, but she'd known after their first time she'd never want another.

"Mom?"

They jumped away from each other when they heard Rachel on the other side of the bathroom door. There was a sharp knock, and then Rachel called out to her again.

She sounded upset.

Teel reached for her robe, and Bobby disappeared into his walk-in closet.

"What's wrong, sweetie?" Teel asked as she cinched her belt around her waist and opened the door. That was another thing that Teel probably shouldn't do with her college daughter—call her sweetie, as if she was still ten or eleven and Teel could fix her hurts with a bandage or a hug.

Rachel's eyes were bloodshot, her lashes wet with tears.

Bobby's closet door opened, and without looking, Teel felt his presence in the room with them.

"What's wrong, Rach?" he asked. He stood behind Teel now, dressed for work in a pair of Levi shorts and a speckled gray T-shirt.

"It was on the news," Rachel said softly. Teel watched her eyes fill. Knowing before Rachel even said it, Teel felt her throat tighten with her own tears. "They said she killed herself."

Chapter 3

TEEL

KEEGAN HAD ALWAYS BEEN Rachel's polar opposite. Bobby called her his little sparkplug until she turned ten and insisted that he stop. They'd always joked when she was younger that she was groomed and ready for the Oscars, right down to her acceptance speech. Drama followed her like her own shadow. When she'd fallen from the top bar of their swing set when she was seven, she'd screamed and cried the whole drive to the hospital. Teel had worried that she'd broken her arm or her collarbone or both. The ER doctor, who looked like a cross between Einstein and Teel's Uncle Dwayne (whom Keegan had always liked) had been gentle and kind, and he'd probably x-rayed every bone in Keegan's arm and shoulder and elbow and wrist at Teel's insistence. There were no breaks, just some bruises that Keegan had recovered from by the following weekend.

Four years younger than Rachel, Keegan had spent her fair share of little sister time, worshipping Rachel and following her around. Rachel and her friends had never been particularly mean to Keegan, but they hadn't ever been especially welcoming either. If Teel had any wishes regarding her daughters, that they had a closer relationship ranked right at the top of the list.

There wasn't a lot of animosity, not these days anyway. There had been little bouts of sibling rivalry here and there through the years, but it had never been anything Teel couldn't handle. But since Keegan had started high school, Teel would like to have seen more of those little spats. As it was, her girls lived in their house like two strangers who happened to rent rooms from the same landlord.

When Keegan was in sixth grade, she and two of her friends had gotten into a fight on the playground. Not just a trading insults and bad words fight, but scratching and hair-pulling, too. Keegan had sworn she was just defending her friend Hannah to their mutual friend Jennifer. The three of them had spent three afternoons in detention writing one essay about the value of friendship and working together. On the afternoon of the third day of detention, Keegan had come home so angry with her teacher and the principal (and still with Jennifer) that she'd sulked down the hall to her room and slammed the door shut. When she'd refused to come out for dinner later that evening and Teel had gone to her room to get her, she'd found Keegan sitting on her bed, weeping, missing half the hair on her head.

Shocked, Teel had said nothing. Instead, she'd stood and surveyed the piles of her daughter's hair on the bed and the floor and the scissors in her hands. For just a moment, Teel had worried that maybe the cutting episode wouldn't be over with just her hair. Though crying, Keegan stared at the scissors in her hand as if mesmerized by what she (and by extension, they) had done or maybe, what they *could* do. What if, God help her, she hadn't come in at just this moment to get

Keegan for dinner, and the girl had started cutting something else? Like the pale flesh on her arms or legs.

Or what if, Teel's mind had roped her in and dragged her down that road even though Teel desperately didn't want to go there, what if Keegan had cut her wrist? Dug in hard enough to find the blue veins there?

"Mommy," Keegan had wailed and pushed Teel into motion. "Mommy, it was her fault!" Keegan cried.

Until that moment, Teel had always thought of herself as a decent mother. She would never have nominated herself for mother of the year, but she wasn't so bad, and she loved her girls with every beat of her heart.

"Keegan, sweetheart," she'd said quietly, and afraid to move and scare her, but afraid to stand still and let those damned scissors start cutting again, Teel had moved to sit by her on the bed. "What did you do? Why didn't you just talk to me?"

"I tried to," Keegan answered as she swiped her hand over her eyes, bringing the point of the scissors far closer to her face and her eyes than was comfortable for Teel to see. "You didn't listen. You said the three of us shouldn't have acted that way on the playground."

"You shouldn't have, honey." Teel had taken the scissors, just like that. Covered Keegan's hand with her own and forcibly taken the scissors. "You know that. That's no reason to do this."

That hadn't been the right thing to say, either, and then Teel had to gather her daughter in her arms and hold her. The tears, the tantrum as Bobby referred to it, lasted another fifteen minutes at the least. When at last Teel and Keegan had joined Bobby and Rachel for dinner, their rice was cold and clumped and their meat was tough and dry.

Bobby had suggested that maybe Keegan needed a little more punishment. Maybe she needed to be grounded, but

Teel had insisted this was punishment enough. Detention. And now this uneven, shaggy haircut.

Teel picked up her coffee cup and took a big drink. The coffee had long since gone cold and bitter, but she drank it anyway. The caffeine couldn't hurt. She wondered now if she'd handled that episode all wrong. If she should have punished Keegan for her impulsive behavior. For the tantrum. If instead of whisking her to the mall to have a stylist save her daughter and finish what she'd started (Keegan had gone to school with a very chic, fashionable haircut the next day,) maybe she should have made her go with her hair shaggy from her own hatchet job.

"Teel?"

She looked up when she heard the tap on her classroom door. Too exhausted to move, Teel nodded to her friend Maggie Hammond to come in. Since this morning, since learning that the girl down the street from them had killed herself, Teel had felt like there was a ton of lead in her ass and she could hardly move.

Maggie Hammond was probably only two or three years younger than Teel, but today, she looked as if she might be fifteen years younger, mostly because Teel *felt* like she could be fifteen years older. Maggie carried her own cup, but Teel knew it was tea and not coffee.

"Hey." Maggie, who taught fourth grade, sat on the stool behind Teel's podium and studied her. "You look like hell."

Teel didn't have any sarcasm in her to answer Maggie. She hadn't talked to Maggie yet this morning, because she hadn't graced the teacher's lounge with her presence. She'd barely been able to function to put her make up on, style her hair, and find something to wear.

On top of everything else at war inside her, and she was still puzzling all of that out, she felt guilty. And not just because her two daughters were alive and well, while Jeannie

English's only child was dead. But because it was all she could think about, as if living down the street from them was enough to make her close enough to feel shock and grief. Probably, being an old childhood friend's mother and being a neighbor didn't entitle her to this level of despair, and yet, there it was. The thought of pretty little Marin English killing herself hurt Teel so deeply; she knew it would never really go away.

Jeannie English might want to tell her to go to hell, because how could she possibly know what this sort of loss felt like. Whatever it was that was pulling Teel under and dragging her around and beating her against the rocks in the undertow, it sure as hell couldn't be grief because her children were okay.

"I can't get my head around this," Teel mumbled. "I can't process this."

When Maggie didn't answer her immediately, Teel glanced up at her. They'd been colleagues for a good fifteen years, and somewhere in the past ten, they'd come to be close friends. The only person she talked to and trusted as much (besides Bobby, of course) as Maggie was her sister. Maggie leaned her left elbow on the podium and rested her chin in her hand. She held her tea cup in her other. She reminded Teel of a sprite, petite and usually lively and bubbly. Today, though, she was quiet, maybe saddened by Marin's suicide as Teel was.

Because a child's death was universally wrong. Didn't matter if you knew the child or the family, it was just wrong. Maggie had known Marin when she was much younger, when Keegan and Marin had been friends. Teel had brought Keegan to school with her occasionally in those late summer days when she came in to get her classroom ready. Back in those days, Keegan and Marin had been inseparable, and so Keegan and Marin would race the halls and draw pictures on

Teel's chalkboard while Teel and Maggie alternately worked on their classrooms and talked about their summers.

"I know," Maggie answered. "I just wish kids could get that it's temporary. Whatever it is, it's temporary. Things'll always get better."

Teel agreed with Maggie, but she couldn't find her voice. She had a feeling she could talk about this until she ran out of words, and her voice was used up, and her face and lips were blue. She would never get her head wrapped around this. She wanted to change it. As always with death, she wanted to deny this. Deny that it was possible. Surely, the doctors were mistaken. Surely, Marin was just sleeping.

And if that wasn't possible, if denying it away and proving the doctors were wrong wasn't possible, then Teel wanted to turn back time. To call Jeannie English at just the moment before it happened and tell her to check on Marin. Bobby had built all but three of the houses in their neighborhood, and Teel had walked the halls of every house he built, and she knew the layout of the English house. She knew how long it would take Jeannie to get from the master bedroom to Marin's room, from the kitchen to Marin's room, from anywhere in that house to Marin's room.

"How's Keegan?" Maggie asked and roused Teel out of her thoughts.

Teel swallowed the last of her cold coffee, set her mug on her desk, and stood up. Rachel had cried. Nothing over the top, but she had cried and burrowed into Teel's arms, needing comfort.

Impulsive, rambunctious, and melodramatic Keegan had stared at Teel when she told her. Dry-eyed. Dead-pan face. No comments.

"I don't know, Mags," Teel finally said. "I have no idea."

Chapter 4

KEEGAN

WASN'T it just like her mother to make her go to school today? In one breath, she told her Marin English was dead and then in the next, she directed her to the shower to get ready for school. Keegan guessed being a "Once Upon A Time Friend" to a dead girl didn't really qualify anyone for grief.

Not that she felt bad about Marin. Well...right now, she didn't really feel much of anything about anything. She'd showered and done her hair and put eyeliner and eye shadow on and bumped into Rachel in the hall and then gone back to her room and dressed in skinny-legged school pants and an oversized school sweatshirt. She'd hoped her mom's mind was too preoccupied to notice the sweatshirt; it was against dress code, but Keegan didn't care.

Mom noticed, though and sent her back to her room to change. Keegan hated school, and she kind of hated all of her teachers, except Fr. Dean (James Dean, and he kind of looked like that old actor, too.) Fr. Dean was her English teacher, and even though Keegan liked Fr. Dean, she sure didn't love English class.

It didn't help that she was Rachel Alexander's little sister. Keegan brought home an occasional B, in the midst of As, but Rachel's GPA was damned near perfect. Not to mention that Rachel was more self-controlled and even-keeled and pleasant to be around.

And then throw in the fact that Mom was a teacher in the Catholic school system, and everyone and their stupid dog at the high school loved her, and you had the final nail in the coffin for Keegan.

Okay, so, maybe that was a little tasteless. The coffin image wasn't really something Keegan wanted to think about. She'd put on a sweater and then stared at a piece of toast for about fifteen minutes before she followed her mom out to the car to leave for school.

She braced herself, figuring her mom would hammer at her about Marin. In fact, she was so worried that her mom would bring that whole deal up, her stomach hurt and she hadn't eaten the toast and had nothing in there to throw up.

But Mom hadn't said a word. Nothing. Keegan was relieved at first, but then she decided it was actually worse than having her mom talk to her. Ask her about Marin—if Keegan had known something was wrong, if Marin had been acting funny.

Keegan had her white slip. Most days she drove to school and then when she got out, Mom came around to the other side and drove on to her school. But today, Mom was driving. On auto-pilot. It was okay, though. Keegan didn't feel much like driving anyway. Instead she'd sat with her backpack between her feet and stared at her hands folded in her lap. Her fingernails looked terrible. She had a hangnail on her thumb that was probably infected. She chewed on it all of the time; her mom was constantly ragging on her about that. So if the hangnail was infected and Keegan chewed on it, did that mean an infection could get inside her? Make her sick?

Sick enough to die?

Keegan stole several quick glances at Mom on the way to school. She looked old; Keegan felt a little sicker when she saw how there were more years on her mom's face today. It wasn't like wrinkles or age spots, but there was just something that made Mom look exhausted and old and worn.

She'd looked away then, because even if she did get sick of her mom, she loved her. And she knew it wasn't nice to think of a parent as worn or old. Her eyes were bloodshot, and Keegan knew she and Rachel had cried this morning about Marin.

But this seemed like more. Like her mom could hardly look at her. Like it was Keegan that was upsetting her.

What could her mom know that would make her not want to look at her?

When her mom turned into the school lot, Keegan took a deep breath, wiped her clammy hands on her pants, and opened the door before the car was even stopped. Her mom might have mumbled goodbye, but she wasn't sure. Keegan had grabbed her backpack and slammed the door and walked straight into school and into the bathroom.

She tossed her glass of juice and then stood there in the stall shaking and trying to throw up more, but there just wasn't anything. Her legs felt like noodles, so she leaned up against the cold, beige metal partition. When she was at home, and she got sick, her mom took care of her. She'd rub her back or hold her hair out of the way and then get her a drink of water to rinse her mouth out. Once when Mom hadn't been home, Rachel had stepped in and taken care of her. It was the first time she'd ever really felt like Rachel liked her.

Keegan braced herself when the outer door opened. She heard the buzz of conversation and lockers opening and closing in the halls, and then the door closed.

"I heard she swallowed a bottle of pills."

"Really? I heard she hung herself."

Keegan rolled her head on the stall wall and closed her eyes. *God. Let the rumors begin.* She didn't want to hear this. She didn't give a damn who they were talking about; it wasn't that she felt any loyalty to Marin. She just didn't want to hear this.

And anyway, how the hell would anyone know? The news people hadn't said jack about how she did it. Only that she had died, an apparent suicide.

"I heard we're going to have a prayer service for her later today."

Keegan struggled to identify the voices outside her stall. She was pretty sure one of them was Tiffany Holmes, but she couldn't tell who the other one was. Tiffany was what all of Mom's books on teenage girls and self-confidence and bullying would refer to as a queen bee. So no doubt whoever she was talking to would be one of her little worker bees. Some wanna be.

People that bullied people like Marin and pushed her until she killed herself.

Except that Keegan knew it wasn't Tiffany this time.

"I heard Mr. Laughlin talking about giving all of us time to talk to the school counselor. To deal with the grief."

Keegan rolled her eyes. So Tiffany and her posse were going to take that road, huh? They'd probably play this for all it was worth, and Keegan thought that was just as bad or worse than bullying someone to death. Ride the coattails of her suicide to get attention for themselves. It seemed a little like rape to Keegan.

Her stomach churned violently, and she quickly leaned over the institutional black-seated, white bodied toilet and vomited something. Since there was no food inside her (she'd hardly touched her dinner the night before) Keegan wondered if maybe it was a lung or something.

The air was heavy with sudden silence. Tiffany and whoever was with her—Brandy Borrowman?—were probably now freaking out about who had overheard their conversation. Either that or figuring out how to add a little more drama to make themselves look even better.

Keegan lifted a shaky hand to her mouth and wiped a little spot of puke from the corner of her lips. She ripped a square of toilet paper off and cleaned her finger and then threw it in the toilet.

"Keegan? Is that you?"

So they must have squatted down to check out her shoes (beat up gray and purple Pumas) and her backpack (orange and white.) Her stomach still roiled, and now her head pounded, but she'd made her presence known and Tiffany and Brandy—she was pretty sure now it was Brandy—weren't going to walk out of here until she answered them.

"Yeah."

"Are you okay?"

"I'm fine," Keegan lied. She flushed the toilet and then took a deep breath. There was no way in hell she was going to make it through this day.

"Honey, did you throw up?"

Puke. She could puke again just from Tiffany calling her honey. She hated when anyone called her cutesy names like that, except Mom and even then, it still grated on her nerves sometimes. Tiffany Holmes called everyone hon or sweetie, and it was so fake, it drove Keegan crazy.

Keegan took more toilet paper and blew her nose. She hated how when you puked, it ended up feeling like you had some in your nose and you had to blow it to clear it. She dropped that piece of sandpapery toilet paper into the toilet, flushed again, and reached for the latch on the door.

"Hey." Tiffany stepped closer to her and put her arm around her shoulders. "Are you okay?"

"Yeah. Fine." Keegan nodded. She pushed past Brandy to get to the sink and washed her hands. A toothbrush would make her feel a little better. Or a cup to rinse her mouth out. No way she could just lean over the sink and use her hand to cup water to her mouth. Not with these two divas watching her. And yet, she couldn't just walk around all day with the taste of puke in her mouth.

"Here."

Brandy handed her a bottle of water. Keegan raised an eyebrow, surprised by the offer. When she didn't immediately take it, Brandy popped the seal and unscrewed the cap.

"Thanks."

Still kind of awkward rinsing her mouth out in front of them after they'd heard her puking just a few minutes ago, but she had to do it. Screw them if they got off on invading someone's privacy that way.

"I'm so sorry about Marin," Tiffany said as Keegan took another big drink. "You were friends with her, weren't you?"

"No." Keegan spit that mouthful out in the sink and then rinsed the sink out.

"I thought you were. Like, in grade school or something."

Keegan stood up straight and looked Tiffany in the eye. Gray eyes. Dark blue eyeliner and tons of eye shadow and mascara that made her lashes look like some kind of model.

Tiffany was gorgeous, but it was only skin deep. Keegan knew the minute she walked out of this bathroom, Tiffany would tell everyone she'd heard Keegan Alexander puking in the bathroom. That Keegan was a wreck about Marin.

Which wasn't even true, but then most rumors weren't.

"Yeah, well, I wasn't." Keegan picked her backpack up and slung it over her shoulder. She walked out of the bathroom and braced herself for the rest of the day.

Keegan ignored the group of kids gathered around Marin's locker, just four to the right of her own. They were all chanting something, and as Keegan swung her own door open, she realized they were praying. Jesus, she thought. Someone dies, and all the freaks come out.

"I cannot f-ing believe this."

Keegan didn't look up when she heard Jess Levine's voice behind her. She did roll her eyes, because it irked her that Jess wanted to use the F word, but didn't have the guts. She grabbed her biology lab manual and her Spanish workbook and shoved her backpack into her locker before closing it.

"Can you? I mean, why would she do it?"

"I don't know." Keegan wished Jess would back off a bit. She was in her face, and suddenly Keegan couldn't breathe. God, what if she puked right here in the hall? Or passed out?

"What're they doing?" Keegan glanced back at Jess. There were papers taped all over Marin's locker, but Keegan couldn't tell what they were.

"Marin's friend Kate kind of made a little shrine by her locker," Jess said quietly. "It's so sad."

Keegan resisted the urge to roll her eyes again.

"I still can't f-ing believe she killed herself. Why didn't she just talk to someone?"

"I don't know," Keegan answered. She had biology first hour, and she was desperate to escape the growing crowd in the halls. But Jess grabbed her elbow and steered her back toward the crowd. "What?"

"You gotta sign the card," Jess told her. "There's a card there for Marin's family. Aren't you gonna sign the card?"

"Yeah, yeah," Keegan mumbled as she yanked her arm away from Jess's grip. "I'll sign the fucking card."

Chapter 5

Teel

THE DOORBELL and the phone rang at the same time. Teel sat still at the kitchen table and willed someone else to magically answer both. She was still bone-tired or something, and she knew instinctually it was actually *or something*. Still shock. Sickened and saddened by such a senseless loss. Grief for a life snuffed out way too damned early. Sympathy for Jeannie and Rick.

No one was going to suddenly appear and answer the door or the phone. No one was around to run interference. Teel had to laugh humorlessly at that one. Run interference? Who did she think she was? She was just a neighbor for God's sake. Since when did neighbors of grieving families need someone to run interference for them?

Rachel was still in class. Modern German History, if her memory served, and Teel wouldn't be surprised if it didn't. Bobby was still working, and Keegan had disappeared into her room the second she'd walked into the house after

school. Teel had gone down the hall and stared at her closed
door for several long minutes. Knock? Ask her how her day
was? Give her some space? At what point did a parent stop
worrying about her own child after her child's acquaintance
committed suicide?

In the end, she'd given Keegan her space and left her
alone. Except really, she'd walked away to give herself some
space. Some alone time. Although she'd felt isolated at school
all day. Even with Maggie coming in to check on her now
and then. Even with her other colleagues sharing her shock
and her sadness over the news.

She snagged the phone as she hurried to the front door.
"Hello?"

She was amazed that she sounded normal. Friendly.
Happy. She supposed that until this morning, she'd been a
regular Pollyana and while she was usually greeted with
smiles and friendly hellos, maybe people got sick of her.
Maybe people got sick of her smile and her contentedness.

"Teel?"

"Yes." The caller couldn't possibly sense that she was irritated with herself for not checking caller ID before she'd
answered. She was in no mood for small talk. Ironically, she
wished it was a telemarketer, because then maybe she could
actually be rude and just hang up.

"Teel, this is Elaine Caldwell from Blessed Sacrament."

Keegan's school counselor? Calling here? Immediately,
Teel's heart was in her throat and then it kind of exploded
out her throat and into her mouth, and she felt like she
was chewing it as she pulled the front door open. Why was
the counselor calling?

She hadn't heard a peep from Keegan since she'd come
home an hour ago.

Glad to see her sister standing on the front porch, Teel
waved her in and then hurried down the hall. She didn't

want to go in all gang-busters and freak Keegan out, but on the other hand, she was the mom and she was scared. She turned the handle and pushed the door open, and for a moment, her heart stopped beating. What if?

She imagined Jeannie walking into Marin's room and finding her daughter dead.

Keegan appeared to be sleeping. Teel stood and watched the steady rise and fall of her chest. Relieved beyond reason, Teel slumped against the closet door behind her.

Thankyouthankyouthankyou

But what if she'd taken something? Was there anything in the house that was dangerous? Could she have overdosed?

"Teel?" Elaine Caldwell again, no doubt wondering if their connection was bad.

Teel shot up straight to look for any evidence that Keegan might have taken something. An empty pill bottle, maybe. The closet door rattled, and Keegan jumped awake. She looked like she'd been on a three-day bender, her bloodshot eyes just about the only color in her face.

"God, Mom, get out," she groaned and rolled over to bury her face in her pillow.

Too relieved to be angry or hurt by Keegan's rudeness, Teel walked out of the room but left the door open.

"Yes, Elaine," Teel finally answered, "I'm sorry. Someone rang the doorbell."

Teel watched Eve, at home in her kitchen. Eve, younger by four years (the same age difference as Rachel and Keegan, though Teel and Eve had always been close,) had been the one to nickname Teel. At two when she was learning to talk, Toniel had come out as Teel, and the name had stuck. Thirty-seven years later, Teel was only Toniel on legal documents. To everyone else in her life, she was Teel or Mrs. Alexander.

Eve, taller than Teel by an inch or two and brunette (Eve looked like their mom; Teel more like their dad) with brown

eyes, had a heart big enough to mother a school full of children, no children of her own to put inside that heart, and an
ex-husband that smoked two packs of Camels a day.

"...concerned about Keegan."

Teel shook her head to clear it and turned away from Eve.

"Why are you concerned about Keegan?"

Well, no kidding, Teel was concerned about Keegan, too.
But something must have happened at school for Elaine
Caldwell to be calling her.

"Mr. Laughlin arranged for any of the kids to come and
talk to us about Marin any time through the day. Keegan
didn't come in."

Teel sighed. Was that all? Because Keegan didn't want to
talk to a school counselor something was wrong? Of course
Keegan was going to have to break at some point and talk to
someone, but Teel was a little irritated to get a call like this
on day one.

"Well, maybe she's not ready to talk about it." Even after
justifying it in her head, this sounded lame, even to Teel.

"That's true, and that's fine. There were several students
who didn't."

"And are you calling all of their parents?" Teel hoped
she didn't sound as defensive as she felt. She and Elaine
Caldwell weren't exactly friendly, but she didn't need to be
rude.

"No. But there were rumors that she got sick this
morning."

"You're calling me based on rumors another student
probably started that my daughter got sick at school?"

Teel looked over her shoulder at Eve and shook her head.
Eve raised her eyebrows and lifted a bottle of wine sugges-
tively. Teel noticed she'd set out two glasses. A glass of wine
might just knock her on her ass right now, because she
hadn't been able to eat anything other than her breakfast

cereal this morning. But she nodded anyway and then turned her attention back to the woman on the phone.

"Well, Keegan skipped her last two classes," Elaine told her. "I just wanted to let you know what was going on. Sometimes teens aren't very forthcoming with their parents."

Teel took a moment to think about Elaine's words. Professionally, she knew Elaine was right and well within her obligation to call Teel and share her concerns. And yet, as a parent, any insinuation that her child might be keeping things from her made her mad as hell.

"I appreciate your call, Elaine," she said, proud of herself for tamping down the flare of anger and defensiveness again.

"Teel, I don't mean to imply anything," Elaine said quietly. "We've had a tragedy at school. It's the first time we've ever had a student commit suicide. I have no idea what state of mind Keegan's in. I just know that she and Marin did have classes together, and that some of her behavior lately has sent up some red flags for some faculty."

Her behavior *lately*?

"Thank you."

"Please let me know if there's anything I can do."

"Thank you. I will."

As soon as she hung up, Eve took the phone from her hand and exchanged it for a glass of white wine.

"Drink."

Teel took a healthy swallow and laughed without humor. "I haven't eaten anything today but a bowl of raisin bran."

"Then sip," Eve corrected herself.

"What's going on, Eve? What the hell is going on?"

"Who was on the phone?" Eve sat on one of the backless stools at the kitchen island. Teel ran her fingers through her hair and then rubbed her forehead with her fingertips.

"Elaine Caldwell. The counselor at Blessed Sacrament."

"Oh, poor baby," Eve whispered. She pushed her glass just

out of the way and leaned over to hug Teel. "Keegan's not taking this well? I was so worried about her when I heard it this morning."

Grateful for the comfort, Teel let herself sink into Eve's embrace, but only for a moment. She couldn't afford to fall apart right now. Not if she was going to drag her daughter out here and make her talk. She could fall apart later, when Bobby was home and the girls were in bed.

"Keegan was fine when I told her this morning," she mumbled as she pulled away from Eve and backed up to sit on the stool next to Eve's.

"Fine?"

"Dry-eyed. Almost bored."

"That doesn't sound like Keegan."

Again Teel sighed and pushed her hair back from her face. This time she left her hands on her head and fingers in her hair and looked up at Eve. "Not at all."

"Maybe she's in shock. It might take a while for it to hit her."

"Well, there were rumors going around today that she got sick at school this morning. And she skipped her last two classes this afternoon."

Eve flinched but said nothing.

"I don't know how to handle this, Eve," Teel admitted. "I don't know what to do."

"Maybe you do nothing," Eve suggested. "Maybe you wait for her to come to you."

"And if she doesn't?"

"Keegan's not gonna do anything stupid, Teel."

Teel shrugged and looked away from her sister's heavy stare. "I bet Jeannie would have said the same thing about Marin yesterday at this time."

Eve nodded, but then she seemed to change her mind. She shrugged and shook her head.

"You can't know that." She sipped from her own glass of wine. "You have no idea what was going on in that house. What led up to this."

"True." Teel stood, picked up her glass and walked across the large, open living room. She glanced at the deck. It was a beautiful day. They should go outside. But she was too tired to walk another step, and the couch sounded more comfortable. She sat and propped her feet up on the big, round coffee table.

"It's just so damned scary," she mumbled.

"Of course it is," Eve agreed with her. She picked up her glass and joined Teel on the couch. "Every parent in the city is going to be triple-checking on their kids every night for a while."

Teel thought about what Elaine had said. Keegan's behavior sending up red flags to the faculty *lately*? She wanted to talk about it, but maybe she shouldn't. Eve might tell her she was imagining the worst, and she needed to settle down because Keegan was going to read this fear inside her immediately, and that could make things worse.

"How's Dennis?"

Eve snorted and laughed at the mention of her ex-husband. "Dennis is Dennis. Why would he ever change?"

"Are you still sleeping with him?"

"Do you really wanna know?"

Teel laughed, glad for the change of subject. Something a little lighter, like her little sister's divorce.

"Well, his lack of change might be due to the fact that he's still getting the best part of you. For free."

"How do you know that's the best part of me?" Eve arched an eyebrow at Teel over her wine glass.

"I heard all those rumors when we were younger."

"Toniel Alexander!" Eve laughed so loud, she covered her

mouth and glanced over her shoulder, obviously wondering if Keegan had heard her.

Teel took a drink and laid her head back on the crème microfiber couch. The room was very soothing, the walls a flat, pale celery and the floor an oak hardwood. She and Bobby had found an area rug with muted greens and sand tones and crème, which really pulled the room together. The cathedral ceiling and the wall of windows in the back of the house created a huge space where it was possible to unwind and still have room for other people.

"Thanks, Eve."

Eve set her glass on the coffee table and scooted closer to Teel. Teel laid her head on Eve's shoulder and thought again about what Elaine Caldwell had said.

Chapter 6

RACHEL

ALL DAY, people talked about it. Rachel didn't get it. Marin was a high school kid. Why did they have to discuss her suicide in every damned class? Sometimes her professors had even picked up on the thread of conversation and just stopped lecturing and said maybe it was more important to address the Marin English story.

Okay, of course, Rachel *got* it. How could she *not* get it? She'd never heard of anyone doing this here, not as far back as she could remember. Six kids had died through her school years; she'd counted them this morning in her rhetoric class. Two were sick with cancer, one when Rachel was just in second grade. The boy who died was in eighth grade. And then a girl from the public high school died when Rachel was a freshman. She had some kind of cancer, too. That right there was weird enough. Two kids from public schools had died in two separate accidents when she was in grade school. And then when she was sixteen, two kids from her school had been killed in a car accident. Drunk driving, so of course Rachel had listened to her mom lecture for hours on end about drinking and driving.

As if Rachel had any desire to drink, let alone get drunk and get in her car and drive.

No one had ever committed suicide. No kids that Rachel knew of anyway. It was just a different kind of weird and sad, and it hung on her like an anchor and chain. It had dragged her down and made it hard for her to move all day.

She'd seen Deacon, but only for a few minutes. He had three classes today, and since it was Thursday, those three classes were each an hour and a half long. He'd been on his way to his last class when she left Modern German History.

She stretched out now on her bed and remembered how he'd hugged her. Tall and broad-shouldered, his hugs swallowed her and made her feel safe. She wished he were here now. Except that would be hard, because Mom and Dad didn't even know she was dating him. She'd never told them anything about him, not even his name. She didn't know why, because she'd had other boyfriends. She'd had to sit through the safe sex talk with Mom at least 87 times.

Maybe by now her mom would trust her. And if not, she could just close her eyes and grit her teeth until her mom got done lecturing. When she was younger, she thought it was really cool that her mom was a teacher. She still did, because those little kids at the grade school loved her. Her mom had gotten teacher of the year twice; she related to those little kids so well.

But her mom being a teacher meant her mom was up on all of the psychobabble crap in all of those books about kids and adolescents and teen drinking and sex and bullying. Mom didn't usually talk like that; she didn't use psychobabble jargon, and she didn't use that crap as a shield to keep her and Keegan at bay. She was a mom, first and most importantly, and she talked and listened to her and Keegan.

But that didn't mean she wasn't totally aware of everything going on and that she didn't lecture them on all that crap.

Rachel figured she should get up and do some homework. She had an essay due for rhetoric next Tuesday. She had a chapter to read for American History tomorrow. Instead, she climbed from her bed and went to stand at her window. She couldn't see the English house since her room faced the backyard. Keegan could, though; her room was across the hall, so her window faced the street.

"Rach?"

Rachel turned from the window to see Keegan standing in the doorway. Her sister looked like hell, and yet Rachel hadn't seen her cry yet. Maybe she and Marin *hadn't* been the best of friends since they were younger. But still. She used to play at her house all the time. Marin had spent a lot of nights over here, too. Rachel had hung out with them now and then, watching movies or playing a make-believe game that let them all be rock stars.

And now she was dead. Just…gone.

No. Not just dead. She killed herself. Killed. Herself.

The thought made Rachel want to puke, but Keegan, standing in her doorway, blocked a quick escape to the bathroom. She didn't feel like explaining her feelings to Keegan. She didn't feel like talking at all, really, unless of course Deacon was here. She wished he were. Then again, she probably wouldn't talk to him. She just wished she could lie in his arms, rest her head on his chest, and listen to his heartbeat.

Keegan squirmed a little bit, like she was uncomfortable with what she wanted to say. Rachel waited silently, figuring she would say something about Marin.

"Will you help me with my biology?" Keegan cleared her

throat and worked hard not to meet Rachel's eyes. "We did a lab today. I have two questions I'm not sure about."

"Really?" Rachel felt the cold disdain paint itself on her face, but she couldn't help it. "Your friend killed herself last night, and you're in here asking me for help on homework?"

Keegan swallowed hard, but from across the room Rachel couldn't tell if she was crying or even near tears.

"Would you?"

Rachel's cell phone beeped to notify her of a text message. Deacon? She ignored Keegan and grabbed the phone from her bed.

Meet me for coffee when I'm done?

She closed her eyes and took a deep breath. The text made her feel better already. She couldn't wait to see him, to feel his arms around her.

"I'll look at it later," she mumbled, still not looking at Keegan.

From the corner of her eye, she saw her sister stand up straight. Irritated that Keegan wouldn't leave her alone, she turned, intending to tell her to get out.

"She wasn't my friend," Keegan said quietly as she walked out of Rachel's room.

———

SHE LEFT THE HOUSE EARLY, because it felt like a frigging mausoleum in there. It was so hot outside today that the air was constantly running, and Rachel had been buried under her blankets reading her American History homework when she decided to hell with it.

Keegan's bedroom door was closed when she left. It was after five, but her mom was nowhere to be found. Her dad wasn't even home yet. Maybe he'd known it would suck to come home, so he was trying to stay away. Mom had acted like a zombie when Rachel had first come home after class. She'd asked her how class was, but Rachel had kept her answer short because she knew her mom wasn't listening.

She hadn't bothered with a note. She'd left the house without a word to anyone. She hadn't changed her clothes; Deacon would like the skimpy denim shorts and pink blouse. She had touched up her makeup and brushed her hair. Put on more perfume. She'd discovered that just a touch of perfume drove Deacon crazy.

One of these days she wanted to drive him crazy enough to make love to her, because *sometimes* it made her crazy that he was moving so slowly.

It was too early for him to be out of class, but she went to the coffee shop anyway to wait for him. The Coffee Bean was just a little corner spot. The building itself looked like hell, and if Rachel ever stopped to think too much about how dirty and old the place was, she would never have set foot inside, let alone drank from their cups or eaten their food.

She found a table near the counter and unloaded her backpack. They didn't have a jukebox, but there was a stereo on the counter. The station varied, depending on who was working and whether or not he or she would let the students touch the dial.

It was too bad the essay she had to write was just a reaction to one they'd read in class. Because maybe she could write about how frigging weird it was to be the neighbor of the girl who killed herself. Even now, with her head bent over her notebook and her pencil flying across the paper, she heard people talking and she heard Marin's name and the words *dead* and *overdose* within the first four minutes of sitting down.

She glanced at her watch once and saw that it was almost six. Deacon should be coming any minute. She wondered if her dad was home, and if they wondered where she was.

"Hey."

"Hi." She smiled when she looked up at him. He grinned and tossed his own backpack to the bench on the other side of the booth.

He leaned over and dropped a kiss on her upturned lips. She watched him go up to the counter and order them both coffee.

Her phone beeped.

Where are you?

She answered Keegan and told her to leave her alone and then turned her phone off and put it in her backpack. She didn't even need it on since Deacon was here with her now.

She scooted over in the booth when he came back. He set the coffees on the table and then sat down by her. This time he kissed her long and hard, and Rachel felt her world tilt back to normal. Marin. Keegan. Mom. None of that mattered when she was with Deacon.

"Get a room!" Someone called from across the café. Rachel felt Deacon move, and she knew without breaking the kiss or opening her eyes that he was flipping the heckler off. Actually, flipping off the room at large.

"I'd like to get a room," she whispered against his lips.

"My roommate's there," he answered. They broke apart, and Rachel let him study her for several long seconds.

"You okay?"

She took a deep breath and shrugged. "I dunno."

"Was she depressed?" he asked as he reached for his coffee.

Rachel bit her tongue before she could respond with sarcasm. Apparently Marin had been depressed or she wouldn't be dead. She wouldn't have killed herself.

"I don't know." She took a drink of her own coffee and wished just for a second that she was at home drinking her mom's.

"Has Keegan talked to her lately?"

Rachel snorted and looked up at Deacon. "Are you serious? Keegan doesn't tell anybody jack. She could've been right there with Marin when she did it, and she wouldn't talk about it."

Deacon squeezed her shoulder.

"My sister's just weird."

"Aren't we all kind of weird when we're her age?"

Rachel thought about what she'd been like when she was fifteen. Hell, what she was like at any age compared to how Keegan was at the same age.

"No. Not like Keegan is."

Chapter 7

Teel

SHE WANTED TO SEE JEANNIE. Well, she didn't really *want* to. But she felt by not seeing her, she was being a bad neighbor. A bad friend. They'd never been the kind of friends to call each other or to go for lunch and share secrets and laughter. But they'd been friendly back when the girls were younger. Friendly enough, and for God's sake Keegan and Marin had been pretty tight once upon a time, so she felt like she should go to her. Offer her sympathy. Offer to help. Deliver that completely ignorant line about 'if there's anything I can do' that Teel herself hated hearing. If she'd been counting at her own dad's funeral a few years ago, she'd probably heard that phrase at least fifteen to twenty times. As if the person who said it could just magically step in and pull the dead person back to life. Breathe them back into that wonderful, vibrant, one of a kind person he or she used to be.

And yet, now that she was on this side of the equation, she felt a desperate need to do something. To help. She knew, of course, there was nothing that could be done. That help-lessness made her head and her heart hurt.

She'd walked down to their house last night. All the while, she'd felt the stares from other neighbors' houses. Were they inside watching her from their windows, wondering what she was doing? Did they think she was caring and brave or just plain stupid? Bobby thought she was caring, but he still thought she was stupid. He hadn't said so, but she'd seen it in his eyes when she left the house.

The English house looked deserted. Not empty, like the parents were at work and the daughter was at school. Deserted like Marin's death had sucked every bit of love and laughter from it. Teel stood in the street in front of the house for a long time. She was scared. Scared to knock on the door and invite the same desperation Marin had felt to her own house, her own family. And yet, she knew she didn't need to invite it. That desperation, that heartache, had come barging in earlier this morning when Rachel had turned on the news and heard that Marin was dead.

She was scared to face Jeannie, too. She'd seen the look of grief in a mother's eyes when her child died too young. The way that grief ate you alive and left you as just a shell of whom you used to be. No parent should ever have to look or feel that way, and seeing it on another parent was a hell Teel never wanted to face again.

But she rang the doorbell and waited for what felt like hours on the porch. It was probably no more than five seconds. The scene from the middle of the night kept playing in her mind. The EMTs. The ambulance and the flashing lights. Jeannie and Rick following their daughter, who was strapped on the gurney the EMTs pushed.

She was just about to give up, when she heard the lock click and the doorknob turn. Her stomach dropped to the porch floor, and she realized she shouldn't have come. She wasn't equipped to deal with this. She didn't know what to say. It wasn't her place.

Rick's bloodshot eyes were not unfriendly, just empty. His hair stood up on end, and he had a day's growth of beard stubble on his face.

If it were Eve or Dennis, she would know. She wouldn't say a word, she'd just step in and put her arms around him or her and hold on.

"Rick, I…" Her voice broke. She looked away, ashamed to be completely whole and content in her home and crying for a loss that wasn't hers.

He nodded and pursed his lips.

"Jeannie?" She said it like a question, but she didn't know why. She didn't want to see Jeannie. She couldn't, now that she was here.

Rick covered his mouth with his hand, as if he had to hold something in. The house was dark behind him. Teel thought of her own house, the whole back wall open to the sunset.

"She's sleeping," Rick finally answered. "Doctor gave her something for nerves."

Teel nodded, grateful that Jeannie could have some sort of escape for now. Maybe if she could get through these first few days on auto-pilot, everything numb, then…*then what, Teel? Was that going to magically make the next six months easier? The next two years?*

"Bobby and I are so sorry," she managed to spit out.

He nodded again. He was younger than her by a few years, but today he looked old.

"How's Keegan?" he asked, and Teel felt a jolt of guilt. Rick had lost his own daughter this morning, and he was asking how her daughter was doing over the loss, and Keegan had yet to express any sorrow.

Teel shrugged, and he nodded, and just like that she'd answered and Rick thought she meant who knows how anyone is with something like this? Or maybe he thought she meant that Keegan was doing as well as could be expected.

She had to get away from him. Her palms were sweaty, and she felt her stomach twist a bit. She was embarrassed that her daughter was as yet unaffected by Marin's suicide.

What kind of friend, old or new, wouldn't be saddened by a suicide?

What kind of mother would hang her daughter out to dry instead of understanding that grief is a personal, immeasurable, intangible thing?

"Please tell Jeannie," Teel's eyes filled with tears, "we're praying for all of you."

"I will."

"Rick, if there's anything we can do…"

He nodded, but he said what Teel had just been thinking.

"Thank you, but there's nothing, Teel."

Of course there was nothing. She nodded and then turned away. She heard the door shut and the lock click before she took a step away.

———

THE CATHOLIC CHURCH holds that suicide is a sin against God. Teel wondered about that. About Marin's funeral. Marin hadn't gone to a Catholic school, but Jeannie and Rick were members of St. Thomas, as she and Bobby had been for the past twenty years. Teel knew the priests; she knew them well, actually, as she had been a teacher at St. Thomas for over twenty years. The four priests there now were kind and fun-loving and giving. But she had no idea how they felt about suicide and what they would do with Marin English and her family.

It wasn't her business, but that didn't mean she could stop worrying about it. She'd been lying here worrying about it for the past hour, and before that, she'd worried about Rachel and where she'd disappeared to tonight, and then she'd told herself she was being stupid. Rachel was old enough to go out in the evenings with friends. There was a time not even that long ago, when Teel wished Rachel *would* go out more often. That she would cut loose just once and have fun.

She glanced at the digital clock. It was nearing two. She wondered what Marin had been thinking about when she died. Who had hurt her so badly? How had she done it? Rumors had already flooded her school; Teel had even heard her fifth graders talking about it. *She overdosed. She hung herself. She slashed her wrists.* It didn't matter, and Teel hated rumors, and she hated people talking, even if they were just sharing the truth. It was human nature, and she knew no one meant any harm by it. It was fear talking, fear and guilt, and Teel was guilty of it, too. She and Maggie had wondered out loud what had happened, and she and Eve had talked about it, and she and Bobby had asked each other how Jeannie and Rick could have missed any signs leading up to it.

It was going to be a long night. She thought about getting up. She hated those nights when her body hurt just from lying in bed when she couldn't sleep. Frustrated at her insomnia and irritated with Bobby, who had gone to sleep as soon as his head hit the pillow and who was now snoring so loud he'd wake the neighborhood if she opened the windows, she turned over to lie on her stomach.

She could read. She was halfway through Elizabeth Kostova's *The Historian*, but she knew she was kidding herself. She would never be able to concentrate, not right now. She wondered what was on TV.

She rolled over again. Her breasts were tender, and she'd never been able to sleep on her stomach for too long at a time anyway. Maybe she could find a movie to watch. She might not process it, but it wouldn't hurt to stare at the TV. She wouldn't have to think.

The church prayed for those who commit suicide, she told herself. They wouldn't condemn Marin. They would pray for her. Pray for God to forgive her. Hadn't she read that somewhere? Even after that sort of death, God would forgive that person. She was sure she'd read that somewhere in her years at St. Thomas. Probably Jeannie and Rick hadn't even gotten around to worrying about that. How could they possibly be thinking about burying their daughter when they'd just lost her? How did you switch gears from planning for college years to planning a funeral?

Teel imagined Jeannie and Rick making the arrangements. The casket. The outfit they would bury her in. The mass itself. What kind of sermon would there be? What would they say on Marin's gravestone?

She sat up, stunned at how ridiculous she was being. It didn't concern her, and even if it did, so what? Why lie awake and worry about it?

Bobby didn't move when she got out of bed. She didn't want to wake him, but she wanted him to comfort her. There was nothing Bobby couldn't take her away from. Her worries and her fears always came back to her after they made love. But when she was in his arms, it was only the two of them.

They'd probably been making love when Jeannie and Rick were learning that their daughter was dead. And then in the morning, they were fooling around in the bathroom when Rachel came to tell them about Marin.

Teel was glad no one would ever have to know that, because the guilt rose up inside her now and almost choked her. She picked up her robe and then pulled the door shut behind her.

Keegan's door was open, although it had been shut earlier when Teel had gone to bed. She stepped into the room, heart in her throat, and wondered how long this terror would last, this worry every time she walked into Keegan's room that she would find something wrong. That she would find her dead. Or trying to be dead.

She was asleep. Teel didn't even need to see her chest moving to know she was breathing. She snored softly. Just enough light came through the transom above her window for Teel to see her backpack on her desk chair and her laptop open on her desk. She must have been working on homework.

Teel made her way back to the kitchen and made herself a cup of hot tea. She jumped so hard she splashed it all over her hand when Rachel shuffled down the hallway and stopped in the kitchen.

"What're you doing?" Rachel asked.

"Can't sleep."

"Me neither."

"Want some tea?"

"Yeah." Rachel sat on a stool at the counter with her chin cupped in her hand. She watched Teel make her tea, but at first she didn't seem inclined to talk.

"Mom?"

"Hmm?"

"There's something I've wanted to tell you."

Teel felt her stomach fall for the second time in less than twelve hours. She took a deep breath and handed Rachel the tea with a steady hand.

"What?"

Rachel hesitated, as if she wasn't sure she wanted to say anything now. Teel held her breath. She'd never pushed either of her girls to talk. She'd always been patient and waited them out.

What if Rachel was pregnant? Good God, could she handle that? What would Bobby say?

"I've been dating this guy," Rachel finally said, and the simple words and the smile in her voice made Teel tremble with relief.

"And?"

"That's it," Rachel answered, but she smiled. "I really like him."

"How long have you been seeing him?"

"Since last summer."

Teel's stomach tightened like Rachel punched her in the gut.

"So long?"

"Yeah."

"What's his name?"

"Deacon. Deacon Samuels."

Teel wished she could swallow the hurt with the tea. Rachel, like kids usually were, seemed clueless that she'd hurt Teel's feelings. Her smile lit up the room, and it was still the dark of night.

"Well. I hope I get to meet him one of these days."

"Yeah. Maybe so," Rachel said, and she took a drink of her tea. Teel left her sitting there and went to the back door to disengage the alarm system. Rachel watched her walk back through the room to the French doors at the back wall.

She stepped out onto the deck and leaned on the railing.

Sometimes there wasn't any reason to get up, because something was always going to knock you down again.

Chapter 8

Teel

THE LAST TIME she wore a dress was probably for a funeral, just like today. Except then it had been her dad's. Never easy, and yet, Teel would be the first to admit that there was a difference in burying an older man who had lived a full, happy life and burying a teenage girl who hadn't seen the world.

She knew without a doubt that the dress she wore to her dad's funeral wasn't going to fit her. The years that had passed since he died had added padding on her hips and her belly. Her thighs weren't so bad, and yet if the dress got hung up on her hips, did it matter if her thighs were as slender and sexy as a Playboy centerfold's?

Her thighs were nowhere near as sexy as a Playboy centerfold's, but she didn't care. Bobby hadn't ever complained, and that was enough for her. She pulled a pair of black slacks from a hanger and stepped into them. Bobby was in the bathroom. He peeked in at her, but he didn't say anything. Sometimes when he'd catch her in the act of zipping a pair of slacks or buttoning a blouse, he would say something flirty about how sexy it was to watch his woman get dressed. That the only thing sexier was watching his woman undress.

Today wasn't the time for a comment like that. Their eyes met, and then he went back to shaving, and she turned her attention back to the rack of blouses in the closet. She chose a gray blouse and slipped it on quickly. Black heels; damn, she hated them. And a black blazer. She would melt the second she stepped out of the Ford Edge at the funeral home.

She stepped into the heels and then hurried back into the bathroom to run a brush through her hair one more time. Thick and full, her blond hair seemed to add another half a foot to her height. She checked her makeup in the mirror and smiled when Bobby mumbled something about her looking damned good. They made a nice-looking couple, she supposed, as she watched him knot his navy and silver tie.

Her heels clunked loudly when she walked across the hardwood. Rachel sat at the kitchen bar with a magazine open in front of her. She stared at the refrigerator, though, and Teel doubted she'd even looked at the magazine once. She looked fresh and feminine in her navy broomstick skirt and lacy white blouse.

Teel wondered again about this boyfriend. Deacon. Deacon Samuels. Apparently he was someone pretty important to Rachel, and again, she felt hurt that she had just found out about him earlier this morning.

She expected to find Keegan in the bathroom, finishing her hair or makeup. When she found the bathroom empty, she went looking in Keegan's room.

"What are you doing?"

Her nerves were frayed, and even as she felt the anger and the impatience with Keegan, she was aware that on a day like today, nothing she felt meant a damned thing because another woman just down the street was saying goodbye to her little girl.

Keegan, face buried in her pillow, mumbled something that sounded like *sleeping*. Teel felt a rush of rage, and she reached out and yanked the comforter off Keegan.

"Get yourself out of that bed and get in the shower. Now."

"Why?" Keegan whined as she reached for the comforter.

"What the hell is wrong with you, Keegan? Today is Marin's funeral."

"I'm not going."

Teel froze as if Keegan had slapped her.

"Excuse me?"

"I said I'm not going."

"What do you mean you're not going?"

"I'm not going." Keegan rolled over and looked up at her. "Marin and I weren't friends. I don't wanna go."

"I don't give a damn what you and Marin were the day before she died." Teel curled her fingers around Keegan's wrist. "You used to be friends with her. You used to go to her house, and you used to spend time with her parents, and you are going to the funeral to pay your respects."

"What does that even mean? Pay my respects? I have no respect for her."

Keegan sprung out of bed and moved closer to Teel.

"I'm beginning to think you have no respect for anyone, anymore," Teel answered. "You will get in that shower right now, or you'll be grounded for the next month."

"So ground me," Keegan shrugged.

Teel caught herself before she moved. The thought had crossed her mind to slap her daughter. She'd spanked both girls when the occasion called for it when they were younger, but she'd never laid a hand on either of them once they'd gotten older.

Keegan suddenly stood up straight and looked over Teel's shoulder.

"This is really disappointing, Keegan." Bobby's quiet words seemed to do what Teel's anger could not. Teel didn't know if he'd thrown the guilt switch or if Keegan was afraid Bobby would follow through on the threat of punishment and make it even worse, but she moved. Teel watched as she grabbed clean underwear and pushed past her and Bobby and out the door.

"You've got about fifteen minutes," Bobby called after her. The door slammed, and Bobby and Teel stared at each other in the remaining silence.

Teel looked away from him when she realized she still hadn't shared with him the phone call from Keegan's school counselor. She hadn't meant to keep it from him. They just hadn't spent that much time together the last couple of nights.

"She needs a come to Jesus meeting, Teel," Bobby said sternly. "I'm tired of this attitude."

"Maybe she's grieving the only way she knows how."

———

TEEL FELT her knees give when they were outside the funeral home. She squeezed the railing on the veranda and held on for a moment. There were so many cars here. So many people. So many kids. How many other mothers had to pause outside the doors of the funeral home and ask for forgiveness because even as they grieved for the family inside, they thanked God the little girl in the casket wasn't theirs?

Shame rolled around in her stomach, but she made herself go on. Bobby walked behind her, his hand on her lower back. Rachel walked at her side, and Keegan, thrown together on a five minute shower and ten minutes to dress and style herself, lagged behind Bobby. She'd put on a gray skirt and a gray vest over a white blouse. Her dark hair, still a little damp, blew just a bit in the lazy breeze. She'd kept it simple, eyeliner and a pale trace of eye shadow. She looked pretty, but she hadn't said a word to any of them on the drive here.

The line inside the funeral home was long and twisted, but at least inside the air was cold and refreshing. Bobby spoke to several people in that reverent funeral home hush that people adopted while they stood in line waiting to offer the family their condolences. Teel nodded to others, some friends, some neighbors, some fellow teachers.

When the line had moved so much they were in the doorway of the viewing room, she could hear the music better and she could see the top of the casket. She looked away quickly, because even though she was damned near forty-five years old, she was suddenly so damned scared of seeing that little girl in the casket she wanted to run away.

What if making Keegan come had been a mistake? What if Keegan was in shock? Afraid? What if Keegan came undone up there? What would she do?

Teel took a deep breath and made herself look at the flowers. Rich, vibrant colors filled the front of the room. They were beautiful to look at, and Teel wished that Marin could see them. What would Marin say if she could see so many people here to mourn her loss and comfort her parents? What had made her so desperate to kill herself?

"Flowers are pretty." Bobby leaned over her shoulder as she signed their names to the guestbook.

"They are." She tried to take a breath, but her throat was tight. She nodded and picked up a prayer card with Marin's name on it.

When finally Teel found herself in front of the casket, she broke. She hadn't yet allowed herself the luxury, because first

and foremost, it wasn't her loss and she didn't have the right
to that kind of grief. Besides that, she had her own household
to run. Her girls to feed and care for. Her husband's clothes
to wash and fold and put away. Her families' tears to dry.
When had there been time to cry? And what if she started
crying and couldn't stop?

Marin's blond hair was arranged to frame her face as it
always had in life. They'd been simple with the makeup, so
she looked sweet and innocent. So damned young.

Teel lowered herself to the kneeler and made the sign of
the cross. Somehow a Hail Mary and an Our Father didn't
seem to be enough. She stared at the tiny pearls of the rosary
woven in Marin's hands, clasped as in prayer. Bobby knelt
beside her and bowed his head.

Mostly, Teel prayed that Marin was at peace now, and she
prayed for God to give her parents some measure of peace.
When she stood again, Rachel knelt down by Bobby and
Keegan hovered behind them. She chewed at her fingernails,
but Teel was relieved to see that she was at least looking at
Marin.

Teel turned to Rick, and the hardest part began. The part
that sounded like a mouthful of lies. But also the part that
meant the most to those left behind when it was all over. She
remembered to this day those who had talked to her and
hugged her and offered their sympathy when her dad died.

Maybe it sounded like lies from this side of the line, but it
sure as hell served a purpose.

"I'm so sorry, Rick." Her voice cracked, and she squeezed
his hand, and then she put her arms around him. He hugged
her back, and it was only a bit awkward, and then he kind of
patted her back, and Teel knew that was kind of a sign that
he wanted her to move on. She stepped back as Bobby shook
his hand, and Teel wondered how Rachel had fallen behind
them.

She glanced behind Bobby and saw that Keegan was standing in front of the casket now. Rachel moved closer to her and draped her arm over her shoulders. Teel drew in a deep breath and turned back to Jeannie.

Petite and so thin she looked fragile, Jeannie reached for Teel without hesitation.

"Jeannie, I'm so, so sorry," Teel cried, and Jeannie cried on her shoulder.

"I just didn't know," Jeannie whispered. "We didn't know, Teel."

"I know." Teel nodded and hoped her words soothed.

"Did Keegan? Did she have any idea?"

"No," Teel answered, although she'd never even asked Keegan if Marin had been acting strangely. She and Keegan hadn't really said much to each other at all since Marin died, and she most definitely couldn't share with Jeannie the things she and Keegan had said. What would Jeannie think if she knew Teel'd had to drag Keegan out of bed to come to the funeral?

Jeannie nodded and wiped at her eyes with a tissue.

"Of course she didn't." She shook her head. "I'm just..." She shrugged. "I just want answers."

"I know," Teel said, and she did know. She would grasp at any possible explanation if she were Jeannie, beg anyone and everyone who knew Marin for answers. But who should know a child better than her own parent?

How well does a parent know his or her child? Teel wondered. How well did she know Keegan?

She stepped back out of the way, reluctant to walk away from her girls. Bobby hugged Jeannie, and Teel heard him offer his sympathy. And then Rachel. She cried and dabbed at her eyes and hugged Jeannie. A touch of a smile in spite of the tears.

And finally Keegan. She let Jeannie take her hands, and

she said something so quietly Teel didn't hear her. Jeannie hugged her, but Keegan was stiff and awkward in her arms.

Teel was amazed to see that her younger daughter was dry-eyed when she stepped away from Jeannie. As a family, the four of them found seats in the back of the funeral home and waited for the service to begin. They prayed with Fr. Dean from the high school and then they filed by the casket one last time on their way to their car.

The funeral mass at the church brought Teel a small bit of comfort. It always helped her to press her grief into a well-practiced, familiar set of rites. To let those deeply engrained prayers and rites take over her mind at least for an hour.

Keegan remained stoic through the mass, while Rachel constantly sniffled and wiped at her tears. The sounds of crying added another layer to the music. Jeannie leaned heavily on Rick during the mass. The kids there, Teel assumed they were all from Blessed Sacrament, fell apart as a unit when two of them sang together after Communion.

The song was an untitled hymn, and it beckoned the listener, the sinner to come to Jesus. Teel felt icy fingers climb her backbone as she thought of what Bobby had said earlier. That Keegan needed a "come to Jesus" moment. No, he hadn't meant it that way, and yet, the music, the words of the hymn, and Teel's worry about Keegan exploded inside her. She glanced at Keegan, who had her arms folded over her chest and a look of sheer boredom plastered on her face.

Chapter 9

KEEGAN

MR. WIGGERS HAD BEEN PROPPED in the corner of Marin's casket. Keegan might have gotten through the whole damned thing untouched if she hadn't seen that stupid stuffed animal. Marin had slept with the navy blue teddy bear every night, even when she spent the night at Keegan's house. She was still sleeping with it the last time Keegan had been over there, which was some random night when they were in sixth or seventh grade. It had been a weird night; it's always weird to go back to trying to be friends with someone after you've already started growing apart and you've found other friends and new interests.

Keegan had stuffed animals too, and she slept with them or at least she started the nights with the animals in her bed. But usually by morning, she'd kicked, pushed or stretched and knocked them all out. The thought of her mom and dad tucking one of her animals in a casket that was going to be lowered into the ground made her sick.

Marin's room was all frilly and pink, the color of cotton candy. Most of the frilly stuff was gone that last night she'd stayed over, but the room was still pink. She had rock star posters pinned on her walls and a big pink bulletin board on her closet door. She tacked snapshots of her family and friends up on the bulletin board. Keegan had liked the idea, and she'd even said something to her parents about doing that in her room.

But it had never gotten done.

She stretched now and straightened her legs out in front of her. It was hot, but not that blistering, suffocating hot it had been earlier in the week. Thank God she'd been able to get inside and change her clothes without her mom catching her. She sure as hell wasn't in the mood for a grilling by her mom. Her dad had left within fifteen minutes of getting home. Keegan had changed into a tank, shorts and running shoes and tore out of there before her mom could stop her. She hadn't run for a few days, and it felt good to stretch her legs and breathe deeply and lose the last few days in the rhythm of her feet pounding the pavement.

When they were little, she and Marin used to come here to the lake at the other end of the subdivision. Keegan always wondered why they called it a lake. It barely qualified as a pond, it was so small. But it was pretty, and it was mostly private. Sometimes the neighborhood boys had run her and Marin off when they came down to dig up worms or scout for garter snakes.

The tall grass around the pond, Rachel called it *fescue* whatever the hell that meant, was dry and brown. Midwest summers took their toll long before August ever started. Nature couldn't keep up with the heat and the humidity. And yet, Keegan didn't know anything other than stretches of burned out grass, air heavy with humidity that sometimes triggered her asthma attacks, and flowers that died no matter how often you watered them.

Marin's hands had looked so delicate. Keegan had wanted to touch her, to touch her hand, but she was scared to. She was a little bit scared that if she touched Marin's skin, death might jump into her and take her with Marin and Mr. Wiggers. Plus, her mom would probably have freaked out and yanked her by the collar and dragged her out of the viewing room. She didn't mean to be disrespectful. Well, maybe she'd meant to be earlier, but not then. Not when she stood there looking at the casket and Marin, in her blue blouse and gray pencil skirt.

Keegan had been frozen there, maybe staring at someone dead, but she was thinking about Marin at school. She looked like a model in that outfit; she always wore skimpy little silver heels with that skirt. Slim, but not string bean skinny, Marin had turned more heads than she would ever know.

Rachel had rescued her. Keegan thought maybe she would still be frozen there in that viewing room, thinking about Marin, if Rachel hadn't stepped up by her and put her arm around her. Frozen, with some new dead person there, and some other family milling about and either wondering who she was or not even seeing her. She felt that inconsequential that she could stand there forever, and no one would notice she was there and no one in her life would notice she wasn't at home or school or where she was supposed to be.

Tiffany Holmes and Brandy Borrowman had been there. Well, Keegan guessed most of the student body at Blessed Sacrament had been at the funeral today. And maybe, of all of them there, five of them were really Marin's friends. Then again, who was she to point a finger at someone for pretending to grieve for Marin? She wasn't her friend, not anymore. She hadn't wanted to go, and she probably shouldn't have gone, but her mom had insisted. It wasn't that she didn't feel bad for Marin and her family. Just that with all of the guilt in her stomach, there wasn't much room for anything else.

What would her mom say? If she knew?

Keegan threw a rock at the lake. It plunked in the water, and she watched the ripple effect move out and fade away.

She'd fucked up, and sooner or later it would all come out and then her mom would hate her. They would all hate her.

She ran the whole way home, and she was winded when her feet hit the front porch. As she stood there, leaned over with her hands on her knees, Rachel backed her crème colored Volkswagon Beetle out of the garage.

Keegan sucked in a deep breath and walked over to the driveway.

"Where ya goin'?"

Rachel stared at her for a moment, but she didn't seem to be thinking about how Keegan was a jerk or a creep or anything. Keegan stepped closer to the car, braced her hands over the door, and leaned in to talk to Rachel. She felt a jolt of need so strong it almost knocked her off her feet.

Keegan wished that Rachel would nod to the passenger seat and invite her to go along. But Rachel only smiled and eased off the brake. Keegan stood up quickly and backed away.

"Meeting a friend," Rachel called as she drove away.

Keegan nodded and waved, but Rachel was already two houses down. Keegan glanced at Marin's house and turned away to go inside.

Maybe she and Jess could go to a movie. No. No way would Mom let her go to a movie the same day Marin

English was buried. But still. Maybe she and Jess could just hang out. Mom would probably be okay with that; she'd probably think it was good for Keegan to be with a friend.

Therapeutic. Except, yeah, Jess would probably want to just sit and talk drone on and on about Marin and how sad it was, and no offense to Jess, but she didn't even really *know* Marin. And besides that, what was to talk about? Marin was dead. Keegan didn't especially want to know how she did it, and she already knew *why* she did it, and she sure didn't want to talk about that.

So she'd just stay home and hope like hell that her dad would get home soon to keep Mom occupied. She knew she was either due for one of Mom's lectures: respect, skipping classes, or even personal hygiene or organization, because her room was pretty bad and going on worse right now, or a heart to heart pow-wow with her. Mom would expect Keegan to break down and cry about Marin, and then she'd get all pissy when she didn't.

The shower made her feel better, but when she was dressed and she wandered out to the kitchen, she still didn't see her mom. That was kind of weird. Had she left the house when Keegan went for a run? But where would she go? Oh God, Keegan almost groaned out loud. What if Mom went back to the English's house? Jesus, she was just going to embarrass herself. Humiliation wasn't going to look pretty on her.

Movement on the deck caught her eye. She turned and saw her then, sitting on the chaise lounge Dad had gotten her a few years ago for Mother's Day. She wore shorts now, not the long kind that she wore when she went anywhere and needed to look her age, and a tank top. She held a glass of iced tea in her left hand, but she didn't appear to be drinking it.

So. If Mom was outside by herself, apparently Keegan didn't rate a heart to heart or even a lecture. Maybe Mom could just tell by looking that there really wasn't much left that was good inside Keegan.

Chapter 10

TEEL

DARKNESS FELL SO SLOWLY that Teel didn't even notice it creep in. Lost in thought or memory or some vague mixture of both, she jumped and knocked her glass over when she heard someone knock on the French door behind her. Thank goodness she'd finished the tea hours ago, and nothing spilled out on the deck.

She looked over her shoulder and saw Bobby standing there holding a big white paper bag. She had no idea when he'd come home, only that he'd run a few errands and probably gone to one of his current construction sites to get a little work done. Probably more to do something with his hands and his thoughts than to actually get anything done.

She was comfortable out here; it had cooled off, though not too much. She didn't really want to move, because for the past several hours (she guessed) she'd just stared across the backyard and far enough into the sunset to see beyond it, where there were painted memories of the girls when they were younger. The girls and Marin. She'd lived the last several hours remembering Marin here at her house, remembering Marin's life and forgetting all about Marin's death.

But the lights in the house looked cozy and inviting. And Bobby obviously had food in the white bag. Maybe Italian or Chinese. Didn't matter. As soon as Teel let herself think about food, her stomach growled.

She climbed up from the lounge chair and pushed the French door open. The house was just a bit chilly, but something smelled delicious. Bobby was at the counter opening a bottle of Chardonnay.

"Want some?"

"Yes, please," she answered as she passed through the living room to the bedroom. Quickly, she stepped out of her shorts and shimmied into a pair of jeans. She left the tank on, but she slipped a white blouse over it. More comfortable now, she rejoined him in the kitchen and took the glass of wine he offered.

"Ziti," he said as he took plates from the cabinet. "Bread. Salads."

"Perfect." She nodded and began taking the food from the bags. "Are the girls eating?"

"Rachel's car's gone," Bobby told her. He sat down at the bar and ripped a piece of garlic bread from the loaf.

"Hmm. She didn't tell me she was going anywhere." Teel swatted his hands away from the bread, took a knife from the drawer, and began slicing the loaf into individual pieces.

"I assume Keegan's in her room," he continued. "Her door's shut."

"I'll get her."

"Have you talked to her? About her behavior earlier?"

"No." Teel sighed and put the knife in the sink. "Bobby, I don't know what to say. I was so damned mad at her earlier, but then when we got to the funeral home, all I could think was maybe it was a mistake. Maybe making her go was wrong, and what if she flipped out."

"She didn't, though."

"No, she didn't," Teel agreed. "But who are we to say how she should act? Maybe she's confused. Angry. Sad. I don't know."

"But don't you think we need to talk to her? About all of this?"

Teel sighed and took a drink of her wine. She set her glass down and then spent a few seconds looking into the glass and avoiding his eyes.

"The day…The day that we found out." She looked up at Bobby. He nodded, and she continued, "Elaine Caldwell called here after school."

"Who's Elaine Caldwell?"

"The counselor at Blessed Sacrament."

Bobby lifted his chin like he was expecting Teel to hit him.

"She said there were rumors around school that day that Keegan had gotten sick in the morning…"

"I don't like rumors, Teel," Bobby said quietly. "You know that."

"I do know that, and I don't like them anymore than you do. Elaine also said that Keegan had skipped her last couple of classes of the day."

That got his attention.

"Then where did she go?"

Teel lifted one shoulder in a lazy shrug. She didn't want to have this conversation. Keegan, though impulsive and a bit reckless at times, had never been the kind of kid to inspire this sort of parental concern or conversation. Teel felt like she was standing on a bridge, considering a jump.

"Elaine also said something about her behavior sending up some red flags for some of her teachers." She took a bite of the ziti and moaned in pleasure. "I had no idea I was so hungry."

"Red flags?" Bobby frowned. "Teel, sit down. You look like you're gonna eat and run."

"I'm going to go get Keegan. She needs to eat."

"Any other bombs you wanna drop on me first?"

This time, it was Teel's turn to draw back as if he had slapped her.

"I don't think that's fair, Bobby," she said softly. "We haven't had a lot of time to talk the past couple of days."

Bobby sighed. "Go get Keegan."

"Do we need to figure this out first? So we appear to be on the same side?"

"Are we not on the same side?"

"Bobby."

"Yeah, maybe we do, but she needs to eat."

Teel wiped her mouth with a napkin and then left the kitchen. There was no noise in Keegan's room, which was unusual. Normally, Keegan had music playing constantly, and she or Bobby or even Rachel often had to tell her to turn it down more than once a night.

"Keegan?" she called as she knocked on the door. Keegan sat like a pretzel on the floor by her bed, a photo album open in front of her legs. She didn't look as if she'd been crying, but she certainly didn't look happy. She looked up at Teel but looked away quickly.

"What?" she sounded petulant, but Teel was sort of glad to hear *something* in her voice.

"Are you hungry? Daddy brought home ziti and bread."

The four of them loved Tuscany's, a small locally owned Italian restaurant, and Keegan often ate an entire loaf of bread in one sitting (although she'd follow that with a week of intense exercise to lose the carbs.) Today, though, Keegan hesitated.

"I'm afraid I'll get sick," she mumbled.

Teel, still angry about this morning, felt her heart melt. She wondered if Keegan had eaten anything since they'd gotten the news.

"You wanna try something else?" Teel asked.

Keegan seemed to make it a point not to look at her. Teel could see her lower lip tremble just a bit like it did when she was a little girl and she was fighting tears.

"Will you fix me some soup?"

"Of course I will, sweetheart." Teel offered Keegan her hand and held her breath until she felt her daughter's hand slide into hers. Gently, she helped her to her feet, and then surprised, but pleased when Keegan stepped close to her, she put her arms around her.

"I'm sorry, Mom," Keegan whispered.

Sorry. Teel felt the weight of that word crawl out of Keegan's mouth and up and over her shoulders and settle in. Sorry. For what? For the way she'd behaved earlier today? For the refusal to show any grief over Marin's death? For skipping classes?

Teel kissed the top of Keegan's head, squeezed her tight and then let her go. This was the first time Keegan had seemed like herself in better than a week, since even before Marin's death. In Teel's mind, that meant it wasn't the time to tear into her and start in with a thirty minute lecture.

"What kind of soup do you want?"

"Tomato," she answered as they walked arm in arm back into the kitchen. Bobby, who had been as angry at Keegan as Teel, folded the second he saw them arm in arm.

"Daddy."

"C'mere, baby." He opened his arms to her. Teel bit her lip

when Keegan ran to Bobby and practically threw herself into his arms. "It's okay."

Teel busied herself warming a can of tomato soup. Keegan hadn't asked, but Teel made her a grilled cheese, too. When Keegan had been a little girl, tomato soup and grilled cheese had been her favorite meal.

"Thanks, Mom."

Teel plated the grilled cheese, sliced it in half, and put two pickles on the plate. "Don't worry about it if you can't eat it."

Keegan watched her set the bowl of soup in front of her on the counter.

"Sit down," Bobby told Teel, and this time she did. She watched him refill his plate with ziti and salad as she dug into hers.

"Is Rachel home yet?" Keegan asked.

"No."

"Do you know where she went?" Bobby asked her.

"She was leaving when I came home from my run." Teel looked at Keegan, surprised that she'd gone for a run. She must have been catatonic out there on the deck. "She just said she was going out."

Teel sighed and rolled her head on her shoulders. She had a dull ache creeping into her shoulders and neck.

"Mm." She took a drink of her wine and dropped the other bomb on Bobby. "By the way, Rachel has a boyfriend."

Chapter 11

TEEL

AT LEAST BOBBY hadn't taken the boyfriend news as hard as Teel had. He hadn't been thrilled to learn that Rachel had a boyfriend, but he wasn't hurt that she'd kept it from them through the summer and into the fall. In fact, he'd reminded her their daughters had always been more forthcoming than most teenagers and they should count their blessings.

Then again, he sounded like a hypocrite when he'd turned around in the next breath and started worrying about Keegan and what those red flags with her teachers were. Teel had told him she intended to call Elaine Caldwell back first thing Monday morning and set up an appointment.

After dinner they'd curled up on the couch together to watch a movie. Or in Teel's case, to stare mindlessly at the TV and forget again about Marin's suicide and the neighbors down the street who were sitting in an empty house, wishing to just hear their daughter's voice one more time.

Bobby had gone to Keegan's room and coaxed her into

coming out to the living room with them. Already in her pajamas at nine o'clock in the evening, she carried her pillow with her and it made Teel think of days when Keegan and Rachel had been her babies and the worst they had to worry about was losing a binkie or which brand of diapers was more absorbent.

"Here for lunch?"

Eve set her purse and keys on the counter and watched Teel for a moment before answering her. Teel's hands seemed to move without her telling them to. They layered spoons full of meat sauce, cheese and lasagna noodles over and over to the top of the glass baking dish. Teel looked down at her hands in time to stop herself from pouring more of the sauce and spilling it all over the counter.

Eve blinked when Teel looked back at her and looked from Teel to the counter behind Teel, where two loaves of bread were wrapped in clear plastic.

"Is that lunch?" Eve perched on a barstool.

"No." Teel shook her head and then shoved a lock of hair off her forehead with the back of her hand. "I think Bobby's going to grill something."

"What're you doing?" Eve asked. Teel turned away from her and leaned over to turn the oven on.

"Well." She stood up straight and took a deep breath. "I woke up this morning, and I felt so empty. Do you know what I mean? Empty, like hollow inside. And I have both my girls here with me."

Teel met Eve's eyes, but she looked away quickly. Bobby hadn't exactly discouraged her, but he hadn't seemed to be behind her one hundred percent either.

"I laid there in bed and thought about Jeannie and Rick and how it would feel to wake up to an empty house forever."

Eve nodded. Teel washed her hands and then poured two

glasses of tea. Eve mumbled a thank you when Teel passed one to her.

"I just can't stop thinking about it," Teel continued. "With Marin gone like that, it's a completely different kind of empty. I just…I hurt for them, Eve, and I feel so useless here, and I feel guilty for who I am and what I have."

"Teel, honey, you can't feel guilty about your daughters."

"I know that. I do. But I can't help it. I feel guilty that I have the girls, and that we're happy. And I feel guilty that I'm sitting here in my home, feeling so lost because their daughter took her own life."

"I think we're all still feeling it, Teel," Eve told her. "It's a tragedy. The whole town reels from something like this."

Teel nodded. Eve worked in the trust department in one of the city's banks. Teel supposed people everywhere had been touched by the teen suicide; something so shocking wouldn't be limited to the education world.

"Anyway." Teel shrugged. "I'm baking. Thought I'd take some of this stuff up to them."

"How're the girls?"

"Okay, I guess. I don't really know how they're supposed to act, so I don't really know."

Eve took a drink of her tea and looked back over her shoulder, down the hall toward the girls' rooms.

"Keegan looked pretty steady at the funeral."

"Too steady, I think," Teel answered.

They both stopped talking and looked up as Bobby came in the back door and up the hallway past the girls' bedrooms.

"Hey." He offered Eve a smile. "How's my favorite sister-in-law?"

"Hungry. What's for lunch?"

"Grilled chicken." He slipped behind the island with Teel and washed his hands. He'd been working outside in the yard. Teel longed to scoot closer to him and breathe in his earthy scent. On Sunday mornings, they awoke early, made love and then had breakfast together on the deck before they got the girls moving to get ready for mass. Today Bobby had been up and out of bed when she awoke. She'd missed his touch, and now as she stared at his back, she wished they were alone and that they could crawl back into bed.

"Stay, Eve," he said to her sister. "We have plenty."

"Thanks. I will."

Both women watched him pick up the plate of raw chicken and carry it out to the deck.

"Does he have a butt?" Eve frowned as she studied him through the glass doors.

"Oh, yeah." Teel grinned. "And a very nice one at that."

"Because his pants all bag on him where his butt should be."

"Trust me. It's there."

"I saw Dennis last night."

Teel raised her eyebrows. "I still don't get why you guys divorced."

"I'd rather not share him with other women," Eve answered simply.

"And yet here you are sharing him with other women."

Eve ducked her head and groaned. "Yeah, well, at least this way I'm free to find someone else, too."

"Not if you spend all your free time in bed with your ex-husband."

"We went for Chinese."

"Still. You were with Dennis. You're as married to him now as you ever were."

Eve looked around the kitchen and finally met Teel's eyes. "Still in love with him."

Teel nodded. "So, again, maybe you should've..."

"Please don't say tried a little harder, Teel." Eve tucked a strand of hair behind her ear. "Please."

"I'm sorry, Eve."

Teel covered Eve's hand with hers. She felt bad for harping on Eve about her divorce, but she hated to see her unhappy. And she'd been unhappy since the divorce.

"Let me tell the girls you're here," she said quietly.

She heard Eve get up and cross the living room, presumably to go outside to the deck. She started to call out to Rachel and Keegan, but she caught herself when she heard their voices.

"...boyfriend."

"Yeah." Rachel's voice. "I've been seeing him for a few months."

"Mom doesn't like him," Keegan said.

Teel flinched. She'd never said she didn't like him.

"Mom doesn't know him," Rachel answered Keegan. She sounded annoyed.

"What's his name?"

"Deacon Samuels."

"Deacon? What? Is he like a religious dude or something?"

"God, Keegan." Rachel, again, even more annoyed. "Deacon is his name."

"That's weird."

"It's not weird. He's really nice."

"Are you sleeping with him?"

Teel couldn't help but be interested in Rachel's answer.

"None of your business," Rachel said. Teel expected her to come storming out of Keegan's room, but she remained alone in the hall.

"Rach?"

"Hmm?"

"Did you know the name *Marin* is Irish? It means 'bitterly wanted child.'"

"God, Keegan, you're such a freak."

Teel ducked back out of the hallway when she heard the

rustling in Keegan's room. Rachel appeared in the kitchen a moment later.

"Hey, Rach." Teel cleared her throat. "Aunt Eve's out on the deck with Dad."

"Cool." Rachel's eyes lit up. "Is she staying for lunch?"

"Yeah."

Rachel took a few steps toward the door and then stopped and looked back at Teel. "Mom?"

"Hmm?" Teel was still wondering about Keegan's question to Rachel that went unanswered. Was she sleeping with this boy?

"Can I invite Deacon?"

"For lunch?"

Rachel raised her eyebrows and nodded. "Yeah, for lunch."

"Sure."

When Rachel went outside, Teel went back down the hall to Keegan's room. She found Keegan at her desk, her laptop open to her MyFriend page.

"Aunt Eve is here," she said softly. She stopped in the doorway, wondering if Keegan was chatting with someone. Jess, maybe.

Keegan, back to the door, jumped and turned quickly in her seat. Teel stepped further into her room, but Keegan hit the power button on her laptop and stood up in one fluid motion.

"Aunt Eve? Is she staying for lunch?"

Teel glanced at the laptop again and then looked up at Keegan. "What were you doing?"

"Talking to Jess," Keegan answered quickly.

Teel nodded, but she wondered why Keegan had shut her computer down so quickly if she'd just been talking to Jess.

"Aunt Eve is staying for lunch, and Rachel is inviting Deacon over."

"So?"

"I'm looking forward to meeting him."

"Well, I'm not." Keegan stepped around Teel and left her standing there alone.

Teel glanced at Keegan's laptop again, and this time she noticed Keegan's geometry book and notebook stacked beside it. An open notebook was tossed haphazardly on the desk, part of it covering the geometry book. Maybe Keegan *had been* talking to Jess. Teel knew they often talked while they did their homework.

She hated how suddenly she was suspicious of every move her daughters made, especially Keegan. She wasn't sure if that said something about her parenting or recent events, since she was letting recent events color her perception of life in her own household.

Chapter 12

Rachel

SHE LIKED that she was finally getting to introduce Deacon to her parents, because she really liked him and she wanted them to like him, too. But she would've skipped the whole This-Is-My-Little-Sister thing if she could have. Keegan could be such a pain in the ass, and lately, she'd been acting like such a freak. Rachel didn't want Deacon to have to put up with any of that.

There hadn't been any need to worry, though, because Keegan hadn't said two words while the six of them sat on the deck and ate lunch. It was cool having Aunt Eve there, though. Rachel loved her; Aunt Eve always made things so much more fun. She'd been really cool with Deacon, and she'd kept the conversation flowing whenever Mom got caught up in her own head.

Probably Aunt Eve had been a save for the day, because Deacon might have thought her mom was a flake as many times as she got quiet and tuned the conversation out. He knew about Marin, but still, Rachel wasn't sure it was normal for her mom to feel so bad about it. Sure, the first day or two it was probably okay, but then you go to the funeral and you feel awful and you tell the family that and then it's over. Not that Rachel wanted to dance or anything, but it was over.

Marin English and her family had been omnipresent in the house for a few days now, and Rachel was ready to get back to normal. Keegan didn't have a clue what normal was, but it would be nice to have her parents back, especially Mom.

Deacon was polite and funny, and Rachel could tell that her parents and Aunt Eve both liked him. He wasn't surfer boy or preppy boy good-looking, but he had pretty eyes and his hair was just long enough and just wavy enough to be messy and cute at the same time. And he was smart. She could tell her Dad liked that about him. They'd spent a while talking about politics, and maybe on a different day, Rachel would have joined in. But she'd seen her mom shut down, and then Keegan had excused herself and carried her plate and glass back into the house.

Rachel wondered what Keegan was doing. She'd been on her MyFriend page earlier, and she'd hollered at Rachel to come and see a video link that showed a little girl singing the alphabet. It was cute, but Rachel didn't really get why Keegan thought she needed to see it. And yet, once in Keegan's room, she'd collapsed on the bed while Keegan chatted online with her friend Jess.

Rachel didn't care for Jess, but then honestly, she wasn't crazy about her sister. Probably, if you asked Mom, she would be clueless, but Keegan had changed a lot since she started high school. Rachel had been content in her small circle of friends, but Keegan had seemed to stick her claws in at the periphery of the popular crowd and climb a little each day. For whatever reason, Keegan wanted to *be* a part of that crowd. Which had turned her into a little bitch, for the most part. And Jess Levine was the perfect best friend for a little wanna-be like Keegan. They were made for each other.

Rachel had felt weird hanging out in Keegan's room, even just for that little bit of time before lunch. She had a couple pictures on her dresser, one of them of her and Jess, and another from homecoming freshman year, with her and Jess and a couple other girls who looked like they'd called it a night hookin' on the corner to go to the dance. Her bookshelf was packed with books with titles like *UpperClass* and *HighClass* and *NoClass*. Rachel wasn't a literature snob; she loved to read just about anything. But she drew the line at books about snotty girls like her sister.

And to top it all off, Keegan always had her damned laptop on. Always. Always on that stupid MyFriend page. Rachel had considered starting one a few years ago, but she hadn't wanted to deal with it. Too much time attached to a computer, and she had better things to do with her time. She'd started working her sophomore year, and even after the little corner bookstore she'd worked for closed and she found herself with a little extra time, she hadn't wanted to chain herself to a computer.

Keegan had sat with her back to Rachel, directly in front of her laptop. Almost like she didn't want her to see the screen. As if Rachel cared whatever the hell she was doing. And then she'd started talking about Marin and how her name was Irish and all that bizarre crap about how the name meant bitterly wanted child. Keegan had acted really weird over this whole deal—yet another reason Rachel wanted it done with and out of the house.

Except now her mom was baking and had enough food to

open the kitchen to the public for dinner tonight. Whatever that was about. When Grandpa died, a few people brought food over, so Rachel got that. But she didn't really get why Mom thought she needed to take care of Jeannie and Rick.

Rachel figured Keegan had been pretty bitchy to Marin since they'd started high school, and Jeannie, at least, had to know that. Most girls talked to their moms about that stuff, and even when they didn't, somehow moms kind of figured things out on their own. And if Jeannie had a clue that Keegan had treated Marin like shit, then she sure wasn't going to want Mom hanging around and doing her favors.

Not her place, though. Rachel had no idea what was going through Keegan's mind, but she sure as hell wasn't going to get involved. She followed Deacon out the front door, happy to be away from the freak family for a while.

"Wanna go for a walk?"

"Sure." She wouldn't turn down time with Deacon, not to mention that she'd eaten far too much, including two of her mom's cookies (more stuff Mom was taking to Jeannie and Rick), and a walk certainly wouldn't hurt her.

Rachel liked that as they started walking, they held hands. It wasn't like she had to reach for him or even that he had to reach for her. It just happened when they were together. She liked the sensation of his skin against hers, and of course it made her want more. But she felt safe when Deacon held her hand or put his arm around her. She felt like her hand belonged in his, like she belonged in his embrace.

"So…" Deacon shrugged as they walked. "This is really bothering your mom, isn't it?"

Rachel looked at him quickly and wondered what he meant. But then behind him, she saw Marin's house and realized of course he meant the English deal. Not the fact that she and Deacon had been dating for a few months.

The English Deal. The English Tragedy. The English

Suicide. The English Affair. Whatever you called it, it still shouldn't be sitting so heavy on her mom, should it?

"Yeah, I guess so."

"I don't get it," he mumbled.

"That's their house," Rachel said quietly, and to his credit, he didn't immediately turn to stare. He glanced at it, but his gaze didn't linger. Instead, he looked back at the road where they were walking and squeezed her hand tighter. "I don't get it, either. I know it's sad, but I wish Mom would let it go."

"No. That's not what I meant," he told her. "I don't get what would make you kill yourself. I don't get what could ever be so bad."

Rachel wished she could pull all those words back in, the ones where she probably sounded like a spoiled brat, ripping on her mom for grieving over a neighbor girl.

"Yeah. I know." She hoped she didn't sound shallow, jumping from one side of the issue to the other. "She never seemed…like the kind of person to do that."

"But what is the kind?" Deacon looked down at her. He wasn't mocking her, she could see that. He looked a little sad, certainly quieter and more pensive than she was used to seeing him. "Ya know? Is there a certain kind of person that just decides one day that it's too much?"

Probably not, Rachel supposed. Because no matter what people projected to their friends or parents or teachers, no one really knew what anyone was thinking or feeling.

"There was a guy," Deacon said quietly, "who worked with my dad. It was years ago. I was probably in eighth grade. His son killed himself. With a gun."

Rachel shook her head. She didn't want to picture that. She didn't want to start wondering about Marin, about how she did it.

"He was nineteen. I don't think Dad ever knew why the kid did it, but it bothered him. Really bad, ya know? Started checking on me and my brother and sister every two minutes. Got to the point that it was driving us nuts, like he was smothering us."

"That's what Mom's doing."

"She'll get past it, Rach." Deacon sounded certain of himself. "But you have to let her go through this process."

"I just...I know it's sad, Deacon. It's sad, and it's stupid. Marin was...She was smart, and she was pretty. I know it's an awful thing, but I don't want this grief, this obsessive grief, to be in my house."

"But it is," he said gently. "Marin was someone your mom cared for her when she was younger. Someone your sister played with. Your mom's gonna feel all kinds of stuff right now. Not just grief. Not just sympathy for her parents. You gotta let it play out. The grief. The guilt."

"Why guilt?"

"First of all, she probably feels guilty for being happy. For being content with you and your dad and your sister."

"That's crazy."

Deacon shook his head. "Not really. I remember Dad saying that stuff to Mom. I didn't get it then, but I don't know...thinking about it now, and seeing your mom so bothered, it makes sense."

"What else?" Rachel looked up at him as they walked. It felt a little surreal to be walking down the neighborhood talking to Deacon about suicide and grief and guilt, and yet, it was kind of nice to have someone to talk to. "You said first of all...what else?"

"She probably feels like she could have done something to stop her."

"But that *is* crazy, Deacon. How could Mom have done anything to stop Marin?"

"She couldn't have, Rach," he said quickly. He stopped walking and turned to her. They were well beyond the

English house now, and yet Rachel felt weird standing in the middle of the street. Guilty. Like Jeannie or Rick could look outside and see her with her boyfriend, doing something as normal and innocent as taking a walk, and hate her for it.

She swallowed hard and looked away from Deacon. He stared at her so intensely, she felt like he could see too far inside her. Though she had nothing to hide, it was discomfiting and she had to struggle to stand still with him.

Guilt. If she felt like this, guilty for standing outside with her boyfriend, then yeah, Mom probably felt like hell for having two healthy, happy daughters.

"Of course there's nothing your mom could have done. But I'll bet every adult that ever talked to Marin feels guilty. Like they could have done something to stop her. To help her."

Rachel nodded. Her eyes burned with tears when she looked up at him again.

"It's okay." He smiled and leaned over to kiss her. Just a chaste kiss on the corner of her mouth. For just a second, Rachel wondered why he would only kiss her like that. She wanted a deep, lingering kiss. She wanted his hands on her, his body pressing hard against hers. Her stomach clenched, and she stepped back. He couldn't very well kiss her that way out here in front of God and the Strattons and Mr.and Mrs.English and everyone else.

Times like these, she felt as immature and stupid as Keegan acted. She wondered if she would ever grow up. If *she* didn't, then Keegan sure as hell didn't have a prayer.

"I know." She nodded her agreement. Probably *everyone* who knew Marin wished they could step in and turn back time and stop her. She'd thought that exact thing just seconds after she'd learned that she was gone.

Without a word, they turned and started walking back

toward their house. Aunt Eve's car was gone; Rachel hated that she'd missed telling her goodbye.

"She's cool," Deacon said, as if reading Rachel's mind, and nudged her shoulder.

"She's a lot of fun," she agreed. "Actually, my mom is usually a lot of fun. She and Aunt Eve…" She shrugged and let her words die off.

"Rach?"

"Hmm?"

"It's okay. You don't have to explain your family to me."

She smiled, but again, she was quick to look away. She did have to explain her family to him, because she wanted him to come back. To see them at their best. To know them, to know that they weren't usually so somber.

"Can I come back?" he asked, when they were leaning against the side of his car. "For lunch? Or dinner?"

She ducked her head and laughed. "I hope you will."

"Good." He pulled her tight against his body and this time when he kissed her, she felt it down to her toes. Maybe it was okay this way, because they were in front of her house and this was a goodbye kiss. Maybe that's the way neighborhoods worked. Maybe Jeannie and Rick wouldn't see her in front of her own house.

Deacon broke the kiss and groaned. "I need to study."

"Me, too."

"I'll call you later."

She nodded.

"Rach?" he called as she headed up the driveway to the house. She turned and looked back at him. He shrugged, like he decided not to say something or he forgot what he was going to say. And yet, she thought she got it. Maybe he was reminding her to go easy on her mom. That it was okay to grieve for Marin and okay, too, for her to go on with her life. Or maybe he was thinking about how it had felt to have their bodies pressed so tightly together, and he wished it could be more.

She nodded again, and then he just grinned that crazy, reckless grin that made her tingle inside and dropped into the driver's seat of his old, beater car and drove away.

Chapter 13

Teel

IF SHE STILL HAD THE GIRLS' red Radio Flyer wagon, she would load it and walk up to Jeannie and Rick's house. There was no way she could carry it all, even after Rachel and Bobby both told her it was way too much food and picked over the delivery to make it look more acceptable. Apparently, she'd cooked and baked too much, much more than was socially normal, and her husband and daughter had felt obliged to critique, and so she loaded a big dish of lasagna, two loaves of bread and a dozen oatmeal cookies into her car and drove up the street.

Jeannie answered the door, and while Teel had wanted to see her, to talk to her, the fact that she opened the door caught Teel off-guard. She'd really expected to find Jeannie in bed, and Rick at home, taking care of her.

"Hi." Teel, so desperate to comfort an old friend, suddenly felt awkward and unwelcome. Jeannie stood in the doorway, her hand still on the doorknob, as if she had no intention of inviting Teel in or even carrying on a conversation on the front porch.

Jeannie pressed her lips together and took a deep breath. "Teel."

"How're you doing?"

Great, Teel thought. She was a teacher, for God's sake, educated in English and communication among other things, and that was the best she could do?

Jeannie sighed and raised her eyebrows. Teel didn't mean to stare, but she couldn't look away. It was as if she could read every second of Jeannie's grief, her sorrow, in the lines on her face and the circles under her eyes.

"Kinda numb, actually," Jeannie surprised Teel by answering her honestly.

Teel nodded.

"It's not supposed to be this way," Jeannie continued. "No one wants to think about death, but let me tell ya, when you do, no one thinks about burying her own child. Shoulda been me or Rick."

Again, Teel nodded, because Jeannie was right. No one ever thought about losing a child. It wasn't the natural order of things.

"It's so damned quiet," Jeannie mumbled. "I'm so used to her music playing or the TV on to the shows she liked to watch."

Teel couldn't help it. She hated herself for standing here on this woman's porch, listening to her talk about the emptiness in her house, and thinking of her own daughters. Of the way Keegan blared music from her room, and the way Rachel always turned the TV to music video channels. The showdown between Rachel, Keegan, and Bobby when the three of them happened to watch *Jeopardy* together.

She gave herself a mental shake. Jeannie deserved more than this. Not to mention, it felt dangerous to stand this close to what had happened and think about her own family. Like there was some kind of curse in the house that might get in her clothes, like cigarette smoke, that she might carry back into her house. To her girls.

"I saw Rachel out here earlier," Jeannie said with a sad smile. "She's beautiful, Teel."

"Thank you."

"Made me think of the time both of them spent the night here."

Teel remembered the night well. Though Rachel was older than Keegan and Marin, she hung out with them occasionally. Marin had asked them both to come over, so Teel and Bobby had taken advantage of the empty house and painted the mudroom and the hallway by the girls' rooms. They'd ordered Chinese, and they'd crashed in the living room and watched reruns of *Matlock* and then made love with the TV and the kitchen light on.

Rachel, thirteen at the time, had said the night at Marin's was okay. The girls had played with dolls, and Rachel had played along. Dolls and then an elaborate art fest that included some drawing, some painting, and some jewelry-making. They'd made friendship bracelets, and of course, Keegan and Marin had exchanged bracelets but Rachel had kept hers. As far as Teel knew, it was still in the top drawer of her dresser, long-forgotten.

"Come in for a minute," Jeannie said suddenly. Teel, shocked by the invitation, quickly stepped inside. She barely squeezed through before Jeannie pushed the heavy front door closed. The room was dark and gloomy, and immediately, Teel felt claustrophobic. Living here in this darkness without the music and the laughter that had been Marin would kill her.

Maybe that's what Jeannie was hoping for.

"Is Rick here?"

"No." Jeannie seemed to brush the question, the thought of Rick away. "Excuse me for just a minute, will you?"

"Of course," Teel answered. She stood just inside the door, still laden with all the food, and waited for Jeannie to come back. The silence was so solid, Teel could hear her heartbeat.

She wondered where Rick was. She wondered where Marin had...done it. In her bedroom? The bathroom? Had she cut herself? Slit her wrists? That thought brought back the afternoon that Keegan cut her hair and the way Teel had climbed around the rage and desperation in Keegan's room to get the scissors away from her.

"You didn't have to do this." Jeannie suddenly appeared again at the bottom of the stairs. She swept in close to Teel and took the casserole dish and the bread and cookies. "I haven't been able to eat anything..."

"You need to eat," Teel said softly. Jeannie turned her back on her again and took the food to the kitchen. "You both need to eat."

"Rick's not here," Jeannie answered absently, and Teel wondered at the way Jeannie seemed so helter-skelter. Dead inside and then bustling around the house like a maid, rather than the mother of a lost girl.

Teel wondered where Rick was. What did Jeannie mean when she said Rick wasn't here? Teel didn't want to think too hard about it; it made her feel sick to her stomach. Without acknowledging what she prayed for, Teel said a silent Hail Mary.

She'd been taught, as a little girl, to say a Hail Mary when someone was in need. When she heard a siren, stop and say a Hail Mary. She wondered now if Marin might still be alive if she'd thought of that the other night.

"I found this," Jeannie said, coming close to Teel again, "after I saw Rachel outside and got to thinking about that night she was here with Keegan."

Teel closed her eyes when she saw what Jeannie was holding. It looked just like the bracelet Marin had made for Keegan, except it had pink and purple threads braided together, and Keegan's (that Marin had made) was pink and green braided threads.

"I thought maybe…" Jeannie seemed to crumble, "that maybe…Keegan would want this."

Teel wondered if Keegan would. Probably not, based on her recent behavior. Which only made Jeannie's offering that much harder to accept.

"Thank you." Teel's words came out in a tight, cramped whisper.

This was wrong. Shouldn't Teel be giving Jeannie something? She didn't want to hear Jeannie saying thank you; it wasn't about that. It just felt wrong to be taking something from Jeannie, from Marin.

"Rick's gone."

This time Teel couldn't pretend not to get what Jeannie was saying. She couldn't ignore it either, not with Jeannie standing two feet in front of her.

"He left?"

How could he do this to her? Teel wondered. How could they not turn to each other to get through losing the child they made together?

"Yeah." Jeannie nodded. "Said he needed some space."

"Oh God, Jean, I'm so sorry." Teel shook her head. Jeannie lowered her head to her hands and sobbed. Without thinking, Teel stepped forward and put her arms around her. "I'm so sorry."

Jeannie cried hard and loud, and Teel cried and held her tighter. She wanted to protect her, to carry her away from the hurt, and yet, she knew she couldn't change anything. Do anything.

"We were having problems," Jeannie said and pulled

herself together. She stepped away from Teel and wiped at her eyes. "Rick and I. We'd talked about a separation. He was...I don't think he was sleeping with her, but he was seeing this other woman..." Jeannie looked up at Teel. "And now I'm afraid..."

Teel raised her eyebrows, certain as to where Jeannie was going. And with no power to reassure her that she was wrong. That it wasn't her fault. Wasn't Rick's fault. The only person who could argue with Jeannie was dead.

"I'm afraid Marin heard us fighting. That she felt she was to blame. Or something. That she was afraid we would divorce. That she'd have to live two lives, one with me and one with him. I'm afraid this is our fault, Teel."

What should she say to that? Teel wished desperately to be back at home with Bobby. She closed her fist around the friendship bracelet in her hand.

"I don't know, Jeannie," she said softly. She couldn't bring herself to mumble something trite and possibly wrong. Possibly dead wrong. "What I do know is Marin was a very smart girl. Very strong. I don't think that would have..."

Jeannie nodded. "Made her kill herself."

The words and Jeannie's voice made Teel shudder inside. Suddenly, she realized how cold it was in the house.

"She cut her wrists." Jeannie was again on automatic. Dead pan. "In the bathroom. I had gotten up. Couldn't sleep. I was wandering around upstairs...And I thought about coming down to get my book to read."

Teel held her breath.

"I noticed her bathroom light was on. I came downstairs. Got my book. Made myself a cup of tea. And when I went back upstairs...maybe ten...fifteen minutes had gone by...her light was still on."

Teel bit her lip, because she wanted to beg Jeannie not to say more. Maybe she needed to talk. *Of course* Jeannie needed to talk and with Rick gone, she had no one but a whole lot of walls to confide in.

"I thought maybe she wasn't feeling well. I put my tea and book in our room. Went back to check on her." Jeannie squinted, but the tears had already begun to flow again. "Both wrists... blood. There was blood everywhere."

Teel sagged against the door behind her.

"I must have screamed." Jeannie shrugged. "I think I was screaming at her. Rick came running. He actually...he stepped in blood, and he slipped and cracked his elbow on the shower wall. Her nightgown...It was pale pink...her favorite color. That night it was just the color of blood.

"Rick called 911. But. We knew..."

Teel could pick up the storyline from there. The ambulance came, and she and Bobby and Rachel and maybe other neighbors had stood and watched the EMTs load the gurney, load Marin's body, and drive away. And then, instead of praying for Marin and Jeannie and Rick, instead of thinking about them, she and Bobby had turned to each other and made love.

Suddenly sickened by her own selfishness served up on a platter, Teel swallowed hard and stood up straight. She couldn't just walk away from Jeannie, but she had to get the hell out of here.

"Thanks," Jeannie mumbled. Teel frowned and wondered what she'd missed. Jeannie had gone from reciting the gruesome details of her daughter's suicide to thanking her. But for what?

"My sisters are coming," Jeannie announced. "They'll get here tomorrow."

Teel nodded. "Will you be okay? Do you need someone to stay with you tonight?"

God, not me, Teel pleaded silently.

"No." Jeannie almost smiled. "Actually, I'd kind of like one more night to myself here. That way, I feel like it's all mine. I feel like everything of Marin's is all mine. Just one more night."

"Okay." Teel agreed. "Okay. Would you call me? If there's anything I can do? Please?"

"I will," Jeannie said, and then she reached behind Teel and pulled the door open. As much as Teel wanted to get out the house, when she found herself alone on the porch and the sound of the front door closing echoed in her head, she felt weird again. Unwelcome. As if Jeannie had been counting the seconds until she could escort Teel out.

She drove home in a daze, half-hoping Bobby would be at the door waiting for her and half-hoping she could avoid him until tomorrow, after Jeannie's words had time to gel inside her. Right now, Teel wanted to fall into his arms, to be safe. She wanted reassurance, not just that life goes on, but that no matter what she and Bobby faced, they would face it together. On the other hand, the thought of being intimate with Bobby while Jeannie suffered just down the street filled her with disgust.

Chapter 14

TEEL

BOBBY'S TRUCK was gone when she pulled the Edge into the garage. A little bit relieved and a little bit annoyed, Teel went inside and hurried straight to the shower. Sunday evenings were usually spent in the living room. Bobby flipped through the channels, though it seemed to Teel that he rarely watched any one show. Teel read, sometimes the paper, sometimes a magazine, and sometimes a book. Now and then the girls would join them. When Rachel sat with them, she claimed the corner of the sectional and curled up with a book. Sometimes a book for reading pleasure, sometimes a textbook to study. Keegan read sometimes, but more often than not, she'd join Bobby in his channel surfing, miraculously keeping up with him enough to comment on just about every show he paused on.

Not this Sunday. Teel turned the water on as hot as she could stand it. Steam filled the bathroom before she even stripped her clothes off. She hoped like hell that she'd shucked the desperation from the English house as well as the clothes. Just in case, she stepped into the shower and rubbed her skin raw. She stood under the impossibly hot water long after she'd finished with the soap and shampoo. Maybe she hoped the steam would seep inside her and smear away the last hour. Jeannie English's voice. Her words. The memories. The images those words had conjured inside Teel.

Bobby came charging in as Teel reached for the faucet. Still dressed for outside work, he looked a million miles away in thought. He pulled up short when he saw her in the shower.

"You okay?"

She wanted to answer him. She tried to answer him, but there were no words for what she felt. For what she'd heard. There was nothing she could say to him that could possibly make him understand what her visit to Jeannie had been like.

Instead, she simply shook her head no. She reached again for the faucet, but Bobby shook his head. Her need for him was stronger than her shame over what they had shared the night Marin died. She stepped toward him as he unbuckled his belt and shoved his shorts and briefs down over his hips. He took her hard, against the shower wall. Still in a T-shirt and socks, he filled her completely, as she dug her nails into his back and held on.

Hard and desperate, they moved together until he came just seconds after she did. Spent, Teel lowered her legs to the shower floor and struggled to catch her breath. It crossed her mind to be glad he'd had her leave the shower water running, because this time had been loud and even harsh. Surely, the girls would have heard them. Maybe they *had* heard them.

Without words, Bobby moved in close to her again and lowered his head to kiss her. Where their lovemaking had been rough and fast, the kiss was slow and tender. Bobby's way of saying he was sorry if he'd hurt her.

She thought of Rick leaving Jeannie, and she poured herself into him. Kissed him with everything, her lips and her tongue and her heart and her body. What if? What if they ever came across something that drove them apart?

"I love you, Bobby," she said the words into his mouth, and he nodded and said them back as he kissed her. But it wasn't enough. She ran her fingers up through the back of his hair and pulled him away so she could look him in the eye.

"Don't ever…ever…leave me."

Even without her sharing the visit with Jeannie, without her explaining the sheer desperation in her touch, he seemed to get it. Without breaking eye contact, he shook his head.

"I'm not going anywhere."

"Promise me." She trailed her fingers over his neck and the beard shadow on his jaw until they rested on his lips. "Promise me, Bobby."

He took her hand and raised it between them. His thumb touched her wedding ring.

"Every day is a promise, Teel," he said and kissed her ring. "Every day."

She nodded and kissed him again and then moved out of his way. She toweled herself dry, and then stood motionless, still naked, and watched him in the shower.

"Honey, go make yourself some tea," he told her, eyes closed as he rinsed the shampoo from his hair. "I'm not going anywhere."

A cup of tea. Teel turned away from him, remembering Jeannie and what she found after she'd made herself a cup of tea.

"Rick left her."

Bobby opened his eyes. Teel saw the regret and sadness cross his face.

"That's awful."

Teel nodded.

"It's not us, Teel."

"I know."

"Go lay down, hon." He reached for his bar of soap. "I'll be there in a minute."

"The girls?"

"Rachel's watching TV. Keegan's on her computer."

She thought about that for a moment, and she wondered again if Rachel had heard them earlier and then she wondered why it seemed that suddenly Keegan was on that laptop every waking moment.

Dressed in pajama shorts and a T-shirt, she padded out to the living room. Rachel was lying on the couch watching a movie. She didn't look at Teel when she sat down.

"Mm." Teel stared at the TV long enough to know that Rachel was watching *Top Gun*. "Tom Cruise."

Rachel glanced at her and smiled. "Easy on the eyes."

"Hard on the heart," Teel finished.

"I have a history test tomorrow."

"Ready for it?"

Rachel shrugged. "I guess."

"I'm glad you invited Deacon over today," Teel said honestly.

"Really?"

"Yes. I'm sorry I wasn't myself, but I did like him."

Rachel's smile lit up the room.

"Did Daddy?"

Teel and Bobby hadn't talked about it yet, but Teel knew him well enough to know he'd liked the kid.

"Yes."

"Mom?"

Teel flinched. Her mind flashed to earlier today, when she'd overheard part of Rachel and Keegan's conversation. When Keegan had asked Rachel if she was sleeping with Deacon. At the time, she thought she'd wanted to hear the answer. Now she didn't want to know, and she was scared to death Rachel was about to tell her anyway.

"Hmm?"

"How do you know when you're in love?"

Teel sighed and laid her head back on the couch. "When you're so full of him inside…and he still gives you room to be you…to chase your dreams…to love your friends and family…"

"That's love?"

"That's a pretty big part of it." Teel shrugged. "At least it is for me."

Rachel nodded.

"Is it love?" Teel asked quietly.

"Maybe."

"Looked like you guys were having a pretty serious conversation out there earlier."

Rachel nodded, but she didn't seem inclined to share any of it with Teel.

"Jeannie saw you," Teel continued. "She said it made her think about the night you and Keegan both spent the night there with Marin."

Rachel's eyes filled, but she looked away. "Mom, I hate what she did. I feel so…bad…for Jeannie and Rick. And I hate what it's done to us."

"We're okay," Teel interrupted her. "You. Dad. Me. Keegan. We're okay. Got it?"

Teel laid her hand on Rachel's leg and gave it a gentle squeeze.

"I thought about her. When we were out there. And I felt…"

"You felt what?" Teel urged her to keep talking. If only Keegan could be this open with her.

Rachel lifted a shoulder helplessly. "Guilty. Like I shouldn't be out there. With Deacon. Since Marin…"

"Sweetie," Teel leaned forward and reached for Rachel's hand. "You can't feel guilty for living. This is life."

Teel heard her own words and wished she could actually live by them.

"It's just…" Rachel frowned. "Whatever it was that…" She shook her head. "Whatever…Maybe if she'd have waited, it would have been better. The next day."

Teel nodded. "Maybe."

"I just wish she would've waited."

"Me, too."

Bobby came out of the bedroom and trailed his fingers over her shoulders as he walked by.

"Tea?" he asked her.

"No."

Maybe she would never drink tea again.

"Want anything?"

"No thanks."

She watched him twist the cap off a bottled beer.

She'd forgotten the friendship bracelet. In her rush to rid herself of Jeannie's words and the oppressive sorrow from the English house, she'd hurried to the bathroom and showered and forgotten about the bracelet she was supposed to have given to Keegan.

Bobby sat down at the other end of the couch just as she stood up. He watched her get up, but he turned to the TV as she left the room. As she feared, he'd picked up the pile of clothes she'd left on the floor. A quick pick through the dirty clothes at the top of the hamper proved useless.

What had she done with the bracelet?

Her hands shook as she made another pass through the

pockets. Again, nothing. She looked on the floor in front of the whirlpool tub, but there was nothing there.

She found it in the garbage can. Hands still shaking, her mind back in the dark English living room with Jeannie, Teel's throat tightened as she snatched the bracelet from the garbage. She felt a flash of irrational anger at Bobby for throwing it away, although he had no way of knowing what it was.

"Teel, sit down for a minute," he said as she walked back through the living room. She raised her hand and told him she'd sit in a minute, and then she knocked on Keegan's door.

"C'min."

Keegan sat on her bed, computer on her lap, back against the headboard.

"Did you see Jeannie?" If Teel didn't know any better, she'd say her daughter was scared.

"I did."

"Is she okay?"

Teel laughed, but her throat was thick with tears and she sounded funny.

"No, Keegan." She sat on the edge of Keegan's bed. "No. She's not okay."

"But she will be?" Keegan asked eagerly.

Teel shrugged. "I don't know. Maybe someday."

Keegan looked away.

"She asked me to give you this."

Teel held the bracelet out to Keegan.

"What is it?"

"The friendship bracelet you made for Marin. Remember? The night Rachel stayed over there with you. Marin made one for you, too."

Keegan took the bracelet without looking at it.

"Oh yeah."

"Do you still have yours?" Teel asked and looked around

Keegan's room. She didn't expect to see the bracelet, but maybe she was looking for a trace of her daughter. The one who seemed to have disappeared and left this cold, unfeeling girl in her place.

"Huh?" Keegan looked back at her. "No. I threw it away."

Chapter 15

KEEGAN

SHE DIDN'T THINK she would sleep. Every time she closed her eyes, she saw her mom handing her that damned bracelet and then she'd look up and instead of it being her mom, it was Marin. She kept thinking about that, and then she must have gone to sleep, because it was Marin handing her the bracelet and Marin saying that pink was her favorite color and she had that dimple at the corner of her mouth and the bandage on her finger where she'd cut herself on a tuna can earlier that day.

And then when Keegan looked up, it was still Marin handing her the bracelet. They were still sitting on the floor of Marin's room, and Rachel was still flopped over Marin's bed, coloring one of those big velvet art things of the Power-puff Girls. But Marin was taller and thinner. The bandage was gone from her finger. Instead, Keegan noticed her manicure. Pretty squared-off nail tips painted some kind of hot, Notice Me pink.

Her ring. Her watch. The skirt and blouse she was buried in. The heels she always wore with that outfit. And then Keegan was awake, and she jumped out of bed and wondered if she was wearing those shoes. Had Marin been buried in those shoes?

Keegan rubbed her eyes so hard she saw kaleidoscope colors and that, too, made her think of Marin. How they'd lay back on Keegan's bed and rub their eyes really hard and then just look at the colors that played on their eyelids. She stumbled in the dark to her window. She didn't want to turn her lamp on. That might wake Rachel, and she didn't feel like talking to anyone.

When she opened her blinds, a waterfall of moonlight and streetlight fell into her room. Desperate for something to do, something to keep her mind off Marin, she turned her laptop on and then sat down on her bed while she waited for it to boot up. Twenty after four. So she *had* slept for a while. She must have been dreaming of Marin all night.

Marin. Damn. Damn. Damn. Sooner or later, they would come for her. Someone had to have told Marin's parents by now. Keegan could just imagine Rick banging on the door and barging in and grabbing Keegan by the collar. Telling her mom and dad it was Keegan's fault Marin was dead.

She was more afraid of Jeannie, though. Just the few minutes at the funeral home, when Jeannie held her hands and asked her if she knew what Marin had been thinking, just that much had been like sandpaper on her skin.

Her stupid computer took forever. It wasn't even two years old, and already it was a dinosaur and it had been locking up on her lately. Pretty sad that she actually liked a stupid beat-up old desktop model at the public library better than her own laptop. Tired of waiting for it to start up, she lay down and buried her face in her pillow.

This wasn't ever going to go away. That's what was bothering her. Keegan had created a mess that had suddenly grown exponentially, and there was no making it go away. It would only get worse.

She stretched and put her hands up under her pillow. For a second, just one second, she thought about him. About that night at the party. How she'd felt all warm and tingly inside when he'd kissed her. The way she'd breathed in the smell of beer and his cologne while he unbuttoned her jeans.

Her fingers touched something now, under her pillow. Something thin and long. Thread. Keegan sighed as she pulled the friendship bracelet out from under her pillow.

She flopped over on her back and wished she could forget it. The bracelet. Marin.

Her mom had clearly expected her to react to the bracelet when she'd given it to her earlier, and she'd been disappointed when Keegan had said she'd thrown hers away.

She got up again, ignored her computer and knelt in front of her dresser. She eased the bottom drawer open and reached in. Fished around through shorts and old swimsuits and even old ribbons given during softball and soccer seasons until she found it.

She pulled it out and then sat with Marin's bracelet in one hand and hers in the other.

———

TIFFANY AND BRANDY followed Keegan around all morning before the bell rang. She had classes with them too, so they kept tabs on her during class and then they'd hurry to follow her between classes. Keegan guessed they were hoping to see her panic and throw up again, only this time they would probably find it more entertaining if she puked on Sean Spanner's shoes. She hadn't wanted to come today. But she hadn't even tried to play the sick card with Mom. Her mom might have been off all weekend, but she'd been cool and collected this morning.

She probably wouldn't get away with skipping again today either, but Keegan held that thought in reserve for later. Just in case. There was still stuff in front of Marin's locker. Keegan was surprised the janitor had left the big piece of paper taped on it, the one with all the Barf Your Lungs Out sweet messages to her, and the pile of teddy bears and flowers on the floor. Just seeing it made her prickle, and she was sick of Jess asking her what was wrong. As if she didn't know, for God's sake.

She did okay until lunch time, when she ran into Sean Spanner. Literally ran right into him. And he didn't recognize her. He was standing just inside the cafeteria, talking to Eric Cole. Keegan had been wandering down the hall, trying to decide if she should cut and walk to the library. Or better yet, home. But if Dad came home for any reason, she'd be busted.

Not necessarily, though. She could hide out in her room, with no music on, no TV. Or she could hang out in the basement. If she was quiet, he wouldn't have any reason to suspect that she ditched and came home early.

No, she'd told herself. Stay and deal with this. If not today, tomorrow. And that was the only thought that kept her moving, one foot in front of the other, to the cafeteria. From now on, everything she did was going to spiral into this huge thing and she didn't have a chance in hell of getting out of it. Soon enough, everyone would know and maybe there wouldn't be any more school.

Maybe it would be worse.

And then she'd turned around at the last minute and smacked right into Sean. He'd barely glanced at her, like she wasn't worth the time it would take to notice her. The first time it had happened, Keegan decided maybe it had been kind of dark in that room, and she'd gotten a haircut and so maybe he had been a little unsure. The second time he'd looked at her and looked away with no recognition, she lied to herself that he felt funny about what had happened and he had to figure out how to approach her about it.

The third time she'd seen him, he'd been flirting outrageously with someone else and she'd had to admit that he didn't know her. That night at the party had been just another night at a party for him. It had been *everything* to her.

She'd bounced off him in the cafeteria, but she hadn't said anything. Instead, she'd backed away and watched him talking to Eric, and she'd had a flash of skin and sex, and she'd turned quickly and hurried from the cafeteria. If Tiffany and Brandy had been around then, they'd have gotten lucky. As it was, Keegan had apparently ditched them after her fourth hour class. She hurried to the bathroom and lurched to a stop just in time. She threw up quickly and wiped the puke from her mouth and then just as quickly, she left the bathroom and slipped out the front doors of school.

She hoped no one had seen her, but really, she didn't give a damn. She had to get away. She had to be alone.

Her phone beeped as she hurried up Fourteenth Street, away from Blessed Sacrament. Text message. Great. Probably Jess wondering where she went.

Backpack slung over her shoulder, she dug her phone out as she walked. Not Jess. In fact, she didn't recognize the number at all.

Leaving so soon, Keegan? Toodles.

Tiffany. She wouldn't have guessed, except for the Toodles. Great. It wasn't just that Tiffany had texted her. Tiffany probably knew everything. From the beginning and maybe even something before that. Someone had given Tiffany her phone number. Most likely that someone would be Jess.

And so it begins, she thought as she walked, head down, hands balled into tight fists. Maybe she should just admit it. Just tell someone the whole story. Nobody at school. She should probably just come clean and tell Mom. But she couldn't. Because she knew that no matter how bad things would get, Mom might still love her. No reason to disappoint her. She hoped to get away with as much as possible, which meant telling Mom as little as possible.

Rachel. Maybe she could talk to Rachel.

Chapter 16

Teel

TEEL SQUIRMED IN HER CHAIR. She didn't particularly like being on this side of the desk. Not in this situation, anyway. Having been a teacher for what sometimes felt like a hundred years, she was accustomed to talking to parents. Having been a parent for nineteen years, she was good at talking to teachers. But not like this.

Elaine Caldwell, though shorter than Teel and very professional, seemed to be looking down her nose at her. She seemed to be saying that her status as the high school counselor made her better able to read the teenagers in the hallways, Teel's daughter included. The hell of it was that these days, Teel couldn't read a damned thing in Keegan, and so maybe Elaine was right. Teel was a good teacher; she loved being with the kids, and it showed. She'd always thought she was a pretty good mom. Never perfect, but pretty good. Elaine Caldwell was making her doubt everything she'd ever done for Rachel and Keegan.

"You're telling me Keegan cut class again today," Teel repeated what Elaine said. Where had this come from? Keegan, though sometimes melodramatic and sometimes petulant (what child isn't?) had never given her and Bobby this kind of trouble. Keegan, though sometimes selfish and sometimes immature (what child isn't?) had never been so unfeeling, so cold to anyone.

Drugs? But a kid cutting class didn't necessarily mean she was on drugs. Besides, Teel hadn't noticed any sudden weight loss or gain or a difference in her sleep patterns. She didn't wander the house jonesing for a fix. She was healthy; her skin was unmarked by needles or scabs from using meth.

"She was here this morning. Didn't show up to any after-noon classes."

Elaine, of the short and spiky dark hair, cupped her chin in her hand and made a face that Teel supposed was meant to convey commiseration. But all Teel could see was her perfect manicure. This woman wasn't on a kid's level. She looked like she belonged in an executive office on Wall Street. Teel believed in being available to children. Being there when they need you. Whether they needed to be taught subtraction or to tell you their mommy and daddy had a fight last night.

"Why didn't you notify me?"

"Because you had already called to set up this appoint-ment. I figured we would discuss it here. And I did call you the last time she skipped."

"Was that the first time?"

"Yes."

Well, that was something, at least. If this was going to be a habit, it was just starting and would be easier for Teel to break for Keegan.

"Her grades are good," Teel commented, because thank God, Blessed Sacrament had an online system for students and parents to keep tabs on grades, assignments, and missing assignments.

"They are good," Elaine said with a nod. With that she eased back in her chair and that quickly, the snooty Wall Street attitude fell away. She crossed her legs—Teel saw gray slacks—and cocked her head, probably to study Teel's face and figure out why her daughter was suddenly dabbling in truancy. "Teel, she's a good kid. She's very smart. I'm just seeing things that don't fit with her, and it concerns me."

"The red flags." Teel nodded.

Elaine nodded in agreement. "Two of her teachers have observed a few changes. She used to contribute to discussion in classes. Ask questions. Converse with them, with other students. She's withdrawn. Daydreaming, maybe, I don't know."

"Which teachers?"

"Biology and English."

Teel sighed. "Can you tell me when this started?"

"Before Marin English killed herself, if that's what you're wondering."

Of course that's what she was wondering. Because she desperately wanted to chalk all of this up to grief. Keegan was only fifteen. It was possible that any of this could be caused by misplaced grief. Grief she didn't understand and couldn't express.

"What else?"

"How well do you know her friends?"

"They're at the house a lot," Teel started, but then she caught herself. Sure, some of Keegan's friends came over (none since Marin's suicide) and yet, how well did she know them? Any kid could play a role for an adult. For a teacher or another parent. "She's with Jess Levine most often. She seems like a nice girl."

"She's not," Elaine said simply. "And from what I can tell,

Keegan's…red flags…started going up when she started hanging out with her."

Teel opened her mouth to answer Elaine, but she didn't know what to say. She couldn't very well ask what Elaine meant when she said Jess wasn't a good girl. And that could mean just about anything.

"No drugs, nothing like that," Elaine continued. "She's smart. She does well in school. But she's a queen. And she's got Keegan riding shotgun."

Teel knew exactly what Elaine meant, but she wanted to play dumb. She wanted to pretend she didn't hear her, didn't understand what she was implying. She wanted to get up and walk out of Elaine's broom-closet-sized office.

"Are you saying that my daughter is a bully?"

"I'm saying her best friend is, and Keegan suddenly seems damned determined to be part of that crowd."

Teel raised her hands and rubbed her cheekbones and then pushed her fingers back through her hair. Sometime just after lunch, a dull ache had lodged itself there along her jawbones. Now it pounded so hard her teeth hurt.

"Marin? Did she bully Marin?"

Elaine winced and then leaned forward again and rested her elbows on her desk.

"I never saw her say anything to anyone, Marin included, that could be considered bullying. But I saw the very sweet, friendly girl that Keegan used to be vanish. And a very snotty, cold-hearted girl took her place."

Teel nodded. It was a struggle to stay calm. To stay sitting. To not run from Elaine's office and home to Bobby. To cry on his shoulder, because how the hell had their daughter become this person Elaine was talking about? To run home to Keegan and read her the riot act, because who the hell was she to throw down everything Teel had taught her about courtesy and compassion and friendship?

And yet, she had to stay calm, didn't she? She couldn't come unglued in Elaine's office, because people talk. She'd no sooner put on a show for this woman than she would walk out into the middle of a busy street.

"I appreciate…"

"Teel, I know that right now you don't like me very much," Elaine interrupted her. "I'm okay when I'm telling you your daughter was accepted into a good college or that your child is being honored for service hours above and beyond those required, yada yada yada. But right now, I'm telling you something you don't want to hear."

And your point? Teel wondered.

"I'm not judging you. I don't know that I would have stepped in with just anyone. So, Keegan's working her way into the A crowd, so what? Welcome to high school; it happens." Elaine stood up and slipped her hands in her pockets. At a distinct disadvantage still sitting, Teel hurried to stand, too.

"I've always respected you. You taught two of my nephews, and they loved you. And I remember helping Rachel with college stuff. She's a good kid. Keegan's a good kid."

"She is," Teel said and hoped she didn't sound as desperate as she felt.

"I just thought maybe…you could bring her back. I like the old Keegan better, and I'm sure a lot of other people do too."

Teel sure as hell did, but she wasn't going to admit to Elaine that she'd noticed some of this same behavior at home. Although, to be fair, Teel hadn't seen a lot of it before Marin's death. What she had seen, though, that cold disregard for a dead girl who had once been a good friend, chilled her to the bone.

"Thank you." She picked up her purse and tucked the strap over her shoulder. She felt burdened, like she was carrying extra weight, maybe a stone mantel like the one on the fireplace at home.

"Please call me. If there's anything I can do."

She spared one last glance at Elaine and nodded and even managed to pull herself together to smile and reach back and shake her hand.

The weight on her shoulders, on her heart, drug her down and though she wanted to run to her car and get the hell out of there, she walked slowly to her car and once in it, sat for a moment. Stunned. Absolutely stunned to have been a participant in that meeting. On this side of the desk.

Her hand shook as she put the key in the ignition. Keegan had better be at home, but she didn't want to talk to her yet. Not yet. She was so raw inside that just the thought of seeing Keegan was abrasive and made her hurt.

She wasn't really even ready to talk to Bobby. Of course she would; she would tell him everything and they would talk about it before either of them came down on Keegan. If that's what you did in this situation. Punish? Or talk?

As she drove, she realized her stomach was in a knot. She dreaded going home. In fact, there was nowhere she could go that could possibly make her feel better. Nowhere. Because there was nowhere she could go right now, no one she could talk to that would make this feeling go away.

She was ashamed. Teel was ashamed of her own daughter.

Chapter 17

TEEL

WOUND TOO tight to sit still and too dazed to string two words together to talk to Keegan, Teel drove across town to Eve's house, praying all the way that she would be home. It was after five, and Eve left the bank around four most of the time. But Teel knew Eve was a busy woman, and this was a gamble.

Her hands still shook against the steering wheel, so she kept her fingers curled so tight around the wheel that her knuckles were white. It had cooled off to a very tolerable, if not pleasant, seventy-six degrees, and she put her windows down and let the wind sweep her hair back from her face.

She felt a rush of relief flood through her when she pulled into Eve's driveway and saw her Sebring convertible in the garage. On auto-pilot, Teel climbed from her car and walked to Eve's back door. It swung open as she raised her hand to knock.

"Hey." Eve eyed her carefully. She reached for Teel's hand and pulled her inside.

"Talk to me." Teel sighed.

"What's—"

"About anything. Just talk."

"I got a cost of living raise today, so now maybe I can afford to go out to eat now and then," Eve started. Teel dropped into a chair at the kitchen table. Eve made better than decent money, and she also loved to cook. Teel had caught her in the act of slicing vegetables. She watched the blade of the knife chop swiftly through squash and onions and then mushrooms.

"I went out last night with some friends. And saw Dennis. At The Dugout." Teel nodded when Eve glanced at her. The Dugout was a sports bar popular with Cardinal and Cub fans. "He was with some little slut that could have probably been our daughter."

"Eve." Teel winced, although she had to admit to herself that it felt good to feel bad for someone else.

"Oh Teel." Eve shook her head. "He's such a bastard, sometimes, I hate him."

"I know."

"But I love him." Eve glanced over at her and then reached up to stop a tear from falling. She sniffled and then wiped her finger on her jeans. "God help me, I love him."

"I know you do, Eve," Teel said quietly.

"I don't know why." Eve shrugged. She focused on the vegetables again. Teel zeroed in on the blade of the knife again, but she looked away quickly when she thought of Marin. Slicing her wrists. Jeannie finding her covered in blood.

"Mom called this morning," Eve continued. She dropped the knife in the sink and then pulled a wok from a cabinet.

"She called you at work?"

"Yeah. To remind me that she's going out of town over the weekend."

"Mom's going out of town over the weekend?" Teel frowned. "Where? For what?"

"She and two of her friends are going to St. Louis. They're going to do some shopping and they're going to a show. She said she'll call us when she gets home on Sunday."

"News to me," Teel mumbled. Then again, she had been a little preoccupied lately, and she had to admit that even if her mother had told her about these plans, she would most likely have forgotten them.

"Hungry?" Eve asked as she lifted the cutting board over the wok.

"No." Stomach still in knots, Teel couldn't imagine eating.

"Guess what I did last night?"

"After seeing Dennis?" Teel raised her eyebrows. "Made a voodoo doll that looked like him and cut something vital off?"

Eve laughed softly. "Maybe next time. I watched the video of Mom and Dad's thirtieth anniversary party."

"Oh Evie." Teel felt a pang at the thought of her sister watching a video that not only showed her and Dennis at a happier time in their lives, but also of their dad, alive and healthy.

"Eh." Eve busied herself with running water to wash the knife and cutting board. "Needed a good cry, ya know?"

"I do know." Teel nodded. She thought of her own night, of standing in Jeannie English's house and listening to a woman fall apart and then going home and feeling like she'd carried the despair from the English house to her own home and the way she and Bobby had pawed at each other in the shower. "I do."

"Can I quit talking yet? You gonna tell me?"

"You can quit talking," Teel answered. "But no, I don't wanna talk right now."

Eve turned the kitchen faucet off and then joined Teel at the kitchen table.

"You and Bobby? You're okay?"

Teel understood why Eve would go there first to worry, after her own failed marriage.

"Bobby's my rock," she said quietly.

"You're okay?"

Teel nodded.

"Then it's Keegan."

Teel stared at her silently.

"I understand. Talk to Bobby first."

"What's the worst thing you did in high school?"

"Mmm." Eve sat back and crossed her arms over her chest. "Smoked pot with Jack Collins."

"Really? Jack?"

The corner of Eve's mouth tipped up in an almost smile. "Which led to me giving him a blowjob in the backseat of his car…during my lunch hour."

"Jack? You gave Jack Collins a blowjob?" Teel laughed.

"He was hot."

"He was a hood."

Eve shrugged. "Still hot."

"Why didn't you tell me then?"

"Because you would've told Mom, and then I'd have been grounded. And I would've gotten a lecture about how proper girls behaved."

"Sounds like you might've needed it." Teel laughed and sat back to dodge the palm of Eve's hand aimed at her shoulder.

"Because you never did that. Right?"

"Not in the school parking lot, no." Teel frowned and shook her head.

"But you did it? You gave someone a blowjob? In high school?"

Teel laughed. "Shouldn't we be drinking to have this conversation?"

"Oh my God, you're embarrassed?" Eve shrieked with laughter. "You're such a prude, Toniel Alexander."

"I am not!"

Eve stood up and headed to the refrigerator. She came back with two bottles of beer in hand and handed one to Teel.

"Truth."

"Yes, I did, but not in the parking lot during the day."

"Then where?"

Teel twisted the top off and took a big drink.

"The hall outside the cafeteria during a basketball game."

"Oh my God!" Eve squealed and laughed. "Seriously? You weren't afraid you would get caught?"

"Does any seventeen-year-old worry about getting caught?"

Eve shrugged, conceding Teel's point. "Who was it?"

"Ted Moore."

"I didn't really know him, but wasn't he a geek?"

Teel lifted a shoulder and took another drink. "He had really pretty eyes."

"Behind those black horn-rimmed glasses." Eve shivered. "You did it for pretty eyes?"

"Oh no," Teel said with a laugh. "He had more than that."

"Really? You slept with him?"

Teel laughed and then rubbed her eyes. "Eve. I'm worried to death about my daughter, and we're sitting here swapping high school sexcapades." She shook her head and dropped her hands to the table.

"Suicide isn't contagious." Eve read the mood change, and the laughter and teasing fell away.

"I'm not really worried that she would hurt herself," Teel answered. She heard the quiver in her voice and prayed that Eve wouldn't ask. As much as she wanted to break down, she knew this was something she had to discuss with Bobby first.

Eve stood up and came around the table. She leaned over and hugged Teel and then kissed her cheek.

"Go home." She squeezed Teel's shoulder and then stepped away. "Talk to Bobby."

Teel glanced at her watch. It was nearing six o'clock. Bobby would most likely be home. What would she do about dinner? She hadn't set anything out to thaw before she'd left the house this morning.

Eve was back at the cooktop as Teel made her way to the back door. She glanced at her and felt a flash of sadness that Eve spent most of her nights alone. In the beginning, Teel would never have guessed Dennis would run around on Eve. He'd been completely absorbed in Eve and their life together.

She wondered what made one man cheat and the next stay faithful. Eve smiled and shook her head, and Teel thought she'd read her mind.

"Call me."

Teel nodded and then stepped into the garage and pulled the back door closed behind her.

Chapter 18

Rachel

USUALLY, she studied in her room, but the house was quiet, too quiet, and sitting in her room these days depressed her. She couldn't concentrate anyway. She kept thinking about Marin. She and Deacon had talked about it, and Rachel knew he was right. It was just going to take some time to get past this whole thing, and she didn't really want to just sit in her room and picture Marin killing herself. She had no idea how Marin had done it, but her imagination had served up several options, to the point that Rachel felt like her thoughts were painted on her walls.

Keegan's door was closed, and Mom wasn't even home yet. So Rachel took her backpack to the dining room and spread her stuff out over the table. Better. The dining room and living area and kitchen were all open and the sun was out, so everything was bright and sort of cheery. Cheerier than her room, anyway.

She opened her biology text book and pulled a pen from

her backpack. And yet, she still couldn't concentrate. She clicked her pen and stared out the window. A few kids rode their bikes up and down the street. Rachel watched them and thought about the days when she and Keegan played outside after school. Bikes. Roller skates. Swing set. Didn't matter what they did, they always went outside after school.

She wondered when that had changed, and then she realized she was getting all stupid sad again and her thoughts made her sound like she was sixty instead of nineteen. Deacon was in class, so she didn't want to bug him. He would text her back; he didn't need to pay attention in class, though he did most of the time. But all the same, she didn't want to bug him. Because what would she say? That she used to play outside and at some point that changed and now she hung out in her room and Keegan hid in hers twenty-four seven?

Not that he wouldn't care, but there was only so much pissing and moaning a person could do before the person on the receiving end got tired of it. She thought about going outside. Taking a bike ride. Going for a run. Nah, that was Keegan's thing. Rachel didn't like running.

She glanced at her cell phone. It was after five. Odd that Mom wasn't home. She usually told them if she had a meeting after school. Maybe she'd just gotten busy checking papers or doing lesson plans.

Restless at the table, not interested in biology homework and still thinking about Marin and Keegan and Mom, Rachel pushed her chair back and stood up. She tossed her pen on the table and went to stand by the window. Two of the kids outside were racing on their bikes. A third, he looked younger than the other two, was just sitting on his bike seat, leaning with one foot on a pedal and the other on the ground, watching them.

Too. Damned. Quiet. She could hear them outside. If she listened hard, she could hear their conversation. They were laughing. The two racing were razzing the other kid, but Rachel didn't want to hear it. Instead, she backed away from the window and wandered over into the living room. She stood at the French doors and watched the neighbor behind their house mow his grass. Even that would be better than sitting in this damned quiet house.

She was surprised to realize she missed her family. She missed the constant buzz of chatter. The TV on as Mom fixed dinner. The laughter they all shared over dinner. The stupid way Mom and Dad flirted while they cleaned the kitchen together.

How long would her family be in mourning? When would it be okay to move on? To take the first step?

At twenty after five, Rachel realized her mom didn't have anything out for dinner. Her stomach was already growling. She wondered again where Mom was, and she wondered what they would eat.

Rachel pulled the freezer door open and rummaged around, looking for a box of cheese sticks. Something to snack on. None. Of course. A box of Girl Scout cookies, but she didn't really want anything sweet. *Pizza. Hmm.* Pizza sounded good.

She closed the freezer and found crust mix and sauce in the cabinet. Okay, so she could fix dinner for Mom and keep her mind off…everything…all at the same time. Win/win.

It was still too damned quiet, though, as she mixed the crust in a big silver bowl. She stood still for a moment and glanced at the window over the dining room table.

She needed some noise. Not the TV. Rachel hated watching the news. It was rare to ever hear anything good, and she didn't want to hear any bad news. Not when they were still shoveling shit from the last bit of bad news they'd had.

Music. Yep. Keegan was in her room, Mom wasn't home,

and she wasn't sure if Dad was, so who was there to care if she turned on some music?

She hurried across the room to the entertainment center under the TV on the wall. Just the thought of music made her feel better. Nothing depressing. No sad songs. No heavy metal noise. Squatting in front of the open doors of the entertainment center, she eyed the stack of CDs. There were more in her room and more in Keegan's room, but surely she could find something here.

She chose The Black Eyed Peas and found the song "I Gotta Feeling." Maybe it was inappropriate, but she was alone for the time being and she didn't care. Or maybe, for her it *was* appropriate. It was time to let Marin rest in peace and get on with it.

Now she wished Deacon were here. She danced in the kitchen as she made three homemade pizzas: cheese for Keegan, ham and pepperoni for Dad, and ham and green pepper for her and her mom. She'd danced with Deacon a couple of times at parties. He was a good dancer; in fact, he was one of those guys so easy on his feet that most people stopped and watched him when he danced. But Rachel liked slow-dancing with him best.

"What're you doing?"

Rachel, now cutting vegetables for a salad, looked up at Keegan. Her sister looked like she'd just rolled out of bed. There was a crease in her left cheek, like the line from the edge of a sheet under her face. Her hair, which Rachel thought had been unruly and messy for way too long, stuck up in some places and hung limp in others.

There was something else, though. Something wistful, maybe. Rachel couldn't pinpoint it, but there was something hopeful about the look on Keegan's face. Like she wanted to believe the song lyrics. Like she was ready to let this Marin stuff go and move on.

"Fixing dinner."

"Why?"

"Because Mom's not home and I'm hungry."

Keegan crossed her arms over her chest and hunched over like she was cold. She came closer and looked at the bowls in the sink.

"Pizza?"

Rachel nodded.

"Did you make me cheese?"

"Yep."

"Thank you."

Rachel nodded, slightly taken aback by Keegan's simple thank you. She finished cutting the vegetables and then tossed them all in a bowl of lettuce.

"Where is Mom?" Keegan asked.

Rachel shrugged. "No idea."

"Do you think she's okay?"

Rachel, wiping the counter off with a dishrag, stopped and looked at Keegan as she slid onto a barstool.

"Why wouldn't she be okay?"

"I dunno. It's just..." She shrugged. "Things are weird right now."

"Things are beyond weird right now," Rachel agreed. "But Mom's fine."

"She could've been in a car accident."

"Keegan, she's fine."

"I skipped my afternoon classes today."

Rachel raised her eyebrows.

"Again."

"Again?" Rachel repeated. "Good luck to you when Mom finds out." When Keegan didn't answer her, she looked up at her again. Keegan stared at the counter and chewed on a hangnail. God, Keegan was such a mess. Which was kind of sad because she could be pretty. "She will find out. You know that, don't you?"

"Yep."

Dishrag still in hand, Rachel studied Keegan, but she was oblivious.

"You need a haircut."

Keegan lifted her eyes to meet Rachel's gaze. "I need a lot more than a haircut, Rach."

Rachel wondered if she was finally reacting to Marin's suicide.

"Want me to take you somewhere? Haircut and mani-cure?" Rachel reached forward and tugged at Keegan's hand, pulling her thumb away from her teeth. "Stop it. That drives me nuts."

"Tonight?" Keegan asked.

"You look like hell."

"Thanks."

"Keegan, what's going on with you? You're like some alien nutcase in my sister's body."

Keegan almost laughed. Rachel danced around the corner of the countertop and took Keegan's hand.

"What're you doing?" Keegan tried to pull away, but Rachel wouldn't let her.

"Dancing. C'mon."

Keegan slid off the barstool, but she stood there by Rachel as she danced.

"C'mon. Swing your butt. Move."

"I can't dance."

"You can dance." Rachel put her arm around her shoul-ders. "Just move, Keegan. You're stuck. You have to move one way or the other."

Rachel wished again that Deacon was there. She would call him later. Maybe she'd go to his dorm room and see him.

God, this sucked. She was so ready to get on with it, and the rest of her family was stuck. Like she'd just said to Keegan.

"Rach?"

"Hmm?"

"What's the worst thing you did when you were in high school?"

Rachel, trying desperately to lose herself in the music, laughed. "Like I'd tell you. You'd sell me out to Mom in a heartbeat."

"Rachel."

"What?" Rachel turned to Keegan, but she didn't stop moving.

"I really messed up."

"What's going on?"

Keegan, her back to the hallway, tensed up when they heard Mom's voice. Rachel looked over Keegan's shoulder as her mom walked into the kitchen. Frazzled. No. That word didn't do justice to the way Mom looked.

She looked like hell. Like Keegan. Only maybe worse, if that was possible.

"Hi."

Mom smiled at Rachel and then stepped further into the kitchen. She leaned over to peek in the oven.

"Who made pizza?" She sounded surprised.

"I did."

"Well, thank you, Rachel," she said sincerely. "I forgot to get anything out for dinner."

"You're welcome."

"Seen Dad? His truck's in the garage."

"Huh-uh."

Rachel wondered why her mom hadn't greeted Keegan. She hadn't really even looked at her. Kind of like Keegan was invisible, and Rachel was just standing here by herself in the living room.

"Did you work late?" Rachel asked her. She picked up the remote from the counter and turned the music down. Keegan hunched her shoulders again like she was cold or like she was trying to make herself small. Invisible. Rachel rolled her eyes when she started chewing on her hangnail again.

"No. Had a meeting." Mom had her back to them. She set her purse on the counter and then turned around. And looked at Rachel. "Went out to Eve's after."

"Oh."

"I'm gonna change clothes really quick," Mom told her. The oven timer beeped. Rachel sighed and walked—the dancing was done for the night—to the oven to take the first pizza out. She glanced over her shoulder as she opened the refrigerator door to get the next one out.

Keegan was gone. Rachel was alone in the room.

Chapter 19

TEEL

THEY ATE ON THE DECK, and Teel thought the pizza was perhaps the best she'd eaten. Because it was good, but it was also made by hands other than her own. Without her having to ask. She didn't have much of an appetite. How could she with the way her mind and stomach were spinning? And yet, she ate three pieces and a salad. Later, when everyone was sleeping and she was awake—she knew she would be—she would be the one chewing Tums.

She hadn't finished the beer at Eve's, and she'd been tempted to have a glass of wine when Bobby poured his. But she'd chosen water instead. It was a beautiful evening, if you didn't count the fact that her youngest daughter had become a stranger. One who skipped classes and aligned herself with a queen bee and treated everyone else as if they were beneath her.

After dinner, Rachel excused herself. She carried her plate inside and put it in the dishwasher—Teel could see her through the French doors—and then disappeared. Keegan, who had eaten two or three bites of pizza, asked to be excused just moments after they all heard Rachel start her car.

Bobby made a point of checking Keegan's plate, but eventually he let her get up. It wasn't as if they had a rule in place that everyone had to eat everything on his or her plate. Or even a certain number of bites of this and that. More that Keegan had become someone new to them, and no one knew how to talk to her.

It was quiet on the deck. Peaceful. Teel wondered if they would ever feel normal again. If they'd ever be like they were a week ago, before Marin English had killed herself.

She met Bobby's eyes and took a deep breath.

Where to begin? With the classes? Cutting classes? With the fact that their daughter was no longer considered a sweet, considerate girl? Would that even worry Bobby? No one really wanted a smartass child, but would it bother Bobby the way it did Teel? She'd read countless books on social skills and the popular crowd and queen bees and bullies and the social hierarchy in school systems. She didn't want to see her daughter in these girls. Mean girls.

But would it be the end of the world to Bobby?

"What time did you get home today?" she asked him, still not really sure what to throw out as the lead card.

"Four-thirty. Trimmed the bushes in the back. Painted some trim work for the spec house on Grove Court."

She nodded. "Keegan got out at noon," she told him.

"She cut classes again?"

Another nod.

"What do we do, Teel?"

"She doesn't contribute to class discussion anymore in English or biology."

"A lot of kids don't," he pointed out.

She nodded. He was right, of course.

"I was also told that her friend Jess isn't a very nice girl."

That could mean a million different things, but Teel let it hang out there. Because she suspected it probably meant everything implied, which made her worry about Keegan even more.

Bobby took a deep breath and ran his fingers back through his hair.

"Drugs?"

Teel shrugged.

"Boys?"

Again, she shrugged.

"Elaine did say that Jess is very popular. And she thinks being popular is very important to Keegan."

"You wouldn't know it these days," he mumbled. "She looks like hell."

"Since Marin's death, yeah," Teel agreed.

"What do we do?"

Teel pressed her lips together and shook her head. "I have no idea."

"She needs to be punished."

"For skipping classes, yeah." Teel stood up and started stacking the dishes that remained on the table. "For deciding being popular is important to her?" She shrugged. "I don't like it. But. Isn't that part of high school?"

"I guess it depends on how far she's gone to get there."

———

BY EIGHT-THIRTY NEITHER of them had made a move to talk to Keegan. To discuss her skipping classes. To hand down a punishment. Teel figured Bobby was thinking carefully about punishment and consequences and what Keegan's next move might be. Teel was just too damned tired to think about it.

Once again, planted in the sofa cushions, her ass felt like it weighed a ton and she didn't want to think about getting up and going down the hall to Keegan's room.

As tired as her body was, she was even more exhausted mentally. The headache that had grabbed hold of her earlier, as early as her first class (because just the thought of calling Elaine Caldwell had stressed her out) had yet to let go. Actually, it was much worse, and she'd taken a handful of Motrin throughout the day. She hated swallowing so many pills, even if it was over the course of a full day. She wasn't prone to migraines. It was stress, and she knew it. Sex might help, but truth be told, she was too damned tired to think about that, too.

She had no idea what to say to Keegan. The thought of confronting her scared the hell out of her. Skipping classes, though frustrating, wasn't Teel's major concern. Let Bobby take care of that. Teel was scared to death of what was going on inside Keegan's head if she'd suddenly jumped ship and left her family values behind and begun swimming toward the shore where the A-list hung out. As a teacher, she'd seen some of these girls in action, even in grade school. It wasn't pretty, and honestly she didn't like those girls much. As a parent, she was new to the whole mess. Rachel had been a breeze.

"Did Rachel ever come home?" Bobby asked, remote control in hand. Teel glanced at him. He looked away from the TV and met her gaze. "Where'd she go?"

"She's not home, and I imagine she went to see Deacon."

Bobby nodded and returned his attention to the TV.

"Did you like him?"

"Hmm?"

"Deacon." Teel sighed and put her feet up on the coffee table. "Did you like him?"

"Yeah," Bobby said half-heartedly. "Seemed like an okay

kid."

She nodded her agreement, even though he wasn't looking at her. "I'm hungry."

"What?"

"I'm hungry," she repeated.

"We just ate."

She shrugged. "Let's go get ice cream."

"Ice cream?" He stretched and looked over her head at the dining room window. Night had leached the light from the sky, but Teel figured it would still be pleasant outside. They often went for ice cream on summer evenings.

"I want a sundae."

He shook his head, but he had to laugh. "And Keegan?"

"Yeah." She put her feet down and stood up. "C'mon. Let's get ice cream."

He turned the TV off as Teel stretched and walked down the hall to Keegan's room. She knocked and opened the door. Keegan was sprawled across her bed, nose in a textbook. The textbook went miles toward making Teel feel better, as if all was not lost if Keegan was studying.

"Hey."

Keegan turned her head to look at her.

"What?"

"You hungry?" If any of them should be hungry, it should be Keegan, since she'd hardly eaten any dinner.

"Not really."

"Ice cream?"

"Really?" Keegan sat up immediately. The grin on her face erased the last several days and a few years, and Teel felt a pang in her chest and actually reached up to lay her hand over her heart. She loved Keegan so much. God knows what they would do to stop the train Keegan had jumped, but Teel loved her so completely that it filled her for a moment and she had to catch her breath.

"Want some?"

"Yeah." Keegan stood up and stepped into a pair of flip flops. "I thought I'd be in trouble."

"Oh, you are," Teel said quietly. She put her arm around Keegan's shoulders and pulled her close. "We're gonna talk about it."

"I'm sorry, Mom."

Keegan's voice was tight with emotion. Teel turned her daughter in her arms and held her.

"C'mon," Teel said as she kissed Keegan's forehead. "Let's go. We'll talk."

"I love you."

Teel raised her eyebrows, but Keegan buried her head in the crook of Teel's neck. There was obviously more going on than skipping classes.

"I love you, too, Keegan."

She rubbed her hand down over Keegan's back, shocked that Keegan felt so bony and small. Her daughters weren't big girls, but they weren't waifs, and Keegan should be a little bigger than this.

Bobby walked down the hallway and looked at Teel. Their eyes met over Keegan's head. Teel prayed that he wouldn't jump to the punishment phase of the necessary discussion. That he would see that something was seriously wrong, and this wasn't one of Keegan's tantrums.

"Hey Sparkplug," he said softly. He reached out and laid his hand on the back of Keegan's head. "How about a Dilly bar?"

Teel breathed deeply, but silently, in relief.

"C'mon." He smoothed Keegan's hair down. "Let's go."

Teel watched as Keegan turned and then melted into Bobby's arms. Again, their eyes met over Keegan's head. Bobby led Keegan to the back door and out to the Edge. Teel was still hungry; she still wanted ice cream. But she thought if she went to bed now, after seeing Keegan break just a little and seeing Bobby comfort her, she might be able to sleep.

Chapter 20

TEEL

THEY HAD LAUGHED. The three of them together had sat outside Dairy Queen and ate ice cream all huddled up against each other (it had actually been a bit chilly) and laughed. Talked. They'd steered clear of the phone call from Elaine Caldwell and Keegan's truancy and Marin's suicide and just talked about everything else and nothing. And they'd laughed.

Until Teel cried. It had felt so good to sit with them and talk, the way it used to be. To hear her daughter's voice, so lively and magical, tell them about playing line soccer in gym and tripping through the lunch line and managing not to run into anyone and make anyone spill his or her tray and the quiz that she aced in Spanish. It felt so good to hear their daughter talk, Teel had found herself overwhelmed with emotion.

"Mom?" Keegan had stopped suddenly, mid-story, and looked closely at Teel. "Are you crying?"

Teel laughed. Bobby reached for her hand and gave it a gentle squeeze. "Where have you been, Keegan Alexander?"

Keegan had only smiled, but she'd looked away from Teel.

"Too bad Rachel's not here," Bobby said, and Teel knew it was his way of easing the sudden tension between them.

"Right." Teel rolled her eyes. "So she could eat half of my sundae."

"You did get a large," he pointed out.

Keegan laughed out loud, and Teel poked her in the ribs. She'd eaten a whole Dilly bar, and watching her, Teel had thought again about how little and frail she'd felt in her arms.

"Keegan," Bobby said and he brushed her hair from her face.

"I know."

"Do you?"

She'd nodded.

"And what would you give yourself as a punishment?" he'd asked her.

"I don't know."

"Well, you're grounded for the next two weeks," he announced, and Teel had thought if things were normal right now, that punishment would kill her. She was always out with her friends. Going to the mall, to movies, out to eat. She and Jess had gone out so often through the summer, Teel had suggested they each pitch in on gas money and Teel's time spent running them around town.

As things were right now, Keegan probably couldn't care less that she'd been grounded. Teel wondered if they were doing the right thing. Cutting her off from friends. Then again, maybe cutting her off from these particular friends was a good thing.

She'd been wrong, of course. Even after sitting with Bobby and Keegan and hearing Keegan talk and laugh and feeling just for a little while like things were back to normal, she'd still lain awake for hours. Bobby had gone to sleep within minutes of getting in bed, and Teel had lain beside him wishing he were awake. To make love to her. To hold her. To talk to her. Make promises that everything would be okay. Promises that he had no right to make, because none of them knew how things would turn out. No one ever really did, did they?

She hadn't been conscious of it, but when she heard the garage door open at ten after four, Teel realized she'd been waiting for Rachel to come home. Furious with her older daughter for taking advantage of the rules they'd done away with, Teel had to fight herself to stay in bed and not charge into Rachel's room and read her the riot act.

Angry or not, knowing Rachel was home must have made her feel a bit better. She groaned and buried her head in her pillow when the alarm went off. Bobby hit snooze and then rolled over closer to her and laid his arm over her waist.

"I slept for an hour," she mumbled.

"I know."

"No, you don't. You were asleep ten seconds after you went to bed."

"I'm sorry." He kissed her neck, just under her ear. She hoped he wouldn't take it any further, because she wasn't in the mood. Not after lying awake all night worrying about Keegan and being angry with Rachel. And resentful of Bobby for being able to put it all out of his mind and sleep.

"It's October," he said as if the beginning of October might mean the end of this hell that had been hanging over their house for the past few weeks.

"And?" She kind of wished he would shut up. Another ten minutes of sleep wouldn't mean much in the long haul, but right at this moment, it would be nice.

"It was pretty cool out last night. Let's turn the air off."

Really?

She bit her tongue. No point in starting a fight before they got out of bed.

The neighbor girl, who just happened to be an old friend of their daughter, was dead. Their youngest daughter was skipping school and hanging out with new friends, friends Teel suddenly didn't approve of, and Rachel was apparently sleeping with her boyfriend of a few months and had done the walk of shame in the wee hours of the morning, and he was worried about the air conditioner running?

"Yeah." She nodded, head still buried in her pillow. "Good idea."

They lay in silence until the alarm went off again, and then Bobby rolled over to turn it off. He leaned back over her and kissed her again.

"Wanna join me in the shower?"

"No."

"You sure?" He nuzzled her neck and let his hand roam.

"An hour, Bobby," she said into her pillow. "One. Hour. I'm dead."

"I'll make the coffee," he offered as he got out of bed.

"Swell," she mumbled after he'd left their bedroom.

She dozed off for all of ten minutes. When she awoke this time, she smelled coffee and she heard the shower running. Still no desire to get in the shower with him. Really, no desire to get out of bed.

And yet, another day, another dollar. She didn't have the choice. She groaned and sat up, more tired now than when she'd gone to bed.

She found Rachel at the dining room table, pencil in hand, eyes on what appeared to be her biology text.

"What are you doing?" she asked as she poured herself a cup of coffee. She added a bit of cream to it and then leaned against the kitchen counter.

"Need to get this done," Rachel answered. "And I couldn't sleep."

"What time did you get home, Rachel?" Teel took a drink and swallowed and stood perfectly still waiting for the coffee to do its magic. Wake her up. Clear her head.

"I dunno." Rachel all but ignored her. She certainly didn't seem to be in the throes of love or in the afterglow of mind-blowing sex.

"Maybe I can help you," Teel suggested as she approached the dining room table. Rachel looked up at her, and Teel noticed the dark circles under her eyes. "I'm pretty sure it was ten after four."

Rachel shook her head and shrugged. "Okay, it was ten after four."

"Where were you?"

"I thought I didn't have a curfew."

"Four in the morning is something entirely different than not having a curfew."

"Whatever." Rachel sighed and looked down at her book again. Teel bristled. She hated that word more than any other in the English dictionary.

"I want to know where you were."

"I was with Deacon, Mom." Rachel stood up suddenly. "Okay? I was with Deacon."

"Where?"

"At his dorm." Rachel threw her hands up in defeat.

Teel shook her head. "Not under my roof."

"Mom…"

"I mean it, Rachel. Not as long as you're living here. It's unacceptable."

"Nothing happened."

"I don't…"

"Nothing happened!" Rachel wailed. "Nothing happened.

Okay? We were studying, and we were lying on his bed, and we fell asleep."

"I don't care, Rachel Alexander. If you wanna sleep with Deacon or anyone else on that campus, you either get your ass home before four a.m. so I'm not lying awake wondering where in the hell you are or you live on campus."

"Mom!" Rachel dropped back to sit in her chair again. "I just needed to get out. To get away from…"

"From what?"

"From this," Rachel yelled. "From this damned house! From you."

Teel flinched as if Rachel had slapped her.

"I don't care," Teel said quietly. "If you live here, you live by my rules. Understood?"

Rachel, eyes glassy with tears, nodded and covered her face with her hands.

Coffee cup still in hand, Teel started back across the hardwood to the bedroom.

"Just so you know, Mom," Rachel said softly, "I'm not sleeping with anybody. Not like that."

"Well, you did last night, didn't you?"

"I slept with him. Slept. In my clothes."

Teel looked back at Rachel over her shoulder.

"I'm a virgin."

Teel stopped walking and turned back to Rachel.

"Are you happy now?" Rachel sneered.

"No," Teel said on a sigh. Still angry, though she wasn't sure now who she was angry with. Still Bobby. Still Rachel. Still Keegan. Throw in Elaine Caldwell, what the hell, she'd been the bearer of bad news. "No, Rachel, I'm not happy."

"And that's exactly why I left earlier," Rachel mumbled. She tossed her pencil down and walked out of the room.

Teel took another drink of her coffee and leaned against the door frame. She hated arguing. With Bobby. With the girls. With Eve. She felt bad for upsetting Rachel. And even worse, she'd come out of her bedroom angry and ready for a fight and taken it out on Rachel. She felt guilty for being angry with Bobby when all he'd done was sleep when she couldn't.

And yet, she felt justified in her anger. She hadn't taken Rachel's curfew away just so her daughter could hop in her first serious boyfriend's bed and come home at ungodly hours. Sure, she'd lost her virginity at seventeen and done things she wasn't proud of, and she knew it was unreasonable to expect anything different from her daughters. And yet, she wouldn't allow it. Not like this. Not under her roof.

Bobby, dressed for work, dropped a kiss on her cheek on his way out of the bathroom as she walked in.

"Have a good day," he called as he headed through the bedroom and out through the living room to leave.

"You, too," she said, alone in the bathroom. She set her coffee cup down on the sink and then stepped into the shower to turn the water on.

She should've joined him in the shower. It would have saved her the blow-up with Rachel, and she wouldn't be so damned cold now, alone in the shower.

Chapter 21

KEEGAN

THEY HADN'T COME for her yet, and already the shit was hitting the proverbial fan. Her mom had gone ballistic on Rachel this morning. How could she not have heard that? She'd been asleep, but her mom woke her up when she gave Rachel hell. Keegan was shocked that Rachel had been out so late, but even more surprised when Rachel had claimed nothing had happened between her and Deacon.

She'd actually got out of bed and cracked her door open just enough to hear them better. Rachel? A virgin? That blew her away. Not that Rachel ever claimed anything different and not that Rachel had guys calling or beating down the door to go out with her. But Keegan thought all girls did it. She thought it was like a rite of initiation when you were in high school. You had to give it up to someone, and the more popular he was, the quicker you were accepted into that group.

Then again, Rachel hadn't ever been popular. She still wasn't.

"Ms. Alexander?"

Keegan looked up at Mr. Sharpe, her geometry teacher. She hadn't been paying attention. Actually, she probably hadn't paid attention in class all year, but right now she was miles away from angles and rays.

"I'm sorry," she mumbled. She heard someone in the back row laugh, but she steeled herself and held her head up to talk to Mr. Sharpe. "What was the question?"

"Maybe you could try tuning us in," Mr. Sharpe told her. He tapped his knuckles on her desk as he walked by. Keegan sat ramrod straight in her chair until he called on someone else.

Then she sighed and slumped back down and tuned out. Again. What did it matter if she paid attention, anyway? She got As, so why couldn't they just get off her back?

Her parents had strongly suggested that she get herself together. They were right; at least last night sitting with them at Dairy Queen, it had sounded easy. Pull it together. Start with hygiene, add a little makeup and dress in normal clothes instead of something old and creepy and huge that was more of a hiding place than an outfit. Fit in with the crowd or else stand out because you look good, not because you look like a freak.

So, at least she looked normal today. No, actually, she looked good today. She knew she did, because she'd seen Tiffany and Brandy do a double-take when she'd walked by them on her way to her locker. That had given her a quick little high, but then she'd remembered who she was inside and she'd crashed and burned even before she got to her locker. Jess had complimented her on her outfit—school pants, yes, but *Hollister* school pants. A gray T-shirt and a bright yellow sweater over it. Three quarter length sleeves, which was okay, because she was kind of cold. She might never warm up. She might be just as cold as Marin, buried in the ground out at the cemetery by the bowling alley.

Her mom was coming unglued. It was scary to watch it unfold, because her mom always kept it together. She'd only seen her mom cry when her grandpa died. Well, and those odd times when she'd get all emotional at stupid, happy things. And movies. Mom cried a lot at movies, but that didn't count.

This was something else. Mom was losing it. She was all freaked out about Keegan, and she didn't know half the story. She was pissed at her for cutting classes, and yet Keegan figured within a week, maybe less, her mom would end up thinking truancy wasn't so bad. She was pissed at Rachel now, accusing her of sleeping around and *that* was totally unlike Mom.

Mom and Dad seemed to be okay, but who knew how long that would last? What if Mom and Dad ended up fighting and stuff? What if they fought and then they ended up splitting up and divorcing? Jess's parents started out with small fights, but Jess said within six months they'd separated. Another six months and they'd divorced. What if her parents got so mad at her they took it out on each other and split up? Just one more thing she'd fucked up.

When class was over, she gathered her books and walked out of the room, not even bothering to look around. People were talking about her; they had to be talking about her. She went straight to her locker and put her geometry book away. Grabbed her health book, thought for a minute how nice it would be to blow it all off and go home. But her parents would really freak if she cut classes again today, after they'd talked to her and then punished her for the same thing last night. This time, her dad might take away her laptop. She'd die without it, and both her parents knew that.

She'd actually been shocked that they hadn't done it last night. But then she'd been shocked when her mom asked her if she wanted to go for ice cream. They'd hugged her. Told her they loved her. Her parents were smart people, but she knew now from experience how naïve they were. How trusting they were, and how badly they wanted to see something good in her.

"Are you feeling better?"

Keegan looked up as Tiffany fell into step beside her.

"I'm fine," Keegan answered and tried to sidestep her. Tiffany moved with her and continued to edge her further left.

"Because Brandy and I noticed you left early yesterday," she said sweetly. "I texted you. Did you get my text?"

"I did."

"I wish you would've answered me." Tiffany made a pouty face and made a left turn at the T in the hall.

"Excuse me," Keegan huffed and shoved Tiffany out of her way. "I need to go this way."

"Oh, I'm sorry." Tiffany kind of laughed like she was mixed up. She looked up and then smiled and acted like she was trying to turn Keegan around. She shoved her right into someone coming their way.

"Hey, Tiff."

Keegan looked up and found herself face to face with *him*. *Sean Spanner*. She held her breath and said a quick prayer that he wouldn't say anything.

"Hey, Sean." Tiffany stepped forward and touched Sean's arm. She looked at Keegan as if to make sure Keegan saw that she was touching him. "Do you know my friend Keegan? Keegan Alexander?"

Sean looked right at Keegan. Right through Keegan. She wanted to look away, because right then she could feel his hands on her. Rough and eager. She could smell the beer on his breath.

"Hey, Kristin." He said it in a rush and smiled at Tiffany again as he moved past them down the hallway.

"I'm sorry." Tiffany sounded anything but sorry. "I thought you guys knew each other."

Keegan felt the rush of heat in her face. She wanted to puke. At Tiffany's feet. On Tiffany's feet. She wasn't picky, didn't matter to her. She wanted to turn and run and run and keep going until she reached her house. Until she could close her bedroom door and shut the whole world out. But she'd promised her mom and dad she wouldn't do it anymore.

It wasn't the promise that kept her standing there. It was the worry that if she got in trouble again, Dad would take her laptop. And if Mom or Dad started looking around on her laptop, she'd been in it much deeper.

"Are you finished?" Keegan asked in a surprisingly strong voice.

"No," Tiffany stepped closer to her and dropped her voice to a whisper, "but I'm pretty sure you are."

Keegan took the blow without flinching and then turned and walked away. She fought the urge to run. To cry. Thank God no one seemed to have seen Tiffany's attack or else no one on this end of the hall cared.

For God's sake, it had been over a year ago. Was the gossip mill so slow that Tiffany had to recycle last year's news?

It hit her as she turned the last corner and stepped into her classroom. Tiffany was creating drama about Keegan because of Marin's suicide. Some kids were still upset about it, especially Marin's friends. But things had settled down, and by targeting Keegan, Tiffany was riling everyone up about Marin again and hurting Keegan in the process. And besides, Tiffany knew there was a connection between

Marin and Keegan. A bigger connection than the friendship that had fizzled out several years ago. Jess had known, of course. But she wouldn't tell anyone, would she?

No one paid her any attention as she slid into her seat. She opened her notebook and kept her head lowered as if she were studying notes. Her face was still burning from being humiliated in the hallway. Tiffany and Sean? Were they friends? Friends with benefits?

She'd realized not long after it happened that Sean Spanner wasn't going to ask her out. She wasn't going to wear his ring. But she hadn't expected to be made a joke of either. It wasn't that she really thought no one would ever find out. After all, wasn't that part of disappearing with a hot guy at a party? Hoping someone would see you sneak off and start talking so that by the time it was over, you might be up a rung or two on the ladder?

She hadn't told anyone about it right away. In fact, it had taken her almost a week to tell Jess. And though she and Jess hung out with a few other girls, she'd never told any of them.

Finally, she felt the heat in her cheeks dissipate. In fact, she felt the blood drain from her face. She wrapped her fingers around the edge of her desk as a wave of nausea moved over her.

Jess. Her best friend had sold her out.

Chapter 22

TEEL

TEEL HATED STARTING her day with a scene. With an argument. She hated sending someone she loved off to face the day on a bad note. Rachel was probably fine by now, but the morning blow-up had stayed with Teel. Instead of playing a math game with her class, she'd done a low-keyed lesson and had the kids work example problems at the board. Rather than reading aloud to them after recess as she sometimes did, she gave them fifteen minutes of quiet time during which they could work on homework or read to themselves. When Marcus Connors got the hiccups during English the same as he did every day, Teel simply smiled while the rest of the class laughed. On other days, Teel had laughed herself to tears at the kid's loud, obnoxious hiccups.

She picked at her lunch and fueled her way through the day with coffee. When the final bell rang, she stood at her door and said goodbye to the kids, and she noticed some of them looking at her, studying her. They knew something was wrong, and God bless them, she appreciated their concern. But she prayed that none of them would ask what was going on. A little compassion in her current state of mind would be her undoing. She couldn't afford to lose it in front of her class.

"What is going on with you?"

She looked up as Maggie stepped into her room and pulled the door closed behind her.

Teel shook her head. She reached for her coffee cup but stopped when she saw that her hands were shaking. Maggie popped open the Pepsi can that she was holding, took a long drink, and settled her butt on the corner of Teel's desk.

"What is it, Teel?" Maggie asked. The gentle tone did it. Teel closed her eyes as they filled with tears. "Oh honey, I'm sorry." Maggie leaned toward her and put her arm around her shoulders. Teel let go for just a moment and cried just enough to notice a tiny bit of relief but stopped just short of coming unglued in the classroom.

When she sat up straight, Maggie was still studying her face and waiting for an answer.

"Just. Having a bad day."

"I see that." Maggie nodded. "What's wrong? Still Marin?"

"No. Not really," Teel answered, though in truth, she supposed Marin had spurred the disquiet in her house.

"You don't wanna tell me?"

Teel pressed her lips together and realized that she *didn't* want to tell Maggie. Her reluctance shook her, because she'd never had any reason not to trust Maggie.

"Just having trouble with Keegan." She decided to keep it vague. "Rachel and I got into it this morning."

"Is Keegan upset about Marin?" Maggie asked. It was a logical question. It was a *normal* question. That her *friend* asked. Someone who had been her friend for years. And yet, she couldn't answer her. Maybe it wasn't the question or the person asking, but Keegan and her attitude that gave Teel pause.

She nodded, because no matter Keegan's intentions or feelings, she was certain everything going on in her house had to do with Marin in one way or another.

"I'm sorry." Maggie reached for Teel's hand and squeezed it. "I hate seeing you like this. My kids were all asking me today if you're sick. They all sense something's bothering you."

Enough of that. Teel wouldn't stomach a school full of kids feeling sorry for her. Wondering about her. Curiosity had a place, but not when it concerned a teacher's private life.

She drew herself up and sighed and then offered Maggie a tired smile. "I'm fine. Functioning...or not," she laughed softly, "on very little sleep today."

"Mmkay." Maggie nodded when Teel stood up. Guilt heaped over her shoulders almost forced her back down to her chair. She was lying to her best friend. And why? Why did she feel the need to lie? She'd trusted Maggie before. She'd trusted Maggie with everything. Almost like Eve.

Eve. Maybe she should call her sister. She started packing things up to go home. Maggie watched Teel close her grade book and pile it with her teacher's reading manual. She didn't believe Teel. Maggie knew there was more going on than Teel had admitted, and she felt slighted and hurt. And yet, Teel couldn't talk. She just wasn't comfortable talking. Maybe on another day.

IT WAS DEFINITELY COOLER OUTSIDE, and Teel was glad now that Bobby had turned the air off. She sat on the deck with a glass of tea in her hand. Keegan was in her room, and when

Teel had checked on her, she'd sworn she'd been at school all day. She didn't seem thrilled about it. Teel had believed her, but she wouldn't admit to Keegan that the only reason she believed her was because Elaine Caldwell hadn't called her.

Rachel wasn't home yet, and that bothered Teel. She needed to talk to her. An apology might be a bit too strong, because even after stewing over the scene this morning, she still felt justified in her position. And yet, she'd gone at Rachel just because she was tired and irritated, and that wasn't fair.

When Bobby came home, Teel had dinner on the table on the deck like she always did before everything had happened. She'd thrown together a poppy-seed chicken casserole and tossed a salad. She thought about opening a bottle of wine, but she was afraid she might be tempted to sit on the deck and drink, and though that sounded heavenly, she knew that avoiding the shadows in her house certainly wasn't going to make them go away.

She felt a dam break in her chest when Rachel stepped out on the deck for dinner. She breathed a huge sigh of relief and wondered if she'd thought Rachel wouldn't come home. Had she thought she would seek sanctuary in Deacon's dorm room?

Dinner was quiet, but not necessarily in a bad way. Bobby and Rachel talked a bit about a scholarship she might be eligible for next semester. It wasn't based on need, but merit. Bobby asked Keegan how school was, and Teel and Keegan both understood that he was asking if she'd cut classes today.

"It sucked," she answered. "But I was there. All day."

"Why did it suck?" Rachel asked her. "Just because you're bored with it?"

Teel saw Keegan raise an eyebrow before she shook her head.

"Just stuff."

"What kind of stuff?" Teel asked her.

"Just." Keegan shrugged impatiently. "Stuff. You know."

"I don't know," Teel answered. "That's why I'm asking."

"You have every book written on the high school social hierarchy," Keegan said in a crisp voice. "Get a clue, Mom."

"What?" Teel pushed. "Someone's bothering you?"

Keegan snorted, but her eyes filled with tears. She blinked them away quickly.

"May I be excused?"

"Was someone bothering Marin, Keegan?" Teel asked. She felt Bobby and Rachel watching her, probably thinking she was going too far, but she couldn't stop herself.

"How should I know?" Keegan sounded bored now. "I hadn't talked to Marin in like…forever."

"Who said something to you today?"

"No one, Mom," Keegan groaned and looked at Bobby. "I have some geometry stuff I need help with."

Bobby nodded. He stacked his and Keegan's plates and then followed her inside. Teel made it a point not to look at Rachel once they were alone. But when she heard Rachel get up to leave and go inside, she cleared her throat.

"Rachel, I'm sorry."

"For what, Mom? Calling me a slut? Suggesting that I'm sleeping my way around campus?"

Teel shook her head. She folded her hands over her stomach and examined her fingernails. No wonder they were a mess. Her hands looked old, pocked with small scars and age spots. But her fingernails, chipped and ringed with hang-nails, looked like those of a teenager.

Disgusted with them, with herself, she looked up at Rachel.

"I didn't mean to imply that," she finally said. "But I won't tolerate that kind of behavior if you're living at home."

"There was no behavior, Mom," Rachel insisted. "We were in his room, studying."

"For nine hours?"

"We fell asleep."

Teel looked away again. "Just don't let it happen again."

"Mom, I don't think he's even interested in that."

"Honey, he's a guy. Of course he is."

"Not with me."

Teel cringed when she heard the break in Rachel's voice. *Not today. God, not today.* She couldn't have this conversation with her daughter today.

"Why do you say that?" she asked. When she looked at Rachel this time, she was staring at her empty plate.

She shrugged. "He just doesn't ever…"

Teel shook her head and rubbed her face with her hands. "Honey, if he loves you, maybe he just wants things…to be right."

Rachel rolled her eyes.

"I know. Let's talk about something else."

"We did fall asleep, and when I woke up and realized where I was, I panicked. Because I knew you would catch me coming in, and I knew you'd be pissed." Rachel laughed, but Teel heard the emptiness in the sound. "And I thought how ironic that was, since you haven't looked at me twice since the neighbor girl killed herself, and suddenly you were going to catch me sneaking in and give me hell, and we didn't even have sex."

Teel stared at Rachel in shock. A hundred things went through her mind. A hundred come backs. A hundred words. And yet, maybe Rachel was right. She'd been so focused on Keegan, what if she had been ignoring Rachel? How many times had she thought to herself that Rachel didn't need something from her because she was in college now? Because if Rachel were living on campus, she couldn't have her mom do something for her.

Rachel, eyes glassy with tears she was struggling not to let loose, stared at her mother, waiting for her to say something.

Teel opened her mouth, but found she couldn't say anything. Where just moments ago there were hundreds of words, suddenly there was nothing. Not one word. She couldn't even take any comfort in the fact that her daughter was still a virgin, that she was guarding her virtue as Teel had probably lectured about hundreds of times through the years.

"I'm sorry."

"You're sorry?" Rachel nodded. "You're sorry. That's great, Mom. Thanks."

Teel lunged when Rachel stood up. She grabbed Rachel's hand.

"What do you want me to say? What do you need me to say, Rach? That I'm proud of you? That I'm so glad you aren't having sex with Deacon? That I'm sorry you think he's not interested in you? That he has to be interested in you, because you're beautiful and smart, and how could he not want to? That it's okay for you to stay over at his dorm room when you feel like it?"

Rachel tugged her arm away from Teel's grasp.

"What do you need from me, Rachel?"

"Notice me," Rachel whispered. "Just remember me."

"I do remember you. I was awake last night…"

"Worrying about Keegan," Rachel interrupted her. "And then when you heard me come in, you remembered that your other daughter had been out all night, and then you remembered to get angry with me."

Teel, stunned at the accuracy in Rachel's words and stunned that her independent, composed daughter had lashed out at her this way, dropped down to her chair.

"Am I right, Mom? Can you at least be honest with me?"

Teel thought about asking Rachel if it was fair that Teel had to worry like this. If Rachel wouldn't be just a bit worried if it were her daughter acting like Keegan. If it was wrong that it still bothered her that Marin English had killed herself and that Rick had left Jeannie to deal with it all on her own.

But she bit her tongue. It wasn't fair; none of it was fair. But it was life. And she was the parent, and it sure as hell wouldn't be fair of her to dump it all on Rachel.

"I love—"

"Mom. Am I right?" Rachel leaned over the table. "Nevermind. You don't even have to answer that."

Teel took a deep breath and laid her head back against the chair. Damn Marin English for unraveling her family.

She felt a flash of guilt the second she thought it. But she couldn't take it back. She wouldn't admit it to anyone, but she really felt that Marin English had yanked the world out from under their feet.

Chapter 23

RACHEL

RACHEL LOOKED up when she heard the knock on her door. She was ready to get up and walk out of the house if it was her mom. Actually, she was ready to get up and walk out anyway. But she didn't think she could stand another night of studying in Deacon's dorm room. Those four walls had felt so confining after a while. She loved being with him, but the room had started feeling like it was shrinking after she'd been there for a couple of hours. At least his roommate hadn't come home. That would have been really awkward.

"What?" she asked when Keegan peeked into her room.

"You and Mom okay?"

Rachel caught herself before she snapped. What business was it of Keegan's what happened between her and her mom? But she didn't really have the energy to fight now, not even with Keegan.

She shrugged. "Yeah. I guess."

"It's my fault." Keegan moved further into Rachel's room.

"Huh?" Rachel closed her book, an old Dean Koontz classic, and looked up at her sister. "Why's it your fault?"

"Mom and Dad are pissed at me." Keegan shrugged. She stood before Rachel's bed looking like a dog waiting to be kicked. "She took it out on you."

Rachel sighed and nodded. "I know." That only drove home the point she'd made to her mom.

"Sucks. Doesn't it?" Keegan laughed, but Rachel thought it sounded more like a sob.

"What does?"

"What doesn't right now?"

Keegan had a point. She had to give her that.

"Did you do your geometry already?"

Keegan nodded.

Rachel watched her sit down on the floor on the side of the bed. Suddenly, she remembered how Keegan had asked her about the worst thing she'd done in high school just last night, before Mom had walked in and sucked the small level of fun they were having right out of the room.

"You haven't slept with Deacon."

Keegan said it more as a statement than a question.

"Keegan." Rachel wanted to scream, but she flopped back on her bed without a word.

"I heard you this morning," Keegan said quietly, almost apologetically.

"Great. That was none of your business."

"I thought everybody did it."

"Guess you thought wrong."

"You seriously haven't? With anyone?" Keegan turned and looked at Rachel. "You weren't lying to Mom?"

"Why does this matter?"

Keegan raised her eyebrows.

"Ohmygod." Rachel sat up quickly. "You did. You did it."

Keegan blushed and looked away. Rachel was torn, a little

bit jealous and a little bit worried. She was nineteen, damn it. In college. Her freak little sister had been with a guy, and she hadn't. But Keegan certainly didn't look excited about sex or about holding it over Rachel.

"What happened?" Rachel asked.

Keegan glanced at Rachel's open door. A mix of curiosity and concern had Rachel leaping off the bed and hurrying to shut her door. She turned on her stereo, too, before she came back to sit on her bed.

She pressed play on her remote and a Leona Lewis CD started playing.

"It was at a party."

"You went to a party?"

"Jess and I did," Keegan answered. She still sat on the floor, but she avoided Rachel's eyes. Rachel watched her pick at the hangnail on her thumb. "I ended up in some bedroom with Sean Spanner."

"Don't know him."

"He's a senior this year," Keegan said matter-of-factly. "He was all over me."

"Keegan." Rachel frowned. This was serious. This was a big deal. "Did he force you?"

Keegan looked up at Rachel with bright eyes. "No."

"You wanted to do it with some guy you didn't know?"

"He plays basketball."

Rachel waited for Keegan to say more, but she didn't.

"And so…what? He plays basketball and that made it okay to just go in a bedroom with him and do it?"

"Mm-hmm."

Rachel shook her head. Freak. Keegan was a freak.

Keegan looked up again and shook her hair away from her face. Rachel wasn't sure she'd had such a good look at her little sister in months.

"I don't want it to be like that," Rachel finally said.

Keegan jumped when someone knocked on the closed door.

"God," she whispered. "Mom is driving me friggin' nuts."

Rachel agreed with her. Their mom had gone a little overboard lately, but on the other hand, maybe she was right to worry about Keegan.

"Rach?" Mom opened the door just a bit and stuck her head in.

"What?"

"Deacon's here."

"Oh!" Rachel jumped off her bed and rushed out of her room. It wasn't until she went outside where Deacon and her dad were sitting on the deck that she realized she had left Keegan sitting alone in her room.

Oh well. It wasn't like Keegan needed to talk about that anyway. She'd been dry-eyed and just flat weird about having sex with some guy she didn't even know.

"Hi." Deacon smiled at her.

She felt her world calm when he looked at her. God, she'd needed to see him.

"I'll go inside," her dad said. But Deacon, who had been leaning on the deck railing, stood up straight.

"Actually, I thought Rachel might want to go for a walk."

"Yes, I do," she agreed and let him take her hand and walk her down the two steps on the deck. They walked across the backyard and then turned to go to the front of the house.

"I was gonna call you." Deacon let go of her hand and put his arm around her waist. "And then I thought I'd rather come and see you."

"I'm glad you did."

They walked in silence for a bit and then Deacon drew her in and kissed her cheek. "Bad day?"

Rachel thought about it for a minute. She didn't want to spoil their time together with all of the crap from her day.

But she wanted to talk to him. All day she'd wanted to hear his voice and talk to him and tell him the awful things her mom had said to her this morning.

"Yeah."

"Your mom catch you coming in?"

"No." She laughed and shook her head. "But she heard me. Ripped me apart this morning."

"I'm sorry. I thought if I lay down by you for a few minutes, I could stay awake."

"'s okay."

Full dark fell as they walked. Rachel realized they weren't far from the little pond where Keegan and Marin used to hang out. She shimmied away from him, took his hand and hurried through the tall grass that she had once told Keegan was called fescue. She'd wanted to be smarter than Keegan, and she'd wanted Keegan to know it.

None of that mattered now, though.

"Hey," Deacon said when she stopped suddenly and he bumped into her. "This is cool."

"Keegan used to come here all the time. Keegan and Marin. They thought they were sly, like no one knew they were here. Some of the boys in the neighborhood followed them, though."

"Things aren't getting better, are they?" Deacon asked her. She dropped gracefully to sit on the ground, legs crossed in front of her like a pretzel. "At home."

"Not yet."

"I'm sorry." He sat down beside her.

She shrugged. "Maybe this is just the way things are now, ya know? Maybe our regular family time is done, and now we're this mess that…"

She stopped talking when he pressed his lips to hers.

"It'll work out." He broke the kiss and then brushed her hair away from her face. "Promise."

She nodded. Sure, everything would work out one way or another, and that didn't necessarily mean good things. And besides, who the hell knew how long it would be before it all worked out? She dreaded the ride between now and then.

"Rach?"

She lifted her eyes to look at him and wished he would kiss her again. Undress her here and touch her. Not a good idea, and she knew it. Even though it was dark, she was afraid someone would see them. The whole neighborhood might be on high alert right now the way her mom was, and if someone saw her down by the pond, taking her clothes off and lying with a guy, alarms might sound, and the whole damned world would know.

"What?"

"I love you."

He touched her lips with his fingertips, and she felt something heavy and syrupy spread from her lips to her fingertips and toes.

"I love you, too."

Chapter 24

TEEL

AFTER THE DISPLAY of concern at work yesterday, Teel made sure to pull herself together before she got out of her Edge today. She sat for just a moment, radio off, and soaked up the silence. It felt good; there was just too much static in her life right now. Finally, when she felt strong enough to go inside and lie through her teeth that everything was fine, and when she figured if she stayed in the car any longer someone might see her and call the nuthouse to come and take her away, she took a deep breath and got out of the car.

She locked it without a backward glance. It was so peaceful this morning. The weather was perfect, and Teel supposed as she walked into the school through the side door by the janitor's closet that maybe God had decided to hold back on that front, since her personal life was turbulent and about to erupt.

She was comfortable in a lightweight jacket and slacks. Three upper grade teachers said hi to her as she headed down the hall to the stairs. She flashed them her old smile and willed them to love the lie. To want to believe that Teel was fine, she'd just had a bad day or two when that girl from her neighborhood had killed herself.

Maggie called out to her as she passed her classroom. Teel waved and hollered that she'd be back in a minute. She unlocked her classroom door, deposited her bag on her chair, and then returned to Maggie's room. Here was the real test. Maggie knew her well enough to see behind the smile and dig past the lie. Teel just prayed she wouldn't, that she'd play along.

"Good morning," Teel said from the doorway. "I'm gonna go get coffee."

"Hang on!" Maggie climbed up on a desk to pin something on the top of her bulletin board. Teel stepped further into the room and leaned her thigh against the desk to hold it steady. "I need some tea."

"Isn't it nice out?" Teel knew she sounded fake, but she couldn't help it. She couldn't drop the act now. Just go with it, she told herself. "Just a week ago, I thought we might melt it was so hot."

"It is nice," Maggie answered absently. "Can you hand me that?" Teel followed Maggie's pointing finger to another cardboard cutout on her desk. She leaned over and grabbed it and then handed it up to Maggie.

"Leaf summer behind and fall into autumn," Teel read Maggie's bulletin board. Maggie was pinning leaf cutouts around the words. "That's cute."

"I'm a little behind," Maggie admitted. "I don't know if I'm getting sick or what. I'm just so tired and blah, I haven't wanted to move lately."

"Me, too," Teel answered truthfully. She reached up for Maggie to take her hand and step off the desk.

"Jack's got a cold." Maggie restacked a pile of papers on

her chair. "And God knows, it's the end of the world when he's sick."

Teel chuckled as they left Maggie's room.

"What is it that turns grown men into babies when they're sick?"

"They wanna regress back to childhood and have Mommy take care of them," Maggie said disgustedly. "He's driving me nuts. Wait'll I get it. No one will be around to wait on me hand and foot."

Teel nodded. Bobby usually took good care of her when she was sick, though she understood Maggie's rant. Bobby, too, tended to want to be babied when he was sick.

"So, how are you? Really?" Maggie asked as they walked down the hall together. "And don't blow me any shit about it being a beautiful day, Teel. Tell me."

Teel glanced at Maggie and saw sincerity and worry in her eyes.

"Well. Life is hell right now, Mags, but I don't wanna put that on display. I slipped yesterday."

Maggie nodded.

"I'm here," she reminded Teel as they bounced down the stairs. "You know that."

Teel felt a flash of guilt for shutting Maggie out.

"I know," she said quietly as they walked into the kitchen. They parted then, Teel going to the coffee pot and Maggie to the tea kettle on the stovetop. Two other teachers and a reading recovery facilitator sat at the teachers' lunch table. Teel listened to them talking about someone sleeping with someone else and her husband finding out. She almost froze in place, imagining her own personal life dissected this way when she wasn't around. But she recognized the names and realized they were discussing a TV show.

Still. Just the thought of being the daily gossip left her

feeling a little sad and a little irritated. She poured her coffee, added a bit of cream, and then turned back to look for Maggie. She waited while Maggie poured hot water over a tea bag and then they walked out of the kitchen together.

"Let's go out for lunch Saturday," Maggie suggested as they made the return trip up the steps to their second floor classrooms.

Teel wanted to say thanks, but no thanks. She and Maggie often went for lunch, or even dinner, now and then. When things were normal. Right now, Teel couldn't think past the present. She didn't feel like explaining that to Maggie, so she simply nodded.

"Okay. I'll see what's going on."

They reached Maggie's door, and Teel kept walking, thinking she'd smoothed her way out of that. She would just tell Maggie tomorrow that she couldn't do it, something had come up.

"Don't blow me off, Teel." Maggie caught her arm, and Teel swung back around to face her. "If you don't want to talk about it, that's fine. I get it."

"Mags…"

"But it might do you good to get away from it."

Teel nodded.

"Whatever *it* is."

"You're right." Teel sighed and nodded. "Okay. Okay. Lunch Saturday."

Maggie gave her arm a squeeze and then she turned back to her classroom. Teel went to her own classroom, but she felt like she was walking in quicksand. Who was she kidding? She couldn't bluff her way through the day. Just this first quarter of an hour had drained her. And she was dealing with a friend. She shouldn't be so exhausted just from blowing off a friend.

———

"SO, GUESS WHAT?"

Teel stood back as Eve marched through the front door. She shut the door and then turned to see her sister setting a big grocery bag on the kitchen counter. It was after five. Keegan was in her room; the girl probably hadn't been out of her room for a solid five hours since Marin had killed herself.

Maybe even before that...

"Teel?"

Teel gave herself a mental shake. Eve was staring at her expectantly. She glanced at the dining room table, where she had her grade book, her lesson plans and a stack of math tests waiting. Her laptop was open too, because she was really behind on entering grades on the Parent and Teacher Together website. If she didn't get that caught up soon, she'd have parents complaining to her principal. She got along well with John Schoch, but she had no desire to step into his office and update him on anything going on in her life that might keep her from getting her work done.

"I don't know, Eve, what?" She shook her head. As much as she loved her sister, she didn't have time for another Dennis story. Not today. Not when she should be getting dinner going, and she had so much work to do, and she should start trying to patch things up with Rachel.

"The son-of-a-bitch is getting remarried," Eve announced.

The words delivered a blow between her shoulder blades. A little more weight. Kind of like she had an anvil on her shoulders and Eve just climbed up on top of it.

"Dennis." Teel raised her eyebrows. "Dennis is getting remarried."

Eve pursed her lips and nodded.

"Evie, the guy's an immature, self-serving ass." Teel's words exploded out of her, but her voice was calm and even. "It's time to let him go."

"I know."

"How can you love him? You deserve so much better."

"The good times were good," Eve said softly.

"Worth this?" Teel threw her hands, palms up, in the air and walked toward Eve. "Really? Is there anything worth being treated this way?"

Eve looked away from Teel and reached for the grocery bag.

"I'm done with him."

Teel would have been glad to hear it if she believed Eve. But she didn't. Eve had been done with Dennis so many times over the past five years; Teel figured she'd be caught up in this dance for the rest of her life. She could've stayed married to him and saved money if she were going to settle for being treated this way.

"Good."

"I mean it this time," Eve promised as if she could read Teel's mind. "He's taking his bride-to-be to Jamaica for their honeymoon."

Teel thought that Eve couldn't mean it this time, if she knew details about their honeymoon.

"Where do you get your information?" she asked instead of sharing her insight with Eve. Teel glanced again at the dining room table, resigned herself to the fact that she would either be yet another day behind or she'd be working until midnight tonight, and then joined Eve at the kitchen bar.

"A friend of a friend," Eve answered.

Teel caught herself again, before she said that maybe a friend wouldn't share all the news with Eve when she was divorced and should be moving on with her life.

"What's in the bag?" Teel changed the subject. She washed

her hands at the sink. Eve slid onto a barstool, but Teel was distracted. What in God's name was Keegan doing? How could she stand to be in that damned little room day after day and night after night? Was Rachel home?

The last thought made her stomach clench. She wasn't even sure if Rachel was home. How had she become *that* mother? *The one who worried so much about one child that she completely forgot the other existed?*

"I brought dinner," Eve said as she dragged her fingers back through her hair. "To thank you for listening to me."

Teel stilled her hands, still holding the dish towel she'd used to dry them. Eve brought dinner. Which meant Eve was staying for dinner. God love Eve, but she didn't have the time or energy to listen to her sister whine about her cheating ex-husband tonight.

"Oh!" She smiled, hoping Eve would buy it, and reached for the bag. "Fried chicken. Smells good."

It did smell good. But Teel rarely ate fried chicken. Too much grease. Too fattening. Indigestion. God knew she didn't need anything else to keep her awake at night.

"How're the girls?" Eve asked.

Teel pulled plates from the cabinet and set them on the counter. She shrugged.

"Not great, Eve," she answered. She didn't feel like getting into it. She'd done nothing but drown in this gloom for the past couple of weeks, and she'd finally decided to tread water and now she was being sandbagged. She wanted a quiet night and an end to the drama.

"How do you do it, Teel?"

"Do what?" she asked as she grabbed silverware from the drawer by the dishwasher.

"Keep Bobby faithful."

She met Eve's eyes and froze mid-action. "Eve. C'mon."

"Seriously. What keeps Bobby faithful to you when

Dennis couldn't keep his dick in his pants for five minutes at a time?"

"How should I know?" Teel shrugged and shook her head. "I don't know, Eve. They're just different. Two completely different guys."

"And Bobby's good, and Dennis is bad. Which means you're a better judge of character than I am."

Teel stared at Eve, anger and impatience growing inside her.

"I never said that."

"You implied it."

Teel shook her head. "Look. I've had it." She stopped when Rachel walked into the kitchen, cell phone in hand. Apparently she had been home. "Why don't you and the girls eat out on the deck? I need to get my grades updated on PATT."

"Hi, Rach." Eve turned to Rachel and smiled. Teel wondered if she'd made her angry. She didn't care. As long as they left her alone, she didn't really care what anyone thought of her at the moment.

"Hi. What'd you bring?" Rachel grinned and Teel saw a glimpse of the little girl she used to be.

"Chicken."

"I'll get Keegan!"

Teel poured two glasses of tea and set one in front of Eve.

"Is it because…"

"I swear to God," Teel turned back to look at Eve, "if you ask me how often I put out, I will never speak to you again. Let it go."

"Actually, I was going to ask if you thought it was because I got married so much younger than you did. If it was too soon for Dennis and me." Eve stood up. "Who pissed in your Wheaties?"

"Just about everybody I've talked to in the past week," Teel snapped. "And I don't even like Wheaties."

She sat down at the table and picked up her red pen. She'd grade the math tests and then she'd start working on updating the grades online. When Rachel and Keegan came out to the kitchen, she completely ignored them. They talked and laughed, and Teel thought as she worked, they sounded like imposters. Certainly not the daughters she'd lived with the past week or two.

When the French door closed behind them and Teel was alone in the house, she sank back in her chair and let out a big sigh. She hated herself when she felt this way. When she was so fed up with life that she took it out on other people. And yet, she was at the end of her rope, and she hated it when Eve started picking at her marriage in an attempt to feel better about her failed marriage.

"Hey."

She looked up to see Bobby in the kitchen. She hadn't heard him come in.

"Hi." She tossed her red pen down, having finished grading the last of seventeen math tests.

"Bad day?"

He crossed the room, planted a hand on the table top and a hand on the back of her chair and kissed her long and hard.

"Is there any other kind?"

"Not lately."

She nodded. "Eve brought chicken for dinner."

Bobby glanced over his shoulder at the three women out on the deck.

"You aren't eating?"

"Not hungry."

"Teel."

She looked up at him and sighed. "Dennis is getting

remarried. So Eve is pining for him. And waxing philosophic and wondering why my husband is faithful and hers wasn't. I'm not in the mood to listen to it."

"Good for you." He stood up straight and looked over at the kitchen counter.

"Have some, Bobby." Teel dragged her laptop closer to where she sat. "I'm just not hungry."

"I think I might go finish painting the trim work for the spec house."

"Okay."

"I'll eat with you later."

She smiled. "That sounds good."

He went to the kitchen for a glass of water, and she turned her attention to her laptop.

"I saw Rick today."

"What?" Distracted, she looked at him over the top of her screen.

"I saw Rick English today."

"Oh." She sat back. "Did you talk to him?"

Bobby shrugged. "Said hi. He looks like hell. Looks like he's lost fifty pounds."

"He didn't have ten to lose."

Bobby nodded. "Exactly."

"Can you imagine?" she whispered. Rather than look at Bobby, she turned to the window and looked at the night seeping into the sky. "Can you imagine...suddenly she's just gone? Can you imagine Kee—"

"No."

She looked back at him and caught him with a look of terror on his face. They stared at each other for a long moment, and then he nodded to the back door and said a nearly silent goodbye.

She answered him with one of her own. Wished like the

devil that she was alone, that she wouldn't have to sit through a goodbye scene with Eve, and then went back to work.

Chapter 25

KEEGAN

HER DAY STARTED off with a run-in with Tiffany before she ever got to her locker. Sadly, she thought things could only get better after Tiffany confronted her and whispered dramatically that she'd heard Marin had cheated on Sean Spanner before she killed herself. Keegan had simply stood and stared at Tiffany, somehow holding it together well enough to fool her. They drew an audience, although Keegan guessed most of the kids gathered around them in the hall hadn't heard Tiffany's opening shot.

"Do you think it's true?" Tiffany had asked and stepped closer to Keegan. It was as if she'd realized she wasn't going to get a reaction from Keegan, so she decided to play it as if they were buddies, into the gossip together. Keegan wondered if Tiffany was trying to bait her into admitting something.

Keegan shrugged. She'd pushed past Tiffany and ignored the eyes boring into her back as she opened her locker. Jess had joined her there and made a loud comment about the losers who had nothing better to do than gawk at someone whose friend had killed herself. Keegan recognized Jess' comment as a notch on her belt, a way to pretend to support Keegan at the same time she let it be known that she was still on the grapevine and still willing to exploit someone's death to stay in the A-list crowd.

She'd almost forgotten the whole incident by third hour. But when Mrs. Caldwell came over the PA system and announced that five people needed to come to her office, Keegan included, the morning and the past two weeks and all of last year came back at her full force.

What had she done now? She wondered as she made her way to the counselor's office. Well...she *knew* the answer to that. But is *that* what this was about? Had someone finally pulled the rope to hang her? Or was this still fallout from skipping classes?

Her heart skipped and then beat so hard her chest hurt. There were two men outside of Mrs. Caldwell's office. Two men dressed in suits and ties. Even if Keegan hadn't watched cop shows on TV, she'd know these guys were cops. No one around here dressed like that. Not even the teachers or Mr. Laughlin.

He only wore a suit on special days, like when grade school kids visited the high school.

"And here's Keegan," Mrs. Caldwell said with a smile. The two men looked at her and gave her a curt nod. Tiffany and Jess were already there. Keegan wanted to be calm, because she didn't want Tiffany to know that she was scared. And yet, she was scared, and it took all of her strength to keep her knees from knocking. She looked away from Tiffany and saw Marin's best friend, Kate Hughes, walking down the hallway.

Keegan felt the life, her resolve to be tough, drain from her body. No, it was more like it was sucked out of her.

There one minute and gone the next. She sagged against the wall at her back. This was definitely about Marin.

"Let's talk to Ms. Holmes first," one of the cop guys said.

Mrs. Caldwell just nodded. "The rest of you can come with me. We'll be in the library. Just around the corner."

"Thank you."

Keegan turned her back on the cops and followed Mrs. Caldwell around the corner. She stared at the floor and almost ran into the woman when she stopped walking suddenly and turned around.

"Good."

Keegan looked up to see what she was talking about.

"Mr. Wright. We're going to the library. Join us."

This time Keegan did feel the blood drain from her face. She shoved her hands in the pockets of her pants so no one could see them shaking. Wishing she could just disappear, she dropped into the first chair she saw in the library. Jess sat down across from her and made faces at her. Keegan knew she was trying to ask her if she knew what was going on.

Since Carter Wright had joined them, Keegan knew exactly what was going on. She folded her arms on the table and then laid her head on them.

What was she going to tell her parents? She could lie. Keep pretending she didn't know what was going on. But if the cops were here, and they'd called Carter Wright in, they knew. Even Tiffany had to know somehow; otherwise she wouldn't have said that this morning about Marin and Sean.

What the hell was she going to tell her parents? They would never forgive her.

Keegan thought back to Marin's funeral. The way Jeannie had held her hands and cried and asked her if she'd known what had made Marin take her own life.

Of course she knew. She'd stood there and lied through her fucking teeth, and now this was karma.

No, not karma, she thought, her Catholic upbringing finally rearing its head.

God. God was pointing His finger. Right at her.

They left her for last, so she was a bundle of nerves by the time the cops came to talk to her. She wondered if it was legal, them talking to her without her parents present. Her legs shook as she followed the two men back down the hall to Mrs. Caldwell's office.

"Keegan Alexander, correct?" The fat cop seemed to do most of the talking. He had thick black hair and five o'clock shadow and friendly eyes, but Keegan was still scared. The other cop—he looked like he was seven foot tall and weighed one hundred pounds—stared at her with hard, beady eyes.

The fat cop had a little notebook out, but he held his pen loosely. He sat behind Mrs. Caldwell's desk, and he leaned back in the chair like he was just there to chat with Keegan about college choices.

She remembered he had asked her a question and nodded.

"Keegan, I'm Detective Smith," he told her. She sat still, didn't acknowledge that he'd said anything. "This is my partner, Detective Rose."

When neither of them said anything else, she looked from Smith to Rose and then nodded. Anything to get out of this.

"We're interested in Marin English." The tall one said. Mom would call him a beanpole.

"Anything you can tell us about Marin?"

Keegan looked from the beanpole to the fat guy and shook her head.

"Were you friends with Marin?"

"No."

"But you knew her?" The fat one, Smith, consulted his notes, so this time Keegan nodded.

"Yeah. We were friends when we were in grade school."

"And she lived down the street from you." He slipped a pair of glasses on the end of his nose and read from his notes. "Correct?"

"Yes."

"You ever talk to Marin? In school? At ball games?"

"Yeah." Keegan shrugged. She couldn't play it like she'd never had anything to do with Marin. Every one of the kids they'd already talked to would have said differently. "We talked to each other now and then."

"What was she like?"

Keegan swallowed hard. "Nice. Fun."

"Nice and fun," Smith repeated. He glanced at his partner. "Sounds like someone I'd want to be friends with. Don't you think?"

"Yeah," Beanpole agreed. "Sounds like a good girl."

"How come you weren't friends with her?"

Keegan took a deep breath. The palms of her hands were sweating. She wished she could rub them over her pants, but that would only call attention to herself and how nervous she was. She wished her mom was here with her. Except that her mom would be shocked about all of this, and she would probably hate her, and that would be worse than sitting here with these cops that were asking her questions like they didn't know anything when probably they knew everything.

"I don't know," she mumbled. "We just. Grew apart. Met new people."

"Grew apart," the fat guy said and wrote something down. "When did that happen? When you were freshmen?"

"Kinda," Keegan hedged. Really, they'd stopped talking in grade school, but there hadn't been anything to it then.

"Kinda. So it wasn't when you were freshmen?"

"More like sixth grade. She invited me to spend the night once in sixth grade. We just…didn't have the same interests anymore."

"Almost like a break-up with a boy and girl? Nothing left in common so you went your separate ways?"

"I guess."

"Were there any bad feelings between you guys? After sixth grade? Freshmen year?"

"Not really."

"Yes or no?" Beanpole, who had been sitting in the chair by hers, stood up. Now, from where she was sitting, he looked like he was nine foot tall.

"No."

The fat one frowned and nodded. He stared at Keegan like he was lost in thought.

"Did Marin have a boyfriend?"

Keegan knew they were going to ask about Carter any minute now. And then they'd ask about Sean Spanner. She wished now that she hadn't eaten that bowl of Lucky Charms this morning.

Lucky, my ass, she thought. Your luck's run out.

"I don't know."

"You don't know?"

"No, I don't," she answered sincerely.

"She ever hook up with anybody?"

Keegan shrugged.

"She ever hook up with Carter Wright?"

"I don't know."

She wondered if her face looked different when she lied.

"And what about you? Do you have a boyfriend?"

Keegan looked up at Beanpole and shook her head.

"It's not true you dated a senior named Sean Spanner?"

Keegan wondered who had told them that: Jess or Tiffany.

"No."

"You never dated him?"

"No."

"But you were with him at a party?" The fat guy consulted his notes again, squinting hard like he was trying to read his own writing, when Keegan was sure he knew all of his lines by heart.

"Yes." Her voice broke, and her eyes burned. *Mom's going to know. Mom is going to know everything.* Keegan squeezed her eyes shut, not to get rid of the tears, but to get her mom out of her mind.

"Ms. Alexander, do you have a computer in your home?"

She winced as a sharp pain nearly ripped her chest apart. Still trying to appear calm, but afraid she was dying because she couldn't breathe, she nodded.

"Do you have a computer of your own?"

"Yes."

The cops both nodded.

"Okay. That's about it for now," the fat cop told her. He smiled gently, like he was her favorite uncle. "You can go back to class."

She wished they would leave the room first, because she wasn't sure she would be able to stand. But neither of them seemed inclined to move.

"Oh," Beanpole said, as if he'd just remembered something. "We might need to ask you a few more questions." He reached to hand her something as she stood up. She took his card without looking at it. "And maybe you could give us a call if you remember anything important about Marin." He shrugged, like he was thinking off the top of his head. "You know. Anything about boyfriends or friends or anything."

"Sure." She nodded and then she slipped out the door. She had to go back to the classroom, because her books were still there. Notebooks. Notebooks that might have private things written in them. Doodles. Hearts drawn with initials in them.

She couldn't get her bearings as she walked. Her legs shook so badly she moved slower than an old, sick person.

Get your stuff and go, she told herself. What was one more day of skipping classes after Mom heard about this?

The classroom was full, but none of the faces was right. Keegan stopped outside the room and looked around, wondering if she'd walked to the wrong class. Then it hit her that the bell had rung and classes had changed since she'd been sitting in the library. Mr. Morgan saw her in the hallway, and he motioned her in. Her things were stacked neatly on his desk. The curious stares barely touched her as she got her books and then turned and walked out.

If she had anywhere to go other than home, she'd have run. But there was nowhere. Just home. Home to her mom and dad, who would catch her skipping classes and get pissed and punish her and take away her laptop.

What the hell would they do when those cops knocked on the door? Because Keegan knew damned good and well they would come.

Chapter 26

TEEL

THE DOORBELL RANG as Teel was putting a small roaster chicken in the microwave for dinner. It would cook an hour and a half to two hours. She had planned to sit down and work on updating the PATT site again and finish dinner later while the chicken finished baking. She heaved a sigh of frustration and stared at the front door as if she might be able to see through it. Even if Eve were in a better mood or if she were here to apologize for going down that road she sometimes traveled (why was Teel's husband faithful and Eve's not?) Teel wasn't in the mood for it. She was completely exhausted, Keegan was acting strangely (even more so than usual) this afternoon, and she really needed to get some work done. She'd never been so far behind, and she didn't like the feeling. Always punctual, always reliable, Teel didn't want her students' parents doubting her now.

The doorbell rang again. She thought about ignoring it. Hiding in the bedroom. Maybe eventually Keegan would hear it and come to the door, and she and Eve could spend some time together. But Teel couldn't do that. She was nothing, if not polite, and she loved Eve. She couldn't hurt her that way. She'd just have to ask her for a little space.

Her heart leapt up into her throat when she saw the two men on the doorstep. Two men in suits. Two men in suits, not carrying Bibles, usually meant cops. Detectives. Teel didn't see any Bibles. She *did* see a nondescript silver sedan in the driveway, though.

Cops. Why were there two detectives standing on her front porch? Her first thought was Bobby. What had happened to Bobby? But she knew it was nothing to do with Bobby. If he'd had an accident, either they would send uniformed cops or else the hospital would call her. She knew instinctively the second she'd seen them that this was about Marin. And Keegan.

She struggled to breathe. To stay upright on her feet. She hoped they wouldn't notice her white-knuckling the door trim with her right hand. White knuckles might imply guilt. She might be choking on guilt right now, because didn't she know something was going on? Didn't she know, deep down inside, that something was happening with Keegan? She might be choking on guilt, but she'd be damned before she admitted anything to the odd pair on her porch.

One was tall and skinny; he looked like a beanpole. The other wasn't necessarily short, but his partner kind of dwarfed him. He was fat, though, and Teel had the unkind thought that he must be a donut-eating cop. She felt a little bad about that, because he offered her a smile and he had kind eyes. But she didn't feel too badly, because she knew this was the beginning of the next circle of hell for her family.

"Mrs. Alexander?"

"Yes." She was amazed that her voice was solid and strong

when she was shaking inside. Dammit all, but she wished Bobby were here.

"I'm Detective Smith." The guy flipped open a badge and held it out to her. Teel tamped down the panic that rose inside her and made a point of studying the badge. *Like what, Teel? Like they were fake cops and this was all for kicks?* "This is my partner, Detective Rose."

Teel nodded. The sun was out, and even though it was afternoon and the sun was now shining on the other side of the house, it was still bright and her head hurt. She wondered if any neighbors were home, and if any of them were gathered at their windows watching events unfold here in front of her house. The same way she, Bobby, and Rachel had huddled by the window and watched the ambulance take Marin away.

Jeannie. Did Jeannie know what was going on? Had Jeannie suspected something going on with Keegan and Marin? She'd never said anything. Though, Teel had to admit the last time she'd talked to Jeannie, the woman had been borderline breakdown. Maybe that was it? Maybe it was all a mistake? A misunderstanding?

She was grasping at straws, and she knew it. Something had happened between Keegan and Marin. If she were honest with herself, she'd admit that she had felt vague stirrings of unease when Keegan had been devoid of emotion through the week of Marin's suicide and funeral.

"We'd like to speak to your daughter," the other guy said. Teel looked up at him, but she didn't answer him. His smile didn't quite work on his face. Too small. Too cold. There was a chip in his front tooth that bothered her. She looked back at the other one, Smith.

"Is Keegan home?" he asked gently.

She snapped out of it. It wasn't going to do anyone any

good, least of all Keegan, for her to stand here and stare at these two like she didn't speak English.

"Yes." She stepped back to let them in. "Can I ask what this is about?"

"Could you get Keegan for us, ma'am?" Smith again.

"Sure." She excused herself and went silently down the hall to Keegan's room. She stood for a moment and listened, wondering what Keegan was doing. What Keegan had done. There had been no noise from Keegan's room for days. No music. No cell phone chiming. No conversation. Just nothing.

Right now, though, Teel could hear the click of the keyboard as Keegan typed. She knocked quietly and then pushed the door open. Keegan, who had listened to her and Bobby the other night and started taking more care with her appearance again, looked cool and collected. She was still dressed in her school clothes, and she'd gathered her hair up in a messy pony-tail. Her eyeliner was precise, and her eye shadow made her eyes seem bigger.

"Just working on a biology assignment," she said before Teel could say anything. Teel glanced at the computer screen, she didn't think Keegan had had time to change anything as she walked in, and caught the words *meiosis* and *anaphase*. Definitely biology.

"Keegan," Teel cleared her throat. She was still shaking, so she slipped her hands in the pockets of her slacks. "There are two detectives here to see you."

Teel watched the color leave her daughter's face. One minute Keegan was her daughter, and pretty and almost vivacious like she used to be, and the next she was pale as a ghost. Her eyes were suddenly so big and round, Teel couldn't see her eye shadow anymore.

Keegan caught her breath and stood up. She slipped past Teel and out the door. Teel looked back at the laptop one more time. Definitely biology. And there were no minimized programs at the bottom of the screen. No other documents open. She didn't appear to be online, chatting with anyone.

Teel fought the need to dash into the bathroom and vomit. Instead, she took a deep breath to calm herself and then went back to the dining room.

"Hey, Keegan." Smith sounded friendly, like he was here to chat with her daughter about the soccer game the night before. Keegan simply nodded. "We just had a few more questions to ask you."

Keegan nodded again, but Teel stepped further into the room.

"I'm sorry. What do you mean a few more questions?"

"We talked to Keegan earlier today at school." The beanpole guy dismissed her with a glance. Teel turned to Smith.

"Keegan's a minor," Teel said with a frown. "Why were you questioning her at school? Without a parent present?"

"Just a few routine questions for her and a few other students, ma'am," Smith answered her smoothly. Teel didn't feel any better after he answered her.

"Keegan, you said a few things earlier that we need to clarify," Rose told her. Teel's heart hurt. Her chest ached so damned badly; she thought she might be having a heart attack. She was angry, yes. It was quite possible she'd never been so angry with Keegan. And yet, it hurt to watch her little girl stand here with these cops. Sort of a paradox, because while Teel looked at the daughter who had grown cold and unfeeling, who was gorgeous even now, standing in front of two cops who were going to do their best to trip her up and expose her in a lie, Teel saw her tiny, helpless little girl.

"You said earlier that you didn't know if Marin had a boyfriend."

Keegan stared at Smith and waited for his question. He simply stared back at her.

"I have no idea if she had a boyfriend."

"And you also said you didn't know if she'd hooked up with a Carter Wright."

"That's right."

"The night you were with Sean Spanner…"

Teel crossed her arms over her chest and tried to take a deep breath. *With Sean Spanner? With? What did that mean?*

"You said you were with Sean Spanner. At a party."

Teel waited for Keegan to correct him. To clarify what she had said. But Keegan simply nodded. Teel's throat was closing, getting tighter and tighter, until she was struggling to breathe.

"Do you know if Marin was at that party?"

"Yes. She was there with her friend Kate."

Smith nodded and pulled his notebook out of his pocket. He clicked his pen and jotted something down. Teel wondered what it was, what other notes were in the little spiral-bound book. What secrets her daughter had been forced to bear to them that she'd kept willingly from her.

"Did Marin talk to Sean Spanner at that party?"

"I don't know."

"Did you see Marin with Sean Spanner at a party last summer?"

"No."

"Did you see Marin with Carter Wright at a party last summer?"

Keegan swallowed so hard, Teel heard it from where she was standing. "No."

"Keegan," Smith frowned and screwed his fat lips up into what appeared to be a mini-frown. "We have witnesses who say they know you saw Marin with both Carter and Sean."

"My God," Teel groaned. She tried to remind herself that

she didn't know the whole story, but the thought did little to calm her.

"And said witnesses claim you were pretty upset because Marin was flirting with Sean Spanner." Rose glanced at Smith. "Isn't that right?"

Teel didn't appreciate the theatrics. Smith had done the damage. She didn't think anyone here needed to hear more.

Smith leafed through his notebook.

"Agitated. Jealous. Extremely jealous." Smith looked up, first at Keegan and then at Teel. He didn't seem to be enjoying this quite as much as the other guy, but his reticence didn't make Teel like him any better.

"Is that true, Keegan?" Rose prodded. Keegan stood straight, but she dipped her head a bit. Just enough for all three of them to know the truth.

"I saw Marin a couple of times with Sean," Keegan said quietly. "I don't remember where we were."

"And did it bother you? Seeing her with him?"

"She wasn't with him, with him. You know. They were just talking."

Smith nodded sympathetically. "Which was kind of even worse, wasn't it?"

Teel blinked at the tears that filled her eyes. Keegan had had something to do with Marin's suicide. No denying it now.

Keegan stood completely still for a moment and then nodded.

"Did you want revenge?" Rose asked her. "Did you get it?"

Revenge. Teel shivered. The phone rang, but she ignored it.

"Keegan, we asked you earlier if you had a computer."

Keegan looked up at Smith and nodded.

"Are you familiar with the social networking site, MyFriend?"

"Yes."

"And do you have a MyFriend page?"

"Yes."

Smith nodded. He flipped his book shut and stuck it back in his pocket.

"That about it?" Rose asked him. Smith nodded, but he looked back at Teel and Keegan.

"Thank you, Keegan," he said quietly. "Mrs. Alexander, thank you for your time."

Teel stared at him blankly as the two of them made their way back to the front door. That was it? A bunch of questions that implied her daughter had hooked up with someone at a party? That her one time friend had hooked up with the same boy?

She stood completely still when the door closed behind the detectives. They'd asked about a computer. They knew more than they were letting on. And this wasn't the end of it.

Alone with Keegan, the tears were suddenly gone, and she was blinded by anger.

"You wanna tell me what that was about?"

"No."

"Let me rephrase that," Teel said calmly. "Sit down." She laid her hand on Keegan's shoulder and pushed her gently toward the dining room table. Keegan sat with her shoulders hunched up and her eyes trained on the table in front of her.

The phone rang again, and Keegan glanced hopefully toward the kitchen. Teel ignored it. She sat down at the table with Keegan and leaned back in her chair.

"Start talking." She folded her arms over her chest. "Lie to me once, Keegan." Keegan pressed her lips together, recognizing the warning in Teel's voice.

"They were at school today," Keegan began in a small voice.

Chapter 27

TEEL

TEEL NODDED. "Yeah, I got that part."

"They talked to us during—"

"Keegan." Teel raised her eyebrows. "Now."

Keegan sighed. "I walked out after they interviewed us."

"You cut your afternoon classes again?"

Keegan nodded.

"Who are you, baby? I don't even know you anymore." Teel covered her mouth with her hand. She swallowed hard, pushed her hair away from her face, and took a deep breath.

Keegan stared at the table again, as if she were unable or unwilling to go on.

"Why were the detectives here, Keegan? What's going on?"

"I don't know." Keegan looked up at Teel with those big eyes. "They never said."

Teel shook her head. "Don't play dumb. You know exactly what's going on. Tell me. Now."

"Because of something on the internet."

"The internet?" Teel repeated. That stepped things up several notches. "Why don't you start at the beginning? When did all of this business with the parties happen?"

"Last year."

"Last year? When you were a freshman?"

Keegan nodded.

Teel examined her fingernails. "Keegan, we're gonna sit here until you tell me every last bit, so you might as well start talking."

"Mom, I can't talk about it."

"No, *you* can talk about it. *Marin?* She can't. She can't tell Jeannie anything anymore."

Keegan flinched as if Teel had slapped her. But she said nothing.

"Let me say this one more time, Keegan Alexander." Teel smacked her hand down on the dining room table. "You are in serious trouble. And I don't even mean with me. You have the police coming to school and coming here to question you, and you're telling me it's about something on the internet. That is huge."

Teel leaned over and poked Keegan in the arm. "You better hear me now. Tell me what the hell is going on, start to finish, and I mean now."

"Jess and I went to a party last year."

"Jess?" Teel remembered Elaine Caldwell saying that Jess wasn't a good girl for Keegan to hang out with.

"She knew this girl who was going. So we went." Keegan shrugged. "There were tons of people there."

"Who had the party?"

"I don't know. Some senior."

Teel kept her mouth shut, though she wanted to rip into Keegan and tear her apart. She wasn't even half way through her story and already Teel wanted to lash out.

"They had a keg," Keegan said softly. "Jess and I didn't drink anything."

Teel wondered if that was supposed to earn Keegan some points. She stared back at her without a word or even a nod, because she wasn't impressed.

"Sean Spanner was there," Keegan continued. Her voice had dropped so that Teel could hardly hear her. "He plays basketball. He's really hot."

Teel bristled. She didn't mind if a guy was called good-looking or a girl was pretty. But she hated hearing young kids talk about other kids being *hot*.

"I wanted to go out with him. I noticed him the first day of school." Keegan drew a shaky breath. "He saw me there. At the party. And he started talking to me. He was really cool. Really nice."

"Really." Teel knew what was coming. She prayed for the strength to sit here and listen to Keegan confess the gory details.

"Jess and I were outside later. And Sean came and talked to me again. He kissed me. So Jess told me to…"

"No." Teel shook her head. "Don't blame this on Jess, Keegan. You knew exactly what you were doing, didn't you?"

Keegan hesitated, but she finally nodded.

"We went in this room. Someone's bedroom."

"Did he rape you?"

"No." Keegan raised her head and met Teel's gaze.

"But you had sex with him?"

"Yes." Keegan nodded. Her eyes were bright with tears.

"You handed your virginity over to some hot guy you didn't even know," Teel began, "in some stranger's bedroom…when you were fourteen."

"Yeah."

Teel licked her lips and looked away from her daughter.

She was afraid to look at her. Afraid Keegan would read the disgust on her face, in her eyes.

"And then what?"

"I thought it meant we would go out," Keegan whispered. "I thought that's what you did when you wanted to go out with someone. When you wanted to be popular."

Teel stared out the window, rather than look at Keegan. "Why would you think that? Why would a guy wanna date someone when he can do her at a party for nothing?"

"Mom!"

Teel turned and looked at Keegan. Her nose was running, and her makeup was smeared with tears.

"What happened, Keegan?"

"It was over so fast. And…"

"And what?"

"I bled a lot," Keegan cried. "I hoped he didn't notice, but he must have. Because the next Monday at school, everyone was looking at me. Whispering. And then Jess asked me about it like a week later."

"Jesus, Keegan."

"I just kept thinking he would ask me out, and then it wouldn't matter. That if Sean said he loved me, it would all be okay and everyone would stop talking about it."

"But he didn't. Did he?"

"I waited all year. For him to ask me out. For him to notice me." Keegan shook her head. "I don't think he even remembered. Doing it. He was drunk. I was just there."

"Exactly."

"And then. Last summer, we were at a party, and Marin was there. Sean kept talking to Marin. But they didn't get a room like we did. They played volleyball. And they danced. And they played cards."

Teel waited silently for Keegan to go on.

"She had his attention. He was doing with her all the things I thought he would do with me."

"Oh, God."

"And then I started seeing them around. I saw them at the movies...When Jess and I went out for pizza. They were dating."

Teel leaned forward and rested her elbows on the table. She dropped her head to her hands and covered her face.

"I found out late in the summer that she was cheating on him. That she was flirting with Carter Wright. Jess said she saw Marin and Carter making out one night at a party. When we were out of town. In St. Louis for that weekend."

"How do you know that you can trust Jess?"

Keegan glanced at her, but she looked away quickly. "I know now that I can't."

"Hindsight's always twenty twenty." Teel directed a look of anger at Keegan, but again, she was quick to look away.

"I don't see what's so bad about what I did," Keegan snapped. "It's no different than when Tiffany Holmes took a picture of this girl at a party. She was topless, because she'd been doing lap dances. Tiffany took the picture with her phone and sent it to a bunch of kids' phones."

Teel took a deep breath. That was bad enough. If Keegan had done that, she and Bobby would have punished her severely.

Lap dances. Teel sunk her teeth into her lip.

"You were fourteen," she whispered. "Fourteen, Keegan. You were just a child. You're still a child. What were you doing? What in God's name were you doing?"

Keegan responded with a lazy shrug. "That girl was sixteen."

"Oh." Teel sat back and nodded. "Sixteen. That's much better."

Keegan sighed.

"What did you do, Keegan? Why are there cops coming here and involving themselves in…in…this…this…behavior." Teel rubbed her face, fingertips smoothing small circles over her cheekbones. Her head pounded so hard, she thought it might split apart. She wished it would. At least that would relieve the pressure.

"I made a MyFriend page," Keegan answered.

"And what did you put on your page?"

"No, it wasn't mine. I made another one."

"And?"

"Pictures of Marin and Carter."

"Pictures of Marin and Carter," Teel repeated.

"Making out."

Teel stared at Keegan for a moment, too stunned to say anything. Too furious to choose the words to convey her feelings. So disappointed in her daughter, in herself that she suddenly felt herself shrink smaller and smaller in the dining room chair.

"I took it down," Keegan said softly. She looked up at Teel as tears spilled from her eyes. "I took the page down—"

Teel pursed her lips, breathed deeply through her nose and leaned forward. "When?"

"I didn't mean…"

"When?" Teel repeated, louder this time.

"After. After Marin killed herself."

Teel stood up. Her stomach pitched and rolled. Keegan cried silent tears. Maybe she needed Teel to put her arms around her. To say it was okay. To say she understood. That she loved her.

Of course Teel loved her. If she didn't love her, learning something like this wouldn't destroy her this way. She stepped away from the table, careful not to step on the pieces of her heart, herself, that were scattered around her feet.

"Little too late, Keegan." Her voice broke. She cleared her throat and took a step backward, away from Keegan. From the truth Keegan had just thrown down. "Don't you think?"

Chapter 28

RACHEL

"WHEN YOU WERE TEN," Deacon said as he popped a French fry into his mouth, "what did you want to be?"

Rachel laughed, but when she realized he was serious, she fell back against the cracked vinyl-covered booth and groaned. "When I was ten? Um…Probably an actress."

"Really?" Deacon cocked his head to study her.

Again she laughed. "No, probably not. I figured all girls were supposed to say that."

"I'm not interested in all girls," he said quietly. "I wanna know what you wanted to be."

"Well, I do know that when I was six, I wanted to be a princess, but…" She sighed and tucked her hair behind her ear. "Ten. I'd say I wanted to join the Peace Corps."

His smile was small and sweet. "Now that I believe."

"I had a cousin who joined the Peace Corps. And another cousin who joined the army. Right around the same time. I gave both a lot of thought." She raised her eyebrows. "Well.

As much thought as a ten year old can give anything for any length of time."

Deacon nodded. "And now? You've never really told me what you want to do."

"I haven't declared my major yet," she reminded him.

"But whaddaya wanna do?"

"I wanna be a doctor," she answered quietly and lowered her eyes to the scarred wooden table top. "Pediatrics or something."

Suddenly Deacon's hand covered hers. She lifted only her eyes to look at him.

"C'mere." He stood and gently tugged her out of the booth.

"What are you doing?" She laughed nervously as Deacon guided her to the center of the old wooden tavern floor. One other couple was dancing, but they appeared to have consumed too much of whatever was on tap.

He wrapped his arms around her waist and drew her in close.

"I think you'd make a great doctor," he whispered. "You'd be good for kids."

She drew back to look at him. "Really? Because I'm horrible with Keegan."

He lifted a shoulder lazily. "She's fifteen, so she's not a little kid. And besides, she's your sister. I think that makes a difference."

"It should mean that I'd do anything to take care of her."

Deacon kissed her cheek.

"What are we doing?" She remembered that they were in a tavern, one that she'd driven by at least a thousand times in her life, but had never been inside. It was just six blocks off campus, and Deacon had suggested they go there for a burger and fries.

"Dancing, Rach." He rubbed his hand up and over her

back. "I've been thinking about how much I want to dance with you."

"Really?"

"Yes, really." He grinned.

"But what if people are looking at us?"

"I don't care. And they're not, anyway."

Rachel didn't know the song that was playing, just that it was country and she hadn't ever cared to listen to it. But when Deacon pulled her tight against his hard body and pressed his lips to her neck, she decided she could get used to it. To the music. To dancing with him.

And maybe it didn't matter if people were looking.

When they'd danced a couple of songs, and finished their Cokes, Deacon paid at the bar and then led her hand in hand out of the bar. It was dark, and the air was cold and damp. Deacon put his arm around her as they walked.

"What about you?" she asked when she realized he'd never told her what he wanted to be when he was ten.

"What about me?"

"What did you want to be when you were ten?"

"Oh." He pursed his lips in thought and hummed a song that sounded vaguely familiar. "Well. When I was four, I wanted to be the Incredible Hulk."

"I'm kind of glad you aren't."

"Me, too. By six, I wanted to be Spiderman."

She ducked her head to hide her smile.

"Hey, every boy wants to be a super hero at some point."

"All the same, I'm glad you don't turn green when you get angry."

"When I was ten," he continued, but he smiled at her comment, "I wanted to be a scientist."

"Like a mad scientist? Or the kind of scientist who would invent stuff?"

"Mad scientist."

She looked up at him as they walked. When he looked at her, she flashed him a grin.

"I love it."

"Well, I changed my mind by the time I was eleven."

"And?"

"Cubs baseball announcer."

"The Cubs?" She flinched.

"Hey, hey." He stopped walking and turned her toward him. "Do you think you can be in love with a Cubs fan?"

Rachel felt his other arm slide around her waist. She tilted her head up just as he leaned in to kiss her.

"I can," she whispered against his mouth, "if that Cub fan is you."

"And when we watch a Cards and Cubs game next summer and the Cards lose, you'll be cool with that? You won't beat me or anything?"

"I promise," she said softly as she kissed her way up his jaw to his ear. "Because it'll never happen."

"Wanna bet?" He jabbed her in the ribs, and she gasped and laughed as she struggled to get away from him.

"Oh yeah." She caught his hands with hers and pushed him back a step. "I'll bet you."

He linked his fingers through hers, and they started walking again. When she shivered, he let go of her hand and put his arm around her. They stopped in front of his dorm and leaned on her car, parked in the street.

Rachel burrowed in close to him and lost herself in his kiss. She forgot that she was cold as he stoked the fire inside her.

"Wanna stay for a while?" he asked.

"What time is it?" She pulled her phone from her back pocket. It was almost eight-thirty. She nodded as she tucked her phone back in her pocket. Pressed together from shoulder to toe, they made their way to his room.

"What about Brandt?" She glanced at his roommate's bed as they stepped inside.

"I think I've seen him twice since the semester started," Deacon said with a shrug. "He spends most nights with his girlfriend."

"In her dorm?"

"She has an apartment on campus." Deacon turned his TV on. "Monday night TV...*Castle?*"

"Sure."

But when they stretched out over his bed, neither of them was worried about the TV. The kisses started slow and gentle. When he slid over to lie on top of her, she felt him hard and ready against her middle. Her fingers tugged at his T-shirt and pulled it up over his back and shoulders. She smoothed her hands over his skin.

"Rach?" He breathed her name against her neck.

"Mm?"

He unbuttoned the top button of her blouse.

"Are you sure?"

"I'm sure."

"Because we can—"

"I'm sure, Deacon." She cupped his face in her hands and drew him back up to kiss him. He groaned when she wiggled to settle more comfortably beneath him. His fingers were magic on her skin, over her stomach and her breasts. She lifted her hips as he eased her jeans down. Caught her breath when he slid his fingers inside her panties.

And then she thought about Keegan. The fact that Keegan had already done this. That maybe Keegan had already done everything, and she was only fifteen. She thought about how her mom had told her she wouldn't put up with Rachel sleeping around, when she lived under her roof.

"What's wrong?" Deacon asked her. She opened her eyes to find him watching her.

"Nothing." She shook her head.

"Something."

"Deacon."

"You were right here with me," he said softly. "I was watching your face. And then you were gone."

She sighed and bent her knees.

"Mm." He ducked his head when he felt her bare skin against his. "I can wait."

"I want to..."

"But?"

Rachel's eyes burned. She dropped her knees and tried to roll away from him.

"Rach, talk to me." Deacon moved to lie beside her. "Tell me what's wrong."

"I wanna do this, but I..."

"What?"

"I'm thinking about Keegan. And my mom."

Deacon's laugh was low like a growl. "Why are you thinking about Keegan and your mom?"

"The other day...when I got home late." She felt his eyes on her as she talked, but she fought not to look at him. "Mom...as much as accused me of sleeping around. And said she wouldn't tolerate it while I was living under her roof."

Deacon nodded. "Moms are supposed to say that."

"I know," Rachel laughed softly, "I know. I just wonder..."

"You wonder what?"

"It's not that I don't wanna do this with you..."

"Rachel, baby, I know." Deacon dropped a kiss on her lips. "Believe me, I know. It's okay. We'll make love. When you're ready. What do you wonder?"

"I found out the other day that Keegan had sex with some guy she wanted to go out with."

"Keegan?"

"Last year."

"But she's only fifteen."

"Exactly."

"So…" Deacon took a deep breath, "you think you might be rushing into this because Keegan did it first?"

That was exactly what she thought, but she hated hearing him say it.

"What if I am?" she whispered.

"Then we wait," he said simply. "Until you aren't thinking about your mom and what she would think or keeping up with Keegan."

"Are you sure? I'm sorry, Deacon. God, I'm sorry."

"It's okay." She could see his smile in his eyes. "Maybe we could do a little better than a twin size bed in my dorm room."

She giggled. "But it won't be in my bed under my mom's roof."

Deacon laughed and dropped over her to hold her.

"I love you, Rach."

Chapter 29

TEEL

COMPLETELY OVERWHELMED, to the point of mental paralysis, Teel left Keegan at the dining room table. She swept through the house like a lonely widow looking for her lost love. She fidgeted with the blinds in Rachel's room and the hand towels in the guest bath, and she avoided Keegan's room completely. Finally, just as it occurred to her that she needed to call Bobby, because he needed to know what was going on, the back door opened and he walked in.

He took one look at Teel, *God only knows what she looked like*, but she felt like she'd been bounced down a train track, leading a freight train destined to crash head on into an Amtrak, and then he'd looked past her to see Keegan sitting at the dining room table. Still. She cried silent tears, which only grated more on Teel.

Part of her wanted to comfort Keegan. To take her in her arms and tell her it would be okay. But part of Teel knew damned well things were far from okay, and that same part of her was so disgusted and disappointed in Keegan, it was probably better to let her sit for a while before she tried to talk to her again.

"What's going on?" Bobby asked cautiously.

The microwave had beeped some time ago. The chicken had probably needed another half hour, at least, but Teel hadn't checked it. She honestly didn't give a damn about baking a chicken right now, and she certainly didn't think she could eat. She wondered now if she could turn the microwave back on; if it cooked a bit longer would it be okay to eat? Then again, she hadn't started anything else, so even if the chicken was okay, there would be no noodles or mashed potatoes or green beans.

Teel took a deep breath and glanced over her shoulder at Keegan, who had moved to cover her face with her hands. Of course she wouldn't want her dad to know any of this.

She didn't know what to say. How did you start this conversation anyway? No holds barred? *Hey, Bobby, Keegan's in trouble with the cops?* Or gently? *Hey Bobby, Keegan isn't your baby girl anymore, and oh yeah, it gets much worse.*

"Keegan?" Bobby asked. She shook her head, face still buried in her hands, and refused to look at him. "What happened?" he looked to Teel again.

"Mom?" Keegan asked from behind her hands. "Can I go to my room? Please?"

Teel felt a pang, a sharp stab of pain in her stomach.

"Yes," she said quietly. "But I want your computer. Out here on the kitchen counter."

Keegan scrambled off the chair and down the hall, quicker than Teel had seen her move in ages. Teel turned back to Bobby, who seemed to deflate when he heard the word computer.

"Whatever this is, it's bad, isn't it?" he asked as he leaned over to untie his work boots.

Teel waited until he looked up at her to answer, and then she simply nodded. Keegan appeared again with her laptop in hand. Her face was splotched with red, and her eyes were swollen. Teel wanted to reach out to her but caught herself just before she did. The hell of it was that she wasn't sure if Keegan was crying for Marin or for herself, because she'd been caught.

Bobby took a beer from the refrigerator and then turned back to Teel. Teel watched Keegan retreat back down the hall to her bedroom and then turned and led Bobby out to the deck.

"It's a little chilly out here," he warned her as they sat down.

She shook her head, not bothered by the cold. By the outside things, the things that didn't matter compared to what was going on inside her house.

"Keegan made a MyFriend page about Marin." Though this was the most damning bit to start with, in terms of the police questioning Keegan, it seemed the easiest to say. Teel couldn't bring herself to think about her fourteen-year-old daughter getting felt up and having sex in some stranger's bedroom, just because she wanted to date someone she didn't know. To be a part of the in crowd. How the hell was she going to tell Bobby?

Bobby took a long drink of his beer and stared silently at Teel, waiting for her to go on.

"She posted pictures of Marin and some boy making out."

Bobby raised his eyebrows. "What kind of pictures?"

"I don't know." Teel shrugged. "But apparently not good."

"Were they really of Marin or did Keegan paste her face over someone else's body?"

"I don't know, Bobby," Teel answered and already her control was slipping. She knew he was spinning this so he could find an angle to defend Keegan. He was angry, of course he was angry, but he would want to call a lawyer and begin whatever process involved for Keegan's defense.

"What was she thinking, Teel?" he asked after swallowing another mouthful of beer.

"Well, that I can answer," Teel said with a nod. "She was thinking about revenge."

Bobby leaned back in his chair as Teel recounted Keegan's story to him. His face went from ghostly pale to beet red and back to ghostly pale. Teel knew him well enough to know every feeling pushing around inside him, vying for control. He was disappointed in Keegan; for giving away something that should have been protected for a special moment. For being at that party in the first place if she was only fourteen. He was angry at the boy who had been so drunk he didn't even remember Keegan the next day. At the whispers that had begun about Keegan, even though they were true. He was probably angry at Teel. Probably he wanted to throw some of the blame for this at her. Maybe he thought she hadn't done enough as a parent.

Though it pissed her off because she thought she had done enough as a mom to at least keep her daughter's reputation intact through high school, Teel understood where he was coming from because she felt the same way. Maybe Bobby hadn't done enough as a parent.

Through the anger, though, she knew that line of thinking was a waste of time. What more could they have done? They had never led Keegan or Rachel to believe that it was okay to be at parties where minors consumed alcohol and teenage girls did lap dances and blowjobs and had sex with whoever was interested. In fact, they'd always preached the opposite, and Teel felt certain that Rachel had never done anything like this.

But what if she was wrong? What if all teenagers were involved in this stuff, and they'd been blind to it with both

Rachel and Keegan, and the only reason they knew now was because someone was dead and someone was pointing the finger at Keegan?

She wondered if she should talk to Rachel about this. Not that she and Rachel were on such good terms right now. In fact, Rachel might tell her to go to hell.

Bobby leaned forward and rested his elbows on his knees. "Everything we do for our kids," he said quietly, "and they're so willing to throw it away."

"I know."

"If I ever get my hands on that Spanner kid, I'll kill him."

Teel winced. She understood the need. She'd thought once or twice, as she wandered the house before he'd come home, about getting her hands on the kid who had taken her daughter's virginity and didn't even remember it or her the next day. She thought it would feel particularly good to give him a good kick in the balls and maybe to strangle him while she was at it. And yet, she knew it wouldn't change a thing. Keegan was no longer her baby girl, and she was still in serious trouble.

Teel thought again of Jeannie and Rick. Of what it must have done to them to lose their only child. Of how it tore their marriage apart. It didn't matter if they'd been having problems; what Marin had done had been the straw that broke the camel's back. No, what Keegan had done had set everything in motion. What a huge, huge responsibility on her daughter's shoulders. And what sickened her was not knowing if Keegan could see past her own sorrow, her own wounds to see just what she'd done to the English family.

"Bobby, I know we're supposed to protect Keegan. To love her. To prove her innocence. But I can't. I can't just pretend it didn't happen. I can't make excuses for what she did."

"Of course you love her."

"Yes, dammit, of course I love her. And I'm scared to death of what's gonna happen now. But I can't make excuses for her. I can't say it's okay that another teenage girl, someone who used to be welcome in our home, is dead because of something horrible that Keegan did."

Bobby dropped his chin to his chest and scratched his head. Teel noticed new spots of gray. She felt her stomach jolt, and she wanted to reach over and run her hands through his hair.

"There might be more to it."

"Excuse me?" Teel cocked her head, sure she hadn't heard him right.

"Yes, what Keegan did is wrong. I feel as bad as you do. I'm…ashamed of this whole thing, yes. But we don't know everything, Teel. We don't know what all was going through Marin's head when she killed herself."

"Bobby." Teel stood up and moved to the railing on the deck. "Really? Keegan posted pictures of her on the internet. We don't even know what the pictures look like. They could be horrible. After what I heard today, I don't even need to use my imagination."

She glanced at him over her shoulder. He met her gaze and answered with a reluctant nod.

"What if it were Keegan? What if Marin had done this to Keegan? If there were pictures of Keegan and that boy she was with circulating over the internet? Even though she pulled the page down, those pictures could be everywhere. You know that."

Bobby steepled his fingers and rested his chin on them. "I do know, Teel. And I know you're exhausted. I know something's going on with you…"

"What?" She stood up straight. "What do you mean? What's going on with me?"

"You tell me."

"Bobby, what do you mean? I'm tired. We've got a hell of a lot going on right now."

"I don't know. You're too tired. I just wondered if you're getting sick. Maybe you need to have your blood checked. Are you taking your vitamins?"

"Marin English killed herself. She used to play at our house. With our daughter. Rachel has a boyfriend, and she's getting awfully close to him. My sister is like Jekyll and Hyde these days, alternately supporting me with the girls and ripping me apart because my husband is faithful and hers cheated. And now the police are questioning our daughter, whom we now know has a pretty wild sex life, in connection with someone's death. How the hell am I supposed to feel, Bobby?"

"Hey." He stood up and crossed to the door before she could get to it.

"Leave me alone."

"I'm just worried about you." He tipped her chin up with his finger. "I'm just worried, that's all. You're frazzled. You aren't taking care of yourself."

"I don't think I matter that much right now."

"Well, I do." He put his arms around her and pulled her close. She fought him at first, angry with him for questioning her behavior, but she gave in and rested her head on his shoulder.

"I thought we could handle anything, Bobby," she whispered. "Now I'm not so sure."

Bobby squeezed her hard and ran his hand up her back to cup the back of her head. "We will handle this, Teel. You and me together."

"I just don't get how. I'm lost, Bobby. I'm at a standstill. I don't know how to get past what she told me."

"I know," he whispered. He pulled back from her to look her in the eye, and she saw that his were suspiciously bright.

"I know. I'll talk to Keegan. You need to relax. Why don't you go soak in the tub or something?"

"I want you with me."

He smiled. "I know. But one of us has to talk to Keegan. We're a team, Teel."

She stared at him for a moment and finally nodded.

"Bobby?" She stopped halfway in the door and turned to look at him.

"Hmm?"

"What would we do? If someone put pictures of Keegan on the internet?"

"I don't know." He shook his head. "I think the first thing I'm going to do is check out her MyFriend page and then close her account."

"If there's something out there, that's not going to take care of it."

"I know, Teel," he answered with a nod. "We'll deal with this one step at a time. Okay? Go. I'll come in and check on you later."

Chapter 30

TEEL

BOBBY'S WORDS stayed with her as she drew a hot bath. They hovered just over her shoulder, and each time she tried to look at them, each time she zeroed in on them to examine them and why they made her feel a little sick inside, they slipped away. She stripped her clothes off, those she put on this morning before going to work. Work. Maggie. The promise she'd made to Maggie to go for lunch this weekend. All of it seemed so far away now. There was no way she would do lunch. There was no way she could face anyone tomorrow at school.

Except she had to. It was her job. She couldn't just not show up. Besides that, no one knew. Except Elaine Caldwell at Blessed Sacrament. And probably the principal. Maybe a few of the teachers.

Who was she kidding? She slid down into the hot water and leaned back against the cold tub. Everyone at Blessed Sacrament knew by now that Keegan and a few other students had been called out of class and questioned regarding Marin English's suicide. Teachers and students alike, and by now, people all over town were discussing Keegan and those other few students and their roles in what happened to Marin.

She closed her eyes and told herself to forget tomorrow. Forget having to walk into school and look at her colleagues, some she considered friends and some she would probably now consider enemies. She needed to let it all go, just for a moment.

And then it hit her. What Bobby had said. He was worried about her. She was tired, too tired. And of course, what he hadn't said. Her breasts had been tender for days, probably weeks, if she were being honest. And she was eating everything that wasn't nailed down. Eating as if for two.

She didn't want to think it, let alone say it. She certainly didn't want to talk about it to anyone. She wondered if Bobby suspected it, or if he really thought she might be coming down with something. As long as they'd been married, and as many pregnancies as there'd been, he probably wondered about it.

There was no way she could have a baby. But there was no way she could not have a baby. She was born and raised Catholic, and she'd been taught that abortion was wrong. But her belief ran even deeper than that. If she were pregnant, she would have to carry this child to term. The baby, if there was one, deserved that much.

Then again, with the hell going on in the house right now, she might not make it to term. She'd had trouble before; she was lucky she had Rachel and Keegan.

Best not to think about it. Not right now. Not yet. She sighed. If she wasn't going to think about that, that left a whole lot of mind to wander back over the last couple of weeks. And she was so tired of thinking about Marin and

Jeannie and Rick. And Keegan. Good God, what were they to do with Keegan?

Forty-five. Teel would be forty-five next May. Too damned old to be pregnant. Too old for a newborn, for diapers and breast-feeding. For preschool and kindergarten. Rachel could have a child; technically, Keegan could have a child. Not that Teel was in any hurry for grandchildren; she preferred to see her girls out of college and married first. But how embarrassing for them if she were to turn up pregnant now.

And how? She breathed deeply, but the lavender scented bath oil wasn't helping her relax tonight. How the hell could she be pregnant? Okay, so maybe Bobby should have taken care of things on his end. But she'd been on the pill for years. Maybe that made her a hypocrite, being pro-life and yet relying on a prescribed contraceptive instead of natural family planning.

So be it, she thought. The pope and the bishop and her priests would disagree with her that it was better to prevent rather than abort. They'd counsel her to pray and watch her cycle, if she were ever to talk about it with them. But she wouldn't. Ever. So maybe that made her a bad Catholic.

She didn't think she was a bad person, though. Well, she hadn't. Up until a few hours ago. Now she felt like a bad person and a horrible parent. What had she ever done to set this kind of example for Keegan? How had she ever given Keegan the impression that it was okay to use other people, to hurt other people to get what she wanted? She'd never been that sort of person.

Hadn't she always taught the girls courtesy? Compassion? Give to those who need. Smile. Live happy and be happy. Where had Keegan learned that it was acceptable to take her clothes off for a stranger just to be popular? How had her daughter become one of those girls?

How?

Teel sat up straight in the tub, no longer able to pretend that she could relax. What was next? What was the next move? Was Bobby talking to Keegan? What sort of punishment did you impose for such a horrible thing? Teel had no idea. She was completely out of her league and completely unnerved by her daughter's apparent lack of remorse.

She drew her legs up and rested her forehead on her knees. As much as she loved her girls, she said a silent prayer that she wasn't pregnant. Imagine how people would talk. *Teel Alexander can't control her youngest daughter, and now she's pregnant again?*

It was more than that, though. She didn't want to do it again. Carry a baby to term. Labor. Raise a toddler into a preschooler into a teenager. She didn't have the patience or the energy for it. And God, think of the risks involved. Health risks for the baby. Teel almost sobbed out loud when she thought about the two Downs Syndrome children she'd known personally; both younger brothers of students she'd had through the years. *Beautiful and loving, yes, but please, God, make this go away.*

She laid her hand over her stomach, already stretched a little too much from her other babies. Her body was showing its age, and she could just see how Rachel and Keegan, especially Keegan, would be appalled by her pregnant belly growing huge and round. Keegan, who apparently chose appearances over true compassion and friendship.

Stop, she ordered herself. Stop. She tuned the little voice in her head out and hurried through the rest of her bath. She even shaved her legs, though she didn't know why. She couldn't imagine wanting to make love to Bobby tonight. In fact, as exhausted as she was, and as disheartened as she was right now, she couldn't imagine ever wanting to make love to Bobby again.

She climbed from the tub and toweled off. Rubbed lotion over her body, purposely ignoring the flabby spots and the stretch marks. No more thinking tonight, she told herself as she stepped into her panties and then her pajama top. She brushed and flossed her teeth, all the while wondering why she took the time. Finally, she pulled her robe on and tied the sash around her waist and left the quiet of the bathroom behind.

The TV was on, but Teel was surprised to find Rachel on the couch. Bobby was nowhere in sight. She thought Keegan's door was still closed, but she couldn't see it very clearly from where she was standing. Rachel glanced at her, but she looked back at the TV without a word.

"Where's Dad?"

"What's wrong?" Rachel asked. She sounded like her old self. The one that had never accused Teel of ignoring her or favoring Keegan. The one that Teel had never wondered about, had never worried about.

Teel almost laughed. *What wasn't wrong?*

"He was in Keegan's room when I came home," Rachel told her. "I could hear them talking. When he came out, he grabbed a beer and went downstairs."

Bobby's office was downstairs. Teel hoped he was down there, maybe working, maybe clearing his head. Maybe both. Keegan's computer was gone from the counter. Had he given in and returned it to her? Surely not.

"Did you guys eat?" Rachel asked.

"Are you hungry?" Teel avoided her question, though not on purpose. There was no way they could keep this from Rachel. She wasn't sure she wanted to anyway. Teel needed a gauge. She needed to know how far out of touch she was, if Rachel had lived this way in high school, if Keegan was the norm, and she was living in some fantasy throwback life.

"No, I ate with Deacon." Rachel shook her head. "But I noticed the chicken still sitting in the microwave."

Damn. Teel groaned. She'd forgotten about the chicken again. She hadn't fed her husband or Keegan. No matter how angry she was with Keegan, this part of life had to go on.

"What happened?" Rachel repeated. Teel looked hard at her daughter. She thought she saw a challenge in Rachel's eyes. *Include me.* Or else what? Teel wondered.

"Oh, Rach." Teel sighed. She sat on the edge of the couch. But remembering the chicken, she jumped up again and started toward the kitchen.

"I took it out of the microwave, Mom," Rachel told her. "But I didn't know what to do with it."

"Thanks." Teel nodded and sat down again.

"It's something about Keegan, isn't it?" Rachel asked.

"Why do you say that?"

"I heard Dad talking. He was very calm, but it sounded like he was laying down the law. Keegan was crying."

Crying? Teel wondered if that meant she'd finally realized that what she'd done was horribly wrong. Hurtful. That she'd torn a family apart. Or was she still just upset for herself?

Teel pressed her lips together and then puckered them, as if for a kiss. "Yeah, Rachel. This is something about Keegan."

"I saw Dad take her laptop downstairs with him."

Teel nodded, relieved to know he hadn't given it back to her.

"What'd she do?"

"You don't know?"

"C'mon, Mom." Rachel rolled her eyes. "Keegan and I aren't exactly close."

"She's your sister."

"She's a snot."

Teel folded her arms over her chest and burrowed into the corner of the couch. "Do you have a MyFriend page?"

"No," Rachel answered. "I think it's dumb."

"Can I ask you something?" Teel cocked her head and watched Rachel as the seriousness of the situation sank into her. She could almost see the moment it seeped into her skin, because suddenly Rachel sat up straight and twisted on the couch to look at Teel.

"What?"

"Did you want to be popular when you were in high school?"

"No."

"Really. I'm not going to judge you. I just want to know."

"No." Rachel shook her head and shrugged. "I had my friends. That was all I needed. None of us cared about being popular."

Exactly what Teel would have said about Rachel and her friends through the past several years. Well...throughout Rachel's lifetime. She'd never given the impression that she needed attention. She was far too self-possessed and private for the limelight. Rachel was so reserved it had often been hard to tell if she was happy, even when she should have been bubbling with excitement. Like her sixteenth birthday. Her high school graduation.

"What did she do?" Rachel's question pulled Teel from her thoughts.

"What?"

"What did Keegan do?"

"She posted pictures of Marin making out with a boy on a MyFriend page she set up. Apparently she wanted to get back at Marin for something."

Rachel seemed to consider her words for a minute, and then finally she looked back at Teel. "That might not be such a big deal."

Teel raised her eyebrows. "Really? You would be okay with someone doing that to you?"

"Well, no. I think it's horrible. But I mean, in terms of Keegan getting into trouble. Like at school or something. Maybe the pictures weren't…that…explicit."

"I haven't seen the pictures, Rachel," Teel told her. "But the police were here earlier to question Keegan."

Teel wished she didn't feel the satisfaction she did when Rachel went pale.

"Oh. Wow." Rachel shook her head. "She said…"

"What?"

"Um." Rachel looked up at Teel and frowned. "She kept telling me the other day that she really messed up about something. But she didn't tell me this."

"Well…the girl she posted pictures of, and God help me, I hope they weren't explicit, but I sure as hell wonder, killed herself. And now her parents are splitting up." Teel stood up. Her legs felt weak. Why couldn't she just shut up? Rachel didn't need to hear this, not this way. Bobby could have told her more rationally. Teel's heart was boiling inside her, she was so angry.

"Did they arrest her?" Rachel asked quietly. Teel bit her lip and reminded herself to think before she spoke. Rachel looked small and frightened, the way Keegan should have looked earlier.

"No, they didn't." Teel padded barefoot across the hardwood to the kitchen and stared at the chicken. She hated to waste it, but better to throw it away, since it hadn't cooked properly.

"But they could," Rachel mumbled. Teel looked over her shoulder at Rachel. "Couldn't they?"

Chapter 31

TEEL

THEY HAD BEEN TOGETHER, but it was less about making love than about anger and mutual disappointment. In their daughter. Maybe in each other. And in themselves. As it had been the day Teel learned that Rick English left Jeannie, it was rough and angry. When it was over, they hadn't turned to each other. Instead, Bobby had lifted himself off her and flopped on his stomach, with his head turned away from her. Teel had rolled to her left side and buried her face in her pillow. She hadn't noticed that he hadn't said goodnight. That he hadn't said he loved her. She didn't think about that until earlier this morning when she got up. Instead, she'd lain awake half the night thinking, worrying about Keegan. Worrying that she might be arrested. Worrying that her daughter still seemed to be more concerned about being shunned by her first sexual partner than about her part in an old friend's suicide.

No amount of makeup was going to do the magic today. Anyone who looked at her would see the newest worry lines around her eyes and her mouth, and anyone who lived in a twenty mile radius of town would know just exactly what put the new lines on her face.

Having to drag Keegan out of bed and practically throw her in the shower didn't help. She understood how badly Keegan wanted to hide, to stay in bed and pretend none of this was happening. Teel had wanted to cry when the alarm went off this morning. But, Teel insisted Keegan go to school. Today was no different than yesterday, she'd told Keegan. The police had questioned her and other students. No arrests had been made. For now, they would stick to routine.

Teel turned the radio off as she drove to her school. Keegan hadn't said a word on the way to Blessed Sacrament. But Teel kept seeing her face when Teel had made the remark that no one had been arrested. The words had shocked Keegan, probably knocked the breath out of her, just as they had done to Teel when Rachel said them last night. Keegan was scared. Teel had just added a true fear to Keegan's list of worries. And yet, fear didn't mean remorse. Regret. Teel still didn't know how to reach out to Keegan, to forgive her. To forget the things she'd told her last night.

She didn't have any idea what Bobby had said to Keegan the night before. They hadn't talked. Not before or after the sex last night. Bobby was up and gone before dawn. She hadn't particularly cared this morning, because she couldn't have looked at him over a cup of coffee and thought to herself how lucky she was to have him or how sexy he was fresh from the shower or how proud she was of the work he did. She couldn't have looked at him this morning, because she was still stewing over Keegan's actions and who was to blame, who was the bad parent.

She regretted that now. Her head pounded, and even the faded, watery sunlight through her windshield made her eyes hurt. She'd washed down a couple of Advil before she'd left, but she wasn't so gullible to believe it was going to take any of this away. She should have talked to Bobby. They should have talked about what he'd said to Keegan. What sort of punishment they would impose on her. What would happen if the police came back. If she were arrested.

If she were arrested. Teel took a deep breath as she eased the Edge into the parking space she'd used nearly every school day for the past twenty years. She felt like an imposter. She belonged here. She loved it here, and until yesterday, most of her colleagues had loved her being here. And yet, today, she was so damned scared to open the car door and get out. To set the day in motion.

People were not kind when this sort of thing blew up and appeared on the town's ticker tape. Teel included herself. Who didn't have an opinion when it came to this kind of stuff? Who didn't mutter that it served someone right for being arrested for DUI? Or for under-aged drinking? Who didn't say things about the parents when someone's teen was arrested for drinking? Who didn't cluck their tongues and shake their heads when someone's kid had an accident because he or she was texting while driving?

It didn't matter that she was a good teacher. Or that Bobby was a good builder, with years upon years of satisfied clients. Or that Rachel was smart or that Keegan was a good kid. Because suddenly Keegan wasn't a good kid. This one selfish act would be enough to pull the world's disapproval down on all of them. It wasn't fair, Teel wanted to shout. It wasn't fair that her good family was going to be ripped to pieces over this, and yet, Teel thought about Jeannie and Rick. And Marin.

Of course it was fair. Keegan had done something bad

that had hurt someone else. Keegan had ripped another family to pieces. Teel knew what everyone was thinking, that she and Bobby had screwed up when teaching Keegan priorities and simple acts of kindness. She and Bobby had failed. Keegan was a bad girl, and bad girls deserved to be punished.

Teel curled her fingers around the door handle and pulled.

Face the music, Teel, she thought. If it were anyone else in this school, anyone else in this town, she knew damned well she'd be thinking the same damned thing. *This time it's us.*

She swung her hip against the door and pushed it shut. Pulled the straps of her purse and her bag up over her shoulder. Her purse and her bag carried so much about who she was inside. Her license to drive, sure, but there were more important things in her slim brown leather organizer and checkbook. Pictures of her daughters. From kindergarten to present. Notes each of them had written her when they were so young their penmanship was atrocious. A tube of Estee Lauder lipstick and a tube of Chapstick. Coupons for fast food restaurants and department stores. A note she'd scribbled to herself a month ago with the name of a song she liked, so she could find it on a CD and buy it. Her grade book and her lesson plans. All the fun things she planned for her students. Pictures her students had drawn for her. The book she was reading now about the Lincolns.

None of that mattered. No one inside this building would care about anything that made up the person she was inside. All they would see when they looked at her was Keegan and what she had done.

Teel reached the side door of the school and pulled it open. She reminded herself to breathe as she stepped inside. And then she remembered something Bobby had said. What Keegan had done was inexcusable, yes. But maybe. God, maybe, there was more to it. Maybe it wasn't simply what Keegan had done that had driven Marin to kill herself.

As she walked through the kitchen, the air grew so thick and hard she felt like she was walking through wet cement. Two upper grade teachers sat at the teacher's lunch table, heads together laughing about something. Teel reminded herself that it wasn't against any rules to laugh about something. It didn't necessarily mean they were talking about Marin or Keegan or Teel.

She decided the least amount of exposure today was a good idea and veered toward the coffee pot. Get it now and then stay in the classroom until lunch time. She wished she'd thought to bring her own lunch. Then she could have stayed there until it was time to come home.

The buzz of conversation stopped as she poured her coffee. So she knew they hadn't been talking about her. But they were watching her now and the second she walked out of the room, the game was on. She wondered for a moment how Keegan was doing. What was being said about her? To her? What had the kids said to her last year? After her tryst with the kid at the party?

Teel made a mental note to look the kid up. What was his name? Spanning? Spanner. Sean Spanner. And Carter. Right? Carter Wright. If she had any hope at all of finding anything else that might have been a contributing factor to Marin's suicide, she had to learn more about the rest of the players.

She swallowed hard as she stirred cream in her coffee. She hated this. Looking at Marin's suicide this way. Making it a game, a contest, and hoping to bring her daughter out of it relatively whole. They were way beyond getting through it unscathed. But maybe Teel could salvage something for Keegan.

"Hey."

Teel looked up at the women at the table. Sixth and eighth grade teachers. Karin Iles, single, sixth grade. Teel had always liked her. What would she know about hunkering down to save your child, though? And Liz Morgan, eighth grade teacher. Married for twenty-nine years, mother of four and grandmother of two. You'd think she might get it, Teel thought. But she knew better. Liz had always been a busy body, always involved in any bit of gossip and always looking down her nose at half the people in this building, Teel included.

Karin stood up and walked closer to Teel.

"Listen," she started, "my friend teaches at Blessed..."

Teel nodded and hoped to cut her off.

"Is it true? Did the police question Keegan yesterday?"

Karin sounded sincere, but Teel told herself not to let her guard down. Especially not in the same room with Liz Morgan.

"Yeah," Teel said quietly. She took a small drink of her coffee. It tasted like metal. She glanced at the coffee pot, but it was the same one she'd been pouring coffee from for several years. It was just her, then.

She hadn't been able to drink coffee when she was pregnant with her girls.

Teel's stomach clenched. She'd forgotten about that particular worry. Wouldn't that just beat all? Teel Alexander's daughter arrested for...for what? Okay, Teel's daughter in trouble with the police. Teel, old enough to be a grandmother, pregnant. God. Her fellow teachers would have hours of material there. Rachel and Keegan would hate her, not Bobby, because he wouldn't be the one carrying the baby. His belly wouldn't get big and round. He wouldn't be all weepy and useless. Her students, all the students here, would be freaked out realizing that people over forty do have sex and do get pregnant.

Her life would be an open book.

Teel gave herself a mental shake. Her life was, as of this moment, an open book. If she were pregnant, that was just another chapter.

"Yeah. The police talked to Keegan and a few other kids."

She wouldn't be petty enough to name names. Not yet, anyway. But she wanted it clear from the word go that it wasn't just Keegan.

"Are they thinking it wasn't a suicide?"

That jolted her awake. What the hell? Were people going to suggest Keegan had a hand in killing her? Good God.

"I don't really know, Karin." Teel felt the weight of her bag and her purse tug at her shoulder. And the weight of the world on her back. Maybe she shouldn't have made Keegan go to school.

And yet. What then? Keegan could just stay home until it all blew over? And when, exactly, would that be? What kind of message would she be sending Keegan if she allowed her to hide indefinitely?

"Is Keegan okay? Should you be with her?"

Teel thought Karin was sincere, but it crossed her mind how hurtful it would be to find out otherwise.

"Keegan's at school, Karin," she answered in a firm, but calm voice. "She's fine."

"Oh." Karin raised her eyebrows. "Well. Good." She smiled and backed away from Teel. Liz Morgan stood finally and went to the sink to rinse her coffee cup out.

"I'm sure it'll all work out fine, Teel," Liz said as she slipped past them and left the kitchen.

Teel wondered now if Karin and Liz had been discussing her and her family before she'd walked in. Or if maybe *everyone* had been talking about them already. She steeled herself for the latter, because it was a more practical thought.

"Thanks for asking, Karin." She excused herself and left

Karin standing alone in the kitchen. How she managed to get upstairs to her classroom on her trembling legs, she couldn't say.

How she planned to get through the rest of the school day, she didn't know.

Chapter 32

KEEGAN

SHE COULDN'T BELIEVE her mom made her go to school this morning. Saying nothing had changed, that she still had to go to school. *Whatever.* Everything had changed, starting with that night at the party with Sean Spanner and ending yesterday when the cops pulled her from her class to talk to her. It didn't matter that other kids were questioned. No one else made that MyFriend page, no one else posted pictures of Marin and Carter.

Speaking of the pictures, Mom would flip when she saw them. Right now, Keegan probably rated a half-step above scum, but when Mom saw the kinds of things she posted, she'd really lose it. Keegan imagined Mom packing her bags for her and kicking her out.

Okay, she wouldn't do that. *Well. Probably not.* But it was going to be bad. She would hate her, and with good reason. And through it all, Mom would probably be freaking out, wondering if she had done all that stuff with Sean Spanner and nothing NOTHING would ever be the same again.

Keegan wondered if her parents would let her live with Aunt Eve for a while. Not that Aunt Eve would be too thrilled with her for this either. Dad had been pretty calm last night. But Keegan had seen that it was a controlled fury kind of calm, not a laid-back, we'll deal with it kind of calm.

Dad had told her to buck up, because the worst was yet to come. *That* made her feel great, because nothing since starting high school had been too wonderful. He'd also said not to talk about it with anyone, but that was proving to be easy, since no one wanted to talk to her. Not even Jess. Like Jess hadn't loved the MyFriend page with all that stuff about Marin.

Jess was a bitch. Keegan had learned that the hard way. Then again, Keegan had learned the hard way that she was no better. She ranked right up there with Jess and Tiffany. Maybe she was worse.

If she lived to be one hundred, she'd never forget the look on her mom's face when she'd started talking yesterday. She'd led her mom through twists and turns of anger and disappointment and hatred and shame and back through anger again. She'd been overwhelmed. Keegan didn't blame her. But she wished that when her mom walked out of the room she would have at least hugged her. Said that even though she was angry, she still loved Keegan.

Something.

The only reason Mom had touched her or spoken to her at all today was to drag her out of bed and make her get in the shower for school. Keegan had never seen her mom so cold. The only thing that brought her any relief, any solace, was that in the middle of the night, she'd tiptoed down the hall and across the hardwood floor to her parents' bedroom door. It had been a gamble, what she might hear. When she heard her mom crying, she'd sagged against the wall in relief because maybe Mom still loved her, and guilt because she hated to be the one to make Mom cry like that.

"So, I guess Marin's mom and dad probably know you did that page, huh?"

Keegan looked up from her notebook. She'd been standing at her locker getting books for her morning classes, but apparently she'd zoned out. She glanced at Tiffany, but she didn't rise to the bait. Frankly, she was sick of the whole game. The parties and the sex and the page and trying to best Tiffany and Brandy and Jess, and she couldn't even summon the loneliness that had settled in sometime after she'd been with Sean and put everything in motion.

She reached into her locker and felt slick, shiny pages with her fingertips. Magazine pages. Great. Someone had been in her locker. Jess knew the combination. Tiffany leaned in closer to her, eyebrows lifted in anticipation. *So Jess and Tiffany were BFFS now?* Keegan rolled her eyes as she pulled the pages out just far enough to see them. Something from a *Playboy* or *Penthouse* magazine, she didn't want to stand there and look at it too long and draw attention to herself. From other students. From her teachers. They were already treating her like she was Adolf Hitler.

"What's that?" Tiffany leaned closer still, but Keegan shoved it back in her locker. She'd seen her name written on one of the pictures. Great. So now everyone was going to go back to talking about her and Sean instead of Marin. Just what she needed.

"Nothing."

"It looked like—"

Keegan slammed her locker door shut, just missing Tiffany's fingertips. "Don't you have something better to do?"

Tiffany laughed. "Of course I do," she snapped. "I just saw you by yourself and felt sorry for you."

"Don't feel sorry for me."

"Okay, I won't." Tiffany shrugged and walked away. Keegan stared after her for several moments. The bell rang. She was late. *Nothing new there*. Hell, maybe she should just turn around and walk out. Go home.

But what was there at home?

She didn't want someone like Tiffany feeling sorry for her. Because with friends like Tiffany and Jess, she didn't need enemies. Too bad she hadn't learned that without the benefit of firsthand experience.

———

RACHEL WAS in the kitchen when she got home. Keegan was embarrassed to feel a little flicker of hope when she saw her. Maybe Rachel would still talk to her. School had been hell. The only thing that kept her there all day had been the thought that cutting too many classes might hurt her grades badly enough that she might end up in summer school.

Her sister was studying something, drinking a bottle of water. She glanced at Keegan when she walked in, but she didn't say anything. At least Keegan didn't read hate all over her face.

"Mom home?" Keegan asked quietly.

"No."

Keegan saw that Rachel was eating an Oreo. Her stomach growled. She'd skipped lunch, choosing to hide out in the library rather than sit by herself in the cafeteria. It couldn't have been any worse if she'd have had a target painted on her back. Marin's friend Kate had sneered at her between sixth and seventh hour and called her a bitch.

That old childhood saying came to mind: Sticks and stones may break my bones, but words will never hurt me. Keegan had stewed over how wrong that was as she'd walked to her seventh hour class. Words hurt. Those kinds of bruises hurt so much deeper and longer than the ones sticks and stones left.

The fact that she'd hurt someone that way only made her feel worse.

"Are there any of those left?"

"Huh?" Rachel looked up. Keegan squirmed when Rachel took her time looking at her. She turned away and dropped her backpack on the floor at her feet. "Yeah. They're in the pantry."

Keegan nodded, still with her back to Rachel, and opened the pantry. She dug out an Oreo and shoved it into her mouth whole.

"You really fucked up, Keegan," Rachel said quietly. Keegan looked at Rachel over her shoulder. Her eyes filled with tears, and her mouth was still full of cookie. She swallowed and choked on the cookie and nodded.

"I know."

"You've got Mom a mess."

"I know."

"I've never seen her like this." Rachel leaned back and stretched her arms over her head.

"She hasn't even seen the pictures," Keegan mumbled.

"What were you thinking?" Rachel picked up her pencil and tapped it on the countertop. "You had to know you'd get caught."

Keegan turned to face Rachel and rested her butt against the counter. She shrugged. "Getting even."

Rachel mouthed the word wow and curled back over her textbook.

"Wow what?"

"Remind me never to cross you," Rachel said without looking up.

"She was dating Sean."

"And Sean is?"

"The guy."

"Oh." Rachel looked up. "The hot basketball player."

Keegan nodded.

"I think you're crazy," Rachel said softly. She glanced up at Keegan and shrugged. "Sorry. But I don't get it."

"Do you hate me, too?"

"Who hates you?"

Keegan sighed. "Everyone at school. Marin's mom and dad."

"They have the right to hate you, don't they?"

"Yeah."

"Do you even feel bad about her, Keegan? Because all I'm hearing is how bad people are treating you, and Marin's dead."

Keegan's throat tightened. She blinked and then ducked her head when the tears started.

"Yes."

"Really?"

"I didn't mean for her to kill herself," Keegan wailed. "People talked about me, after what I did, and then people were talking about her. I didn't think she'd…"

"You didn't think," Rachel repeated and nodded.

"So you hate me?"

"No, I don't hate you." Rachel sat up straight again. "I just don't get you."

"Didn't you ever wanna be popular?" Keegan heard the edge in her voice. She knew she sounded pathetic, but she couldn't stop herself. She'd had so many words stored up from days, from weeks of not talking to anyone and she'd had *these* words locked inside forever. Since she'd had sex with Sean and walked out of that room feeling like she'd left so much more than her virginity there. She'd felt so empty since that night, and she hadn't wanted to say *that* to anyone. Thank God, she hadn't said that to anyone, because she could just imagine all of them, Tiffany, Brandy and Jess and all the guys, throwing *that* back in her face at school.

She'd shoved the magazine pages deep into her backpack when she left school. Lewd pictures of women, with her name and Marin's name on them. Phone numbers and guys' names, including Sean and Carter's. That had hurt. She'd even cried, a tiny sob as she'd thrown her backpack over her shoulder and walked out of school. She'd managed to hang onto the tears until she was a few blocks away.

"No," Rachel answered her now. "I didn't like half the kids in my class. The popular ones. Why would I wanna change who I was just so I could hang out with them?"

"Do you think I did that?" Keegan's voice was a gruff whisper.

"What?"

"Did I change? To be with them?" Keegan looked up boldly and met Rachel's eyes. "Or is this really me? Am I really a bitch?"

Rachel held her gaze, but she was slow to answer.

"I…" She shrugged. "I don't know, Keegan. You've been like this, so obsessed with this crap, for so long. I don't really know the real you anymore."

Keegan squeezed her eyes shut. She couldn't stand to look at Rachel for another minute. Rachel, the perfect sister. The kind one. The compassionate one. She didn't even have to try, and everyone loved her.

She took a deep breath and then leaned over to pick up her backpack. "Would you take me to Walmart later?"

"Why?" Rachel, who had already gone back to her book,

looked up again. "There's a whole box of tampons in the bathroom."

"No." Keegan shook her head. She wiped at her face with her fingers. "I need...I need a new lock for my locker."

Rachel opened her mouth, but apparently changed her mind. Instead, she just nodded.

Chapter 33

TEEL

STILL ON AUTO-PILOT, Teel pulled out of the school parking lot and headed home. She was happy as hell to leave school for the day, but she had no burning desire to go home. Home meant dealing with Keegan. And she was no closer to knowing how to do that now than she had been yesterday when her daughter confessed to the parties, hooking up... Was it hooking up if it was only one guy, one time... *Was it only one guy, one time?* How would Teel ever know? How would she ever trust Keegan again?

And the pictures. The...what? Teel asked herself as she drove through town. How could everything look so normal? Her life had shattered yesterday, and here everything was the same. The convenience stores still advertised gas for ridiculous money and cartons of cigarettes, and sub shops still had two for one prices and the chiropractor's office on the corner still had that stupid little jingle on their sign: 'Have a nice fall? See us on your next trip.'

Revenge scheme? Was that it? Teel had been hurt by friends, and she'd been angry at friends. But she'd never felt a need for revenge. Nothing on this scale. She wondered again about Bobby's theory. That maybe there was more to Marin's suicide. It was possible. Marin might have had other kids bothering her. She might have been pregnant. She might have been reacting to the tension in her house if what Jeannie said was true.

But it didn't matter. In Teel's mind, her daughter had thrown a knife and it had hit her target, and whether it was the death blow or not, Keegan was guilty.

Her head still hurt. There had been a brief respite, just after lunch, when the pain had eased. But it was back, and now she was so tired, she could barely keep her eyes open. Maggie hadn't said a word. She'd simply walked into her classroom and put her arms around her. The first bell had just rung, and there were a handful of students in the room. Teel had wanted to protest, to ask Maggie to leave her alone. But she'd needed the support. The friendship. Instead of arguing, she'd thrown her arms around her friend and hung on, all the while thinking about how bad things were probably going to get and praying that Maggie would still walk into her room and care on the worst day, whatever it might bring.

Maggie had steered Teel to the farthest corner of the room and turned her away from her students. She'd stood with her arm protectively around Teel's waist until the tightness had eased in Teel's throat and she'd blinked the tears away.

"Okay?" she'd whispered.

Of course not. Maybe not ever again. But Teel hadn't said that. She'd pulled herself together and nodded and plastered a cheery Mrs. Alexander smile on her face when she'd turned back to her classroom.

And she'd ended her day even bigger. A sit down chat with her boss. He'd even splurged and bought her a Coke. Teel wished now that she'd been able to drink more of it; the caffeine might have done her some good.

Concern. She'd definitely seen that he was concerned for her and her family. For Keegan. And his school. That burned, and yet, she couldn't blame him. Well, she could, and she did. But she knew if she were in his shoes, she'd feel the same way. Her daughter had been questioned by the police about a student's suicide. That alone implied guilt, even without an arrest. How would the parents of her students feel about that? How would they feel about her? Would any rally around her and show support or was this going to end up feeling like a witch hunt?

Not so much a witch hunt, after all, she was right there in her classroom for anyone to find. More like a burning at the stake. How long would she be welcome on her job?

You're getting ahead of yourself, Teel, she thought. For God's sake, nothing's happened. Nothing official. A teen suicide might merit investigation, but that didn't mean anyone would be arrested. It didn't have to mean she and her family would be shunned. Liz Morgan's son had been arrested for drinking and driving when he was seventeen. That had blown over fairly quickly. He hadn't hurt anyone, but he'd wrecked his car and done several hundred dollars' worth of damage to the bank building where Eve worked.

Eve. God. She needed to call Eve. She wondered when Dennis was remarrying his new bimbo. If Eve was still over him, or if she'd already waffled and decided she'd forgive him if he brought her flowers and that one package Eve could never seem to turn down.

Rachel's car was in the garage. At least she and Rachel had had a civil conversation last night. About Keegan. She missed Rachel. She missed sitting with her over a glass of tea and cookies and talking. Rachel used to talk to her about her future, her plans for medical school. About a movie she'd watched on the Lifetime channel or a book she'd just started or finished. Now it seemed their every conversation revolved around Keegan.

Keegan. It always came back to Keegan. Is that what Keegan had wanted? Was there a problem at home that Teel had been completely blind to? Did she and Bobby not give Keegan enough attention? God, that can't be it, she thought. Obviously she wasn't the perfect parent, but she'd always been involved in her girls' lives. So had Bobby. Neither of the girls had ever wanted for attention or love.

So, what, then? That whole in crowd thing? Seriously? Being "Someone" meant that much to Keegan? Teel couldn't wrap her mind around a fourteen-year-old Keegan allowing a guy to use her. She pulled the Edge into the garage, careful to watch Rachel's car beside her so she didn't bump it.

Her first time had been less than great, and she'd been three years older than Keegan. And she'd been with a boy she'd been dating for a few months. She leaned back against the headrest in the car and closed her eyes. It had to have hurt, and then to have to hustle around and find her clothes —had she even fully undressed?—and for this kid, Spanner? to be drunk and then coming out of that bedroom with people watching her.

Teel felt her eyes burn again. It wasn't what she'd wanted for Keegan. For either of her girls. She'd never dreamed that she'd be privy to any details, and mostly, she didn't want them. Because now that she had them, she couldn't stop imagining how hurt and embarrassed Keegan must have been.

She wondered if Keegan had come home that night. Or if she'd spent the night at Jess's house. If she'd come home, had there been some sign? Something she'd missed? Surely a mother should know when something so huge happened to her baby girl.

It wasn't rape, though. Keegan had told her that. It wouldn't stop Bobby from tearing the guy apart limb from limb, but Keegan had made it clear she'd wanted to do it.

She sighed when her cell phone rang.

"Hello?"

"Mom?"

It was Rachel. She wondered if she and Keegan would ever talk again. Beyond the cold, stilted words they'd had this morning or the burning hot, emotional words exchanged yesterday.

"What?"

"When are you coming home?"

"I'm in the garage."

"Oh."

"What's wrong?" Teel asked as she pushed her door open and climbed out of the car.

"I dunno. Keegan's kind of freakin' out."

Teel shoved her phone in her pocket and hurried into the house. Keegan's bedroom door was closed. She stood for a moment and listened. Nothing. No music. No voices. No crying.

Rachel appeared at the other end of the hall. She motioned for Teel to come to her.

"What do you mean? Is she in her room?" Teel asked quickly.

"She is now. But she asked me if I hated her, and she just started crying."

Teel took a deep breath and then tucked her hair behind her ear. She rubbed her hand over her neck and then let it drop.

"What'd you tell her, Rachel?"

"You think I'd tell her I hate her?"

Teel shrugged. "I guess you're an adult, and you're entitled to how you feel."

Rachel shook her head. "I don't hate her. I just don't get her."

"That makes two of us," Teel mumbled. She dug her phone from her pants pocket and set it on the counter.

"Mom?"

"Hmm?"

"Are you okay?"

Teel glanced at Rachel, touched that she would ask. How easy it would be to say no. To break down. To cry.

Rachel didn't deserve that.

"I'm fine," she assured Rachel. "Just tired."

"You and Dad are okay, right?" Rachel fidgeted with a pencil and then started packing up her books.

"Why do you ask that?" Teel leaned on the counter. She hated to see Rachel grab her things and rush out of the kitchen like she couldn't stand to be in the same room with her. Teel had to fix dinner. She'd like to have Rachel's company, some conversation. Something normal.

"I don't know." Rachel shrugged. "This is just weird." She continued to avoid Teel's eyes. "I saw a for sale sign in Jeannie and Rick's yard. And I haven't seen Rick around since...well...It's just been Jeannie and her sisters..."

"Dad and I are good, Rach." Teel covered Rachel's hand with hers. "This is weird. It's really weird, and it's really hard. And probably it's going to get worse, before it gets better."

Rachel looked up then, and Teel saw that she was fighting tears. "But it will? Get better?"

Teel saw a ten-year-old Rachel asking for reassurance, rather than her nineteen-year-old college student.

"It will."

Rachel nodded, grabbed her backpack from a barstool, grabbed her book in her other hand and disappeared down the hallway.

Teel slumped against the counter. "It's gotta get better," she whispered to the empty kitchen.

Chapter 34

TEEL

SHE'D PICKED up a Clear Blue Easy last night, but she hadn't used it yet. Teel didn't have the guts. She was scared out of her wits that she was pregnant, *how wrong to be that worried about it on this end of life, as opposed to the scary high school and college days,* and the only way she could deal with the fear was to fold it up into a tiny little square and tuck it away in the back of her mind.

Rachel had caught her before she left to go to Walmart, and Teel had held her breath. She was afraid Rachel would want to go with her, and the last thing she needed was to be sneaking around Walmart, trying to hide a pregnancy test from her daughter. But Rachel had only asked if she would get a new padlock for Keegan's locker. She hadn't explained anything, but it wasn't that hard to figure out. Someone was jacking with Keegan, apparently someone Keegan had trusted and given her combination to.

Teel didn't like shopping discount stores on a good day.

She couldn't drive through the parking lot without grumbling and even cussing a blue streak some days, and she hated how half the city seemed to congregate in every aisle. Some of the cashiers took three years and a day to ring up her purchases, and she always spent too damned much. Even if she went in for a ten dollar purchase, she never left without dropping at least fifty.

Last night, she'd parked at the end of a row and walked almost leisurely to the automatic doors. It had been cool out, but not uncomfortably so. Bobby was at home watching a movie, and she hated to think it, but babysitting Keegan. They'd locked her laptop in the closet in his office, though Bobby had told Teel when he'd gone through it the night before, he hadn't found anything incriminating. Some emails to and from Jess about boys and who was hot and who wasn't and how much of a bitch someone named Tiffany was. But no pictures.

Teel had told him Keegan said she'd taken down the page with the pictures of Marin. Apparently, she'd decided they didn't need to be anywhere on her computer. Maybe still on her camera. Her phone. They probably needed to take the phone, too. At least for a while.

But with Bobby at home with Keegan and Rachel out with Deacon, Teel reveled in being alone. She'd breathed deeply outside, and the air had been so fresh and cool it had almost zapped her headache. Inside, though she only needed a home pregnancy test and a padlock, she got a cart and pushed it up and down aisles she didn't need to walk. She compared prices on Surf and All laundry detergent, though she'd used Tide for what seemed like a hundred years. She studied the nutrition information on six different kinds of breads, before moving on and not putting any in her cart.

In electronics, she moved slowly through the DVD aisles, and the boxed TV series made her sad. All the shows

they used to watch together as a family. *Gilmore Girls.*
Everybody Loves Raymond. It seemed so unfair that those
fictional families were packed so neatly into those little
boxes and displayed with their smiling faces on the covers.
Teel's family had had smiling faces for years, and no one
had cared to look too closely. Now that there was bound to
be drama, everyone was going to stop and take a closer
look.

She picked up a padlock in the hardware department and
wondered who had been bugging Keegan. What had he or
she put in Keegan's locker? She didn't wonder enough to ask
Keegan. She still didn't know how to look at Keegan and
pretend that yesterday's words hadn't been said. She didn't
want to talk to her, because she was still so angry. Angry
about what Keegan had done to herself, but even more (and
it pained Teel to admit this, because it was possibly the most
selfish thought she'd ever had) angry that Keegan had drug
the whole family into this mess.

Who knew there were so many home pregnancy tests
now? Two young girls stood head to head in that aisle and
giggled as they tried to decide which brand to buy. Teel
watched them and thought how easily it could have been
Keegan. Pregnant. At fourteen. Maybe not pregnant by the
grace of God. Neither of these girls wore wedding rings, and
Teel would bet that neither of them was a day older than
sixteen.

She looked away when they finally chose a box and
turned to walk out of the aisle. A week ago, if she'd have seen
them in this aisle, buying a pregnancy test, she'd have judged.
She would have judged the girls, and she would have judged
their parents, most especially their mothers. The hell of it is,
even with what Keegan had confessed to the other day, Teel
still felt that snap judgment inside. She still didn't understand kids who wanted to grow up so fast. What was there

about adulthood that was so appealing that teens were suddenly racing each other to get there?

Apparently, she'd missed the boat. Because while she loved her life, and while she was happily married and she loved her kids, she couldn't say she wished she'd been able to jump into a life of working and worrying about money and worrying about her children and their health and their education and her husband's business any sooner.

She dropped a Clear Blue Easy box in the cart and continued on through the store, stopping when she saw Christmas trees. Christmas trees? But. It was just August. And hot. And they were just back in school.

Except. Well. Marin had killed herself in September. Teel moved slowly to a fully decorated tree on display. It was gaudy and ugly, and it made her stomach ache. She reached out and fingered a dusty gold bell. October. They were nearing the middle of October. Where was the Halloween stuff? What was the rush with Christmas?

She looked around and realized she'd walked right through the Halloween costumes and decorations. Keegan and her friends, Jess and a few girls Teel didn't know, had dressed in costume last year and gone to a party. She wondered now if that had been the party. Doubtful. Keegan had been dressed like a monkey and Jess had been a banana. Probably not many teenage boys would want to make out with a girl dressed like a monkey.

What would Christmas be like for Jeannie and Rick? She hadn't seen the for sale sign in their yard the day before, but small wonder. She'd been a million miles from earth as she drove home. She saw it this morning, though, on the way to work. It had chilled her, and she'd turned up the heat in the Edge for about two minutes, and then she'd started sweating and had to turn the heat off and put her window down an inch.

She couldn't imagine a Christmas in her home, without one of her daughters there. Not like the future, where maybe her girls would be married and unable to come back every year, though that would be hard enough. But gone. Dead. It would all be empty. Pointless.

She ached so deep inside, thinking about Jeannie and Rick, and the divorce and the move that she felt sick. Her eyes burned, and she was afraid she might cry. Right there, in the middle of Walmart, she might break down and sob. And God, wouldn't everybody know then? As if they didn't already.

Pushing the almost empty cart back toward the check-out lanes, Teel saw Liz Morgan and her husband. Just who she wanted to talk to. She hoped she could duck into a side aisle, but Liz looked up and saw her.

"Hey, Teel. How're you holding up?"

Funny how she was furious with Keegan and willing to dole out any punishment she could think of, which apparently right now was the silent treatment, but completely unwilling to let anyone else judge her daughter.

Holding up? For God's sake, the police asked Keegan a few questions. That was it. Zip. Let it go.

"I'm fine, thanks, Liz." She smiled, though her lips felt cold and stiff and it suddenly hit her how pathetic little was in her cart. *The Clear Blue Easy box. Shit. Shit. Shit.*

If Liz looked down and saw it, everyone at school would know before the first bell rang.

Teel angled her cart as if she were going to walk down a stationery aisle. She noticed Liz crane her neck to look at her cart, but she prayed the box was tossed in at just the right angle and Liz wouldn't actually be able to read the words.

Wouldn't it be great if the whole damned school knew she'd bought the pregnancy test, and she hadn't even talked to Bobby about it yet? It'd be even worse if Liz assumed she was buying it for Rachel or Keegan.

"Gotta get some groceries," Liz said with a smile, and Teel called goodbye as she turned her back on the other woman and pretended to be interested in a pack of Sharpie permanent markers.

She let her hand fall away from the markers as she glanced to her left and saw that Liz was gone. *Thank God.* Permanent markers. She looked from the Sharpies to a bag of five erasable pens. She prayed that what Keegan had done was erasable. That the pictures she'd posted hadn't been the driving force behind Marin's suicide.

That someday her family might pull itself back together and be normal. She wouldn't even ask for happy right now. Just normal.

Ready to get the hell out of there, Teel'd grabbed the lock and the pregnancy test and walked away, leaving the cart parked there. She stood in the express lane, and then she worried that Liz might come back by or she would see someone else she knew, so she grabbed a magazine to cover the items in her hands.

A women's magazine. Her eyes caught the big bold letters on the side, announcing a featured article about cutting stress from your life and living fancy free. Teel almost laughed. *If you thought you could cut stress from your life and live fancy free forever, the joke was on you.*

Teel had learned that the hard way.

She yanked the keys from the ignition and pushed her door open immediately. She was still scared. If anything, today was worse, because Liz might have seen that damned box. But she couldn't hide out in her car every day. This was her place of employment, but more than that, her classroom, her students were her joy. She loved being here; she loved the kids. She would dare any of her colleagues to say something to her.

And go from there.

Hiding only made her look guilty. That thought tripped her up. She adjusted the straps of her purse and her bag on her shoulder to hide the way her steps had faltered. Guilty. Well, maybe she was guilty of poor parenting, because Keegan was guilty of...something. Teel didn't want to take the time to put a name to what Keegan had done. Thoughtless, selfish and stupid worked well enough for now.

Teel intended to take a big breath to fortify herself, to steel herself for whatever lay in wait inside the school building. But Karin Isles walked up right behind her, and Teel figured if hiding made her look guilty, then needing to fortify herself to face a possible attack made her look guilty *and* defensive.

"Good morning." Karin's smile was so genuine it was contagious. In fact, it made Teel forget everything and smile as she returned Karin's greeting.

Teel wasn't surprised to find Liz already at the lunch table, drinking a cup of coffee. She wondered if Liz had a life at home or if she lived on the school grapevine. She gave Liz a once over and noticed that her hair had gone completely gray and that the fingers around her coffee cup were so thick that her wedding ring seemed to be choking her.

Still hoping like hell that Liz hadn't seen the box or that Liz had a shred of human decency in her and wouldn't say if she had seen it, Teel gave herself a mental shake and walked toward the coffee pot. She wasn't an uncharitable person, and she didn't like feeling so hateful toward anyone, especially someone she saw on a daily basis. This mental half-crouch she was in was making her whole body and head and heart hurt. She felt as if she were a snake, coiled tight and ready to strike at anyone who spoke out against her or

Keegan. Or like a mouse, poised and ready to run and hide as a huge cat's paw descended on her.

She poured herself a cup and added cream and tasted it. Metal again. Damn. She'd loved the smell of coffee when she was pregnant, but she'd never been able to drink it. It had never tasted good and four of five mornings, she'd be in the bathroom tossing it back up. Which was interesting when she couldn't sprint and get to the teacher's lounge and restroom and had to use the student girls' room.

"Morning, Teel."

Teel looked up as a smiling Liz approached her.

"Hey."

"Coffee?" Liz nodded at Teel's cup as she refilled her own. "Must have been negative. I remember how you couldn't keep a swallow down when you were pregnant with the girls."

Teel lifted her chin. At least they were alone in the kitchen.

"Unless."

"What?"

"It *was* for you. *Wasn't* it?"

Teel thought quickly. She would never allow any of them to think one of her daughters was pregnant. She would just have to play to any compassion Liz might have buried inside.

She nodded and set her cup down. "It doesn't taste great."

Liz gave her a knowing smile. "Bless your heart," Liz said with a laugh. She reached out and squeezed Teel's shoulder. "I wouldn't want to be starting over."

Teel opened her mouth to say something, but Liz turned and walked out of the kitchen before she could decide what. Should she tell Liz she hadn't even done the test, therefore she didn't know that she was starting over? Should she laugh it off and say it was negative, but the stress was killing her? Should she appeal to Liz's desire to be a part of a big, juicy secret and tell her Bobby didn't even know yet? That she didn't want anyone else to know until she could talk to Bobby.

No. Teel walked to the sink and poured the coffee out. No. Because Liz Morgan would twist that around and soon the whole school would think she was having an affair and the reason she hadn't told Bobby was that the baby wasn't his.

"I just met Liz on the steps," Maggie said as she swept into the kitchen. She grabbed the boiling tea kettle from the stove and poured water in her cup. "She had this big ol' smile on her face. Think she got some last night?"

Teel nearly dropped her cup. She snorted and looked up at Maggie. Their eyes met, and the laughter bubbled up and out, almost explosively.

Maggie dropped a tea bag in her cup of hot water, and they walked side by side back to their classrooms.

"Still on for lunch?" she asked when she stopped at her door.

Teel opened her mouth to say no, but Maggie put a hand up to stop her.

"If you don't want to, Teel, I understand. But."

"But what?"

"Maybe it would be good for you. To get away from everything for a couple of hours."

Maybe it would. But Teel knew better, and she suspected Maggie did, too. First law of parenting. You could remove yourself physically from a situation, but you could never really get away from everything for any length of time.

Parenting was a full time, forever job.

Chapter 35

Teel

WHEN EVE TAPPED at the front door and let herself in, Teel was on the phone with her mom. She was a heap of nerves, bundled so tight she thought she might combust if she didn't keep moving. Her mom had been alternating between worrying about Keegan, stewing over the terrible things Keegan had done (and she didn't know the half of it,) and catching Teel up on her recent trip to St. Louis, as well as the state of her yard and her trees and plants. Teel didn't know if she was just talking, trying to take Teel's mind off everything else or what. But she was happy to let her talk, as she held the phone between her ear and her shoulder and scrubbed the refrigerator out.

Eve, dressed in old jeans and a plain yellow T-shirt, plopped her purse and keys on the counter, which Teel knew was a declaration that she was in for the long haul. All the biting words between them from the last few days had been tossed aside, the hatchet was buried, including the handle.

Squatting in front of the refrigerator, sweat trickling down her back, and a nasty kink in her neck from holding the phone for so long, Teel twisted just enough to see her sister and catch her eye.

She mouthed 'thanks,' and Eve simply nodded. Rather than pester Teel about who was on the phone, Eve opened the cabinet at the far end of the counter and started pulling out odds and ends, including the rolling pin Teel hadn't been able to find the last time she'd needed it. Teel appreciated how well Eve knew her just then; she had joined in cleaning because she knew they'd get more said than if Teel stopped and they sat together on the deck. Lack of movement would tie Teel's tongue, and she'd sit and stare at the houses and the trees and the way the setting sun melted into the horizon, and she'd feel worse instead of better.

"Mom?" Eve asked when Teel stood a few minutes later and said *thanks* and *goodbye* and *I love you, too.*

"Yeah."

"She pretty upset?" Eve was dusting the rolling pin and the salad shooter and everything else she'd pulled from the cabinet. Teel had to laugh, though she felt like laughing too hard would make her cry and if she started crying, she might never stop.

"She is," Teel mumbled, "And she doesn't know half of what Keegan did."

"So it's true?" Eve asked. Teel pushed the sleeves of her sweatshirt up and eyeballed the refrigerator contents, scattered helter-skelter on the countertop. "Keegan did it?"

Teel nodded and grabbed the milk and juice. "I can't believe this, Eve," she said softly. "I can't believe the mess she's made of things."

Eve set the salad shooter down and stepped closer to Teel. Teel felt something inside tear as Eve put her arms around her. She cried softly for a moment, but she was still afraid to let go. To cry it out. Those kinds of tears were for the dark of night in Bobby's arms.

"Is she here?" Eve rubbed her hands up over Teel's back.

Teel stepped back and wiped her eyes.

"She's in her room." She took a deep breath and then picked up the ketchup, mustard, and Miracle Whip to put them in the refrigerator door. "She's always in her room. She won't come out here with us."

"Teel, she's hurting," Eve said gently. "She's probably embarrassed. Ashamed. Scared."

"I know." Teel swallowed hard. "I know. I just…I don't know…I don't know what to do. I don't know how to talk to her. What to say."

"Because of the pictures? Of Marin? Have you seen them?"

"No, and no." Teel continued to restock the refrigerator and considered what to do next. Maybe a good old-fashioned scrub for the oven. Self-clean never seemed to do a damned thing anyway. "She had sex with some kid at a party last year. She thought it was her ticket to the in crowd."

"Keegan?" Eve dropped the lid to the tea kettle. It clanged hard and loud on the counter and then fell to the floor, making even more noise. "Sorry," she winced and leaned over to pick it up.

Teel nodded.

"When she was a freshman?"

"Apparently, the guy's never even looked at her since. Like he doesn't remember her or what happened." Teel spoke quietly, aware that Keegan could come out of her room and hear them at any moment. "And he probably doesn't, because he was drunk when it happened."

"Oh Teel," Eve whispered. "I'm so sorry."

"How could I have missed this, Eve?" Teel squinted as tears filled her eyes again.

Eve shook her head. "Huh-uh. Don't do this. It's not your fault. It's not…"

"Really?" Teel said sarcastically. "Shouldn't I have known that Keegan was doing this? Shouldn't I have known that she was sneaking out to parties and having sex and dealing with gossip and…"

"How?" Eve asked and stopped Teel's rant. "How could you have known? Keegan's sharp, Teel. You know that. She's a damned smart girl, and she's a teenager. This is what teenagers do."

"It is? This? Screw around with a stranger just to be cool? Start a campaign against an old friend because she's dating the boy she messed around with?"

"It's a bit extreme, and yes, considering that she's your daughter, it's very extreme," Eve admitted. "But, you can't blame yourself. This isn't your fault."

"How can it not be my fault? I raised her…"

"You and Bobby raised her together," Eve corrected her. "And you and Bobby raised Rachel together. Has Rachel ever done anything like this? Anything?"

"No."

"Shit happens, Teel. Keegan messed up. Assigning blame isn't going to change anything."

Teel nodded. "So. Everybody knows?"

"Yeah, probably everybody." Eve shrugged. "They don't matter. Nobody matters, but you and your family. Okay? One day at a time, we'll get through this."

"What about Marin's family?"

Eve took a deep breath and exhaled slowly. She met Teel's eyes and nodded.

"I know. I know." She threw her hands up in surrender. "It matters. They matter. It all matters, and it just makes it worse. I know, Teel."

"She could've gotten pregnant, Eve."

"I know."

Teel turned away from Eve and closed the refrigerator.

"I just keep thinking about it. About my baby. With some boy in some strange bedroom. If it hurt. What she was thinking. What's been said to her. About her."

Teel leaned against the refrigerator. She ducked her head to her hands as the tears came again.

"I keep thinking about it, and it hurts. It hurts me so much that she'd do this, and that I wasn't there for her..."

"You couldn't have known," Eve reminded her. Teel tensed when Eve laid her hand on her back.

"I hate it that I wasn't there for her to talk to," Teel said again, "but Eve, I'm so angry and I'm so disappointed, I can't talk to her. I can't be there for her now."

"Teel, it's okay." Eve squeezed her shoulder. "It's okay. You need time. It's just gonna take time."

"I feel like a horrible mom," Teel cried. "She probably hates me. But I can't even look at her right now."

"Then let Bobby be there for her until you can," Eve said gently. "You're not alone. You have Bobby to lean on. Bobby's crazy about the girls, Teel. You have Rachel to help you. You have me."

Teel turned and leaned her back against the refrigerator.

"I know, Eve." She nodded. She rubbed her face again and tucked her hair behind her ears. "I know Bobby and I are in this together, but she's my daughter. I feel like I let her down, and I feel very much alone with that."

"You didn't let her down." Eve shook her head. "Honey, she let you down. You've taught her right from wrong, and she made a bad choice. That doesn't make her a bad kid. It means she made a bad choice."

"Having sex when she was fourteen was a bad choice," Teel told Eve. "What she did to Marin is different. It's so much bigger, Eve."

"I know."

Quiet fell between them, but it was a good quiet. Teel still hurt all over, both real and imagined pains, but she felt better for having talked. Knowing that Eve hadn't taken her angry words too personally eased some of the burden from her shoulders. She finished restocking the refrigerator, and then she started on the cabinet next to it. Canned goods. She could work on it for the rest of the evening, although at some point, she would need to start dinner.

"How's Rach?" Eve asked a while later.

"Okay, I guess."

"This is hard for her, too."

"It is."

"Is she home?"

"She's at class." Teel, tired of squatting, sat on her butt in front of the cabinet. "She hasn't been spending much time here. She's either at class or with Deacon."

"He seemed like a good kid."

"Yeah, I guess so," Teel agreed.

"You're just worried about her getting serious with Deacon."

Teel glanced up at Eve and smiled. "Of course I am."

"This is hard, Teel," Eve said quietly. "But it'll pass."

"Have you heard from Dennis?"

"No." Eve raised her eyebrows. "I'm assuming he's on some beach, drinking and screwing his new bride's brains out."

"You okay with that?"

Eve shrugged. "I guess. It's time to move on."

"What in the world does he have that keeps you going back?"

Eve blushed and laughed softly. "He's got some moves."

"Apparently."

"I was out the other night," Eve said hesitantly. "Just went for dinner with a friend. And ended up hanging out with another friend. This guy Dennis and I know."

"A guy? You sure you're ready for that?"

"We drank a couple of beers and watched a soccer game on ESPN at the bar." Eve grinned. "It was just...fun. I guess."

Teel nodded. "Do I know him?"

The doorbell rang. Eve offered Teel a hand and helped her up from the floor.

"No, you probably don't know him," she answered. Teel glanced down the hallway at Keegan's closed bedroom door as she crossed the hardwood to the front door.

Her stomach clenched when she recognized Detectives Smith and Rose on the front porch.

"Mrs. Alexander."

"Detectives." Her voice was as cold as her hands. She crossed her arms over her chest. "What can I do for you?"

"Is Keegan home?"

"Yes."

"We'd like to speak with her again if we could." Smith looked past Teel into the family room. Teel felt Eve's presence behind her.

"Is it really necessary?"

"It is, Mrs. Alexander." Teel heard the regret in his voice. She must have swayed on her feet, because suddenly Eve's hand was on her shoulder. "Could you let her know we're here?"

"I'll get her," Eve whispered and then her hand was gone from her shoulder, and Teel was cold and her legs trembled. She wished she could rewind time and go back two years.

Keegan had changed into jeans after school. Face scrubbed clean of makeup, she looked to be no older than twelve. Teel's heart quickened. She needed to call Bobby.

It was time to put aside her anger and be there for Keegan. She had to be strong.

"Ms. Alexander, we'd like to ask you a few more questions." Rose.

Teel stepped back to allow them to enter. She intended to usher them to the dining room table.

"We'll need her down at the station, Mrs. Alexander," Smith said apologetically.

"Excuse me?"

"We'd like to talk to Keegan at the station."

"Why?"

"Standard procedure, m'am," he answered.

"You spoke with her here last time," she reminded him.

"Yes, m'am." He nodded. She considered punching him. Pictured his teeth going down his throat. She'd never hit anyone. Anything. Rather than his teeth going down his throat, it would be her knuckles sore and bruised and an arrest for assaulting an officer of the law.

And it wouldn't change what was happening with Keegan.

"We just have a few more questions for Keegan. We'd like for her to take a look at some stuff on our computers."

Teel wished again that Bobby were here. Keegan looked at her with huge, haunted eyes. Teel felt as if she were in a car, bearing down on a doe that was too skittish to move out of the road.

"Mommy?"

"It won't take long," Detective Rose said. "Mrs. Alexander, maybe you could drive her down?"

Keegan looked at Teel. Tears dripped from her already raw and swollen face.

"Mommy, please. Please don't make me go."

Teel glanced at Eve.

"Go."

Eve hurried to the kitchen and grabbed Teel's purse and keys. Teel stood rooted to the spot, looking from Eve to the detectives who waited for them on the front porch. Her daughter looked so small, so fragile, caught there in the middle.

Her stomach rolled.

"Go. I'll call Bobby." Eve rushed forward then and hugged her. "I'll wait here for Rachel. You go."

Teel nodded and finally her body moved. She and Keegan walked down the hall. She felt like an executioner as she helped Keegan into the Edge.

Chapter 36

KEEGAN

SHE CRIED ALL the way to the police station, and still she knew it wouldn't change the way her mom felt about her. She wasn't crying about Marin, not right now. Keegan was so damned scared, she thought she might pee her pants. At least they'd had her mom drive her, instead of throwing her in a cop car like they do on TV. But that didn't make the shaking stop. She huddled in her seat and tried to make herself as small as possible. Maybe the smaller she was, the less she would feel the fear and nervousness.

She kept her hands together, folded like in prayer, but she didn't pray. If her own Mom couldn't forgive her, then she doubted God would. She shoved her folded hands between her legs to try to warm them, but it didn't work. Afraid of seeing someone that would know her, but even more afraid of watching the landmarks of her life pass by as she was being taken to the cop shop, she kept her chin ducked low and her eyes on her jeans.

Stupid, stupid, stupid. God, she'd been so stupid. Who even cared about Sean Spanner anyway? He was a dick, and he'd hurt her and didn't even remember any of it, and he even acted like a stuck-up dick at school. *Let Tiffany have him.* Why had she done this? Why had she tried so hard to get back at Marin? Just because she'd been so stupid about Sean didn't mean she had to do something so mean to Marin.

They couldn't have the pictures, could they? She'd taken the page down after Marin killed herself. She'd taken it down, and she'd deleted the pictures from her phone. They'd probably just heard rumors from kids at school, so it wasn't like they were going to make her sit and look at the pictures of Marin and Carter.

What if they did, though? What if someone had taken pictures of her and Sean? And that's what she was going to have to look at now? That couldn't be it, though, because they'd been in a dark bedroom. The only light had come from the window, and that was only through the small slit where the curtains didn't quite meet. Besides if someone had pictures of her and Sean, they'd have surfaced a long time before now.

Unless someone had found some gross pictures online and cut and pasted her and Sean's faces on them. She'd considered doing that with Marin.

When the car stopped and Keegan looked around to find herself in front of the police station, she almost threw up. *This was real.* She was really in trouble.

Pleasemompleasemompleasemom...

The cops met them just inside the door, but then the beanpole one, Rose, excused himself and disappeared down a hallway to the left. The other guy, Detective Smith, escorted them to a small square room. Despite his gentle manner and the way he touched her back quickly like a guy on a date ushering his girl to a table, the room scared her.

She'd seen enough cop shows to know this was an inter-rogation room. There was a table here and four chairs. Nothing else. The tabletop was nicked and scarred; and the chair Smith led her to rocked on uneven legs.

He asked if she wanted anything to drink and then offered her a soda, but she shook her head no. Her stomach burned and the thought of trying to put anything in it right now made her want to puke. She smoothed her icy hands over her jean-clad thighs to dry her palms. It didn't help.

They sat in the room for a few minutes, after Smith excused himself, but she and Mom didn't speak. Keegan had no idea what to say to Mom. She wished her mom would at least reach over and take her hand or something, but she sat still as stone with a deep frown chiseled in her forehead. Keegan would have thought the cops were watching her, but there was no window or mirror. Just four solid dingy white walls, badly in need of a paint job.

Her body hummed with nervous energy, but she was too scared to get up and pace the room. Instead, she bounced her leg faster and faster, until she drove herself nuts with it. She chewed on her fingernail until it bled. She didn't wear a watch, and she'd left her phone at home, so she had no idea what time it was or how much time had passed since she'd been brought in.

She jumped when the door opened again and the two detectives came back inside. Keegan almost heaved a sigh of relief, until she noticed that the beanpole guy was carrying a laptop computer.

Oh God. If they were going to look at pictures, at the pictures she'd posted, it would probably be better if her mom wasn't in here.

"Keegan," Detective Smith said as the other guy turned the computer on. He sat across the table from her, and her mom sat beside her. Keegan watched the other guy type something. How could they do this? She'd taken the page down. "We just have a few more questions for you about the webpage and Marin. Okay?"

"It wasn't a webpage," she said softly. "It was just a MyFriend page. And I took it down."

"Mm-hmm." Smith nodded and pulled his notebook from a pocket on the inside of his sport coat. "Took it down in September. The day Marin English killed herself, correct?"

Keegan looked away from him, but she nodded.

"Well, the owners of BeMyFriend," here he looked at her mom, "that's the full name of the social network your daughter is involved with."

Her mom nodded.

"The owners archive all information for three months. So," the guy plopped his butt on the corner of the table and looked hard at Keegan, "that means that even though you took the page down and the general public can't access it, it's still out there."

Keegan swallowed hard.

"Now, in another two months, it would have been gone. But it's there, and we've had a look at it."

"I'm sorry," Keegan mumbled.

"Do you realize that anything you put on the internet never really goes away?" Smith asked her. "Sure, the official page will be out of the archives in a few months. But did you ever stop to think how anyone in the world could right click on those pictures and save them? And do whatever they chose with them?"

"No."

"Was that your intention?" the other guy asked.

"What?" she cried. Her mom slid her hand along the table and then laid it over hers.

"Never-ending revenge?" the cop continued. "Did you hope that when Marin was in college and looking for a job that her prospective employers might happen on these pictures?"

"No." Keegan shook her head. "No. I didn't know they'd never go away. I just…"

"Just what, Keegan?" Detective Smith asked her.

"I just knew that she was cheating on Sean with Carter. And I wanted Sean to know."

"And the best way to make Sean aware of that was to create a page on the internet and upload explicit photos? Photos of two minors engaging in sexual acts."

Keegan heard her mom's sudden, sharp inhale.

"I didn't know how else to get his attention," Keegan whispered. "He acted like he didn't know me—"

"Even after you'd had sex with him? He didn't recognize you at school?"

"No, he didn't."

"So this was your way of telling Sean Spanner that his girlfriend was cheating on him?" Detective Rose turned the laptop so she and her mom could see the screen. The picture was of a topless Marin, hands in Carter's hair, his open mouth pressed to her skin.

"Yeah."

Detective Rose turned the computer back around and tapped a few more keys. Keegan wondered if Jeannie had seen the page. She hoped not. She couldn't imagine how horrible that would be for Jeannie to see this after Marin was dead.

"The pictures were uploaded from a phone?"

Keegan nodded. Okay, so now her mom knew she hadn't cut and pasted anything. This was the real deal.

"Did you take them?"

Again, she nodded.

"So…based on the series here…" The cop made a show of

studying the pictures and then looked up at Keegan. "You watched the whole thing."

Keegan didn't hear a question, so she simply stared at him.

"Why? Why not get your pictures and go?" Rose asked her.

"Does it matter?" her mom asked. "Really?"

Keegan swallowed another mouthful of snot and tears and wiped her eyes. "When I did it...with Sean...it was horrible."

The room was silent while Keegan thought about what to say. "TV and movies and books make it sound so great. I guess...I guess I got caught up watching them. Wondering about it."

"Wondering about how come Marin got to date Sean and probably sleep with him and how come she could have sex with other boys and it all worked out and nothing was okay for you?"

"Detective," her mom said softly.

"Goes to motive, Mrs. Alexander," Smith said quietly.

"I didn't mean to hurt her," Keegan wailed.

"Didn't you?" Rose asked and fixed a heavy stare on her.

"Well, I did, but not like this. I just wanted Sean to know. I wanted them to break up. And then I thought it would be over."

"And instead she killed herself," Rose said with a shrug.

"Oh, come on," her mom said quickly. "You can't know what was in Marin English's head the day she killed herself. There might have been a hundred other things bothering her. Jeannie English, herself, told me that she and Rick were having trouble. Maybe that had something to do with it."

"That's true." Detective Smith nodded. "And it's possible. But that doesn't change the fact that your daughter did this."

Keegan waited for her mom to argue, but she didn't say anything.

"Mrs. Alexander, Keegan could be charged with a felony," Smith told her.

Keegan felt the bile in her throat, but she clamped her hand over her mouth and fought to control herself.

"A felony?" her mom whispered. "What charge?"

"Cyber-bullying. There've been a handful of cases around the country."

"Oh God."

Keegan's stomach dropped when she saw the color drain from her mom's face. She sat on her hands, hoping to stop the trembling.

"Keegan Alexander, you have the right to remain silent. Anything you say can and will be used against you in a court of law…"

"Mommy, please," Keegan cried and lunged for Teel. She noticed the flinch, the way Teel wanted to draw away from her. It only lasted for half a second, but Keegan felt it in her bones. Her mom still blamed her, and maybe she would never forgive her.

"Baby." Her mom finally put her arms around her, but Keegan still felt cold. This wasn't love. This was parental obligation.

"Mrs. Alexander, we'll have to follow the arrest procedures. Write up an arrest card. Get her prints. Be aware that this is a relative felony, which means the judge will decide if it'll be treated as a misdemeanor or felony."

Keegan buried her face in her mom's shoulder and waited, but her mom didn't say anything.

"Because there are no previous incidents and because you are an upstanding family in the community, we'll release her to your custody pending her appearance in court."

"Mom!" Keegan wrapped her arms around her mom as the cops tried to pull them apart.

"It's okay, Keegan," her mom said as she pulled away from her. Her face was streaked with tears and mascara. "It's okay. I'm right here. Dad's coming."

"Mom, I didn't mean for this…"

"C'mon, Ms. Alexander," Rose said and gave a firm tug on her arm. Her hands slipped, and the cops pulled her away from her mom. She caught her breath as cold metal handcuffs clicked around her wrists drawn behind her back.

"Do you have to handcuff her, for God's sake?"

"Mom, I'm scared," Keegan cried as they led her out of the room and left her mom sitting there alone.

Her teeth chattered as Detective Smith questioned her and filled out what he called an arrest card. His desk was a mess of paperwork and two coffee mugs and a battered desktop monitor. Keegan felt like she was a bug under a microscope, so she was careful not to look up at anyone. So what if they were cops? None of them got why she'd done what she'd done. She wished a million times over now that she hadn't taken the pictures. That she'd never been with Sean. That she'd never gone to that party or become friends with Jess. But she couldn't undo any of those things, and no one here knew or cared why she'd done them. No one knew she hadn't meant for Marin to kill herself.

She read the top line of one of the papers on Smith's desk over and over. Detention screening instrument. Detention. She knew it didn't mean school detention, but she wished it did. Smith filled out the arrest card and then turned his attention and his black pen to the screening instrument and started writing down numbers. She wondered what it meant, and she wished she could see the number he wrote at the bottom of the page.

But then he looked up and dropped the pen.

"Okay." He stood up and took her arm and led her away from his desk. He led her to another cop, this one in uniform.

"Officer Randall's going to get your fingerprints," Smith explained, "and then we'll need your picture."

A mug shot? Shit. The guy rubbed each of her fingertips with alcohol. Then he dried them thoroughly, though her hands were still clammy. She shook so badly, the cop had a hard time getting her fingerprints. Three of them he had to redo, because she smeared them. He was patient, making sure she rolled the pads of her fingers slowly from one side of her fingernail to the other.

"Okay, these are rolled fingerprints," he told her. "Now I need you to press your fingers here." He pointed to the bottom of the card, where there were ten small boxes, one for each of her fingers and thumbs. Keegan remembered the year she had turned six. Her parents had taken her and Rachel to the state fair. They had free fingerprinting there, and they stored the fingerprints on a CD and gave them to parents. Keegan had been scared, thinking there was a pretty good chance she was going to be kidnapped. Her dad had picked her up and carried her around the fair and promised her nothing bad was going to happen.

Now she was being fingerprinted again and she was crying again, and something bad had happened, only she had caused it. And this time her daddy couldn't make it better.

Chapter 37

TEEL

OF ALL THE moments of the day, from getting out of bed and making herself go to work and knowing that Liz Morgan knew she might be pregnant and holding her breath wondering when Liz might blow the whistle and tell everyone, to every moment of Keegan's arrest, it was the picture that haunted Teel. The picture of Marin with the kid named Carter.

And not because it was Marin. *Really Marin*, not Marin's face cut and pasted on someone else's body. It wasn't that that kept coming back to get her when the quiet had claimed the night and everyone else was sleeping. *Although that had thrown her.* She hadn't even realized it, but up until that moment, she'd hoped that Keegan hadn't really done it. That her daughter hadn't really put something so private and so intimate out there for the world to see.

As deep as that realization had cut, that wasn't what bothered her about the picture. And it wasn't even that Marin was dead. That had settled inside her and become a part of her, like an arthritic ache in her bones.

It was seeing that picture, a very young Marin, obviously naked and obviously caught in a very grown-up moment with a boy, and the fact that the picture made Teel really visualize her baby girl having sex with a stranger at a party. Up until that moment, it had hurt but in a distant way. An abstract way, because what mom in her right mind could just instantly absorb that news and roll with it and *just get it*? Seeing the picture had made it solid—a true visual of Keegan, naked or at least half so—on a bed, under a heavy, maybe muscular male body.

Every time Teel closed her eyes, she saw it. Well, every time she closed her eyes, she relived the whole damned day. But it was that flash of reality that was unraveling her slowly and painfully. She was an insane mix of feeling, twisted inside with anger and sadness and jealousy and fear. Angry with Keegan, hell yes. For so many things, not the least of which being the pictures that may have driven Marin to suicide. Angry about her sneaking out and being at a party where there was alcohol and sex and God only knew what else. The sadness, again, was more about Keegan than Marin at this point. Teel would never live a day when she didn't think about Marin, but right now the sadness inside her was all tangled up with the anger and the jealousy because here was her daughter who had thrown a hell of a good thing, a good life, a good reputation, a good opportunity for a posi-tive future out the window.

Out the proverbial goddamned window, and God, how she hated that window. Maybe if it were real, she could at least open it and escape. But it wasn't, and she lay beside Bobby, mind and heart racing so hard she thought she might have a heart attack.

Bobby had charged into the police station as they were

running Keegan through the arrest. Fingerprinting her. Getting her booking photograph (Teel couldn't bear to think of it as a mug shot.) He was angry and ready for a fight, but when he saw Teel, he deflated. She knew him well enough to know he wanted to cry, and that he wouldn't. He'd been tightlipped, simply asked her what was going on, and she'd held herself together and told him they were arresting Keegan on charges of cyber-bullying. Bobby had immediately tried to argue with her that they couldn't prove what Keegan had done had led Marin to suicide, but Teel just shook her head and said no, they said they couldn't prove that. But it didn't change what Keegan had done to break the law.

She explained to him, just as Smith had to her, what a relative felony was and that they would have to wait for Keegan's hearing to know exactly what the hell was going on. He'd asked her why she hadn't called him, even though she knew Eve had called him for her. Her hands had been shaking far too badly and her brain was on overdrive, and trying to make that phone call while she drove to the police station could have resulted in more shit to wade through. He'd grumbled about Keegan needing a lawyer, and he'd acted as if it were Teel's fault that she hadn't insisted a lawyer be present.

Maybe so, she'd agreed. But Keegan was guilty, and there was no road around that, and Teel was standing in that corner. It wasn't that she wanted Keegan under arrest. That she wanted Keegan found guilty. That she wanted Keegan in a juvenile detention center. It was simply that her heart, her mind, had shattered and she was simply stuck on the thought that Keegan was guilty. That her daughter was guilty of something so selfish and so wrong. And if Keegan was guilty, then Teel was guilty, too.

The police had released Keegan to their supervision, and

they were told she was not to leave the house with the exception of approved leave. Which, for Keegan, amounted to school. Like she would want to show her face there again.

Like Keegan would be welcome there now.

Home confinement. Her fifteen-year-old daughter was remanded to their supervision under home confinement for cyber-bullying a classmate. Teel felt that same, insistent pain in her chest, and she laid her hand over her heart. The sweat from making love with Bobby had long since dried, and she'd put her pajama shirt and panties back on, but she was sweating again. And cold. And too damned wired to sleep.

She sat up, intending to slip out of bed and find something to read or watch on TV.

"Lie down," Bobby grumbled without looking at her.

"I can't."

"Teel, you need some sleep."

They'd talked after they brought Keegan home. Eve had made a pot of chili and left it in the refrigerator for them. Keegan had gone to her room, and Teel had reheated the soup and she and Bobby had talked. She'd confessed to him that she was afraid he blamed her, because she blamed herself, and he'd held her and promised he didn't. They'd talked about how Keegan was a good kid, and she'd made a bad choice that had led to other bad choices that had led her to this serious trouble.

It had made her feel good, good enough to want him to hold her and make love to her, but not good enough to not feel guilty. Eve had taken Rachel out for dinner and then when she'd brought her home, Eve came in to check on all of them. She'd asked if there was anything she could do and when Teel had said no, Eve cleaned the kitchen and kissed Teel's cheek and exacted a promise that Teel would call if she needed her. Now the girls were tucked away for the night in their rooms and she and Bobby had made love and they lay curled together in each other's arms, and she'd confessed to him that she thought she was pregnant.

And that Liz Morgan had seen her with the pregnancy test box in her hand at the store.

She'd felt his body tense, and she wondered if he was pissed that she might be pregnant, that she'd bought a test for someone to see, or that Liz had been nosey enough to make sure she saw it. Worried that Bobby was angry with her and angry about a baby, she'd taken the offensive and reminded him that she hadn't gotten herself pregnant, and that his equipment was just as much to blame as hers. He'd muttered that he was too old for a baby, and she'd asked him just what the hell he thought she was, and that had been it for the night.

"I can't sleep, Bobby," she said softly. "I can't. I can't make today go away."

In the darkness, she could see his darker form flip over and then she saw him put his arm behind his head. He lay on his back and looked at her.

"Do you wanna talk?"

She laughed. "Really? Do I wanna talk? I think I'm all talked out."

"Do you ever think about what it was like when it was just me and you?"

Teel turned backwards in the bed, so she could see him better in the darkness. Of course, now and then she thought about life before the girls. The easy way she and Bobby could come and go. No responsibility, none like that of raising children. Sometimes she missed the spontaneity they used to have, but not really. There had been years when things were different, when they didn't have that much time for each other, when the girls were younger. But now the girls were older, and she and Bobby had their lives as parents and their lives as a married couple. Friends. Lovers.

She wouldn't trade a second of the time she'd spent with her daughters. Just thinking about it made her want to throw up.

"Sometimes," she admitted. "But it makes me feel guilty."

"I don't mean that I would want it that way again." He rolled to his side to face her and reached out to touch her. She closed her eyes as his fingers grazed over her legs. "It's just so much to worry about."

"I know." She covered his hand with hers when he stopped moving. "I'm so scared for Keegan, Bobby, and I still can't even look at her, I'm so angry."

"It's just gonna take some time." His voice was gruff with emotion.

"Is it? Do you really think that one day I'll just wake up and I'll be over this?"

"Do you love her, Teel?"

"God, Bobby, I love her so much it hurts."

"Then yes, I really think you'll just wake up one day, and you'll have figured out how to process it and put it away, and it'll be okay."

She laughed in spite of herself.

"Did you get a psychology degree from one of those online universities?"

He brought her hand to his mouth and kissed her fingers. She traced the smile of his lips.

"C'mere." He tugged at her and she leaned willingly toward him and kissed him. But she pulled away from him when his hands began to roam.

"That's how we got ourselves in trouble, Bobby Alexander."

"We're old people," he answered. "Old people don't get themselves in trouble."

"No, but we embarrass our families just the same."

"Where're you going?"

"See what's on TV."

"At one in the morning?"

"Yeah. Maybe I'll watch the Home Shopping Network."

"Great. Leave the credit cards in here with me."

She laughed as she padded to the door.

"Teel?"

"Hmm?"

"I love you."

Oddly enough, his vow brought it all back all over again. She slid her hand up the doorframe to hang on when her knees buckled.

"What're we gonna do?" she whispered.

"We're gonna get through it. Together."

She stood for a moment, even after she heard him turn over. She loved him. And she needed him, and they had to get through this together, because anything else was unthinkable. And yet, she found the TV remote and lay down on the couch filled with resentment that even in this horrific mess, he could turn over and go to sleep while she lay awake and worried.

Chapter 38

T<small>EEL</small>

TEEL HAD FALLEN asleep on the couch just after two, awakened a little before three and gone to bed. When the alarm went off at five, she could have sworn someone was whacking away inside her head with an ice pick. While Bobby was in the shower, she opened the pregnancy test, said a little prayer, and then peed on the stick. With a jittery stomach and a dull headache that had the potential to explode into something mind-boggling if she let her mind go and thought about everything that had happened yesterday, she waited the two minutes for the results.

"There's just something wrong with this," she mumbled as Bobby toweled himself off and stepped into his briefs. "I'm old enough to be a grandmother."

"Jesus, Teel," he muttered. "Let's don't tempt fate."

"I don't believe in fate."

"Then let's not tempt God," Bobby told her as he combed

his hair. "I'm pretty sure He's not too happy with any of us right now, anyway."

Their eyes met in the mirror. He raised his eyebrows. "Well?"

She sighed and hurried into the small alcove in the bathroom to check the test stick she'd set on the back of the toilet. Her stomach, baby and all, hit the floor between her feet when she saw the plus sign.

"Son-of-a-bitch."

"You're pregnant?"

"Apparently so."

"Wow."

"Bobby, I can't..." She laid her hand over her chest as pressure built inside her. Her throat tightened and made it impossible for her to talk.

"First things first." He stepped closer to her and kissed her forehead. "Let's call Dr. Cash and make an appointment and make sure."

"Make sure what?" she snapped. "We have sex every friggin' night of the week. You're still fully loaded..."

"Whoa, whoa, whoa!" Bobby backed away from her. "This is my fault? I'm the one who always wants sex? Maybe we should've planned for this..."

"Planned for this? Planned to have a baby when we're damned near fifty?"

"You're forty-four, and that's not what I meant."

"I can't do this. Not now. I can't."

"So, what? Are you saying you want an abortion?"

"No!"

Someone knocked on the door. Teel turned her back to the door and pressed her hand over her mouth.

"What's up?" Bobby asked when he opened the door.

"Is everything okay?"

Teel swallowed hard when she heard Rachel's voice.

"It's fine," Bobby answered quickly.

"Okay. Just wondered. I...um...I thought maybe Mom was sick."

"Mom's fine. She didn't sleep much last night."

Teel knew Rachel wouldn't let it go until she said something. She took a deep breath for courage and then turned to look at her daughter.

"Didn't go to bed til after three," she said and offered Rachel the dregs of a smile, "so I overslept."

Rachel studied her suspiciously. Teel wondered how much of their argument Rachel had overheard. "I made the coffee."

"Thanks, babe." Teel nodded. She leaned into the shower to turn the water on.

"Are you going to work?" Rachel asked her.

"Of course I'm going to work."

Bobby left them alone, presumably to get dressed.

"What about Keegan? Is she going to school?"

Teel drew another deep breath and puffed her cheeks out as she exhaled. "I don't know."

Rachel, still watching her suspiciously, nodded. "Okay. I'm gonna go do some reading."

Teel nodded. When Rachel was gone, she closed the door and sagged against it. Get moving or give in, she thought. But she knew if she gave in, that was it. She'd crawl back into bed and not get up. Maybe not for another three years, when Keegan was eighteen and could move out and go to college.

Besides, maybe if she went back to bed for the next three years, this other mess would go away. A baby. Good God, they didn't need a baby. What the hell was she going to do? She couldn't have a baby now. Not at this age. Not with everything such a mess with Keegan. What if Keegan ended up in some kind of juvenile home? And Teel was carrying another baby? It was ridiculous. Why the hell hadn't they done something? Why hadn't Bobby had a vasectomy? Why hadn't she had her tubes tied? What in the hell had they been thinking?

She peeled her clothes off and stepped into the shower. The hot water went a long way toward making her feel human, but she was no happier when she rinsed off ten minutes later. Bobby stood at the mirror, shaver in his hand.

"Are you going to call your doctor?"

"Yes." *What? Like she thought she was pregnant, and she wouldn't call her doctor?*

He finished shaving, and she started working on her makeup.

"What about Keegan?" she finally asked.

"What about Keegan?"

"Do we send her to school today?"

Bobby sighed. "What I wonder is if she'll be allowed to be at school today."

Teel said nothing, but she'd wondered the same thing. In the back of her mind, another question nagged at her, but she didn't want to acknowledge it.

"It's a Catholic school," Bobby continued. "I'm sure she's not the only kid there who's having sex, but probably the only one…"

"Don't say it, please?" Teel's eyes met his in the mirror again. "Why are you being such a jerk about this? Last night you tell me we're gonna get through this together…"

"What the hell did I do?" He put his shaver away and slammed the drawer closed. "Yeah, if you're pregnant, I had a hand in it. But it wasn't just me, and don't even tell me you don't want sex."

"I'm not telling you that, and I don't wanna argue, and I have to walk into a Catholic school today and see if I still have a job, and I feel like I'm gonna puke, and I wanna know what to do with Keegan. Can you just answer that?"

"They'll stand by you."

She shook her head. "I don't think so."

"Teel, you've been there over twenty years. You're a good teacher. Your kids love you."

"My daughter might be charged with a felony," she said quietly. "How welcome is a teacher in a classroom full of young, impressionable minds, when her own daughter commits a felony act that may or may not have led to another student's suicide?"

"You're really that worried about this?" He moved closer to her and rested his hand on her waist.

"I'm really that worried about it." She nodded.

"I'm sorry."

She pressed her lips together and looked away from him.

"I heard it. On the late news last night," she mumbled.

"I know." He nodded and then leaned his butt against the bathroom cabinet. "Okay. I have some trim work I can do here. Need to run a few errands and check a few job sites. I'll do that early, before Keegan's awake. Make sure I'm back here to work when she'll be up and moving around."

"So we have to babysit her."

"Maybe for now." He shrugged. "I honestly don't think she's going to do anything to get into more trouble. But I think for appearances…for the hearing or trial or whatever… that someone needs to…"

"Babysit."

"I guess."

"And that's okay? You don't need to be out somewhere?"

"I'll have the guys handle things," he said. "Maybe if I need to do something, I can go out after you're home later."

Bobby left her alone; she figured he'd go ahead and run his errands now. And he'd probably pick up a cup of coffee somewhere rather than drink the cinnamon coffee she smelled in the house. Teel applied her makeup, but it didn't hide the worry lines or the dark circles under her eyes. She styled her hair, dressed quickly, and went out to get her own coffee.

Rachel sat at the dining room table, reading and making notes. She was bundled up in sweats and a big, fluffy robe. The fingers of her left hand were curled around a coffee cup. The TV was on, though she didn't appear to be paying much attention to it.

"Dad leave?" Teel asked.

"Yeah," Rachel answered without looking at Teel. "Said he'd be back in about an hour."

"Okay." Teel considered breakfast options, but she wasn't hungry. She'd never been one to eat a lot so early in the morning, but she preached to the girls about how important a good breakfast was and therefore, tried to eat something to set a good example.

She didn't think she could do it today.

"What were you and Dad fighting about?" Rachel still wouldn't look at Teel.

"Rach, Dad and I argue sometimes," Teel told her. She crossed the hardwood floor, the soles of her black loafers making a loud click. She crossed her arms over her chest. "Married people argue. Sometimes they have huge blow out fights. Doesn't have to mean anything, okay?"

Rachel nodded and sat back in her chair. She fiddled with her pencil, and Teel knew she had more she wanted to say.

"What?" Teel asked gently. "What's wrong?"

"I wish I could talk to you about Deacon."

"What about Deacon?"

Rachel glanced up at Teel, but she was quick to look away. Teel waited and wondered what was bothering Rachel. Of course she wanted to know, but she didn't want to know. She didn't think she could take any more intimate details about either of her daughters.

In the awkward silence that hung between them as Rachel wrestled with what she wanted to say or ask, and Teel prayed that the moment would pass without her learning that Rachel had slept with Deacon, the TV seemed to grow louder and Teel became aware of what was being said.

"...Keegan Alexander, the daughter of Robert and Toniel Alexander, was arrested yesterday on charges of cyber-bullying, in connection with fifteen-year-old Marin English's suicide..."

When Rachel finally looked at Teel, her eyes were wet with tears.

"I feel sorry for her, Mom," she whispered, apparently having forgotten her worries over Deacon.

Teel nodded. "I know."

"She's so alone right now."

Teel stepped back, absorbing Rachel's words like a physical blow. Keegan was alone because her own mother couldn't forgive her or show her any love.

She glanced at her watch. It was almost six-thirty. Teel hated the thought of going to work, but she hated the thought of standing here in the kitchen and being judged by one daughter for how she was treating the other daughter even more.

"I'm gonna go into work early," she announced. It made sense. She could beat everyone else there and hide in her classroom. "I need to work on lesson plans, and I have social studies tests to grade." True enough, but really, she just couldn't admit to Rachel that she was running from her unspoken accusations.

"Sure, Mom," Rachel said quietly, and Teel felt exposed as if Rachel could see right through her.

Teel took her coffee cup to the sink, dumped it, and rinsed it. She started back across the family room to brush her teeth and grab her purse from the closet.

"What's going on?"

"Huh?" Rachel looked up from her book and followed Teel's gaze to the window.

"There're people in the front yard," Teel mumbled. "What the hell?"

She saw a sign, just as she reached to pull the front door open. The word *murderer* caught her eye, but she was opening the door and stepping onto the porch before she realized these were people here to judge and torture the family, *Keegan*, for what she had done.

Teel saw three people move forward on the lawn, closer to her. A woman, probably close to her age, a young man, probably not much older than Rachel and a young girl, maybe Keegan's age. They each held buckets, and as they closed in on Teel, who froze, suddenly unable to move, they drew the buckets back.

This is what it's like, she thought, for all of the families who love those kids who do something wrong. For all of the good kids who make bad choices, for all the kids like Keegan. For the families whose children kill someone in a drunk driving accident. For all the families of the bad kids, the truly bad kids who raise real guns and fire real bullets and kill classmates and teachers.

The blood, she knew instantly it was blood from the smell and the texture, splashed over her gray sweater and her black slacks. She felt the warmth of it on her bare arms and on her face. She cried out, involuntarily, and for just a moment, for one God-awful moment, she felt it on her lips and almost tasted it.

Crying and gagging, she turned to the side of the porch and vomited. She was vaguely aware of the voices, the chanting. Something about *murder* and *jail* and *Keegan*. She had to get inside before Rachel came out. She didn't want Rachel or Keegan to see this.

They were still there, still chanting as she turned her back to them. She cringed as another warm splash hit her from behind. When she looked up, Rachel stood in the doorway, horrified by what she saw.

"Ohmygod, Mom!" She rushed outside and reached for Teel's hands. "Ohmygod. Oh God. Did they hurt you? Mom? Are you okay?"

"Sssh." Teel nodded. She shook so violently she couldn't move. "I'm fine, Rach. I'm fine."

"Is that blood? Is it? Did they hurt you?"

Rachel was rambling, on the verge of a break down, and Teel wasn't sure she was too far behind her. She had to get them both back inside.

"I'm not hurt," she said calmly. "Get me a towel."

Teel let Rachel pull her inside, but she didn't want to step on the hardwood with the blood on her shoes.

"Go to hell!" Rachel yelled out the door.

"Rach, don't." Teel still shook, but her voice was made of steel. She was afraid the vultures on her lawn would attack Rachel, throw blood on her or something even worse. She was afraid anything they said right now would be taken out of context in the news later today.

She was afraid they would wake Keegan. As unresolved as her feelings for Keegan were right now, she didn't want her to see her like this. This would traumatize her baby; more than anything that had happened yet, Teel believed this would be Keegan's undoing.

"Leave us alone, you fuckers!" Rachel yelled, and Teel squeezed her hand hard. She almost laughed, just a little bit proud of her oldest for trying to stand up for the family. But she was still scared of a million things that could come of this, and she desperately needed Rachel to close the door and get her a towel so she could make this go away.

"I'm sorry, Mom." Rachel was crying now. She closed and

locked the door. "I'm sorry, but it's not fair. They don't even know us."

"It's okay." Teel nodded. "It's okay. Just get me a towel. Please."

"Okay. Okay. Towel," Rachel talked to herself, repeating the words *okay* and *towel* over and over as she disappeared through Teel's bedroom door.

Teel stared at her trembling hands. Hands that had loved and stroked and cared and raised two beautiful girls. Hands that would do the same for a third baby. Hands that ached to fight, to claw for justice.

"Mom?"

Damn.

Teel looked up at Keegan. Hands that had never been more useless.

There was blood in her left eye, and she had to blink several times to see Keegan clearly.

"Ohmygod, Mom. What happened?"

"I'm fine," Teel said, still calm, though she was a wreck inside. "Sweetie, I'm fine. But I really need you to go back to bed. Could you do that for me? Please? Everything's fine."

"Is that blood?" Keegan asked.

Rachel appeared with the towel.

"Thank you, babe." Teel took it, but then she wondered if she should call the police first. "Call Daddy. Please."

Rachel nodded. Keegan sobbed as she stared at her.

For the first time since this whole mess had blown wide open, Teel desperately needed to hold Keegan and this time an animal's blood, rather than Marin's, kept her at a distance.

Chapter 39

TEEL

SHE HAD no idea what Rachel said to Bobby, but it seemed like mere seconds passed before the back door flew open and he ran down the hall toward her.

Still standing on the welcome mat, worried about dripping blood on the hardwood, Teel looked up as he came to a stop in front of her.

"Are you hurt?"

"No."

"Goddamned people," he muttered.

Keegan had left the family room when Teel wasn't looking. She'd hated for Keegan to see her like this, but the fact that she'd disappeared so suddenly bothered her even more.

"Rach," she said quietly, "would you check on Keegan, please?"

"Yeah." Rachel nodded and hurried down the hall.

"C'mon." Bobby reached for the towel and squatted down in front of her.

"Should we call the police?" she asked. Kneeling in front of her, he helped her slip first one and then the other shoe off.

"You bet we're calling the police," he answered. "But let's get you out of this first."

"Do they need to see it?"

"Teel, I'm not gonna have you sit there in blood soaked clothes until they can send someone out." He shook his head almost violently. "This is disgusting. Trespassing on our lawn and then attacking you this way. Jesus."

"What if it had been Keegan?" she whispered.

Bobby shrugged. "Doesn't matter who, this is disgusting."

Once her shoes had been wiped clean, as clean as they could be and Teel could still see blood on them (didn't matter, she'd never wear them again) Bobby stood and pulled his cell phone from the case on his hip.

"Let me get a picture for the cops," he said, obviously still furious. Teel stood still for him, but her skin was crawling. She itched all over, and she longed for a hot shower.

Once the call was made, he took her by the hand and led her to their bathroom.

"Are you okay?" he asked when he'd closed and locked the door, and they were alone.

She started to say yes, but she couldn't. With Bobby home, and Rachel with Keegan, she cracked. He caught her as she swayed on her feet and held her up with an arm around her waist. He leaned into the shower and turned the water on and then began peeling the bloody clothes from her.

"It's okay, Teel," he said to her over and over again. "It's all gonna be okay."

She cried, and she tried to talk, to argue. Nothing was okay, and nothing was going to be okay. Keegan might be found guilty and placed in a juvenile home or maybe prison, who knew? They could be fined ungodly amounts of money, and she was probably going to lose her job. People would talk. Bobby might start losing construction jobs. She was pregnant again, for God's sake, and even if everything worked out okay and Keegan was sentenced to community service, nothing would ever be the same.

Once this kind of thing happened, it never really *unhappened*. It would never really go away. It would always be like a shadow that clung to Keegan. There would always be someone who would learn about this and take it upon themselves to exact justice for Marin.

Bobby listened to her, though Teel figured he didn't catch half of what she was trying to say. His hands were gentle as he removed the clothing she'd just put on not even an hour earlier. He tossed everything in one small pile on the floor by the tub and then, fully clothed, he stepped into the shower with her.

He continued to talk to her, in a soothing voice, telling her it was okay. Telling her he loved her. That they were in this together. He washed her hair and bathed her as if she were a child, and maybe at this moment she was as helpless as a child. She watched his blue jeans turn deep, dark blue as they soaked up the water.

When he'd rinsed her hair and smoothed his hands up and down her arms and legs, he held her and let her cry. She stopped trying to talk and buried her face in his neck. The water turned lukewarm first and then as it grew colder, Bobby turned it off and grabbed a clean towel.

She let him pat her dry, and then stood, lost, until he came back with a clean bra and panties for her.

"What're those for?" she asked when he set down a pair of sweatpants.

"For you to put on," he answered. "I don't want you to get chilled."

"Bobby, I gotta get to work."

He shook his head. "No. You're not going to work."

"I have to…"

"No. You're under too much stress as it is. You might be pregnant. And now this. This was…this was a horrible shock for you. Just take the day…"

"I can't afford to just take the day," she argued. "My job's probably on the line as it is."

"Sweetheart, you need to take the day at home."

"Then they win." She tossed her hands in the air as if admitting defeat. "I'm not gonna let them win. They had no right to do this."

"No, they didn't. You're right." He stepped closer to her and cupped the back of her head in his hand. "We're not gonna let them win, but today might be theirs. Okay? Can you honestly tell me you could go in today and look at that classroom full of kids and concentrate?"

Teel started to answer, but he bent his knees to dip lower and look her in the eyes.

"Honestly? Could you do it?"

She mouthed the word *no*, but she couldn't force herself to actually say it.

"So maybe you're being responsible. You're not capable of teaching today. You need this break. I'll call."

"No." She shook her head. "Let me at least do that."

"Okay." He stared at her a moment longer. "You call school. I'll call the police."

She nodded and finished dressing. He was right. She was freezing, and even the sweats and thick socks didn't help. The kitchen and family room were empty when she went back out to make her phone call. Keegan's bedroom door was open, though, so she took that to be a good sign.

Her shoes were still on the throw rug in front of the door. A flash of movement just outside the door caught her eye, and her heart hammered before she realized it was Bobby. Cleaning the porch off, most likely.

With trembling fingers, she dialed the school office and asked for Mr. Shoch without telling the school secretary who was calling.

"Hello? This is Mr. Shoch."

Teel turned away from the hallway, suddenly not wanting Keegan to hear her talking. She walked over to the French doors and stared out across the backyard.

"John, it's Teel Alexander."

She could tell from his hesitation that he was surprised she was calling. Or was he? Maybe it was just that he'd heard the news, of course, and he didn't know what to say to her. Maybe he was putting all of his ducks in a mental row and putting his words in order to fire her.

He couldn't just fire her, she knew that. It was a Catholic school, so there would be a meeting between John and the priests, the pastor of the church. Still, her stomach knotted at the thought.

"Teel. I'm sorry to hear what's going on."

He sounded sincere. But how the hell could she know what was going on in anyone's mind right now? She knew what she'd probably be thinking, and though she'd never go vigilante and throw a bucket of blood on someone accused of a crime, she would judge.

And yet, she'd always liked John. They'd worked together for nearly ten years. All of the teachers respected him, and he seemed happy to work with each of them, as well as the students.

She hated that she would be forever second-guessing all of her relationships now. Already, this whole damned mess had been jacking with her and Bobby. The strain of the past few weeks was trying damned hard to get a wedge between them.

And now she'd wonder about her friends. Her colleagues. Her boss.

"Thank you," she said quietly and continued. "We had an incident here this morning."

"What happened?" he asked. She told herself he was asking because he cared.

"There were people in the yard." She shook her head as she talked, still stunned that it had happened. *Appalled* that it had happened. "I stepped outside to see what was going on. They had posters…"

"I'm sorry. You don't need to deal with that."

"I was ready for work." She pushed herself to go on. "In fact, I was almost ready to leave. When I stepped outside, three of them…threw buckets of some kind of animal blood…"

"Oh, no." Still sounded sincere. "They threw blood at you. Didn't they?"

"Yeah."

"Stay home. I'll take care of it."

"John, I'm sorry. I hate missing a day."

"Take a day, Teel," he said firmly. "It's okay, and you need it."

She breathed deeply and, she hoped silently, through her nose. She prayed that he meant it, that she hadn't just set the wheels in motion that would crush her and take away her job.

It wasn't the money. It wasn't a lot, and they didn't need it anyway. She loved what she did. She loved the kids. She still thought about the first class of kids she taught, and they were old enough to have children in her class now.

"Thank you."

"I'm going to check in with you later this afternoon," he told her. "Did you call the police?"

"Bobby did."

"Okay. How's Keegan?"

The kindness in his voice hit her hard. She felt it in her knees and her stomach and her heart and throat.

Clearing her throat, she answered that Keegan was very badly shaken up about all of it. He made some kind of noise low in his throat that sounded like commiseration. She prayed she heard him correctly.

"She's a good girl, Teel. It'll work out."

"Thanks."

She said goodbye, clicked the cordless off and stared out the French door. She'd never wanted to be outside, to be free more than she did at this moment. And yet, she was safe here.

Keegan would not have that luxury if she were sentenced to any kind of detention center. She would desperately want her freedom, and she would feel so alone, locked away in some sterile correctional center. Tears burned Teel's eyes. She let them fall.

Chapter 40

RACHEL

SHE'D SKIPPED CLASSES TODAY, and she felt like a renegade as she and Deacon walked hand in hand. Like one of her professors or the college dean was going to approach her at any moment and confront her. Ask her why she was out gallivanting around town if she'd missed her classes earlier. She knew it was stupid. Well, it was more than stupid. She was a freak, and each day she was more and more aware of that, and she wondered when exactly Deacon was going to realize it and walk away.

There had been days she'd played hooky in grade school and high school, though they had been few and far between. Since her mom was a teacher, Rachel felt bad any time she exaggerated an illness just to stay home. True, there were times when her dad worked around the house, and he'd taken care of her when she was sick.

Today was the first time she skipped a college class. It felt all wrong, and she kept thinking she needed to call the office or her professors and tell them she wouldn't be there and why. She was such a freak, so many years of following the rules, toeing the line. God, compared to Keegan, she was borderline OCD with massive control issues.

Then again, she guessed she'd rather be the quiet control freak than be in Keegan's position.

But she hated being so uptight, so afraid of living. There was a tiny part of her that envied that wild streak in Keegan. Not that she wished she'd have done what Keegan did. She wouldn't wish to claim any of it as her own. But Keegan had spunk; she'd always had a spark inside her that Rachel didn't understand.

"So. Tell me," Deacon said as they walked. It was chilly, and the wind coming in off the Mississippi was brisk. Rachel shivered and pulled her jacket sleeve down over the hand that wasn't wrapped tightly in Deacon's. "Tell me what's going on, Rach."

She laughed, but her eyes filled with tears.

"It's a mess, Deacon," she told him. "Everything is just a mess."

He nodded. They stood together at the railing around the park and stared at the raging river waters.

"I just can't believe my little sister did all this stuff," she mumbled. "I was afraid to wear my shorts a little too short for the dress code, and she's out at a kegger when she's fourteen, having sex with someone she doesn't know. And then..." Rachel shook her head. "Those pictures of Marin. I just...I don't get that. Of all of it, that's the part I just don't get."

Deacon leaned on the railing and looked at her.

"Don't do that," she said as she reached for him.

"It makes you nervous, doesn't it?" he said gently.

"Deacon, everything makes me nervous. You know that."

"You're careful," he answered with a shrug. "I like that about you."

"I'm a control freak." She looked away from his inquisitive eyes. "I hate that I'm so uptight." She laughed again, but this time her voice broke, and she was crying. "I used to want to…"

"What?"

"I used to want to be like her," she admitted. "Like Keegan. She just…she lives life, no holds barred. And look where it got her."

Deacon took his time answering her. She watched him as he looked at the gazebo and the parking lot and the abandoned warehouse buildings across the street.

"She's impulsive," he finally said. "Not always a bad thing. Not always a good thing." His gaze settled on her face again. "I only really know Keegan through you. But I don't think she's a horrible person. She made a mistake."

"She made a horrible mistake."

"True."

"It's just…*She* did this, but now it's become about my whole family. My mom's afraid she's gonna lose her job, and I know that might sound selfish of Mom…"

"It's not selfish. Actions have consequences. Keegan's actions are gonna hit every one of you."

"My mom's a good teacher." Rachel pressed her lips together, wishing she could quit crying. "She loves what she does."

Deacon smiled. "You know what I hope?"

"What?"

"That I'm around when this is over and I get to see the real Teel and Bobby Alexander."

"Really?"

"Absolutely."

Rachel laughed again despite the tears.

"I want that, too. I want them to have the time to get to know you."

"I'm not going anywhere," Deacon promised her. "You get this look in your eyes sometimes, and I know you're afraid. Of me. Of us." He drew her against him and brushed his lips over hers. "Trust me, Rachel."

"Even if...I'm not ready...to make love with you?"

"I'm not in any hurry," he answered sincerely.

She nodded and slid her arms around his waist.

"There were people at our house this morning," she whispered.

"What kind of people?"

"They were there...with posters...that said mean things about Keegan."

"Oh, man."

"And Mom didn't want Keegan to see them. So she went outside. I don't think she realized, at first, what it was about. But then she stepped outside, and they threw buckets of blood on her. All over her."

"Oh, God." Deacon put his arms around her. She pressed into him, feeling secure in his arms. "Did Keegan see it?"

"Yeah, she ended up coming out of her room. Mom looked so..." Rachel thought for a minute to find just the right word, "vulnerable. And then Keegan saw her, and I think it just...I think Mom just broke inside. She was covered in blood, and her clothes were sticking to her, and Keegan was...She was so scared."

"Were you? Scared?"

Rachel nodded against his shoulder. "Mom's so strong. It's like I know that no matter how bad something gets, Mom's strong enough to handle it. I've never seen her look so small. So helpless."

"I'm sorry."

"I keep thinking about what Keegan did. I mean, it's like

this is all wrong. Everything's wrong. Marin English killed herself, and now everything is about Keegan. I feel like it's wrong to worry about Keegan, but she's my sister. And I keep thinking how this is like all those news stories. All those stories you hear about where some kids kill another kid. Or some crazy, depressed teenager walks into a school, guns blazing, and takes out like twenty people, and the whole world hates that kid."

Rachel pushed away from him and stood up straight.

"I feel like we're *that* family, Deacon. Like everyone hates us. All of us, and it's not fair. I don't even care about me. I don't want people to hate my little sister. She was wrong, but God, she didn't mean this. I know she didn't mean for any of this to happen."

"C'mere," Deacon said and grabbed her wrist before she could walk away from him. "You know what? You are that family, and you're not that family, Rachel."

"We're just like them."

"Sort of," he said. "You aren't. Because you're a good, loving family. You have both parents at home, and anyone out here looking in can see how much they love you. How much they do for you and your sister. You love them. By God, you've been raised so right you can't even walk left. You can't bend a rule without making yourself sick with guilt. Your parents made you that way. They made you responsible. That's an incredible thing these days."

"And what about Keegan?" Rachel swiped at her tears. "What did they make Keegan?"

"Independent. Secure. So secure that she lives in the moment, trusting that she's got a safety net. She's creative. She's boisterous, or at least you said she was."

Rachel nodded. "And the rest of the world will see her as selfish, irresponsible and immature."

"That's the rest of the world." Deacon shrugged. "The rest

of the world might see you as *that* family. People who love you and your family would never see that."

"I don't even want the rest of the world to think that!" She wailed. "They don't know us. How can someone judge us by this one thing? They don't know that Mom cries about some of her students and the stuff they deal with at home. They don't know that my dad gives all this money to organizations to help people. They don't know that Keegan's crazy about animals and nurses sick birds and raccoons back to health. That she cries when she watches sad movies. That she's scared inside and that's why she thinks she needs to be popular. She's just so scared of being alone she needs to know people like her. How is it fair that they can think that about us, and they don't even *know* us?"

Deacon stroked his thumb over her lower lip, and her eyes met his gaze.

"That's why you are that family, Rachel," he said softly. "Because every time a kid makes a bad choice...uses poor judgment...the whole world condemns that family. Without knowing anything about them."

When he reached for her, she went willingly into his arms, laid her head on his shoulder and cried.

"Thank you."

"For what?"

"Just...listening. Being here for me."

"I'm always here."

She lifted her head and turned her face to look at him. "I feel like a jerk, because I know there's so much going on. But I just...I wish my parents would look at me. Remember I'm there. Not that I'm there to help them. But that I'm there. And this hurts me, too."

"They know that."

"I know." She nodded. "When I left the house earlier..." She stopped, uncertain about confessing these feelings.

"What?" he urged her to go on.

"Mom and Keegan were curled up together...laying on Keegan's bed. Mom had her arms around her, and they were sleeping. And for just a minute..."

"You wished you were Keegan."

Rachel nodded. "I don't, because I..."

"What?"

"I wouldn't wanna be...that girl." Rachel sobbed. "I don't wanna be Keegan. I don't wanna be that impulsive, thought-less girl who did something so awful. But...I wanna know that Mom and Dad love me."

Deacon pulled her close again. "I know. I know this is hard, Rachel. But God, I know they love you. They love you so much, and maybe it's not fair, but right now they need you. They need you to be strong for them."

"I know."

"So let me do it." Deacon kissed her forehead. "If you need to be loved right now, let me do it."

Chapter 41

KEEGAN

SHE JUST KEPT PICTURING her mom, covered in blood, standing by the front door. Keegan felt like she could smell it, but she knew better. She couldn't smell anything; it was all in her head.

Still, she felt like she was going to throw up, and the smell of blood was making it worse. Keegan thought she would go crazy from being in her room forever, well, since September anyway. Right around the time Marin killed herself.

Climbing the damned walls. Not like she could go anywhere, though. Not that she'd want to now. She could never show her face again. Not that it mattered. She'd fucked things up so badly, no one was going to want to hang around with her. Her friendship with Jess had been superficial at best, and Keegan wondered how she could see that so clearly now, with blood in her eyes, when she hadn't seen it with perfect vision over a year ago.

With Marin dead, and knowing now that Jess was no

better than Tiffany and Brandy, and worst of all, knowing that she worse than all of them, Keegan was alone. Truly alone.

She'd had Mom and Dad today, kind of all to herself. Rachel had been really good to her, just sitting with her after that thing with Mom happened. Keegan couldn't even decide if it was real at first. She woke up and thought she'd heard voices outside, so she got up and stumbled out to the hallway and there was Mom. Covered in blood and Rachel was yelling out the front door, calling someone fuckers.

At first, she thought she was dreaming. But then she'd seen that look on Mom's face, and there was just something about the way she looked like she was about to shatter, like a cartoon character. Now Keegan could picture that, little pieces of her mom splintering off and falling on the floor. The hardwood that Mom had been determined not to step on when she had blood on her shoes.

Rachel had stayed in her room with her after Dad came home and took care of Mom. She hadn't said anything, but that was better. Keegan couldn't think of anything Rachel could have said that would have made her feel better. Probably, anything Rachel would have said would have just made her feel worse.

Dad had called the police; Keegan didn't get up again, but she heard her dad outside talking to someone. And then it had gotten quiet in the house. Now and then she could hear Dad downstairs or out in the garage. She was so sick of being in her room, lying in her bed and staring at the same four walls, trying to sleep. Seemed like the only thing to do to pass the time was sleep. It was the only way to get from one day to the next.

But Keegan wondered what the point was. Why did it matter if she made it from one day to the next?

She woke up once to find her Mom curled up behind her

in her bed. Keegan could tell from the deep, even breaths she took that she was sleeping, and she hadn't wanted to wake her. So she'd just lain there as still as she could and for just that little while, she'd felt safe. Safe, as she hadn't felt in a long, long time.

But then she'd gone back to sleep, feeling safe with her mom's heartbeat at her back, and she'd had that stupid dream. It was a school morning, and Marin was dead, but Keegan still had to go to school. She was so mad at her mom for making her go, she didn't pay any attention as she opened the door to get in her mom's car.

But then as she slid into her side of the car, she smelled it. She smelled blood, and then she looked at the driver's side, and instead of her mom sitting there, it was Marin. Covered in blood, head to toe, just like Mom had been earlier. When Keegan had screamed, Marin had turned her head and smiled at her. That same, stupid smile that everyone always said made her so pretty. Her own parents had always said Marin was pretty, and then teachers and coaches started talking about how pretty Marin was, and then finally it was the guys at school who had a thing for Marin.

Still screaming, in the dream, Keegan had turned sideways in her seat and flattened herself against the door. Marin didn't move, didn't threaten her, and yet Keegan couldn't stop screaming. And then from the corner of her eye, she saw movement in the backseat and when she turned her head, she realized Sean and Carter were there. Not covered in blood, but mud. Their jeans and boots were caked with mud, and their faces were streaked with dirt. A shovel lay across their laps, and Keegan knew immediately that they'd dug up Marin's grave and that's how she was sitting there in Mom's car looking at her.

She reached behind herself to get the car door open, but

Carter leaned around her seat and grabbed her hand. She cried, begged him to let her get out, but he wouldn't let go.

"Keegan."

"Please, just leave me alone."

"Keegan, sweetheart, wake up…" Mom's voice.

Keegan still struggled with the hand that bound her; she still needed to get out of the car, away from Marin. But now she was hearing her mom's voice, too.

And then someone squeezed her hand really tight, and Keegan looked around the headrest on her seat to look at Carter.

"Keegan, you're dreaming," her mom said.

Awake, but afraid to actually open her eyes, Keegan lay in her mom's arms. It felt so good to lie there with Mom. She didn't want to see her. To look at her. Because what if Mom still had that look in her eyes? The one that kind of seemed to say *you're not my daughter*. Or maybe *I love you, but only because I have to*.

"Are you okay?"

Keegan nodded her head without opening her eyes.

"Wanna tell me about it?" Her mom propped herself up on her elbow. Keegan could feel her watching her.

"No."

"Might help."

"No."

"You know you can talk to me, Keegan."

Great. Sounded like Mom was crying. She hated doing this to her parents. Making them so sad and so angry. Shaming them. She'd never considered what any of this would do to them. She'd never considered that what she'd done would ever go beyond breaking Marin and Sean up.

It wasn't like she'd wanted Marin to kill herself. It wasn't like she meant for those pictures to end up all over the internet. She hadn't meant for Rick and Jeannie to see any of it.

She hadn't planned on the pictures following Marin through her life and into adulthood and messing up her job or a family she might have. She'd just wanted Sean to see that Marin wasn't the super sweet girlfriend he seemed to think she was.

"I don't wanna talk."

"You know we might not be in this situation if we'd have talked more in the first place."

"Yes, we would be, Mom. I messed up. I didn't mean for any of this to happen."

"Did you think about what you were doing? Did you think about talking to me? Or Rachel, even?"

Keegan had snorted. "Rachel thinks I'm a freak. At least you have to listen."

"I don't have to, Keegan." Her mom tucked her hair back behind her ear and then smoothed her fingers over her cheek. "I want to."

"No, you don't, Mom. I see how you look at me."

"How do I look at you, Keegan?"

"Like you wish you could claim I wasn't yours. Like there was a mix up at the hospital and you got the wrong baby."

That had done it. Keegan had hurt her mother deeply enough that Mom had let go of her hand and got out of bed and left her alone. Without a word.

Keegan, so cold where her Mom had been pressed up against her, rolled over to lie flat on her stomach. She buried her face under her pillow and squeezed her eyes shut.

Why had she said that? Why did she keep saying that kind of shit to her mom?

Because she wanted her mom to fight her. To argue. To swear that it wasn't true and promise her that she loved her. That no matter how bad she'd fucked everything up and even though she'd had sex when she was only fourteen and even though she'd plotted stupid revenge against a girl her mom knew and liked, and even though she'd as good as killed someone, her mom loved her.

Maybe actions speak louder than words; God, how often had Keegan had that drilled into her when she was little? Sure, a lot of kids get that at school, but God, when your mom was a teacher besides being a mom, you were pretty much spoon fed that shit from birth. Actions might speak louder than words, and it had been nice to sleep with her mom holding her.

But then again, how hard did it have to be to just lie down and close your eyes and sleep? Who's to say that Mom hadn't pretended she was Rachel? Maybe she'd pretended that to get past the revulsion she felt when she looked at her younger daughter.

Maybe her mom needed to see proof, needed to see actions. But Keegan needed to *hear* it. She needed to hear those words. Daddy had held her that first night, when the detectives came and questioned her. He'd held her and told her they would work things out and that he loved her.

Keegan crept out of her room and down the dark hallway. It was the middle of the night, but she hadn't looked at her clock. Time didn't really mean that much to her right now. It was either dark outside, or it was daylight. Didn't matter much when she was stuck in this stupid house in her stupid room.

She glanced at her parents' bedroom door and wished they kept it closed. Then again, what did it matter? She went back down the hall past her bedroom door and glanced into Rachel's room almost disappointed to hear her sister's soft snoring.

It'd be nice for Rachel to get in trouble once. Real trouble, not Mom getting all psycho over her falling asleep with Deacon. Trouble like flunking out of school or getting pregnant. Keegan's stomach clenched, and she shivered. *Nice,*

*Keegan. God, what a freak. Wishing shit like that on Rachel. With
a sister like you, she doesn't need enemies.*

With trembling fingers, Keegan keyed in the alarm code
and then went cautiously back through the living room to
the French doors. She didn't slow down when she thought
about the people in the front yard that morning. The blood.
Her mom.

She didn't care. Really, it was too bad she hadn't been the
one to walk into that.

She slipped outside quietly and then sat in her mom's
lounge chair. It was a clear night, and the sky was filled with
stars. But she was cold. She bent her knees and circled her
arms around her legs.

She didn't think about the stars, about whether or not she
was going to be serving some kind of detention or jail time
(although that had been all she could think about right after
they got home from the police station.) She stared at the stars
and wondered when she'd last heard her Mom say she loved
her. When her mom had last really meant it.

If she ever had.

Maybe Mom couldn't do it. Maybe they were just too
different, and if she were more like Rachel everything would
be fine.

She considered that for a moment. Be more like Rachel.
Dress like Rachel. Act like Rachel. Talk like Rachel.

Be Rachel, and maybe Mom would love her.

Keegan's eyes burned and then her skin itched where the
tears trailed over her face. Too much trouble. It was too
much work to be like Rachel, and besides that, it was just too
late.

Rachel would never have done what she did, so no matter
what she did now, her mom would never be able to see her
through the blood and the dust. Even when it settled.

Keegan was different now. Marked. She didn't even need

to wear a blazing letter on her chest; people could see it when it wasn't even there.

Unlovable.

Maybe it wasn't her mom's fault. Maybe she was just unlovable.

Chapter 42

TEEL

THE BLOOD HAD SPLASHED over her arms and her shirt and even splattered her face, and she thought of the miscarriage. The second one, the way the blood had soaked through her shorts and then streaked her legs.

The girls didn't even know about the miscarriages, and so she found it funny that she would lie in bed and chase sleep and think about those babies. Keegan was not the middle child, no matter how you looked at it, and so it wasn't about birth order.

There had been three of them, one before Rachel and two between Rachel and Keegan. The first had been hard. So hard to be young, well, they'd gotten married a little later and gotten pregnant a little later but still…In terms of pregnancies and motherhood, aren't you always young the first time? She and Bobby had wanted that baby so badly, and she'd ignored her mother's advice and purchased baby clothes and blankets and newborn diapers and then one day, just after the end of the school day, she'd sat at her desk grading English worksheets and felt a twinge in her belly.

The twinge hadn't bothered her. But by the time she left the school to go home to Bobby, she'd been in the grips of full-blown abdominal cramps and she'd known that baby wasn't meant to be. Her second pregnancy had ended with beautiful Rachel, and she and Bobby had given her the moon any time she'd reached a fat little hand for something and made a noise that resembled anything like *Daddy* or *Mommy*.

The miscarriage with the blood, the bad one, that one came when Rachel was just a year old. And though she'd told Bobby it was silly to blame himself, she often wondered if by making love too soon after Rachel and getting pregnant so quickly, if they'd done something to hurt her body or her chances of carrying a baby to term. Intellectually she knew that was ridiculous. Though doctors didn't advocate for women to get pregnant immediately after giving birth, it did happen and most women and babies were fine.

She'd been further along than the first miscarriage, and she'd suffered through what seemed like hours of labor pain and Bobby had taken her to the hospital and Dr. Cash had said there was nothing he could do. The blood was so sticky and thick, and she remembered how it had seemed unfathomable that this blood had once been part of her baby.

The blood today had been warm like that, and a little sticky, but not thick. If she breathed too deeply, she could still smell the cloying scent, and she gagged and then Bobby stirred in his sleep. She didn't want to wake Bobby. He had to be on site at six am, so he needed his sleep and besides what good would it do for Bobby to be awake? He'd held her earlier, until she'd finally drifted off to sleep, but dreams woke her, and she couldn't decide what was worse: the dreams or being awake and feeling the blood splash over her.

Funny that she would be thinking of those babies now.

God knows there was so much she should be thinking about. And yet, no amount of thinking was going to change anything. Part of her thought she should get up and figure out how to help Keegan, but then part of her wondered just what the hell could be done to help Keegan. Exhausted and body aching from lying awake so long, she rolled to her back and turned her head on her pillow to look at Bobby.

He wore his age so well. Even now, after the blood and dealing with Keegan and the looks her colleagues were sneaking in the hallways, she could look at him and see how attractive he was. She didn't quite feel the stirrings of desire she normally would, but that was okay. Not tonight.

Maybe it was just the blood. The sudden onslaught of warm, sticky blood would disturb anyone, and so maybe it was just the tactile memory of the miscarriage and maybe that's why she couldn't sleep for thinking of her babies.

The second one was a boy. She'd failed to give Bobby a son, though he'd never complained. He loved the girls just as much, if not more, than she did. They'd have named him Robert Michael, after Bobby, if she could have carried him to term and given birth.

Maybe it was the pregnancy test stick she'd used just this morning before the blood.

Maybe it was Keegan. Fear of losing her. Or maybe it was the fear that they already had lost her. Teel still felt the burn in her stomach from what Keegan had said earlier. She might never forget Keegan's words, and she would never forget the way she said them.

She hadn't told Bobby. How could she? It wasn't as if Keegan was right; Teel didn't wish that Keegan were not her daughter. She would never wish that about either of her girls; what kind of mom would wish her child *wasn't* her child?

And yet, Teel hadn't been able to look at Keegan then. She hadn't been able to find words to answer her. True, it had hurt. In about a million different little ways, it had hurt. After all she had done for Keegan, all she had given her, how could she possibly think that she didn't love her? That she wasn't proud of her? It had hurt her to know years of motherhood had been useless in making Keegan understand how much she loved her. And it hurt her to think her daughter might really, truly feel that way. If Keegan wasn't just adding a little dramatic flair to the already crazy-as-hell life in this house, and she truly thought Teel didn't love her, it broke Teel's heart.

She couldn't stand that her baby might feel so alone. But she didn't know how to change it. Lying with Keegan, holding her in her arms had started the healing process for her. She had a long way to go before she could accept all that happened. She would have trouble with the F words, the forgiving and forgetting, but holding Keegan in her arms had been the first step.

She wondered about the dream that had made Keegan cry in her sleep. Was it about that kid? The one who had hurt her? Or was it about Marin? Or something completely different? Teel hated to admit it, but she didn't *know* Keegan. She obviously didn't know half of what was going on in her life and in her head and heart. She had hoped that when Keegan awoke there in her arms, she would let go and talk.

And instead, she'd dropped that damned bomb that was still lodged like shrapnel in Teel's chest.

Did she really look at Keegan like she didn't want to love her? Like she wished she'd been switched at birth? Good God, she hated to think Keegan saw that in her eyes.

The guilt had eaten away at her all night. She hadn't been able to eat anything, though she'd fixed dinner for the rest of them. She'd wandered the house like a ghost, and yet, she felt as if she were the one being haunted.

It wasn't that it was true, that she wished Keegan weren't her child. That she wished she had someone else as a daughter. But good God, how many times through the years had Teel wished Keegan could be more like other kids? Like the easy kids. The well-behaved, thoughtful kids. She'd wondered a hundred times over why Keegan had to be the impulsive type, and why she always seemed to have to talk her down from some dramatic escapade.

Why couldn't Keegan be more like Rachel?

Teel hadn't told Bobby what Keegan had said, because she hadn't wanted to admit to him that she felt that way sometimes. That she compared Keegan to Rachel or to other kids in Keegan's class or other kids Teel had taught through the years, and sometimes it bothered Teel that Keegan was who she was.

She hated herself. To have been carrying this around inside for how many years, wishing she could remake her child, make her into someone she's not and to have been called on it suddenly, by that child, sickened her.

Keegan had freckles over the bridge of her nose, and she wore a pencil's worth of eyeliner daily. She laughed loud and hard when she was happy and she found something funny, and Teel missed that laughter. She played with Barbies until she was seven, and then she'd announced that she was too old for them and she'd boxed them all up and left the box for Teel to take to Goodwill.

When she was in third grade, she'd shared her lunch with a boy in her class. Every day. From what Keegan had said, the kid didn't have much at home, and every day he brought a sickly-looking brown banana to school, and it made Keegan cry one day after school when she told Teel about it.

Teel had started sending two sandwiches to school with

Keegan when she took cold lunch, and she'd sent double the cookies or chocolate, proud of her daughter for caring about someone else.

Teel wondered where that boy was now. She couldn't even remember his name. Why couldn't it have been someone like that? If Keegan had to *do it* (she hated that phrase, but really which euphemism for sex worked when you were applying it to your fourteen-year-old daughter?) why not someone like that? Why not a nice boy?

How many nice boys are big in the popular crowd, Teel? They might be okay; they might be polite in school and fun on the football field and the good all-American boy type with other parents. But how many of them would turn down a four-teen-year-old ready and willing to unzip her pants for them?

Enough. She slipped out of bed and went to stand at the window. Halloween was coming, and she hadn't even started thinking about some fun stuff for school. *School.* Did she even have a job? Could she blame them if they did ask her to resign?

What would she do? If she didn't teach, what would she do? But that wasn't really it. It wasn't just that she loved teaching, it was that she loved teaching at St. Thomas. She loved being in a Catholic school. She loved her colleagues; every last one of them was a part of her life, even Liz Morgan. And even though she didn't care for Liz, she was a constant in her life and right now she needed those constants.

Without realizing it, she'd smoothed her hands over her belly as if she were trying to touch the baby she might be carrying.

She didn't want another baby.

Just thinking about it made her sick inside. Thinking about a baby, all the work involved, and she was already stretched pretty thin. What would it do to Keegan? Rachel might be okay. Mortified that her mom was pregnant and so old, but she would most likely adjust. *But what about Keegan?* If she already felt like Teel didn't want her, what would adding another baby to that equation do?

Should she abort this baby? Could she? No. She couldn't even consider it for ten seconds.

But what about Keegan?

Thirsty, she left the bedroom and padded across the hardwood to the kitchen. Glass of water in hand, she turned and saw Keegan sitting on the lounge chair on the deck. Her breath caught, and she moved slowly across the room to stand at the door.

Keegan's hair blew gently in the breeze. She sat with her knees drawn up to her chest, but her feet were bare. Teel imagined she must be cold.

She wondered how school had been going for her before. She didn't really remember talking about it. Asking her if she liked her teachers this year. It was almost like life with Keegan began when Marin killed herself; she couldn't put herself back too much further in time unless she thought about Keegan's younger years.

But high school. Teel suddenly felt like the high school girl on her deck did belong to someone else. What if Keegan wanted that? To belong to someone else? Teel pressed her hand over her heart and squeezed her eyes shut.

Don't go, Keegan, she thought. Please don't go.

Knowing that Keegan had to be going stir crazy in her bedroom, Teel hesitated to open the door and have her come back in. And yet, she couldn't just leave her out there on the deck. It was chilly. Keegan didn't need to get sick on top of everything else going on.

She opened the door. Keegan didn't even look at her.

"Aren't you cold?"

"Leave me alone," Keegan whispered. "Please? Just leave me alone."

Teel stepped back into the house, but she thought better of it. She closed the door behind her this time and then squatted down beside Keegan.

She reached for her and cupped her chin in her hand. Keegan stared at her with bloodshot eyes.

"No. I'm sorry, but I can't." Teel stroked her thumb over Keegan's cheek. "I can't leave you alone. I'm gonna do everything I can to get you through this."

Keegan stared at her expectantly, but she looked away when Teel opened her mouth again to say something.

"Don't. I know it's your job to say it. Let's just pretend you did, and now you can go back to bed."

"Why are you doing this? Why are you pushing me away like this, Keegan?"

Keegan didn't answer her. Instead, she pulled away from Teel and stared across the deck.

Hurt by Keegan's harsh tone, Teel felt a window closing inside her. She was done with understanding for today.

"You need to come inside," she said firmly.

"I don't want…"

"I said you need to come inside. Now." She stood up, bones popping as she did. *Yeah, let's have a baby, old woman.*

"I hate you," Keegan snapped as she climbed off the lounger and threw the French door open.

Teel closed the door behind her, went down the hall and reset the alarm system, and then went back to bed. Bobby, still asleep, curled up close behind her and threw his leg over hers.

Usually she loved sleeping in his arms or with her stomach and chest pressed up against his back, but she couldn't take it tonight. Her head was swimming with Keegan's words, and her heart hurt, and she couldn't breathe.

She needed to be able to move, and Bobby was deadweight in his sleep.

She gave him an elbow and breathed in relief when he finally rolled away from her.

She glanced at the clock. Only quarter after one.

Chapter 43

Teel

IF EVER THERE were a day that she wanted to drive right by the school parking lot, it was today. She was afraid. So much more afraid to walk into the school right now than the day after she'd seen Liz at Walmart. She'd taught her girls never to be afraid of anything, and she still felt that way. She still believed in living, not hiding, but she desperately wanted to hide today.

She felt like every driver of every car she passed could see her, really see her and know who she was and what Keegan had done. She could already feel how closely she would be watched today, by her fellow teachers and students alike. Her skin already itched, like someone was holding a magnifying glass over her to get a good long look. Strangely, she wished they would keep looking. So they would see deeper and know who she was and who Keegan was and not judge her just from what had been said in the news.

With her stomach in knots and her heart in her throat,

she parked her car. And sat. Karin Isles knocked on her window as she walked past and waved, and Teel waved and then wondered where in the hell the smile she'd delivered had come from. God, she wanted to go home and crawl back into bed.

She was angry with Keegan all over again. Not even about yesterday. That was something completely different. Today she was angry with Keegan for making her a coward. For making her afraid to face a building full of people whom she had been close to for twenty-some years.

And yet, was that Keegan's fault? Keegan had done something wrong, but that didn't mean Teel couldn't get her ass out of her car and get to work. A didn't equal B here; there was no logic to it. Buck up, Teel, she told herself.

Bobby had been gone when she got out of the shower. No goodbye. No kiss. Apparently, he had work to do. Rachel was with Keegan, and she'd promised to stay home as long as she could. She hadn't argued, but she hadn't looked too thrilled about babysitting her fifteen-year-old sister. Teel just hoped that Bobby had lit out so early so that he could be back home to work and keep an eye on Keegan.

She wondered if it was necessary. No, she didn't believe Keegan was going to do anything stupid. She thought monumental thoughtless acts like Keegan's were once in a lifetime. But she wondered if it was necessary under the law for one of them to be at home with her at all times. It just wouldn't work. Bobby had to be out on site, and right now, as far Teel knew, he had three sites going. It wasn't like she could ask her mom to sit with Keegan; her mom stayed busy with friends and card games and luncheons. She loved Keegan and Rachel, but Teel couldn't ask her to bend her brain enough to be on Keegan's side and not harass Keegan about what she'd done. Bobby's family amounted to a brother who lived in

Arkansas, and his dad and stepmother, who now lived in Florida.

Eve would be happy to help, and Teel knew it. But she wasn't going to ask Eve to miss work for something wrong in her family. Apparently, this was her mess. It was her child who had been arrested, so it fell to her and Bobby to figure things out.

When Liz Morgan pulled her Hyundai into the parking lot, Teel knew it was time to move. She had no desire to walk into work with Liz, but she couldn't cower out here in her car and let Liz see that.

She made a show of checking her bag and her purse and then pulled the keys from the ignition and opened the door of the Edge.

"Morning, Teel," Liz called from her spot two cars over.

"Hi, Liz."

Teel shut the door, beeped the lock, and fell into step beside Liz.

"Rough day yesterday, I hear," Liz said quietly. She sounded sincere, but Teel wasn't about to talk. She had no plans to share what had happened with anyone here, other than John Shoch, who already knew. Most likely, everyone here knew about what had happened, and most likely there had been enough gossip to embellish what had happened to something that involved knives or guns and Teel's blood. But she had no desire to comment, to set the record straight.

She simply nodded.

"How's Keegan doing?"

Teel wondered how to answer that. She couldn't lie and say Keegan was swell, no matter how badly she wanted to. It was too much of a lie, and she didn't have it in her to pull it off. She couldn't tell Liz all about Keegan, because not only did she not want to share anything about Keegan with Liz, she just didn't know. Keegan had become such a stranger to her, she only caught rare glimpses of her baby girl and maybe when hell froze over, she'd admit *that* to Liz. Teel raised her eyebrows and answered Liz with a shrug. "As well as can be expected, I guess."

"Kids these days." Liz shook her head. "They never stop to think about what they're doing and how it will affect people around them."

It was true, and it was the same thing she and Bobby had said time and again. But it pissed her off to hear Liz say those words. At least she was rational enough to recognize that no matter what Liz said to her today, it would be wrong, and it was going to make her mad.

"I guess some things are just learned the hard way," Teel answered. She pulled the school door open and held it for Liz before stepping in behind her.

"Shouldn't you be at home with her?"

Okay, now this was the nosy, busybody Liz she knew.

"Bobby and I have that all worked out." It was a lie, because while they'd talked about it yesterday morning, she had no idea what Bobby's agenda was today.

Liz's smile was patronizing. "You got yourself a good one there," she told Teel. "It's good you have his support."

Teel was taken aback by Liz's comment. She smiled but said nothing. She watched Liz walk the short distance to the kitchen and wondered what that meant. Yes, Bobby was very good to her. But did she have his support? Was this really all on her? Did Liz really just suggest that she was to blame for Keegan's mess and that it was up to her to fix things, and it was just a good thing to have her husband's support?

Really? Did other people see it that way? She thought marriage and child-rearing were something done together. Yes, in the olden days, things might have been different. But Teel didn't believe in the old way of doing things. She didn't believe she, alone, had led Keegan down the wrong road, and she felt like fixing this was just as much Bobby's responsibility as her own.

Then again, Liz Morgan was probably one of those wives who had sex on Saturday evenings and every other Tuesday, after the ladies of the church meetings. She probably made her husband's lunches every day and referred to him and the boys in her family as the men folk.

"Hey Teel." John Shoch laid a comforting hand on her shoulder. Teel gave herself a mental shake. Here she was in the middle of this hell with the whole world watching, and she was standing in the hallway thinking bad things about a coworker.

"John."

"Doing okay?" John asked.

Compassionate and understanding, she believed that he was concerned. But she was still afraid of everything she might have to say to him before this was over. Starting with *Keegan's being put in a juvenile detention center* and possibly including *Oh, hey, I'm pregnant. I might need some time off to get myself together if I terminate this pregnancy.*

"Hanging in there," she said with a nod.

"Office door's always open."

"Thank you, John. I appreciate it."

"Except when it's not," he added with a laugh. Mr. Shoch's office door stayed open unless someone was sent to his office for disciplinary reasons. It was rare, but Teel knew there had been a few instances when he'd had to close the door and dole out a good dose of anger and punishment.

She appreciated his attempt to lighten the mood, so she laughed. But laughing felt wrong, and in that instant, she pictured herself stepping out onto the porch and getting the blood thrown at her, Keegan wandering down the hallway and seeing her like that.

Keegan walking away from her on the deck last night, telling her she hated her.

She made it to her classroom before she had to answer any more questions. Maggie fell into step behind her and parked her butt on the corner of her desk.

"Doin' okay?"

God, but she hated that question. And they were only two days into act two.

She nodded, too tired and already too frazzled to answer her.

"Who subbed yesterday?"

"Mr. Shoch."

"No way." Teel couldn't help it; she laughed again.

"I hear the kids thought he was pretty cool."

"Should I worry about my job?"

Maggie snorted over her tea cup. "You wanna job swap that man and be the principal?"

"Not a chance in hell," Teel answered.

"I'm figuring you're going to cancel lunch Saturday."

"Mags…"

"It's okay. I know you've got too much on your plate."

Another expression Teel was already tired of. Why were people so predictable? Who had authored the expressions of support, anyway? Everything said was so trite, so useless compared to Teel's heartache.

"Just call me," Maggie was saying. "If you need anything, even if you need someone to wash your car or walk your dog, just call me."

"We don't have a dog," Teel mumbled. Maggie grinned.

"I know. But you get my point, right? Let me know how I can help you. Tell me what I can do."

Teel held Maggie's gaze for a moment. "Just believe in Keegan for me, because she's so lost right now, Mags. Pray for her?"

"Done, of course." Maggie nodded.

"And me?"

"Done."

"And don't take anything I say personally, because I am so damned mad at the world, and everything is just grating on my nerves, and I don't know how much more I can take."

"Say whatever you need to. You can't run me off that easily."

Teel felt bad for the mean thoughts that had gone through her head ten seconds ago. Some people were in your corner, twenty-four seven, and if you felt cramped there instead of safe, then that was your problem. Teel figured maybe this was a good time to work on some of her own problems.

And maybe she should start with her relationship with Keegan.

Chapter 44

TEEL

TEEL SHIVERED. The rain had started just after ten this morning, and it hadn't let up. Normally, Teel enjoyed thunderstorms. There was a charge in the school, in the classrooms when it stormed. The dark clouds hung over the school, and the kids lingered at the windows expectantly. Teel understood; she tended to hover behind them, waiting for a streak of lightning and then counting *one Mississippi, two Mississippi* until the thunder followed.

Today, the kids had watched the sky, and Teel had sat at her desk or stood at her podium and glanced at the windows. She'd taught spelling and religion, and all the while she taught religion, she'd wondered who the hell she was to stand in front of these kids and talk to them about loving their neighbors and giving to those in need and following the commandments.

She'd dropped in at the clinic yesterday on her way home from work. Just a quick trip to the lab for a blood test. It had taken less than fifteen minutes, and yet, it was such a huge test. Teel had been sick all night; she'd barely been able to eat the pork loin she'd had in the crockpot all day for dinner. She hadn't eaten this morning. Instead, she'd gotten out of bed before Bobby, after lying awake half the night, and thrown up.

She hadn't discussed it with Bobby, but she still didn't know if she could have another baby. She couldn't have an abortion, but she could not wrap her mind around another pregnancy. How at-risk would this pregnancy be? The tension in her house was so thick, it took her breath away, and it hadn't been much better here at work.

It just scared her to think about what her having another baby would do to Keegan. What would Keegan think of her being so tied up with a new baby?

Usually, on a rainy school day, the only time she had to brave the rain was to the car and back. Today, though, she'd gotten a call from Dr. Cash asking her to come in after school. The call came late morning, and she'd been a terror since. Rather than take it out on her class, she'd assigned them independent seatwork and sat and stewed at her desk.

Why would he want to see her other than to tell her that yes, she was pregnant, and yes, at her age, a pregnancy was a huge risk and to present to her all the possible complications? It was only sprinkling when she left school around four, but by the time she'd parked at the clinic, it was raining buckets, and Teel stepped in three big puddles before she got to the front door.

She'd been called back to the exam room about two seconds after she'd sat down. But she'd taken her clothes off and slipped the lovely gown on, open to the front, and sat on the edge of the table and waited.

Teel liked Dr. Cash; she always had. But other people liked him too, which meant long waits and plenty of frustration over time wasted. Finally, after twenty minutes of staring at the walls decorated with posters of diagrams of the female reproductive system, and twenty minutes of wondering if she were pregnant, she closed her eyes and took a deep breath. This was making her crazy. *Stay calm, Teel. As soon as Dr. Cash comes in, you'll get your answer.* But when she opened her eyes, she found herself staring at the rack on the wall that held informational pamphlets about things like menopause and estrogen. Her eyes skipped over all of it and landed on birth control options.

She immediately thought of Keegan, and how lucky they were that she hadn't gotten pregnant, and then before she could even think about everything else, she wondered how she would know if Keegan *had* gotten pregnant. She hadn't learned about any of this until a year later, and if Keegan had gotten pregnant, she could have gone to the planned parenthood office and had an abortion and Teel would be none the wiser. At the very least, Keegan could have gone to planned parenthood and seen a doctor and gotten on birth control, and Teel wouldn't have to know any of it.

Teel's heart was racing when the door finally opened, and Dr. Cash walked in. She didn't know any of this for a fact. Normally she would think she had no reason to believe any of this about Keegan. And yet, a month ago, she'd never have believed she had any reason to worry about Keegan getting into this kind of trouble.

"Teel." Dr. Cash shook her hand. Teel hated sitting in only a gown and shaking hands with her doctor, even though they'd done the same thing for the past twenty years.

"Dr. Cash."

He stepped back and leaned against the counter behind him and crossed his arms over his chest.

"How're you feeling?"

Teel raised her eyebrows. She wasn't a newlywed, anxious

to know the results of this test because she wanted a baby. She was desperate to know if she was pregnant, because she...what? What good was it going to do her to know? Still. She wasn't interested in small talk.

"I'm a mess," she answered simply. "Everything that can go wrong at home is going wrong."

Dr. Cash made a sympathetic face and nodded. "What about you and Bobby? You guys doing okay?"

"Yeah." She winced. *Maybe not everything. Dear God, don't let that go wrong. Please, don't let that go wrong.*

"How's Keegan?"

Teel shook her head. "Not good."

"Have you thought about taking her to see someone?"

"You mean a doctor?"

"A counselor...a therapist. Someone for her to talk to."

Teel closed her eyes as they blurred with tears.

"No. I guess I just want her to talk to me."

"Is she? Talking to you?"

"No. She tells me she hates me and to leave her alone."

"Teel, I know that's hard for you. But you might think about finding someone for her. She's going through something huge, and she does need to talk. To get her head together. That's the first part of leading her through this."

"But I'm her mom," Teel cried. "Shouldn't I be the one to listen?"

"Yes, if Keegan's willing to talk to you. But she's not." Dr. Cash stood up straight and approached her again. "What about you? What's going on? Are you working?"

"Yes."

"Are you sleeping?"

"No. Not really."

"Well." He lowered his head to look at her over the tops of his glasses. "I'm going to suggest you start taking better care of yourself."

"Oh, God."

"Let's go ahead and do an exam while you're dressed for the occasion."

She couldn't appreciate his humor today, so she simply laid back and put her feet in the stirrups.

"I had the lab do a quantitative blood test," he explained as he sat on the stool at her feet. She closed her eyes and wished she were anywhere but here. "You'll remember that a quantitative test measures the amount of hCG in your bloodstream."

Because she'd had three miscarriages when she was younger, she was familiar with the jargon. Rather than simply check for hCG in her blood, he'd done a test to measure how much hCG was in her blood. Once she conceived, the levels of hCG should continue to increase rapidly.

"Your numbers are pretty low," he told her. She wanted to squirm, to move, to get up and run when she felt him touch her. She made herself lie still and kept her eyes closed. Funny, when she'd first gone to an ob/gyn when she was so much younger, they'd told her to keep her eyes open. She guessed so she wouldn't imagine horrible things. Right now, though, she had to squeeze them closed because she was thinking about Keegan. Again. Keegan on someone's bed with a guy on top of her. Hurting her.

Keegan would never forgive her for this. She would never forgive her for being pregnant, and if she managed to have this baby, Keegan would always resent it.

"I can't have this baby, Dr. Cash."

She didn't know she would say the words until she heard her voice.

"Well. You are pregnant, Teel," he answered matter-of-factly. "Are you telling me you want an abortion?"

God, she hated that word.

"No. But."

"Your numbers are low," he repeated. "Miscarriage is more prevalent with mothers in your age group."

She was too relieved to hear that to be offended, and she was angry at herself for being relieved.

"I can't do this to Keegan," she mumbled. "She accused me the other day…"

She couldn't say it. She hadn't even told Bobby that Keegan said she always looked at her like she wished she weren't her child. How could she repeat such a horrible thing to this man? Even if he was her doctor? Even if he had delivered Keegan?

"I just…I can't…"

"Let's just wait and see," he suggested.

"Do you really think I'll miscarry?"

"It's possible," he answered. "But if you don't, you're probably looking at a high-risk pregnancy."

Teel reached to wipe the tears from her face.

"You might want to start thinking about your future." He stood and pulled his latex gloves off.

"What do you mean?" She started to sit up, but he waved her back down.

"Let's just do the whole routine, so it's out of the way."

She lay back down on the table and put her right hand behind her head as he pressed his cold fingers over her right breast.

"A tubal ligation. At least."

"We just never talked about it," she said quietly. "I never dreamed I'd be in this situation at my age."

"Maybe now's a good time to talk about it."

She could just imagine that conversation. First she'd tell Bobby the pregnancy was real. Caution him that she could miscarry. Or she could have a high-risk pregnancy. And oh by the way, did he think she should have her tubes tied? Or maybe at her age, she should just dive in head first and have a hysterectomy. It was like a drive down life's freeway in the passing lane. Sex and babies and the end of an era of her life all in one breath.

"Yeah." She nodded. "We will."

She was still more worried about Keegan than anything else. How the hell was she supposed to tell her daughters that she was pregnant? What would Keegan do?

So distracted, she didn't realize Dr. Cash was finished with his exam until the door closed behind him. She hadn't heard a thing he'd said after he suggested she talk to Bobby about permanent birth control.

If she were being honest, she would admit the thought of having her tubes tied bothered her. Not that she wanted more children, but it did bother her. It made her feel like a part of her life was over. Like she was closing the door on something huge, and once closed, that door would never open again.

And yet, if she'd closed and locked that damned door a long time ago, she wouldn't be pregnant right now when her teenager needed her most.

She sighed. What about Rachel? God forgive her, she'd all but forgotten Rachel these past few weeks. She couldn't mother the two daughters she'd had for the past fifteen and nineteen years. How the hell was she going to manage a newborn?

She wondered what God would think of her if she prayed for a miscarriage.

Chapter 45

TEEL

BOBBY HAD dinner ready when she got home. She felt guilty for the way her stomach turned instantly when she smelled the barbeque sauce. He'd added the sauce to the leftover pork loin she'd made last night for dinner and made homemade fries.

Rachel sat by herself at the bar. She looked up at Teel as she nibbled on a fry.

"Hey, Rach." Teel set her purse on the counter and then kissed Rachel's cheek. "How was your day?"

Rachel leaned into her, so Teel put her arm around her shoulders.

"It was okay," she answered. "Daddy made dinner."

"I see that." Teel nodded. "Smells good," she lied.

"Where were you?"

Teel glanced at Bobby. What had he told the girls?

"Had an appointment."

"With who? A student? Parents?"

Bobby met Teel's gaze and barely shook his head. So he hadn't told them anything. Teel hated lying, but she wasn't ready to discuss the baby with Rachel or Keegan.

"Yeah. Parents." She took glasses from the cabinet and filled them with ice. "Where's Keegan?"

"Where else?" Rachel mumbled.

"Would you tell her dinner's ready?"

"I've told her three times."

Teel stopped moving and looked at Rachel. "Is she okay?"

"Other than being a freak? Sure, she's fine."

"Rachel."

"She was working on some homework or something. Did you get her assignments for her?"

"I did," Bobby answered. He fixed a plate for Teel. She had to fight to stand there by him and not run for the bathroom. "I also spoke with Roni Andrews."

"Who's that?" Rachel asked. "Some guy you work with?"

"No." Bobby picked up a bottle of red wine and glanced at Teel. She shook her head. He raised his eyebrows, but she turned away from him, afraid that Rachel would pick up on what they weren't saying. "She's a lawyer. I talked to her about Keegan."

"Really?" Teel filled her glass with water and poured Rachel tea.

"Is she young?"

"Why would you ask that?" Teel turned to her.

Rachel shrugged. "I don't know. Roni sounds like a young girl. I'd think you'd want someone with a lot of experience to help Keegan."

"I've heard very good things about her," Bobby assured Rachel.

"What did she say?" Teel asked. In the back of her mind, she was thinking about Keegan. That she needed to get Keegan out here with the family. They'd left her isolated far too long; it was time to move past this phase, whether it be their punishment or her self-imposed banishment to her room.

"Is she pretty?" Rachel asked.

"Why would you ask that?" Bobby glared at Rachel this time.

She glanced at Teel and then shrugged. "I don't know."

Teel wondered why Rachel would ask these questions about someone Bobby had talked to about helping with Keegan. Was Rachel that concerned about her and Bobby? And why would Teel let Rachel's questions bother her? What did this woman look like? Was she young? Was she married? Was she someone Bobby might prefer to spend time with right now?

Teel took a drink of water and eyed Bobby's wineglass. Bobby took a drink of wine and then swooped her into his arms and kissed her. She laughed in spite of the day she'd had. In spite of the month they'd all had. She couldn't help it.

His lips were smiling over hers, and he was laughing, too. Rachel groaned and pushed away from the bar. "Gross."

"Get your sister," Bobby told her without turning away from Teel. "Did we make a baby?" he whispered the second Rachel left the room.

Teel turned her face away from him. He sounded like he wanted this baby. Like he really wanted to do this again. When he rested his forehead against her cheek, she smoothed her fingers over his jaw. Maybe he did. Maybe he felt cheated that she hadn't given him a son.

"Yes."

He flattened his palm against her stomach.

"Don't, Bobby," she pleaded. "We need to talk about this. Before we talk to the girls."

"Okay." He kissed her again and then backed away from

her grinning like a twelve-year-old boy who just got a peek at his first girlie magazine.

Rachel appeared in the kitchen with Keegan trailing behind her.

"I'm not hungry," Keegan announced.

"You need to eat something," Teel told her.

"So do you. Sit down." Bobby leaned forward and set her plate on the counter. She eyed him suspiciously, afraid that he would blurt something out about the baby.

What would he say when she told him she didn't want it?

Keegan sat in the chair furthest from Teel's, which was where Bobby usually sat. She folded her arms on the bar and then rested her head on her arms. Teel watched her, remembering a time when she was four and she'd done the same when she was supposed to be eating dinner. She hadn't felt well, and she'd just put her head down and gone to sleep.

Teel's eyes blurred, and she looked away.

"Roni wants to meet with us tomorrow," Bobby announced.

Teel wanted to know why Bobby had to refer to her as Roni. Why wasn't she Mrs. Andrews? Or even Ms. Andrews? Why was she obsessing over this? Who cared how Bobby referred to the attorney he'd talked to about Keegan? Who cared if she was a hot little blonde number with sexy legs and pretty eyes? If she could help Keegan, what did it matter? And why the sudden jealousy with Bobby? He'd never given her cause to worry in all the years they'd been together.

"Okay," Teel agreed. "That's good."

"Who's Roni?" Keegan asked without lifting her head.

"The attorney who's going to help you, Keegan."

"I don't need an attorney," she said softly. "I did it. I did something wrong, and it hurt somebody."

Teel sat back, surprised to hear Keegan admit that she'd caused someone pain.

"You still need a lawyer," Bobby told her. "Sit up and eat, Keegan."

"I'm not hungry."

"Eat," he repeated and looked at Teel, as if to include her in the order.

She managed to get half of her sandwich and a couple of fries down, which was more than Keegan ate. Teel figured she'd lose it later, but she'd deal with it then.

"May I be excused?" Keegan asked quietly.

"Honey, you need to eat."

"I can't, Daddy," she wailed. "I can't eat. My stomach hurts."

Teel pressed her lips together, hurt by the interaction between Bobby and Keegan. Why was Keegan so angry with *her? Why just her?* She dragged her fingers through her hair, angry with herself for being jealous of Bobby and Keegan. Keegan needed someone, didn't she? Even Dr. Cash had said so.

"Want some soup?" he asked her.

"No."

"Milkshake?"

"No."

Teel watched the tenderness on Bobby's face turn to worry as Keegan stood up and shuffled back to her bedroom.

"We're punishing her, so you offer her a milkshake?"

"Let it go, Teel."

Rachel took her plate to the sink. "I'm going to meet Deacon to study."

Teel watched in silence as Rachel rinsed her plate and then put it in the dishwasher. Her daughter's hands were pretty. Long, elegant fingers. No age spots or freckles. She still wore the birthstone ring she and Bobby had given her when she'd turned sixteen. Her nails were short and rounded, each of them perfectly shaped.

Afraid, but knowing she had to do it, Teel looked up at Rachel's face. Her cheekbones were prominent, especially now that she had so little to smile about. She wore a turquoise blouse, open at the collar at the base of her long, graceful neck. Her blond hair was pulled up in a messy bun.

She was gorgeous.

When had Rachel become a woman? *Had* Rachel become a woman? Should Teel know? Should she ask? Did she want to ask? Not really. But was it part of her job?

"What?" Rachel finally noticed Teel staring at her. She swallowed the last of her tea and then rinsed her glass out.

"Nothing."

Teel's hand shook as she reached for her own glass. She had no idea what was going on in Rachel's life right now. Sure, she knew that Rachel had a boyfriend. She'd even met the boyfriend. But what else? Was she in love with him?

Was she sleeping with Deacon? Had the argument she and Rachel had the other day sent her running to Deacon's arms? His bed? Was she being careful? Did she really need to worry about this? If Rachel was nineteen and in college, was it Teel's place to ask?

Of course it was. She was Rachel's mother. Mothering someone you loved didn't just stop because that someone reached a magic age.

"How is Deacon?" Teel asked.

The smile on Rachel's face answered one question. She was head over heels in love with him.

"He's good."

"Anything we need to talk about?" Teel hoped she sounded casual, but she could tell by the way Rachel's eyebrows shot up that she'd missed it by a longshot.

Rachel actually laughed. "Really?"

"Rachel."

"I'll be back before midnight."

"Rachel, your mother is talking to you."

Rachel glanced at Bobby as she walked out of the kitchen.

"No, Mom's just asking if I've slept with Deacon yet."

Bobby turned to Teel with such a look of horror on his face, she laughed.

"You were asking that?"

She shrugged. "I thought I was being subtle."

"Is she sleeping with him? She's too young to be sleeping with…"

He trailed off, and Teel figured he was thinking about Keegan.

"We should send them to boarding school or something through the teen years." She pushed her plate away. "This is harder than the terrible twos."

"You're done?" he asked with a nod toward her plate. "You didn't eat much."

"I can't. Stomach's a mess."

"Because of…"

She shook her head, because she hadn't heard the back door open. Rachel was still in the house.

"Tell me about this lawyer you met with."

"She thinks she can help. For one thing, Keegan wasn't given the opportunity to have a lawyer present at questioning. And then she said something about proving culpability. She asked where Keegan took the pictures. I didn't know for sure. From what she said, it would be really good if Keegan took them at a party. They couldn't have expected privacy at a party. Kind of changes what Keegan did."

"I don't know where she took them." Teel stood up and scraped her plate over the garbage can. "That's not what I meant anyway."

"What did you mean?"

"What's she look like?"

Bobby laughed. "The lawyer? Did Rachel rattle you?"

"Mr. Alexander, you better start talking." Teel pointed a fork at him. "I'm old. I'm already fat. I'm gonna get huge. I cry all the time, and who wants to make love to someone who looks like she swallowed a watermelon?"

"I do," he answered immediately. "In fact, I'm up for it right now."

She laughed.

"She's short and wide. And she has mousy brown hair. And she wears horn-rimmed glasses."

"She's pretty hot, isn't she?"

"She is, but I have the hottest woman in the world. Why would I need to shop around?"

"You window shop."

"Who doesn't? I saw you checking that guy's ass out last Sunday when we left church."

She laughed and slugged him as he stepped closer to her and put his arms around her. "You are terrible. I was not!"

He backed her up against the counter and rubbed his middle against her.

"What do you think? Quickie? My office?"

"Ohmygod." Rachel stood at the end of the hallway and stared at them. "Ohmygod. I am so outta here."

Teel laughed and buried her face in Bobby's shoulder.

"I thought you were gone," Bobby said with a laugh.

"Oh, I am now. Wish Keegan wasn't comatose in there," Rachel mumbled. "I'd share that with her."

"Go. Mom and I are busy."

Still laughing, Teel felt her heart squeeze and ache. This is the way it used to be. Always joking and teasing and laughing. All four of them. Oddly enough, she wished Keegan were standing with Rachel right now, laughing, embarrassed, and as freaked out as Rachel.

It would be normal. She was afraid they would never be normal again.

"Eh," Rachel groaned again as she walked down the hall to the garage. "I need to bleach my ears and eyes. Yuck."

"Hey!" Teel lifted her head. "That's harsh!"

"Goodnight, Parental Units."

Teel looked at Bobby. He grinned.

"Really?" she asked. "Now? Still?"

He pressed into her again. "What do you think?"

"What about Keegan?"

"She's doing homework."

Teel stroked her thumb over his lips. "You know what I love about you?"

"What?"

"You keep me young."

Chapter 46

Teel

FOR THE SECOND TIME TODAY, Teel sat more than half-naked in a cold room, waiting on a man. At least this time, she was wearing panties and her blouse. Nevermind that it wasn't buttoned, and she wore nothing under it. At least this was Bobby's office, and she was sitting on a leather loveseat and she'd just had mind-blowing sex. Making love with Bobby was never bad, never boring, but there were times he still blew her mind and left her begging for more.

She would have begged for more tonight, but they had too much to talk about. Way too much going on for them to act like teenagers and go at each other against his desk, only to end up on the floor with rug burns on their backs and knees.

Bobby had gone upstairs to check on things, make sure Keegan was in her room and not wandering the house. She should use these few moments while she waited on him to piece together her argument on why they couldn't have this baby. But that thought led her to thoughts of abortion, and she just couldn't think about it. The mental argument she'd had with herself all day regarding the baby and having an abortion had worn her out, and even though she should be thinking about it right now, she wasn't.

Instead, she was sitting on the loveseat, with her head back and her eyes closed, and she was damned near asleep when Bobby came back. She was so exhausted, and romping all over the room with Bobby had left her pleasantly warm and tingly. She figured she could probably just sleep right there, sitting up on the loveseat.

He closed the door with a swing of his hip and then a gentle kick with his foot. Wearing only his faded blue jeans, he crossed the room and handed her a bottle of water. She leaned against him when he sat down beside her.

"She okay?"

"She was reading something," Bobby answered. "At her desk."

"Good to see her get out of that bed."

He put his arm around her and trailed his fingers up and down her arm.

"So. Tell me about this baby."

Teel took a deep breath and leaned her head back again to look up at him.

"I'm pregnant."

He grinned.

"You're happy about this? You want to have a baby? At our age?"

"It's been done."

"I don't think I can do it."

"You're healthy…"

She shook her head. "I don't mean physically. I don't think I can do the whole baby thing over again. The sleepless nights. The diapers. Bottles. Preschool. I don't want to do it again."

"And yet...here we are."

Teel nodded. "Here we are."

"You're not saying..."

"No. I don't want an abortion, but...Bobby, have you thought about what this baby will do to Keegan?"

He sighed and nodded his head from side to side. "It might do her good, Teel. Get her mind off of all of this."

Teel shook her head and stood up. She paced the office, trying to find the words to tell Bobby how worried she was. Trying to find the courage to tell her husband what their daughter had said to her the other day.

"The other day..." She swallowed hard. "The other day, when the people...were here."

He nodded. She stopped talking when he got off the couch and approached her. She almost pushed his hands away, but he simply buttoned her blouse half-way.

"When it was all over...and you were busy...I laid down with Keegan. Held her in my arms. And we slept."

"I know. I watched you."

She smiled, but her eyes blurred with tears. She ducked her head and tried to wipe them away.

"She was dreaming. I woke her up. Tried to get her to talk to me."

"And?"

"She said that I look at her like I wish she wasn't my child. Like I wish that there'd been a mix up at the hospital and that I brought the wrong baby home."

"Honey, she's just lashing out. She wants to hurt us."

"No, Bobby, she's lashing out at me. Not us. Me." Teel set the bottle of water on his desk. "And it's not just that. This is real, Bobby. She's really lost right now. What if she really believes that? What if she really believes I don't want her? And then I turn around and tell her I'm pregnant?"

Bobby dropped and sat on the edge of the loveseat.

"Because here's the thing," Teel plunged ahead, "I've never wished that she weren't my child." She looked up and boldly met his eyes. "But I've wished more than once that she could be more like other kids."

It killed her to say it. She sobbed openly, and she looked away from Bobby, afraid that he might agree with Keegan. That he might decide she didn't love Keegan enough and that he didn't love her as much as he thought he did.

"Teel." He stood up again and reached for her hand.

"I feel like everything going on with her is my fault. Like I've caused some huge rift. She's desperate to get back at me, and in that attempt to hurt me, she's lost her way back here. She's hurt so many..." Teel leaned into him and cried. "She's hurt so many people, but mostly she's hurt herself."

"It's not your fault," he said quietly. "It's just something that happened. It just happened. Keegan knows you love her."

"I don't think she does," Teel protested.

"Then tell her."

"I tell her that every day. I give..."

Bobby shook his head. "I know you do everything for Keegan and Rachel. I know it. I see it. But Keegan's still a kid. And she's immature at that. She needs to hear the words just as much as she needs you to do things for her and care for her."

Teel sighed. "I thought I said them. I thought I told her I loved her."

"Well, just in case you didn't, maybe you should."

She nodded against his shoulder.

"What did Dr. Cash say?"

"He said my numbers are low, Bobby, and that at my age

and with the problems I've had in the past, it's very possible I'll miscarry."

"And that's what you're banking on?"

She opened her mouth to answer him, but she thought about how harsh that sounded.

"Do you really wanna do this? You're really happy about another baby?"

"I didn't ask for it," he answered simply, "but here we are. Of course I want this baby. This is you and me, Teel. We made this baby. Just the same way we made Rachel and Keegan."

She licked her lips and nodded. "Great. So I'm already a bad mother to this one, too."

"You're under a lot of stress."

"That's no excuse."

"I admit it's not the best time." He shrugged. "Especially not with things the way they are with Keegan. But the lawyer sounded positive. Like we could get the charges dropped. Or at least that Keegan wouldn't be charged with a felony."

"Keegan's legal issues might be the least of our problems, Bobby."

"I think we're gonna be okay. All of us."

"And," she took his hand and lay it over her stomach again, "how will you feel if this baby is another girl?"

"Happy."

"And if I do miscarry, are you going to blame me?"

"Why are we dealing in blame these days? That's not us, Teel. You and I don't do blame and finger pointing. Why would you do this now?"

"Because I'm more concerned about Keegan than I am about this baby."

"We'll be okay."

———

AFTER SHE SHOWERED and put on her pajamas, albeit early, Teel knocked on Keegan's bedroom door. She waited for Keegan to acknowledge her and then tiptoed in as if Keegan's floor were made of eggshells.

"Whatcha doing?" she asked. She wished she still had her school slacks on, because she had nothing to do with her hands. At least if she still her had slacks on, she could stick them in her pockets.

"Finishing a biology assignment," Keegan mumbled as she closed her book. She sat at her desk, but she was wearing pajamas. Teel couldn't remember the last time she'd seen Keegan dressed to leave the house with her hair and makeup done.

"Dad said he got your work for you."

Keegan nodded, but she was uncomfortable with Teel in her room. Teel could tell.

"Maybe tomorrow we'll be on the road to getting things ironed out. Meeting your lawyer and stuff."

Keegan shrugged. "Whatever."

"Don't you wanna get back to normal?" Teel perched on the edge of Keegan's bed.

"What's normal, Mom? There is no normal anymore, is there?"

"School. Friends. Don't you…"

"Friends? I don't have any friends. Remember? I'm either the slut who fucked Sean Spanner or the girl who killed Marin English. Who wants to be friends with someone like me?"

Teel raised her eyebrows. "How about the girl who could sing the alphabet backwards and do the moonwalk better than Michael Jackson? How about the girl who made straight As and loved Saturday morning cartoons? Where's she at these days?"

"Gone."

"I think people are a little more forgiving than you're giving them credit for, Keegan."

Keegan's laugh was cold and empty. "Right. Starting with you. Right, Mom?"

Teel longed to go to Keegan and put her arms around her. But she knew Keegan wouldn't tolerate it right now.

"You know what? It doesn't concern you. What I did is none of your business, so you need to just let it go."

Teel wondered what would have happened in her home, growing up, if she or Eve would have spoken to their mother this way.

"Well, that's where you're wrong. I'm your mother, and when you're fifteen, everything you do concerns me. Everything you did affects me and your dad and Rachel."

"Maybe what happened with Marin. But what happened with Sean is my business."

"Don't you wanna talk about it? About the way he hurt you..."

"I never said it hurt."

Teel groaned. She was getting nowhere. Maybe Dr. Cash was right. Maybe Keegan did need to see a professional.

"Can I ask you something?"

Keegan simply stared at her.

"Was he the only one?"

"What?"

"The boy at the party? Was he the only one?"

Keegan opened her mouth to answer Teel, but she seemed to think better of it. She pursed her lips and cocked her head at Teel.

"At the party? Was he the only one at the party?" she finally asked. "Are you asking me if I set up business at the party?"

"God, no, Keegan." Teel threw her hands up as if to show Keegan surrender. "Of course not. I'm just asking if there's been anyone since. If we should get you on birth control. You should at least be careful."

Keegan laughed again, but the sound only chilled Teel.

"So…Rachel is the freak who's scared to sleep with her boyfriend. And I'm the slut who's sexually active at fifteen. Is that it?"

"Why do you do this, Keegan?" Teel sighed and leaned against the wall. "Why do you keep pushing me away?"

Keegan looked away, but Teel saw her eyes fill with tears.

"I love you." Teel took a step toward her, but she stopped when Keegan turned to stare at her. "I love you so much. Do you know that?"

"Whatever."

"Keegan…"

"Lemme alone."

Teel reached for the doorknob, but she stopped and looked back at Keegan. She was hunched over her desk now, head on her folded arms, her whole body shaking.

She couldn't walk out. She couldn't walk away, no matter that Keegan had told her to leave her alone. Instead, she hurried back across Keegan's room and leaned over her to put her arms around her.

"Keegan, it's okay."

Keegan lifted her hand to throw Teel off.

"Leave. Me. Alone."

It wasn't the scream that did it, but the look in Keegan's eyes. Sheer hatred. Teel covered her mouth with her hand and backed away from Keegan.

She couldn't have another baby. Not even because of what it would do to Keegan. She couldn't have another baby, because she couldn't take any more of this heartache.

And no one had the power to hurt her like her daughters.

Chapter 47

TEEL

IF IT WAS hard to get out of bed yesterday, today was worse. She hadn't slept more than a few hours, and when she did sleep, she dreamt about the baby. First she dreamt that she miscarried, and somehow they knew it was a boy. Then she dreamt about the baby's baptism, and how Rachel's friends thought the baby was hers, because Teel was too old to be a new mom again.

Only the thought of meeting with Roni Andrews later in the evening could drag Teel out of bed. She had to imagine the meeting as a big blank page, where they would be able to write their own ending to Keegan's problem. It was all she focused on as she walked, half-asleep, through her shower and her morning routine. A table with the key players present, though she couldn't picture Keegan there. It hurt too much to think about Keegan. She'd crawled into bed last night before nine, ignoring the English and reading worksheets she should have graded. Ignoring the phone when it rang and Rachel when she knocked gently on the door to tell her Aunt Eve had called. If she could just pretend last night hadn't happened, then maybe she could get through today.

So, a meeting of the key players who would currently remain nameless, a blank page and maybe somehow they could get Keegan's arrest watered down and maybe somehow they could turn a corner and start over.

Half-way through mission impossible—her makeup and hair routine—Rachel brought Teel a cup of coffee. She should have said no thank you, but she'd have had to explain why. Right now, Rachel seemed such an odd combination of hopeful and needy, Teel couldn't afford to give her only half her attention. Not with the way Rachel had been so angry with her just a week or two ago. Not with the way Keegan had banished Teel from her life.

She took a small sip of the coffee, winced at the metallic taste, and tried to smile at Rachel.

"So are you excited?" Rachel asked. Teel met her eyes in the mirror. Excited? How did Rachel know about the baby? Surely Bobby hadn't said anything. "About meeting Keegan's lawyer? Do you think she'll keep Keegan out of jail?"

Teel took a deep breath and tried to smile at Rachel.

"I wouldn't say I'm excited," she finally said. "Hopeful, I guess."

"Dad seems to think it's all gonna go away."

Teel wished it would be that simple. The fact remained that no matter what happened regarding the arrest, Keegan had changed, and maybe she and her youngest daughter would never be close again.

That did it. She ducked into the smaller, private alcove in the bathroom and vomited.

"Are you okay?" Rachel asked when she came back out to her sink.

"Yeah," Teel said quietly. "Fine."

"Mom, you don't look good." Rachel reached out and tugged at the waistband of Teel's slacks. "You look like you've lost ten pounds."

"Well, I need to lose another ten," Teel said with the dregs of a smile.

"You're worried about Keegan."

Teel nodded. "Of course I am."

"I heard her crying last night. In her sleep."

Teel squeezed her eyes shut.

"It's okay. I...um..." Rachel shrugged and averted her eyes. "I sat with her. For a while."

Teel smiled, for real this time, but she felt a flash of envy. Why could *everyone else* comfort Keegan?

"Thank you."

"I just want this all to be over, Mom."

"Me, too, Rach. Me, too."

"I want our lives back. I want you and Daddy back."

"Oh, honey." Teel opened her arms to Rachel, who still wore her pajamas. "We love you. You know that."

Rachel nodded, but Teel heard the little hiccups that meant she was trying not to cry.

"I love you so much," Teel repeated. She held Rachel as tight as she could. "And I miss you, Rachel. I miss you. But... I'm so worried about Keegan right now."

"I know." Rachel backed away from her. She tucked her hair behind her ear. "Me, too."

"Do you know how much I appreciate what you've done to help us? Since this started? Do you know that, Rachel?"

She nodded, but she wouldn't look at Teel. Instead, she wiped at her eyes and then ambled out of the room, playing with her hair.

Teel brushed her teeth and then dumped the coffee down the sink. She finished her makeup, and she styled her hair, and then she avoided looking in the mirror, because she was afraid of the person she would see.

Maggie was waiting for her in the kitchen at school. She steeped her tea while Teel grabbed a bottle of water from the soda machine. Liz Morgan asked her how she was doing, and Teel simply said she was fine and thanks for asking. When Mr. Shoch asked her how she was feeling, she could only smile and nod, because her throat tightened up and her eyes filled with tears.

"We haven't told the girls yet, but I'm pregnant," Teel said to Maggie once they were alone in her classroom.

"Wow." Maggie's face was a mix of excitement and horror. "When it rains, it pours, huh?"

"Bobby wants this baby, Maggie. He's really happy about it."

"And you don't?"

"Would you? If you were me?"

"I wouldn't want another child, if it were me pregnant," Maggie said slowly. "But I'm not you. You're…Teel Alexander. You're a good person. You're a happy person. I could see you wanting another baby."

"That was the old Teel Alexander," Teel answered. "I have nothing left inside to give another baby. I don't even know how to reach my youngest daughter now. She hates me."

"Happens to so many people, Teel." Maggie touched her hand. "That whole teen rebellion thing. She'll be okay."

"It's different, though, when it happens to you, Maggie." Teel studied her friend's face. "We're not like just like them. Like all the rest of them. This is me and Keegan. And it hurts a hell of a lot more when it's your kid lashing out and hating you."

"There's a fine line between love and hate, Teel," Maggie told her. "And she's walking that line, waiting for you to yank her back over."

"I don't think so." Teel shook her head and started unloading her bag.

"Who's the safest person in the world to hate?" Maggie asked. She leaned across Teel's desk and curled her fingers around Teel's wrist. Teel looked up and met Maggie's eyes. "Your mom. You can hate the absolute hell out of your mom." Maggie raised her eyebrows. "Right? You can hate your mom to kingdom come. Right?"

Teel didn't answer her.

"And why? Why can you hate your mom with such a passion?" Maggie pushed her for a response.

"Because your mom will always be there," Teel whispered.

"Because your mom will always, always, always love you. And she'll be there waiting when you realize how wrong you are, that you don't hate her."

Teel dropped into the chair behind her desk. Maggie squeezed her wrist.

"You hang in there," she said firmly. "Do you hear me? Hang in there, and she will come around. Okay? It might tear you apart before it's over, but she will come around."

Teel nodded. "I just never...I never thought in a million years...that this would happen. That we would be just like everyone else."

Teel rode her emotions like ocean waves through the rest of the day. She managed to swallow the swell of tears when she had to, when she was faced with two students fighting in the hallway, when she came face to face with Liz Morgan in the teacher's lounge and Liz asked if she'd used the pregnancy test yet. She'd lied through her teeth and told her no and that she wasn't that concerned about it. She picked at a ham sandwich at lunch time and managed to eat a bite of it before lunch was over and she threw it away.

On the drive home, she got a text message. She wasn't one to text and drive, but she had to check it when she saw that it was Rachel's number. Rather than read it and drive and cause an accident, she pulled over into a dentist's parking lot and opened the message.

Just wanted to tell you I love you. Deacon and I are going to a party later. I'll be home before midnight.

The flood of tears surprised her, though it shouldn't have. She sat for a moment, in the parking lot, and cried. She didn't care anymore who saw her, who recognized her car or plates and saw that she was crying. Didn't everyone know by now what was going on? Didn't everyone know that Keegan had been arrested? Didn't everyone know what Keegan had done?

It wouldn't be long before everyone knew she was pregnant. Including Keegan. And then all hell would break loose, and her family would continue to unravel until maybe there was nothing left. Maybe just she and Bobby left with nothing but the frayed threads that used to bind their family.

When the sobs were under control, she put the Edge in drive and pulled out of the dentist's lot. She dreaded going home. Keegan would be in her room. Bobby would be working, and she knew it wasn't fair that Bobby was working from home every day and not spending time at his construction sites. He had capable builders, yes, but he loved being on site. He loved the physical labor. That love was evident in his lean, strong body and his more than successful business.

And yet, she didn't want to go home. The house that she used to love had become a prison to all of them, and they were being held in the worst time of their family life. Depression and sorrow permeated the whole house, and with just one breath, it filled her and left her almost paralyzed.

She climbed slowly from the car, careful not to bump Bobby's truck as she got out. The sun was out, and it reflected in the puddles yesterday's downpour had left in the streets. It was chilly, though. The trees across the street, the woods behind those houses blazed with yellow, orange and red leaves. Ordinarily, this was Teel's favorite time of year.

The house was quiet when she walked in. Rachel wasn't home, and Bobby was either downstairs or out in the shed behind the house. The silence grated on Teel. She decided to change her clothes and then turn on some music so she wouldn't feel so alone. Just until Bobby was ready for dinner.

She changed quickly, choosing a pair of worn, comfortable jeans, thinking how sad that she had to look to clothing for comfort. As she turned to leave the bathroom, she noticed the bottom drawer of the vanity wasn't quite closed. It was the drawer where they'd always kept their medicines and bandages and first aid things. She wondered absently if Bobby had cut himself while working.

She nudged the drawer closed with her foot and then headed back to the kitchen. It was only four o'clock. They weren't to meet with Keegan's lawyer until six. She had to find something to fix for dinner, which was hard to do when all food tasted like paste and made her want to vomit.

Deciding she'd ask Keegan what she wanted for dinner and insist that she come out to the kitchen while she cooked, Teel went down the hall and tapped on Keegan's closed door.

When Keegan didn't acknowledge the knock, she tried again.

"Keegan, what do you want…"

She stepped into the room, heart beating so hard it hurt. Keegan was asleep, but something felt wrong. The room was too still. Even with the laptop having been gone for several days, there was something too still and quiet about Keegan's room.

"Keegan?"

The blinds were closed, and it was gloomy and dark. Teel

flipped the light switch and glanced at her daughter, unmoving, on the bed.

"Keegan?" She moved closer to the bed and touched Keegan's leg, hidden beneath her comforter. "Keegan, honey, why don't you come out to the kitchen with me?"

Still nothing. Teel moved closer yet and stood at the head of the bed. She noticed a bottle of water on the desk. She leaned over, knowing that Keegan would probably wake up and take a swing at her, and shook Keegan's shoulder.

"Keegan?"

She leaned closer still when she noticed Keegan's fingers curled around something. Amber. Round.

"Keegan?" Teel shook her harder. "Keegan?"

Heart hammering dangerously hard now, Teel reached for Keegan's hand. It was cold. She pried the bottle out of Keegan's hand, already screaming, though she had no idea what she was saying.

It was an old prescription for Lortab, from when Bobby had fallen at a construction site and broken his collarbone. He'd done damage to his rotator cuff and dislocated his shoulder. The doctor had prescribed Lortab after the surgery on his rotator cuff.

"Keegan?" Teel shook her hard. "Ohmygod. Keegan? Keegan, wake up!"

Keegan looked pale, but then she'd been in her room for days on end, with no sun and no fresh air, and Teel suddenly couldn't remember if she'd been this pale last night when she'd come into her room.

"Bobby!" Teel ran to Keegan's door and yelled. "Bobby, please?"

She hurried back to Keegan's side and touched her hand again. Leaning over Keegan, she felt her chest rise and fall. She nearly slumped in relief that Keegan was still breathing.

"Keegan Alexander!" She shook her again. "Keegan, goddammit, wake up! Bobby, help me!"

She dropped to her knees beside Keegan's bed. She needed a phone. She needed to call 911, but she was afraid to leave Keegan's side.

"Keegan? Keegan, wake up!" She was crying now, too hard to make sense, but she kept talking to Keegan. "Bobby! Bobby, I need you!"

Finally she heard him. She heard the back garage door open and bang back against the wall. Then the back door and his footsteps as he ran inside.

"Call 911!" she yelled.

"What the...What? Ohmygod..."

"Call 911!"

Bobby disappeared from Keegan's room. Teel leaned over Keegan's bed, stroking her hair off her forehead.

"Don't you die on me, Keegan. Don't you leave me."

It crossed Teel's mind as she knelt at Keegan's bedside that it hadn't been six weeks ago that this nightmare started. When that ambulance came and took Marin English away.

Just like them. We're just like them.

"No, we're not," she argued aloud. "No, we aren't, Keegan. We're not just like them. We're not just like anyone. This is you and me, kiddo. You and me. Wake up, baby. Wake up. I love you. I love you, Keegan. Please? Please don't leave me."

She was still talking, still crying when Bobby's hands pulled her gently away from Keegan. She turned on him, ready to fight him off, when she realized there were strangers in the room with them. Paramedics. With a gurney and a bag of tricks they would now use to try and save her daughter.

Chapter 48

T EEL

THE LIGHT in Keegan's room was brash and yellow, and Teel felt chilled as she stood helplessly and watched the paramedics examine Keegan. She was vaguely conscious of Bobby's arms around her, but she couldn't be bothered to look at him. She desperately needed to touch Keegan. To hold her hand. To be connected to her. Will life into her.

"She's not breathing!"

"What?" Teel struggled against Bobby's arms. "What? She was breathing just a minute ago." She tugged hard, trying to get away from Bobby. What if these two boys, they hardly looked old enough to drive a car, didn't know what they were doing? What if they screwed up and cost Keegan her life? "She was breathing just a minute ago."

"Teel, step back," Bobby said calmly. Teel ignored him and struggled to get away from him and close to Keegan.

She melted, though, when the paramedics dropped into

place and began doing CPR. Her knees were liquid, and Bobby caught her on the way down.

"Oh, God," she whispered. "God, help her."

After what felt like hours, the paramedic breathing for her straightened.

"What're you doing?" Teel asked quickly. "What are you doing? Why are you stopping?"

"Pulse is steady," the other guy said. Teel leaned around him to see Keegan. She still looked pale, though now Teel could see blue around her lips.

She watched impatiently as the paramedics moved Keegan to the gurney and started an IV. Keegan's body was limp, her arms fell from the sides of the gurney. Teel's stomach turned. One of the paramedics gently lifted Keegan's arms to her sides and then strapped them down.

Teel broke loose of Bobby's grip and stumbled to Keegan's side. She sobbed out loud again when she touched Keegan's cold, clammy skin.

"What're you doing?" she asked as one of the paramedics placed an oxygen mask over Keegan's face.

"Giving her oxygen, m'am."

"Teel." Bobby put his hands on her waist.

"Oh God, Bobby," she cried. Under the mask, Teel had seen that Keegan's lips had turned a slightly bluish color. "Oh, God."

"C'mon, Teel." Bobby tugged at her. "Let them out. Let 'em do their job."

Teel backed away, but she strained to hold onto Keegan's hand. They rushed Keegan out the hall to the family room door; Teel ran behind them. She glanced back at Bobby, scared to go without him.

"Go!" He nodded. "I'm coming. Just go."

Scared. God, she was so scared. What if—? What if she—? Teel climbed into the back of the ambulance with Keegan and sat beside her, holding her hand. Keegan still slept, though she seemed to be coming around. A couple of times she twisted and turned in her sleep, as if she was in pain or having a bad dream.

How awful, Teel thought. How awful for Keegan to have swallowed those pills, thinking she was going to escape and then to be stuck in some horrible nightmare.

"Keegan," Teel leaned over her, "Keegan, please. Please wake up."

The ride was short and still too long, and then suddenly the ambulance rolled to a stop, and everyone was moving again. Teel stepped down and backed out of the way. She needed to be with Keegan, but the paramedics asked her to stay back. She looked around wildly, searching the parking lot for Bobby.

They hurried Keegan in through the emergency doors, and Teel followed them, still looking over her shoulder for Bobby.

"Ma'am?"

She stopped short when a short brunette in pink scrubs touched her arm.

"You'll need to wait here."

"I can't—"

"You'll have to. Let them take care of her."

Teel spun on the ball of her foot just as Bobby rushed in.

"Where is she?"

"They took her back," Teel said quietly. She looked up at Bobby, desperately needing him to be strong for her. To put his arms around her. Tell her that Keegan was going to be okay.

Just like always, he reached for her and pulled her hard against his body and locked his arms around her. She rested her forehead against his shoulder and cried.

"We can't lose her, Bobby," she whispered.

"We're not gonna lose her," he answered. "She's gonna be okay."

"How do you know that? How do you know she's gonna be okay?"

"She just is, Teel," Bobby said impatiently.

"She's too young. She's too damned young to die. It would all have gone away, if she could've just given it time."

Bobby tried to interrupt her, but Teel raged on.

"She's gonna be sixteen. She'll be driving. Wanting to go to the spring dance. She's too goddamned young to die. To want to die."

"Teel," Bobby's whisper broke. This time she reached for him and pulled his head down to her shoulder. "She's gonna be okay. We have to believe, she's gonna be okay."

Teel felt eyes all over them as they stood in the middle of the ER waiting room and cried. She didn't care. Nothing mattered right now. Nothing but Keegan.

"Teel?"

Teel looked up when she heard her sister's voice. Eve ran through the automatic door so fast she nearly clipped it.

"Ohmygod." Her eyes were bloodshot; her mascara and eye shadow was streaked and smeared around her eyes. "Is she okay?"

"We don't know yet." Teel shook her head. "She seemed to be…in the ambulance…she seemed to…Like she was coming around…"

"Oh, God." Eve put a hand on each of their shoulders. "I'm so sorry. I'm sorry."

"She's gonna be okay, Eve," Teel said. She wondered if she was channeling Bobby, because she sure as hell didn't feel as confident as she sounded.

"Teel, what about Rachel?" Eve asked her.

"Oh, God." Teel's knees dipped, and Bobby backed her into a chair. "I forgot about Rachel. I keep forgetting about

Rachel. I'm so caught up in Keegan, I keep forgetting about Rachel."

"What do you want me to do?" Eve asked calmly. She dabbed at her eyes and then wiped her hand on her slacks.

"She has to know," Teel whispered. "She needs to be here."

"Okay." Eve nodded. "Okay. I'll call her. I'll find out where she's at. And I'll go get her. She shouldn't drive. Not...not today."

"Thank you." Teel nodded. She watched Eve walk over to the corner of the room and flip her cell phone open.

"What did she take?" Bobby asked.

Teel looked up at him, surprised by his question. Of course he couldn't know. She had been holding the pill bottle, and she'd given it to the paramedic in the ambulance.

"Lortab."

"Son-of-a-bitch."

"Bobby."

"It was my prescription."

"Bobby, no." She reached for his hand. "No."

She watched his face for a moment, but he seemed to be lost in thought.

"What?" she finally asked him.

"Trying to remember how many of them I took. How many would have been left."

The same brunette nurse approached them with a clipboard and started talking about insurance. Teel wanted to snap the clipboard in half, but Bobby simply took a deep breath, rubbed first his right eye on his right shirt sleeve and then his left on his left sleeve, and took the form from her.

"Rachel's with Deacon," Eve said as she rushed back over to them. "He's bringing her here."

Teel nodded.

"Did she say anything?" Eve asked and nodded toward the nurse who had brought the clipboard. "About Keegan?"

"Red tape." Teel dragged her fingers back through her hair. "God, this is making me crazy. I need to know. I need to know what is going on." She stood up and crossed to the desk where the little nurse was now sitting. "Can you please let me see my daughter now? I need to know what's going on with her."

"Let me go check."

Teel rested her elbows on the counter and covered her face with her hands. Again, the thought of Jeannie English finding Marin covered in blood came to mind.

She lifted her head as her stomach clenched and tightened again. The nurse was still gone. Bobby was still filling out paperwork.

"Ma'am?" The nurse hurried out to them. "You and your husband can see her—"

"Mom?"

Teel froze when she heard Rachel's voice. She turned, wondering how the hell she and Deacon had gotten to the hospital so soon. Ready to read Deacon the riot act for driving so damned fast. Rachel ran through the waiting room and flew into Teel's arms.

Torn, Teel hugged Rachel close. She couldn't just walk away from Rachel, but she was desperate to see Keegan.

"Mommy?" Rachel sobbed. "Why did she do this? Why'd she do it, Mom?"

"Oh, God." Teel ran her hands over Rachel's back and up and down her arms and then over her face and into her hair. She realized she was checking to make sure Rachel was whole. To make sure she was healthy, unscathed. Because she'd missed too damned much with Keegan. "Rachel, I don't know. I don't know, baby."

"Where is she?" Rachel asked. She turned her head to look at Bobby. Teel noticed Deacon standing beside Eve, his eyes a little bloodshot.

"In an exam room," Bobby told her. "Let's go."

Bobby led Teel and Rachel down the hall behind the nurse. To Teel's surprise, she didn't stop Rachel from coming with them. The hallway seemed to go on and on, and Teel was dying to get to Keegan. To be at her side. To touch her. Talk to her.

But then they were outside Exam Room C1, and Teel stopped so suddenly, it was as if she hit a wall. She couldn't go in. She couldn't see Keegan like this. Her heart beat so hard, she couldn't breathe.

She bent over at the waist and sucked in a deep breath, the same way she'd done a million years ago in PE class after running too many laps.

"What is it, Teel?" Bobby asked. "What's wrong?"

"I can't. I can't do this."

"She needs you."

"I can't, Bobby. I'm scared. I'm so scared."

"How do you think she feels?" Bobby snapped. "You are her mother. She needs you."

Teel stood up straight. She lifted her chin and turned her face from him.

"C'mon," Bobby said, this time more gently. "Be strong, Teel. Be strong for Keegan. She needs you. And me. She needs all of us to be strong for her right now."

"I'm scared."

"I am, too," he whispered. He cupped her chin in his hand and leaned so close she thought he was going to kiss her. "I've never been so fucking scared in my life. But whatever we feel, she must feel a million times worse."

Teel pressed her lips together, aware of Rachel watching their every move. Bobby's blue-eyed gaze burned through her, until she nodded.

"I know. I know, Bobby, I do. I just keep thinking. I keep

thinking what if? What if I wouldn't have walked in there? What if I'd waited…"

Bobby shook his head. "Not now. No what ifs. Okay? Later. Between you and me. Not now."

"Okay."

Teel took a deep breath and then turned to the closed curtain of the exam room. She reached for Bobby's hand, but instead she felt Rachel slip her fingers in hers. Teel squeezed gently and then led them into the room.

Keegan lay pale and lifeless. Teel felt her breath catch. Had there been a mistake? Was she—? She walked further into the room. An IV was attached to a needle in the back of Keegan's hand. Teel wondered absently what was in it.

"Keegan?" Her voice was gruff.

Keegan's eyes stayed closed, but she turned her head.

"Keegan? Please? Please look at me."

"Keegan?" Rachel's voice was quiet and scared. "Are you okay?"

Keegan opened her eyes, but she didn't turn to look at them.

"Oh, God," Teel sobbed. Her knees gave, and this time she simply let go and dropped to the floor. "Oh my God, Keegan. Oh, God."

Keegan finally turned her head. Her eyes were dull but wide with fear.

"Mommy?" she croaked. "Mommy, I'm sorry."

Chapter 49

TEEL

TEEL CLIMBED to her feet and closed the distance between herself and Keegan. She leaned over the bed and pressed her lips to Keegan's forehead.

"It's okay, Keegan," she whispered. "It's all gonna be okay."

Teel heard a male voice in the room, and she turned to see Bobby talking to the ER doctor. She wanted to know what he was saying. She needed to know what he was saying, what they had done to Keegan. If there was any possible permanent damage. And yet, Keegan was crying silent tears and when Teel took her hand, she squeezed her fingers and Teel wouldn't walk away now. Not after so many days and weeks of Keegan's cold shoulder.

"Mrs. Alexander?"

Teel stood up and turned to the doctor. She tried to pull her hand away from Keegan, so she could shake the doctor's outstretched hand. But Keegan wouldn't let go. Instead, Teel shook the doctor's hand with her left, unwilling to pry Keegan's fingers from hers.

"I'm told you found her and called for help."

"No." Teel shook her head. "I found her, but my husband..." She looked over the doctor's shoulder, but Bobby was gone. Despite Keegan's fingers gripping hers painfully tight, and the quiet murmur of Rachel's voice talking, soothing Keegan, Teel felt Bobby's absence. She needed him there with them. She wanted him there with his family.

Dr. Beck, as he'd introduced himself, continued talking, telling her that they'd given Keegan activated charcoal to prevent her body from absorbing the Lortab. Teel fought to listen to him as he told her they'd considered an antidote to counteract any serious effects, but they hadn't used it. According to him, Teel had found Keegan almost as soon as she'd lost consciousness and the quick response had saved her.

"We're moving her to ICU," he told her. Funny how those words made her shiver with fear, her little girl in the ICU. She guessed it hammered home how grave the situation was, and yet, didn't she already know that after watching the paramedics resuscitate her?

"From the ICU, she'll be moved to the third floor, where she'll be on suicide watch."

Suicide watch. Teel held her breath for a moment. Keegan was alive, but this wasn't over. Of course a suicide attempt brought with it serious repercussions. Her daughter was alive, but she might not want to be. They were going to admit her. *To the psych ward. And watch her so she couldn't attempt to kill herself again.* Teel wondered how long she would be kept there. How long until she could bring her daughter home and love her back to happiness, *if* she could love her back to happiness.

"Okay."

"She's a very lucky girl," the doctor said with a glance at Keegan and Rachel.

Teel nodded, but she was still distracted.

"I'm sorry. Do you know where my husband went?"

"Said he needed to make a phone call."

"Okay. Thank you."

———

TEEL HATED THE ICU. Not just because of the constant beep of the monitors and the steady stream of medical personnel in and out of Keegan's room and down the hall and back up the hall. Not just because of the sheer dire straits patients were in when they were admitted to the ICU. She hated that she couldn't get close to Keegan. She had to sit at her bedside for a few minutes at a time and try to reassure her that everything was going to work out okay.

"I'm scared." Keegan's voice was scratchy and small.

"What are you scared of?"

"That I won't wake up."

"You will," Teel promised her. "It's okay. I'm right here."

"Before. I just. I wanted to sleep. I didn't mean to hurt you, Mom. I just thought it would all just go away if I slept."

Teel traced her fingertips over Keegan's cheekbones and down her nose and then across her chin.

"I have never been so scared, Keegan," she said softly. She felt tears sliding off her face, and she reached to wipe them away. "You have no idea how much I love you. I was so scared."

"I'm sorry." Keegan frowned, and Teel hurried to calm her. She traced her fingertips over her face again and then leaned over to kiss her cheek.

"Sssh…It's okay. Everything's going to be okay," Teel whispered. She felt a twinge, low in her belly, but she ignored it. "It's all gonna be okay now."

"But what if I have to go to jail or something?"

"We'll figure something out. Let's just get through this first, okay? You and me."

"Where's Daddy?"

"He's at home with Rachel."

"Is he mad at me?"

"No, sweetheart, no one is mad at you."

"But you were."

"I was disappointed, Keegan, yes. But only because I love you so much. And I want…so much more for you than what you took for yourself. You deserve so much more."

"But I killed Marin."

"No, you didn't. She made that choice." Teel winced as another twinge, a stronger one, twisted her belly.

"But I hurt her."

"You did, and that's what hurt me. It was so unlike you. None of this was like my Keegan. I didn't know where you were in the middle of all of this stuff."

"I wanted to be like them."

"But the most beautiful thing about you is how you aren't like them. How you aren't like anyone else in the world," Teel said softly. "You're special, Keegan. I wouldn't want anyone else to be my daughter. I have everything I'll ever need with you and your sister."

"But I know I do stupid stuff."

"Hush," Teel said gently. "You need rest."

"I'm scared, Mom."

"Trust me, Keegan. I'm right here. I will always be right here."

———

BOBBY CAME IN THE MORNING, and they waited together in the hall, while they checked Keegan's vitals and once they decided she was stable, moved her to the third floor. Teel ignored the cramping that was almost constant now, but she knew what it meant. She wasn't ready to think about it. She certainly wasn't ready to tell Bobby. Right now what mattered to her was getting Keegan settled, though she had no idea *how* to do that. Keegan huddled in her bed, curled up in the fetal position, possibly more afraid of the psych ward than anything else in her life at the moment.

Once home, and it had taken Bobby hours to talk Teel into leaving, she washed Keegan's bed sheets and blankets. She'd considered cleaning her room, a true top to bottom dusting, vacuuming cleaning. But Teel was a little bit afraid of what she might find and a little bit afraid of breathing in the same room where Keegan had tried to kill herself. She couldn't think past finding Keegan and how first the skin around her lips and then her lips themselves had turned blue. The way the paramedics had resuscitated her. In the end, she left Keegan's room untouched, except for making her bed with fresh, laundered sheets.

"What?" Bobby asked later when he found her in the kitchen fighting tears.

She shook her head and closed her eyes.

"I called Keegan's lawyer," he told her. "Yesterday. After…"

She nodded.

"Rescheduled for the week…after Keegan's out of the hospital."

"Okay."

"Roni's going to check in with us when Keegan is released. See how she's doing. We'll go from there…See if Keegan's ready…"

Teel wished she could answer him, but she simply nodded again.

"She said she's talked to the DA. I just hope we can get this all over with soon."

"Me, too," Teel whispered. "Me, too."

"Eve said she'd be by a little later, and your mom called. She wanted to know how you were doing. And how Keegan was doing. I told her we were all kind of living minute by minute right now. And that Keegan was stable, but she'd been admitted."

"Thanks." She rubbed her hand over her stomach, wishing she could ease the cramps. Should she tell him? Should she tell Bobby? And then what? Would he whisk her right back to the ER and demand that they save the baby? Or would he finally take the rose-colored glasses off and realize this baby wasn't meant to be?

"I called Schoch for you." He sounded distracted. "Told him you wouldn't be in today. And that you'd call him later."

"Thank you," she said quietly. "You've taken care of everything."

Bobby, staring at the French doors, shook his head and then looked back at Teel. "Everything but what matters most."

"Bobby…"

"I'm gonna take a drive around and check out the sites. See if there's anything I can do."

She understood. He needed something to do with his hands. Something hard and physical to pound out his anger and his fear.

"Just…call me. Okay? If you need me?"

"I will," she said with a nod. She stood on her tiptoes to kiss him, but he turned his head and her lips only brushed his cheek.

When he was gone, even with Rachel at home, she was lost. Like she could wander the house and never find herself or the happiness they'd all had here just months ago.

She needed Bobby to put his arms around her. She needed someone to hold her, while she cried out the visions, the images of Keegan's pale face and blue lips. Bobby had made her snap out of it yesterday, as much as she could, for Keegan's sake.

But she felt it. All of the fear, the shock of finding her daughter that way was still coiled tight in her shoulders. Still wrapped around and around her chest and her heart, and she felt as if she'd spent the past eighteen hours poised on the brink of a huge exhale, and she knew that when she let it go, when she plunged, she would break.

The cramping was dull, but persistent. Eve dropped by, and Teel was tempted to tell her that she was pregnant and that she was miscarrying. But she didn't. Perverse, perhaps, but Teel needed to keep this loss to herself. She didn't even want to share this with Bobby. Besides, he was still reeling from Keegan, and this was one thing Teel could shield him from, so why not? Bobby had been her rock through all of this, and she could see the toll it was taking on him.

Eve stayed for a while. She'd taken the day off, so she'd dropped on the couch and then tugged Teel down with her. Rachel had wandered out of her room and the three of them had snuggled together and stared blankly at the TV and now and then at each other. Each of them cried, and sometimes they all cried together.

While Eve was there, the doorbell rang. Teel, mindful of the day she'd had the blood thrown at her, was hesitant to get the door. Eve patted her hand and told her to stay put; she'd get it.

"Teel?" Eve called.

"Who is it?" she asked Eve as she joined her at the door. She looked up and saw Jeannie standing on her porch. Her knees felt weak, but she stepped out onto the porch with her. Eve closed the door gently behind her to give them privacy.

"I um..." Jeannie licked her lips and looked around Teel's yard. Teel took that opportunity to study her. To study Jeannie's face and her eyes and her skin and her body. To see what sort of mess she could have been. Jeannie's once vibrant happy face was gaunt and sad. Her eyes were dull, though they were glassy at the moment. She looked old, like she'd aged five years in the past month, and just because Teel hadn't lost Keegan didn't mean she didn't feel it. Didn't know just exactly what Jeannie dealt with every day of her life.

She'd come so, so close, and she'd gotten a glimpse of this pain, and she'd begged God and she'd been lucky. Luck was all that had saved Keegan, because Teel knew that Jeannie had begged God just the same way she had. She'd just been a little too late.

"Is she okay?" Jeannie finally asked.

Teel shrugged and shook her head. "I don't know. I guess...physically. They admitted her. To the..." Thankfully, Jeannie nodded so Teel didn't have to say the words.

"I just..." Jeannie sighed and finally met Teel's eyes. "I don't know what happened with them. But..."

Surely Jeannie knew about the pictures? Teel held her breath and wondered what to say.

"Jeannie, I'm so sorry."

"They both made bad choices," Jeannie said quietly. A tear rolled off her cheek, but she made no move to wipe it away. "I can't say that I don't blame Keegan for what happened. But I'm glad she's okay."

Teel felt a pang, a severe jolt of pain, but this one was in her chest. It took her breath away. Just hearing Jeannie say that she blamed Keegan made her hurt. She knew if she were Jeannie, she would feel the same. But in these roles, Teel was the mom. The mom of the girl who might be to blame. She wanted to lash out, to protect Keegan.

"Thank you." Teel nodded.

"Take care of her." Jeannie nodded her head toward the house, and Teel nodded and then without another word, Jeannie turned and walked away.

Chapter 50

T EEL

LATER, when the dark had come again, and it was after ten, and Bobby wasn't home, Teel paced the hardwood. She imagined her footprints had left a dull trail across the family room. Bobby had come home and gone a few times, but this last time he'd left just after seven and he wasn't home yet. Each time he'd left, he'd told Teel where he was going, what errands he was running, what spec home he would be working on, but this last time, he hadn't.

Deacon had called Rachel, and she'd talked to him right there while she sat on the couch with Teel. From the answers she'd given him, he'd asked about Keegan, and Teel took that to mean that he was concerned. About Rachel and Keegan. Rachel had texted him on and off all day, too.

Teel was happy for Rachel, almost at peace with the fact that Rachel was in love. *Almost.* It was good to know that someone was there for Rachel, especially when Teel knew she hadn't been attentive enough to her lately. And yet, with everything that had happened, Teel wasn't ready to let anyone claim to love Rachel the way she did. She vowed to herself to make more time for Rachel, and yet, even as she did, she wondered how it would happen with losing this baby and Keegan in the hospital.

It hurt Teel knowing that Keegan wanted that kind of love, that kind of attention from a boy when she was so young. So much better to wait and let that kind of love find you. It hurt her to see Keegan floundering with friendship, too. She needed friends to surround her and rally her back to the happy girl she used to be.

Rachel kept dozing off on the couch. Each time her eyes closed, Teel fought the panic that climbed inside her. She kept remembering Keegan with her eyes closed, not breathing, and then she would wonder where Bobby was. She didn't want to be alone, but she didn't want to keep Rachel awake, either. Her stomach hurt. Not cramps this time. Fear layered over the top of the soup she'd fixed for dinner and the ice cream she'd eaten with Rachel made her want to throw up. Just thinking about Keegan's room down the hall nearly drove her over the edge. In fact, she thought as she continued to pace, she wanted to move. To get as far away as possible from this house and the memories that haunted it.

When Rachel went to bed, she wandered the house in silence, but eventually the quiet was so loud it hammered on her last nerve. She called Bobby's cell again, but he didn't answer. When she put the phone down, she turned the TV on again.

Earlier, she'd called John at school and talked to him about Keegan. She was now officially on leave. She'd never taken any personal time, and a small part of her felt a bit lost. The rest of her, though, needed to be at Keegan's side until she regained her strength. Mentally and physically.

Funny. She'd felt eyes all over her at work, and she'd felt a knife or two buried to the hilt while there, but she already missed it. The comfort of her routine. The support from her friends, which apparently far outweighed the wounds the knives in her back left.

Still wishing for the power to turn back time, although she knew that wasn't the answer because it only meant she wouldn't know about anything Keegan was doing and not that it hadn't happened, she went to get ready for bed.

As she'd feared all day, she'd started bleeding. God had listened to her prayers; he'd given her back Keegan and taken the baby that Bobby seemed to want. Even though she hadn't wanted to have another baby, and even though she'd make the same trade again and again for Keegan or for Rachel, she felt empty inside.

Too empty, even, to cry. Instead, she stepped into the shower and let the hot water drum over her stiff shoulders and neck. It didn't make her feel better. Instead of not thinking about the baby she'd just lost, she thought about the morning she'd done the test and then gone outside and had buckets of blood thrown on her and how Bobby had walked right into the shower with her.

When the water turned cold, she turned it off, dried off and put on long pajama pants and a sweatshirt. She was chilled now, but she didn't think it had anything to do with the water. Where was Bobby? She fixed herself a glass of tea, though she didn't want it, and then walked down the hall to Rachel's room, surprised to find her awake. She was propped up on her pillow, against the headboard, reading.

"You okay?" Teel asked quietly.

"Can't sleep now." Rachel shrugged. She closed her book. "Where's Dad?"

"Must be busy," Teel said with a smile. "I'm sure he'll be home soon."

"Do you think he's okay?"

"Yes, I do." Teel nodded. "I'm gonna go finish grading some stuff and writing the rest of the month's lesson plans to take over to John tomorrow. For the sub."

"Okay."

She worked until almost midnight, and then exhausted, she gave up. She turned the light off and left her books on the dining room table. The TV was still on, though she had no desire to watch anything, because as make-believe went, her life topped it all to hell these past few weeks.

But she wouldn't go to bed without Bobby. Instead, she lay down on the couch to wait for him. She surfed the channels just like Bobby, not caring that she caught a word from each program and had no idea what was going on. She cried. For the baby she'd lost, alone.

She cried for Keegan. For Rachel. For herself.

She slept, and when she heard the key in the lock and woke, her neck was stiff from lying with her head on the arm of the sofa. She swung her legs around and sat up and watched him. He walked with his eyes on the floor, and he rubbed his neck with his hand. She glanced at the clock on the microwave. It was after two.

Never in all their marriage had either of them stayed out like this without a phone call. Without a reason like a party with friends or a night out with Eve.

"You're still up?" Bobby looked shocked that she was awake.

She stood up and folded her arms over her chest.

"Where were you?"

"Just. Out."

"Out? Where?"

He shook his head and walked past her. She followed him into their bedroom and closed the door behind her.

"Bobby?"

He turned to her, eyes bloodshot and face haggard.

"I was at the tavern."

She shook her head. "Not until two in the morning. They close at midnight."

"Let it go, Teel."

"What? Just tell me. Where were you?"

"I was at the tavern, and then I just drove around."

"You just drove around for two hours, after you sat around drinking for hours?"

"I didn't drink that much. I just needed to be out...To be away from the house."

She studied him and for the first time in over twenty years, she wondered if she would know. Would she know if Bobby cheated on her? She'd always thought she would. But she'd always thought she'd know if her daughters were mixed up in something over their heads. There was no neon sign that lit up when someone had sex. She hadn't known when Keegan did it, how the hell could she ever know for sure about Bobby?

Because he made vows to you, she told herself. Because that's not us.

"Were you with someone else?" she whispered. She hated herself for asking. Because Bobby had given her everything, he had been her only strength through all of this, and if he needed to lean on someone, was she really going to hold it against him?

Yes. She was. Because they were a team. They were getting through this together, and if he needed to lean, she was there for him.

"Teel, God, no." He shook his head. "No. I would never do that to you." He stepped closer to her and cupped her face in his hands. "Don't make this about that."

"Then what is this, Bobby?" She covered his hands with hers. "What is this? Make me understand this."

"I just. I sat at the tavern on Twelfth and State. Hard Times." He shrugged. "Seemed fitting."

"You drank alone?" she asked. She moved her hands from his and touched him. Her fingers flew over his face, as if she were reading his emotions in his skin.

"I only drank two," he answered. "Then I drove around for a while."

"But why?" The words squeezed out sideways, around the knot of tears in her throat. "Why alone? Why not come to me? Talk to me."

"We almost lost her." His voice broke, and suddenly he was sobbing. "We almost lost Keegan, and it's my fault."

"No, no Bobby, it's not."

She pulled his head down to her shoulder and held him as tight as she could. He shook against her as he cried. Teel's tears were silent, but she kept her lips pressed to his head, and her hands moved steadily over his back and his shoulders.

"It's not your fault, baby," she repeated when he stood up straight. He dragged his hand over his face, but he couldn't uncolor the red in his eyes.

"It was my prescription. I was here with her, and if you hadn't come home when you did, she would be dead. Keegan would be dead."

"It's not your fault. How could you have known?"

"Look me in the eye," he said gruffly. He snatched her arm and squeezed hard enough to make her stand still. "Look me in the eye, and tell me. Tell me you don't blame me. That you didn't feel that instant rush of blame when you found her."

She shook her head slowly. "I never blamed you. I just needed you. I needed you to help me with her, because," she swallowed hard, but the knot in her throat wouldn't ease, "because we're in this together. Bobby Alexander, you and I do things together. We've never been about blame. Didn't you just say the same damned thing to me the other day?"

"This is different. We almost lost her!"

"But we didn't!" Teel yelled. "We didn't. We came so damned close, I know. But we didn't lose her. And now..." She stepped closer to him. The painful knot in her throat broke, and she could hardly speak. "And now...we have to help her. You and me. Now we help her. And day by day, we put this family back together."

"If she'd died. Would you blame me then?"

"No. Goddammit, no. Stop it, Bobby!" She gathered a fistful of his shirt in her hand. "I love you. I love you. I need you with me. Not out by yourself feeling guilty. Talk to me. Just talk to me."

"I didn't know." He pulled away from her and paced their bedroom. "I didn't know she was...hurting like this. I thought we'd talk to her lawyer, and it would go away, and she'd be fine."

"It's okay."

"You knew."

"Just because of how much she hated me. She hated me for a few days, and that's not like Keegan."

"But you knew, and I didn't."

Teel backed away. She'd taken Motrin, but she was still cramping. The worst of it was over. The baby was gone. But she was still bleeding.

"There's something else we need to talk about," she said quietly.

"What?" Bobby looked at the closed door. "What's wrong?"

Teel looked away from him, ashamed to face him and tell him, even after she'd just preached to him about blame.

"I'm bleeding." She ducked her head to her hands and crumbled, but Bobby was there. His arms closed around her, and together they fell to sit in the middle of their bedroom floor. "I'm sorry, Bobby. I know you wanted this baby."

She felt a crushing pressure in her chest, and she wondered again if she might be having a heart attack. Bobby didn't say anything, and she was afraid to look at him. She was to blame for this; there was no getting around it. She had asked God to take this baby.

"You were right," Bobby finally said. "Having this baby would have hurt Keegan."

"Doesn't make it right," she mumbled. "We made this one just the same way we did Rachel and Keegan."

Bobby hooked his finger under her chin and made her look at him. He shook his head.

"We've done this before," he reminded her. "Nature's way of taking care of things."

"I prayed. I actually prayed for God to take this baby."

"How many teenage moms do you think pray for God to take their babies? It doesn't work that way."

She thought it had worked exactly that way, but she was too damned tired to argue.

"He gave us Keegan," Bobby whispered. "This is the way it's supposed to be. Me and you and our girls."

Chapter 51

TEEL

TEEL MARVELED at how she could feel solid, strong even, when she walked into her school and then fall apart within the first two minutes of being inside. She hated how any kindness shown, be it from friend or foe, could draw out instant tears. She had always been this way, and she suspected a lot of other people were the same.

It was her students who first took hold of her emotions and ran—her current students and all of the older kids she'd had in her room in previous years. They saw her walk into the building and bombarded her before the door closed behind her. Cold air whooshed in around her, but the arms thrown around her and the way the kids said her name warmed her instantly.

She looked ahead, down the hall, as the kids swarmed her. Liz Morgan stood just outside the kitchen and watched her. Teel wondered what she was thinking, but she decided she didn't care. These kids weren't going to catch anything from

Teel; family matters weren't contagious. Teel hugged them back, each of them, as long as she could take it. In the back of her mind she wondered how much they knew. Surely they all knew Keegan had been arrested, but did they know Keegan had…? Did they know Keegan had attempted suicide?

It bothered her so much to think those words. To say them. Not because of the stigma that might now be attached to Keegan's name. She was beyond caring what people might think about her daughter, what they might think about her.

She eyed Liz again. Okay, she wasn't beyond it. She was scared to death that everyone in this building, with the exception of Maggie, saw her as a failure. As a bad mom. She was scared that they all thought Keegan was a screw-up, that they might have all just placed odds on what Keegan would do next. Drugs? An unwanted pregnancy? Another suicide attempt?

Finally, the kids' arms around her felt confining. She loved them, and she thanked them and she promised them that she was okay and she would be back, and then she found her teacher voice and directed them up the stairs to their classrooms. Her throat ached as she watched them go.

She felt a strange mix of guilt and sadness. Maybe she wasn't a good mom. She was resigned to the fact that she had to stay home for a while. She *wanted* to be at home with Keegan, to care for her and to spend time getting to know her again. And yet, she wanted to be here, at school, living the daily life she'd carved for herself years ago.

"Teel."

She turned to see her fellow teachers lined up along the wall outside the kitchen. All of them, lined up like soldiers going to battle. Teel approached them slowly, almost like they were a firing squad and they might open fire at any moment.

"Is Keegan okay?"

Teel searched Liz's face for any sign of arrogance. For the usual smug grin that drove Teel to anger quicker than lightning. It wasn't there. Somehow Teel knew the sincerity on Liz's face was more than skin deep.

Liz had asked about her child. No one who is a teacher, let alone a mother, could not be deeply affected by an attempted suicide.

Teel nodded, but when she tried to speak, she could only cry. Liz stepped forward and reached out to Teel. She took her hand and squeezed it, and Teel was grateful for the support.

"I just can't believe…" Teel started.

Liz nodded. "I know."

Teel dabbed at her eyes. "You never think…" She looked from Liz to Karin and Maggie and the rest of the teachers, the rest of her colleagues. "You just never think it's gonna happen. Not in your family."

"Give her my best, okay?" Liz said quietly. "Let me know if there's anything I can do. Anything."

"Thank you, Liz." Teel nodded as Liz gave her hand a final squeeze and walked away. The rest of them nodded and echoed Liz's words, and the blanket of caring words both soothed her and irritated her like steel wool on a sunburn. Everything was too close to the surface, and every kind word scraped her skin and made her bleed.

Karin Isles gave her a quick hug, and then she and Maggie were left alone in the hallway.

"I am so, so sorry," Maggie said quietly. "What can I do? Please let me help you."

Teel shook her head. "There's nothing, Maggie. I just need to be with her until she feels stronger. I just…can't be here when she's in the hospital."

Maggie nodded. "Okay. I'm gonna miss you. I'm gonna pray for you guys. For things to settle down now."

"Thank you."

"What about you? How're you feeling?" Maggie raised her eyebrows. Teel knew she was referring to the pregnancy.

She shook her head. "Lost the baby."

"Oh God, Teel." Maggie clapped her hand over her mouth. "Oh God. This is hell for you."

Teel shrugged. "Maybe this is how it's supposed to be."

"I know," Maggie agreed. "I know you want to be there for Keegan, without a newborn." Maggie touched Teel's arm. "I also know that no matter how ambivalent you felt about this pregnancy, it bothers you now that it's out of your hands."

Teel nodded. "It does." She took a deep breath. "But it's... I'm okay. I'm just so...I'm so worried about Keegan."

"I know."

Teel glanced at her watch. "You should go. I need to go talk to John and get back home."

"Is Bobby with her?"

"Yeah. I need to get home so he can go to work."

"Call me. For anything."

"I will," Teel said with a smile. Her eyes blurred with tears as she watched Maggie hurry up the steps. She wasn't sure she would ever feel that light on her feet again.

She found John in his office. Whatever bravado she'd mustered the rest of the way down the hall to the office collapsed inside her when John stood up, laid his hand on her shoulder, and then closed the door.

"How is she?"

Teel had already grown so tired of this question; not because she didn't want the comfort or support, but because she was so ill-prepared to answer. Maybe they had gotten lucky with the OD, and Keegan would suffer no physical effects.

But, how *was* Keegan? *Really?* Teel couldn't answer that.

She was scared. Keegan had told her that earlier this morning when she'd been allowed to visit her. In the fifteen minutes she'd been able to spend with Keegan, she'd watched her daughter cry. Keegan had told her she was scared to go to sleep, because she was afraid God wouldn't let her wake up after what she'd done. She was having nightmares, too, apparently, and Teel knew they were about Marin. But Keegan hadn't said anything else, and then Teel had been ushered out of the room and off the floor and away from Keegan.

She was scared of what was to come in the real world, too. Teel knew Keegan was afraid of the lawyers and the charges and the consequences to come. That was one fear she shared with Keegan, that they all shared with Keegan.

Teel shook her head and dropped into the chair in front of John's desk.

"She's okay, I guess," she answered.

"It's gonna take some time." He nodded and slowly sat down in his own chair. "She's at home, though?"

"No. She has to stay...in the hospital for two weeks."

John flinched. "How're you holding up?"

She hated this question even more than the one about Keegan. She was a grown woman, and she had no idea what she was feeling or how to put any of her feelings into words.

Rather than answer him, she looked away. Through the window behind him, she could see the church across the street.

Throat tight with tears again, she shook her head. "You're just...You're never prepared for something...like this. These kinds of things. They don't happen to you. It's always someone else's problem."

He nodded, but said nothing.

"And then it does happen, and..." she shrugged. She

closed her eyes slowly and then half-laughed and reached to dry her eyes. "I'm sorry."

"It's okay."

When she looked at him, he was relaxed back in his chair, as if he was prepared to spend the day talking to her. Just the thought brought her comfort.

"I...um..." She took her lesson book from her bag, which she'd put on the floor. "I planned through November. Graded the assignments I had at home..."

"You didn't have to do that."

"I needed to," she admitted, grateful when he nodded. She couldn't begin to tell him how lost, how empty she'd felt yesterday when Bobby had disappeared. There were some things you just didn't talk about, no matter who asked or how much he or she cared.

"We'll keep in touch," he said to her now. Still reaching into her bag, she looked up at him quickly.

"Do I still have a job here, John?"

"Why wouldn't you have a job here?"

Now his relaxed pose and expressionless face unnerved her.

"It's a Catholic school. My daughter was arrested for..." She raised her eyebrows and shrugged. "I'm sure my family's been dissected over several family dinners lately."

"Kids make mistakes," he said simply.

"Catholic school," she repeated.

"You've planned through November," he told her. "Check in with me. Let me know when you're ready to come back. We need you here. You need to be here, after you get Keegan back on her feet."

She drew a shaky breath and then nodded.

"Does that make me a bad person? My daughter needs me at home, and I need to be here?"

"You're taking the time you need with her." He stood up.

"And I know you well enough to know you'll make sure she's ready before you ever call me. Makes you a good teacher who's a good mom."

"Okay." She stood up and picked up her bag and purse. "Thank you, John."

"Absolutely. Let us know if there's anything we can do. For you or Keegan."

She nodded, unable to speak again, and walked blindly out the door. She hurried down the hall, too undone to stop and talk to anyone else. She all but dived into the Edge and pulled the door shut firmly. Silence breathed around her. She leaned her head back and closed her eyes.

Recovery, she thought. This is recovery, Keegan's and mine, and it hurts just as much as breaking.

Chapter 52

RONI ANDREWS WAS INDEED a hot little blonde, with long, thick lashes and a perfect smile. Bobby didn't seem to notice. He was more concerned about Keegan, and that coupled with the past nights they had spent together grieving and praying and loving made Teel more sure of him, of their marriage, than she'd ever been. The worry they'd lived the past two weeks, while Keegan was away from them at the hospital, had built a solid wall around them—not to shut anyone out, most especially not Rachel, but to redefine them as parents and strengthen their resolve, their determination to save Keegan.

Roni (Teel still wanted to refer to her as Ms. Andrews, but the lawyer insisted on being called Roni) was gentle and kind with Keegan, who spoke very little. Keegan was still pale, and she was skittish and easily spooked. She answered Roni's questions, which led her through the entire tale of sex and revenge again. It still hurt Teel as much now as it did the first time she heard Keegan talk about it, but she put her poker face on and kept her mouth shut.

It was surreal, sitting in a renovated office of an old warehouse turned office building, listening to this girl who barely looked old enough to be a college graduate talk about defense strategies for her daughter. It was surreal that her daughter and the term *lawyer* be linked in the same sentence, same room, same world. Like she'd said yesterday to Liz and John, you never expected this to happen to you or your family. And once it did, you were stuck in a tailspin, and life kept moving and passing you by.

The thing was *Keegan was guilty*. Not necessarily for driving Marin to suicide. Teel wasn't sure they could ever prove that, since Marin had left no note. And yet, Keegan had posted graphic photos of Marin taken when Marin had reason to believe she and the boy she was with had privacy; Roni's words, though Teel had to agree with them.

The police hadn't mirandized Keegan soon enough to Roni's liking and, though Teel had been present and should have known better and didn't because she was broken down to what she'd thought then was her last nerve, they hadn't given Keegan the opportunity to seek counsel. According to Roni, mistakes on their part.

Sort of a draw. The police had known when they questioned Keegan that she'd posted the pictures due to the IP address from which they'd been posted. But they hadn't followed procedure, and now Roni had a leg to stand on.

Teel's head pounded as she listened. When she thought no one would notice, she wiped her hands on her pant legs, but it didn't help. She felt like she was back in high school, like she'd just been caught screwing around with some boy in the locker room or smoking in the girls' bathroom. And the hell of it was knowing that if she felt that bad, Keegan felt a hundred times worse.

Teel wondered if it mattered that Keegan had no previous run-ins with the law, that she'd always been an exemplary student. But she didn't ask. She left the talking to Bobby and trusted him to ask the right questions. He asked Roni about Keegan's lack of a record of any sort and the fact that she was a good student, and Roni agreed that these factors counted in their favor.

But it wasn't enough. They left Roni's office with a small bit of hope, maybe more than they'd had when they walked in. For Teel, it wasn't enough. They'd been on this roller coaster too damned long, and Teel was desperate for answers. For *the* answer. For the only answer she could bear.

She wondered if it would be over then. Not counting any sentence or probation or community service, would it be over? She figured Keegan would get something more than a slap on the wrist, and maybe at this point she wouldn't admit it to Keegan, but she felt like Keegan should do *something* to make up for what had been done. But would it be over? Would it be enough to the rest of the world? Or would they still torture Keegan? Would she face people who wanted to throw buckets of blood on her? Would she meet people who would hate her the instant they realized who she was? That she was *that* Keegan Alexander? The one who'd posted pictures of that girl who'd killed herself?

Teel had always believed herself to be a woman of conviction. She believed in punishment for rules or laws broken. She believed Keegan should do *something* to right her wrong. And yet, maybe Teel was learning that more than a woman of conviction, she was a mother who desperately needed to protect her own. She wouldn't stand and parade and proclaim Keegan's innocence; she would accept that her daughter had made a bad choice that had hurt someone, that had hurt an entire family. She would accept it and forgive Keegan and pray that the rest of the world wouldn't stereotype her. That no one would see Keegan as one of those kids, one of the bad seeds that deserved to have the book thrown at them.

After watching her daughter suffer through these past two months, seeing her pull away from her friends and her family, living with her through the tears and the heartache and the hatred all driven by fear, by the need to fit in, after kneeling at her side and begging her to live, to fight back, Teel hoped that she herself had changed. That she wasn't one of those people who would look at another girl like Keegan and make assumptions about who she was and throw judgment at her without knowing, truly knowing her.

Some kids, some people were bad. Some were good. Teel felt like Keegan had given her a precious learning opportunity. One she could have done without and would have, if given the choice. But it had happened, and Teel prayed that the next time she heard this story in the news that she would stop and think before she reacted with the usual disgust.

Keegan had been through enough. Teel hoped that when the dust settled, the people around them, the people in town would look past the story to the girl.

———

"MOM?"

"Hmm?" Teel looked up from the magazine she had been flipping through. She had no idea what she'd been reading; she had no idea what the magazine was. Keegan was curled up on one end of the sofa, and Teel was stretched out on the other end. It was a cozy day inside, but outside the wind whipped the branches of the trees hard enough to strip them of their crisp, dry leaves. Halloween was less than a week away, and this year, Teel had nothing planned.

Nothing. No classroom games. No pumpkin-shaped

math worksheets. No fun cartoon-vampire window clings. No jack-o-lantern on her front porch. No candy in the pantry. It felt a little strange, and more than once when it occurred to Teel that she was late with the decorations or candy, she'd almost jumped to get moving and get it taken care of. Reminding herself that she wasn't playing along was weird. Teel was a doer, and it was taking her time to learn to be idle.

And yet, spending these quiet days with Keegan made the lesson easier to absorb. Due to her suicide attempt, her extended hospital stay, and her shaky hold on her emotions now, Teel, Bobby and Keegan together had chosen to go to Blessed Sacrament and talk to Mr. Loughlin. Teel thought it entirely possible that Keegan might end up expelled from the Catholic high school. It didn't matter anymore. She couldn't imagine that Keegan would be able to return there anyway, be comfortable there, surrounded by eyes that wouldn't stop staring and mouths that wouldn't stop talking, whether they were saying mean things to her or about her. They'd withdrawn Keegan for the semester, accepting incompletes in her classes, and decided she could make up her schooling in the summer. It wasn't the best answer, but it was the better of their two options.

Keegan spent her days trailing Teel like her shadow. Teel welcomed the closeness, the togetherness, but she worried about Keegan's neediness. She drove her to her appointments with the psychiatrist, but Teel wasn't allowed to be present and wondering what demons drove, *haunted,* her daughter made her hurt inside.

They talked a lot, but not *always* about consequential things. Keegan talked about Marin, about how Keegan had been wrong to be jealous of her and that she wished she'd never gone to Carter's house and taken the pictures. One day Keegan talked about the night at the party, the night

she'd had sex with Sean Spanner. Teel struggled with that
one; she didn't *want* to know but she *had* to know, so she sat
with Keegan on the couch and listened to the details. She
learned that Sean had been drinking, and the smell of beer
on his breath made Keegan feel sick. That he hadn't
undressed her all the way, just yanked her jeans down and
out of the way and ripped her panties off and shoved them
in his pocket. That he'd bitten her neck and pinched her
hips and left bruises. Teel was glad Keegan couldn't look at
her as she told her these things, because it broke her heart
to know there had been bruises. There had been physical
evidence of what had happened, of what Keegan had done,
and Teel had been so busy living that she hadn't even
noticed it.

What kind of mother didn't notice a bite mark on her
daughter's neck? How could she not have noticed any mar on
Keegan's perfect skin?

"Can I tell you something?"

Teel caught her breath. Each of Keegan's confessions,
discussions had started this way. Could she tell Teel something? And each time, Teel wanted so badly to say no, to say
she didn't want to know. That she *couldn't* know any more.
But *she had to know*; she had to know what Keegan had done,
what she was thinking.

"Yes."

"That night…"

"The night of the party?" Teel wondered what more
Keegan could say about that night.

"No. The night…before I…took Dad's pills."

Teel nodded when Keegan looked at her.

"I came out of my room. Rachel was gone. And you and
Dad weren't in the kitchen."

Teel waited patiently, already afraid of what Keegan
would say.

"I looked for you. And when I didn't find you up here, I went downstairs."

Oh God. Teel winced, dreading but knowing what Keegan was going to say.

"I heard you and Dad talking. In his office."

"Oh, Keegan." She tossed the magazine on the coffee table and scooted around the couch to touch her. To hold on to her.

"I thought that…" Keegan's nose was running. She sniffed and then reached for a tissue from the box on the table. "That if you had another baby…it was okay. If I just…closed my eyes and went to sleep. I thought…"

"You thought what?" Teel whispered.

"That you wouldn't miss me."

Teel wasn't sure how she was supposed to react to Keegan after a suicide attempt and while she was seeing a psychiatrist. Maybe she shouldn't let Keegan see how badly she was hurting. Maybe she was supposed to be stronger than that. Or maybe instant, honest reactions were best.

It didn't matter. She couldn't have hidden the way her heart dropped to her gut and made her feel sick. She couldn't have hidden the tears, the way she couldn't help but cry out loud.

"C'mere," Teel said as she reached for Keegan. Thank God, Keegan scooted across the couch willingly. "Don't you ever, ever think that, Keegan Alexander." Teel closed her eyes when Keegan's head rested on her shoulder. "How could you ever think Dad and I wouldn't miss you? That it wouldn't tear Rachel apart to lose you? How could you ever think that?"

Keegan mumbled something, but between the two of them crying, Teel didn't catch it. She let it go for now, and simply held on to Keegan.

"I missed you, and you weren't even gone," Teel whispered. "I love you so much, little girl, and my life would never be the same without you. We'd never be okay without you."

Keegan pulled back from Teel, just enough to lean on the couch. Her skin was still deathly pale, except the bruised hollows under her eyes.

"Even after what I did?"

"No matter what you ever do," Teel answered. "Being disappointed...being angry...Keegan, that's part of being your mom. It's part of loving you."

"Did you get pregnant because of that? Because you were disappointed in me?"

Teel sighed and leaned her head on the couch. Side by side, they stared at each other, neither of them willing to break eye contact.

"I got pregnant because I got pregnant. Sometimes that happens. Sometimes women try and try and try and never get pregnant."

"Does Rachel know?"

Teel took a deep breath. "No, we didn't tell her. Keegan..."

"What?"

"I lost the baby."

"You lost it?" Keegan's big eyes filled with surprise and sadness. She laid her hand over Teel's stomach.

"I did." Teel covered her hand.

"Is it my fault? What I did...did it cause you to lose the baby?"

"No." Teel squeezed her hand. "No."

Keegan raised her eyebrows. "Promise me? Because I feel like it's my fault."

"I promise you. At my age, the risk of miscarriage was higher. And...it's happened before. It absolutely had nothing to do with you."

"You've miscarried before?"

Teel kind of wished Bobby was home, because she felt like she was bleeding inside. Not the baby, not really bleeding. She felt like her heart was bleeding.

"Yeah. Once before we had Rachel and twice after Rachel was born and before we had you."

"I didn't know that."

"Maybe I should have told you guys." Teel shrugged. "It just…never came up."

"So. Rachel and I were lucky?"

"Dad and I were lucky to have you. Both of you. And Keegan, we still feel that way. You two are so different, but we love you both. We love you both the same. Do you get that? Do you know that your dad and I will do anything for you? Anything at all."

Keegan answered her with a half-nod. She looked away from Teel. Her eyes settled on the coffee table, but Teel could tell she was far from the couch where they sat.

"I just wanted to be myself. To be away from Rachel. To be someone outside of you guys."

"And you will be," Teel told her. "You are. You're beautiful. You're fun and smart. And honey, by changing who you are inside to be one of them, you aren't being yourself. You can't change who you are for someone else. People who expect that aren't friends."

Keegan nodded. "I know." She glanced at Teel again. "I know that now."

They sat quietly for a few minutes before Keegan spoke again.

"Do you think it's too late?"

"For what?"

"For me. To be normal. Is everybody gonna hate me now? For what happened to Marin?"

Teel stroked her fingertips over Keegan's cheekbone. "I honestly don't know. But what I do know is that you have to let those people really see you, to see who you really are and then maybe they'll see past all that other stuff."

"Mom?"

"What, sweetie?"

"Thank you. For being with me. I know…" Keegan shrugged away the words she was struggling with.

Teel nodded and then drew her close again.

"You're always welcome." She kissed Keegan's cheek. "Always."

Chapter 53

Rachel

RACHEL WASN'T USED to missing classes. In fact, she hated it, but this time it had been an emergency with Keegan. She'd talked to her professors and all of them had been very understanding and very concerned, both about Rachel and Keegan. They'd even copied their notes for her, which had been a lifesaver. She had reading to catch up on, but she'd learned very quickly in August when classes had first started, college was mostly about independent reading and studying.

She tossed her books in her backpack and slung it over her shoulder. Mom was at home with Keegan. She had to keep reminding herself, because she kept thinking about everything and she'd get a jolt in her chest, like a heart attack or something. She'd forget that Keegan was okay, that she was at home with Mom. Rachel kept picturing Keegan as she was in the ER, looking so small and breakable.

She'd never call her a freak again. Rachel had no idea

Keegan was so mixed up. If anything, she thought she was the real freak, the one that didn't belong with the rest of the family. She was quiet, and the rest of them loved to talk. Rachel always found it hard to think of things to talk about, so mostly she just didn't. She hated crowds, preferred to spend time with one friend or Deacon or even alone. Parties scared her, and God knows, kids who didn't party weren't cool.

It had never really mattered to her, though. That Being Cool thing. She had a few good friends, friends she'd made at the beginning of high school. True, they were gone now, away at college, but they kept in touch with email and texting.

How ironic that she considered herself the odd man out in their family and then Keegan stepped off that ledge. Rachel hadn't told her mom, but she hadn't eaten anything the first three days after Keegan did it. She couldn't. Everything felt like sand in her mouth, and she kept throwing up, and so she'd just stopped trying. Not permanently. She wasn't in danger of developing an eating disorder. She was just scared to death and then some because she'd almost lost her little sister.

Rachel kept thinking about a day when she was thirteen and Keegan was nine. Rachel had been in her room doing homework, and Keegan came in and somehow sensed that she'd had a bad day. At school that day, she'd been accused of stealing something from another girl's book bag, and she hadn't done it. No amount of talking could change her teacher's mind, and she'd had to write a two page essay on stealing and how it was disrespectful to the person she stole from. Keegan had brought her a bag of M&Ms, the ones Mom had just bought her the night before at the grocery store, and put them on her desk. Then she'd started cracking jokes like a comedienne on *The Tonight Show*, and Rachel had tried so hard to ignore her. She'd finally caved, and the two of them had laughed like hyenas until Mom had come in to see what they were up to.

Keegan had changed so much since she'd started high school that Rachel had forgotten that part of her sister existed. The good-hearted, compassionate part. The crazy girl who would say anything to get a laugh.

How could she have gone on? If Keegan had done it? If those pills had killed her, how could Rachel have picked herself up and gone on?

Rachel felt the tension drain from her neck when she saw Deacon waiting for her in the hall outside her classroom. She was grinning like an idiot, but she was beyond caring that he knew she was crazy about him. They were both well beyond that stage of their relationship. She hadn't meant to do it, but she'd fallen so in love with Deacon, never stopping to think about how wide open she was for heartache. He was worth the risk.

"Hey." She stood on her tiptoes and kissed his cheek. "What're you doing here?"

"Got outta class early and thought I'd come down here and wait for you."

As they walked hand in hand to her car, they swapped stories about their classes.

"How about lunch?" he suggested.

She opened her car door and dropped her heavy back-pack to the driver's seat.

"Um."

"What? What's wrong?"

"I kinda…thought I'd go home. Check on Keegan."

"Okay." He nodded. "Not a problem."

"Wanna go with me?"

"Do you think Keegan'll be okay with that?"

Rachel raised her eyebrows. "You were with me at the ER, Deacon. You're family now."

"Then I'd love to go with you," he said as he leaned over to kiss her.

"Good. Get in."

———

KEEGAN AND MOM had been cuddled together on the couch when she and Deacon showed up for lunch earlier. Not long ago that would have bothered Rachel. It would have hurt her. But Keegan's suicide attempt had painted things a different color. Rachel had only had a moment of longing to curl up with her mom and Keegan.

Instead, she'd made them all lunch. Sub sandwiches and chips and soup for Keegan. Her sister wasn't eating much, and that worried Rachel. But Mom had sat with Keegan for the better part of an hour while she slowly finished the cup of chicken noodle soup Rachel had put in front of her.

They'd eaten together for dinner, too, the family and Deacon. Rachel had appreciated her mom's invitation for Deacon to stay. Since his books were in the car, he agreed, and then they'd gone downstairs and cracked their books and studied together for a couple of hours.

When she'd come home after taking Deacon back to his dorm, Dad and Keegan were watching a movie together. Her mom was making cookies. Rachel had made a production of smelling the baking cookies, to make sure her mom hollered at her when those already in the oven were done, and then she'd gone to her room to find a book to read.

She almost draped herself over her bed to read, but she decided against it. There was room on the couch for three;

she could read while Dad and Keegan watched the movie. When she turned to leave her room, Mom stood in the doorway.

"Cookies ready?" Her stomach growled. Teel smiled, but she shook her head.

"There's something I need to tell you."

"Oh, man." Rachel's stomach dropped. Maybe she didn't want cookies after all.

"No, it's okay. Just something…" Teel sighed. She put her arm around Rachel and walked her back into her bedroom. Rachel sat when Mom sat on the edge of the bed. "Something Keegan overheard. That I guess I need to tell you, too."

"What, Mom? What's wrong?"

"I was pregnant." The words kind of tumbled out like Mom couldn't stop them. "I just found out the other day."

"What?"

"Dad and I were waiting to tell you and Keegan." Her mom kept talking. "I've had miscarriages before. Before you were born. And when you were little. So. I just wanted to wait a while before I told you. Just in case."

"What happened?"

"I miscarried."

"When?"

"A couple of weeks. It's okay, Rachel. I'm fine. Dad's fine. It's just…Keegan overheard Dad and me talking about it. She asked me earlier today. We talked about it, and I feel like you should know, too."

"How do you do it?" Rachel asked, but her voice caught and the words came out a little crooked.

"Do what?"

"How do take all of this…stuff…and stay standing? So much has happened…How do you just…keep going?"

"Because I have to," Mom answered simply. "It's okay,

Rach. We're all on the same road now, right? We're all moving in the same direction. Things are gonna be okay."

Rachel's eyes burned. "I keep remembering. What happened. But it's like…" She closed her eyes and thought about how to say what was in her mind. "It's like I'm remembering with my body…with my heart…instead of my head. And I get so scared…Like it's all happening right now, and we might lose her this time."

Mom frowned and then she nodded. Her eyes got all glassy.

"I know. I know exactly how you feel, because I feel that way all the time."

"I hate myself sometimes. For all that mean stuff I said to her. All the times I called her a freak." Rachel wiped at her eyes. "I didn't know. I didn't know she was so sad."

Mom shook her head and reached for Rachel's hand. "No more hating yourself. Okay? Nobody in this family is allowed to hate him or herself. Keegan's home. And we're going to help her. And we're going to heal right there with her."

Rachel nodded.

"And Rach?"

"What?"

"If you need to talk to someone…if you need more than Dad or me can give you, it's okay. We can do that. We can do whatever you need."

"Thanks, Mom."

Her mom pulled her up from the bed, and together they went back to the kitchen to check on the cookies. Neither of them had heard the timer, but Bobby was in the kitchen gently scraping the warm cookies from the sheet. He snitched one and then looked up to see he'd been caught.

"Gotcha."

Her dad grinned at her mom. "Guilty."

"Gimme one," Rachel said as she reached for one.

"Keegan, wanna cookie? And some milk?"

Keegan looked up at them and nodded. Rachel wondered how her mom could stand it, if she looked at Keegan curled up on the couch like a little kid and saw her like she was that night in the emergency room, the way she did.

Chapter 54

TEEL

THE DA'S office was a little bit like Roni Andrews' office and really, a hell of a lot different. Martin Stone's office was in the courthouse, which was in an old office building with a new facelift. The sprawling building was fancy white stone and sexy chrome and glass. The interior walls were a cool gray, and the carpet was institutional blue. Martin's office was on the first floor, and out the window of the conference room next to his office, Teel could see the parking lot. Not exactly an inspiring view, but on that particular city block, Teel wasn't sure there was an inspiring view to be had.

The aesthetics didn't matter all that much to Teel. She could be checking into a five-star hotel, and she wouldn't notice. Because she and her family were here to determine Keegan's future. At Roni's office, though she'd felt like she was a kid facing punishment from the principal, she'd had hope. Roni was on their side, and she had offered them an inch of hope when they'd thought there was none.

Martin Stone was on the other side of the law. Martin Stone didn't necessarily have Keegan's best interests in mind. He was there to ensure that justice was done, for Marin or the state or whatever the hell, it didn't matter. He hadn't been planning strategies to keep her daughter out of the juvenile system.

Besides that, he was a formidable man. Teel was tall enough that it took a big man to make her feel short. Martin Stone made her feel short. He was also robust, making about four or five of Bobby. When he greeted them, he seemed distracted, which did nothing to make him likeable in Teel's book. This was her daughter's future they were about to sit down and draw.

He brushed crumbs from his mustache as he led them to the conference room. She wondered what he'd been eating before they'd come in. She hadn't eaten much at all today, because her stomach was a pit of nerves. Keegan had tried to eat, but she'd thrown up after only half a grilled cheese sandwich.

Introductions were made once they were inside the conference room, and Teel was somewhat mollified to see that he was more attentive. They sat at the long rectangular table, Keegan's side, the defense, Teel guessed, on one side and Martin Stone and an assistant on the other.

Stone scanned a few notes and then put his file folder down and looked right at Keegan. Teel felt her stomach clench, and her heart caught and then tripped and hammered the hell of out her chest, and then the man offered Keegan an almost gentle smile.

"Keegan."

Teel saw Keegan sit up straighter. Her face couldn't get any paler; she looked like a ghost already. The only color in her face was still the dark bruises under her eyes.

"Yes, sir."

Teel was grateful to hear the courteous words, but Keegan's voice was tiny. As small as she'd become lately, Teel figured she'd probably lost ten pounds, if not more. Keegan looked almost like a bird perched there, ready to fly away.

"How are you?" he asked sincerely.

Keegan, ready to be questioned yet again about the night of the party or the pictures she'd taken, appeared stunned with his personal question. She raised her eyebrows and then looked to Teel and then Roni, as if asking how she was supposed to answer him.

"I'm okay," she whispered.

"You're at home now? For the rest of the semester. Is that right?"

"Yes."

"I understand you attempted suicide." He sat back in his chair and studied Keegan. "Why did you do that?"

Teel was taken aback this time. Why did they have to dig up these bones? Keegan was still reeling emotionally from everything that had happened, and Teel worried that any little thing or any big thing might set her back. She'd gone through the house and gotten rid of the drugs that were no longer necessary. Those that were, she'd locked in the safe in her and Bobby's closet. She'd taken razor blades from the girls' bathroom and hidden them in the closet. She felt ridiculous for doing it, arguing with herself that Keegan was damned near sixteen and not a toddler. And yet, Keegan was possibly the emotional equivalent of a toddler right now, and she wasn't entirely convinced that Keegan wouldn't try something again. In the hospital, Keegan had been on suicide watch. Teel wondered when *she* would stop watching. If Keegan had tried once, Teel wasn't sure that any amount of healing would stop her from that sort of downward spiral in the future.

"Because...I did something really stupid, and I hurt my

friend. And her family." Keegan's eyes filled with tears, but to Teel's surprise, her voice was steady this time. "And I hurt my family."

"Do you feel that you can make restitution to the English family?"

Keegan hesitated. "What does that mean?"

"Can you make it up to them?"

Keegan cocked her head and stared at the DA like he'd suddenly turned green. "How could I ever make up for what I did?" she asked and shook her head.

"Keegan, I'd like to offer you a pretrial diversion."

Again Keegan looked to Teel and Bobby and finally Roni to understand what the man said.

Roni gave Keegan a slight nod and then turned to Stone, as he started to speak again.

"Keegan is here because of violating a cyber-bullying statute." Stone raised the corner of his mouth as if he was shrugging. "I don't like what she did. No one likes what she did. Was it threatening violence? No. Did she do it repeatedly? No. Has she shown remorse for the act of taking the pictures and posting them online?"

He stopped and looked at each of them.

"I believe she has," he continued.

"She has," Roni agreed.

"You're very young, Keegan. I'd hate to see a bad decision change your whole life," he said as he leaned forward and folded his hands on the table. "I understand you're lying low for the rest of this semester, but I want you back in school, full time, next semester."

Roni nodded, but Keegan simply stared at him. Teel held her breath, scared to believe he meant anything he said.

"Until next semester, I want you reenrolled and working one on one with a tutor. Said tutor will work with all of your teachers at Blessed Sacrament to make sure you complete this semester of study. I also want you to continue seeing Dr. Brennan until she believes you are stable. If, in a year, you've fulfilled these conditions, I will use my prosecutorial discretion, and I won't file charges against you. None of this will even go on your record, and you won't have to go through any court appearances."

They all sat silently, paused as if waiting for someone to hit play on a remote control and nudge them into action. Roni glanced at Teel and Bobby and finally Keegan. Teel and Bobby both nodded, and Teel wished silently that Roni would fill out whatever paperwork was required and sign on the dotted or solid line and get them the hell out of there before Martin Stone changed his mind.

Bobby thanked Martin Stone and then Roni and shook her hand. Teel barely had the presence of mind to nod and mumble her own thank you.

When they filed out of the conference room a while later, Keegan still white as a sheet, Teel cried tears of relief. Keegan made it three steps before her knees gave. Thankfully Bobby was there to catch her.

"Daddy," Keegan cried softly.

"What? What is it, honey?"

"Is it really over?"

"The hardest part is over," Roni assured her. Teel appreciated the way Roni touched Keegan's shoulder and even how she gave it a gentle squeeze. And maybe she was right, the hardest part was over. This was better than she and Bobby had hoped for, and Teel was so relieved, she felt like she'd lived the last two months in a two dimensional world. Like the worry and fear over Keegan had sucked the life out of her and everything around her, and now suddenly, she was breathing again, and the black and white around her was gone, and there was color.

But maybe for Keegan, the hardest part was going to start

again tomorrow. Maybe just getting out of bed was hard for Keegan these days. She was sleeping with Rachel, so Teel thought it was kind of hard for Keegan to go to bed at night. And maybe each appointment with her psychiatrist was hard, maybe not as hard as each was for Teel, when she was an outsider and was left to wonder what Keegan was telling *someone else*.

And maybe, for Keegan, starting school in January would be the hardest part. Maybe leaving Blessed Sacrament was a good thing for Keegan. Maybe she couldn't have settled back into her place, her group of friends, and Teel was glad for that, to be honest. She didn't want Keegan near any of the girls who had driven her to want to be just like them. Right now, Keegan didn't want that, either.

But maybe starting at the public high school in January, when everyone else had been going there at least since August if not for a year or longer, was going to be the hardest part for Keegan. It was a huge school, and the student body was five times that of Blessed Sacrament. It could provide Keegan a safe place to hide; it could give her the opportunity for a new start, and it could provide her a lot of enemies who tortured her over what had happened.

The not knowing scared Teel to death. The thought of Keegan walking into the school by herself scared the bleeding hell out of her.

Teel reminded herself to breathe. One day at a time. They would all get through this together, one day at a time.

———

THOUGH THE MEETING with the D.A. had gone better than she and Bobby had hoped for, they didn't go out to celebrate. Now that they'd met with the D.A., and now that they knew what to expect, exhaustion hit Teel full in the face, like a brick between the eyes. She figured Bobby and Keegan felt the same way.

Something about the house felt more welcoming, cozier. Teel still wasn't ready to think about Keegan's room. And yet, for the first time in such a long time, she was truly happy to walk inside her house. To be home.

Rachel was at the kitchen bar reading, but she shoved the book away when they walked in.

"What?" she asked. She hopped off the barstool and looked from Teel to Keegan and then to Bobby. "What happened? What's going on?"

"The D.A. offered Keegan a pretrial diversion," Bobby answered her.

"What? What does that mean?" Rachel hurried to Keegan and took her hands. "What does that mean for Keegan?"

"She has to have a tutor to help her here at home for this semester, and she has to go back to school in January." Bobby leaned on the counter. "And she has to keep seeing her doctor for a while. If she does that, he said he wouldn't file charges, and none of it would go on her record."

Rachel raised her eyebrows. "That's it?" She turned to Keegan with a grin on her face. "That's it? It's over?"

Keegan nodded, but she still looked worried. Shell-shocked. Teel put her arm around Keegan's shoulders.

"It's gonna be okay, Keegan." Teel allowed herself a smile. She kissed the top of Keegan's head. "It's gonna be okay."

"For me." Keegan's words caught, and suddenly she turned into Teel and cried. "It's gonna be okay for me, but Marin's still dead."

"I know." Teel wrapped her arms around her. She looked at Bobby over Keegan's head. She'd been so caught up in what would happen to Keegan, she'd all but forgotten about Marin.

"Keegan, there is no proof that what you did caused Marin to kill herself," Bobby reminded her.

"I know, but I know I hurt her," Keegan cried against Teel's shoulder. "I just wish I could take it all back."

Teel had wondered before, back when their world had started to fall apart, if Keegan would ever grieve for Marin. She had been so cold anytime Marin's name was mentioned. Maybe that had been guilt. Guilt and fear were pretty powerful emotions, and it was entirely possible that self-preservation had smothered the grief over Marin's death.

Teel watched Rachel dig through the refrigerator. Bobby picked up the phone and grabbed Rachel and pulled her away from the refrigerator and close to his side.

"Let's have pizza," he suggested.

Teel nodded, though she still wasn't hungry. It wasn't really over, only the first hardest part. Now came the rest of it, and Teel suspected it would be just as bad, if not worse than what they'd already faced together.

"I think I want to move," she told Bobby, later that night. Rachel and Keegan were in Rachel's room. Teel thought they were watching a movie, though she wasn't sure. Rachel had been glued to Keegan's side all night, and Teel knew Keegan was happy to be close to her. But she also knew Keegan was exhausted, and she needed to rest.

Bobby lay behind her, his legs spooned behind hers, his arm over her waist.

"It was good to come home tonight," she continued, "but...I just can't get past it. I don't like her room. I don't wanna ever have to be in that room again."

"I know," Bobby agreed. "Me, too. I've been looking at some lots."

Teel sighed in relief.

"We'll build it with a good foundation," he told her. "Just like us."

She smiled, even though he couldn't see her. "Aren't all Alexander Homes built with a good foundation?"

He kissed her neck, just below her ear. Teel turned her head when he leaned closer to kiss her again, but then she slipped out of bed and grabbed her robe.

"Where are you going?"

"Checking on the girls," she answered.

"Remember when they were little, and we'd end up with both of them in bed with us?"

"Part of me wishes they were that little again," Teel said softly. "Then maybe we could've..."

Bobby shook his head. "Let's not do that. Let's not second guess ourselves, Teel. We're all doing the best we can."

She stared at him for a moment, loving the lines around his eyes and the beard shadow on his jaw. Finally she nodded to him, leaned back over the bed and kissed him, long and sweet.

"I love you."

He turned out the lamp as she walked out of the room. The house was cold, and she realized they were already into November as she crossed the hardwood and went down the hall to Rachel's room.

The girls were asleep, but Rachel's TV was still on. Teel was tempted to turn it off, but she didn't. When they were younger, it scared them both to wake to a completely quiet, dark room.

There had been enough fear lately. Why add the fear of the dark back into the equation? She stood by the bed and watched them sleep for a few minutes and then turned away, and tears blurred her vision.

"Mom?" Keegan said quietly as Teel stepped into the hallway.

"Hmm?"

Keegan didn't answer her. Teel walked back into the

room and knelt down beside the bed. Keegan reached for her hand.

"I'm scared to go to sleep," Keegan finally whispered.

"It's okay." Teel squeezed her hand and with the other, she brushed her hair from her forehead. "I'm right here."

Keegan closed her eyes, and Teel watched her slip back into sleep.

About the Author

Tracy is the author of the Lorelei Bluffs women's fiction series, the Williams Legacy, and several stand-alone women's fiction novels. She has recently dabbled in contemporary romance, as well.

Also by Tracy Broemmer

Also by Tracy Broemmer

Women's Fiction Novels:

Luther's Cross (Writing as Therese Kinkaide)

Luther's Cross 10th Anniversary Edition (Tracy Broemmer)

Fairytale (Writing as Therese Kinkaide)

Small Hours (Writing as Therese Kinkaide)

Picket Fences

Two Story Home

Green-Eyed Girl

Say Everything

Come Home For Christmas

Sketching Litchfield Lake

Ever, Again

Safe as Houses

Damsel

Every Little Thing, Lorelei Bluffs, Book 1

Two A.M., Lorelei Bluffs, Book 2

Blind, Lorelei Bluffs, Book 3

Leaving July, Lorelei Bluffs, Book 4

Hesitation Marks, Lorelei Bluffs, Book 5

Four Letter Words, Lorelei Bluffs, Book 6

See Kate, Lorelei Bluffs, Book 7

Loved You More, Lorelei Bluffs, Book 8

A Lorelei Ending, Lorelei Bluffs, Book 9

I Do, Lorelei Bluffs, Book 10

Truth Is, The Williams Legacy, Book 1
Other People's Ugly, The Williams Legacy, Book 2
Omissions, The Williams Legacy, Book 3

Contemporary Romance Novels:
Destiny's Calling: Your Future Is Waiting
Wedding Day Shenanigans
Holiday Fling
The Kiss Off
Something Like Love

Love, Nashville, The Mississippi Queen Trilogy, Book 1
Forever, Duncan, The Mississippi Queen Trilogy, Book 2
Always, Jess, The Mississippi Queen Trilogy, Book 3

Gettin' Hitched, The H Books, Book 1

Contemporary Romance Novellas:
Indian Summer, A Novella
Dear Jaclyn Perris, A Novella

Contemporary Romance Short Stories:
Perfect Pictures, The Wine Tasting Series, Traminette
Coming Home, The Wine Tasting Series, Edelweiss
Save Me Every Dance, The Wine Tasting Series, Rosé
Marry Me, The Wine Tasting Series, Shiraz
Birthday Wishes, The Wine Tasting Series, Muscat
Dad Jeans, The Wine Tasting Series, Vignoles

www.ingramcontent.com/pod-product-compliance
Lightning Source LLC
Chambersburg PA
CBHW030617250626
47154CB00006B/1828

* 9 7 8 1 9 5 1 6 3 7 0 4 0 *